ALSO BY EDIE MEIDAV

The Far Field: A Novel of Ceylon

Crawl Space

LOLA, CALIFORNIA

EDIE MEIDAV

LOLA,
CALIFORNIA

FARRAR, STRAUS AND GIROUX | NEW YORK

Farrar, Straus and Giroux
18 West 18th Street, New York 10011

Copyright © 2011 by Edie Meidav
All rights reserved
Distributed in Canada by D&M Publishers, Inc.
Printed in the United States of America
First edition, 2011

Library of Congress Cataloging-in-Publication Data
Meidav, Edie, 1967–
    Lola, California / Edie Meidav.— 1st ed.
      p.   cm.
    ISBN 978-0-374-10926-4 (alk. paper)
     1. Friendship—Fiction.   2. Families—Fiction.   I. Title.

  PS3563.E3447 L65 2011
  813'.54—dc22

                      2010046275

Designed by Abby Kagan

www.fsgbooks.com

10 9 8 7 6 5 4 3 2 1

Back in that long-ago century, ladies wishing to see greater beauty in life traveled backward on wagons, looking into a popular, smoky and distorted mirror that let them see the world—land, trees and sky—as far more picturesque than any reality could ever hope to be.

In this limited way, during a limited time, the female half of the species found their freedom.

—*Eden Always*
Victor Mahler
Freedom Press
Berkeley, California, 1984

And what happens to the selfish ones?

—Rose's diary, 1983

LOLA, CALIFORNIA

1984

Rose crossing a square in Spain, could be Valencia or Granada or any of the places where two girls stay the summer after high school, sleeping under rowboats or in flowerbeds, in hostels or pensions with balustrades and mites made venerable and happy by tourists, but it happens to be a less trafficked area of Barcelona, not far from where Senegalese vendors pray. Rose is all chrysalis, bruisable and diffident, aware of contours, thrilled by the people she will meet, the ones who will reveal all her possible faces, still hidden in magic invisible cloak sleeves.

She is crossing a newly washed square toward Lana in a white T-shirt called a wifebeater and does it matter whether she holds aloft two drinks and one straw or one drink with two straws and whether the drink is horchata or limonata and that in a shaded patio Lana sits awaiting Rose with some dark-browed man they have just met?

The man doesn't matter: he just spells the name of some new adventure together. Rose's tongue inches forward, all is potential. The surface of her skin could be a plum's, ripe and ready for anything, because someone just granted her new sap: at that point, Rose is still included in Lana.

All that matters is crossing toward her friend, their bubble mostly unburst, Rose no longer an observer, now someone deserving to take breath and live, every footfall commuting what had been one long and lonely life sentence.

What goads her on could be as happenstance as the single brush of an arm as they stride along a railway platform, enough to act as a million fireflies of encouragement in the dark of all they leave unsaid. Rose, crossing toward Lana, shivers. They will never be lovers, they have been newly set loose on the world, fairly oblivious to everyone else. Masters or meteors: two girls at seventeen.

EDIE MEIDAV

LOLA, CALIFORNIA

Vic has been, for years, losing his appetite. This happens on death row. In the last thirty days he has lost fourteen pounds and much of his eyesight.

"What's the matter, boss?" the guard Javier asks. "You want to look like a war victim?"

"Who do I want to look like?" Vic's fingers hover over yet another food tray, its edges webbed with grime, as if sensing radioactivity. "Who's looking?"

"Food smells bad today?"

"The body doesn't want food," says Vic. The day before, he'd had a consuming hallucination that some old friends from early school-boy and surfing days in America awaited him in the prison courtyard. In a fancy suit he had gone out to bless them. Then he argued with some official that he wasn't ready to follow the guy into a cold corridor. Too tired, he had to get back to bed.

Later Vic talked to Javier about how nice and thoughtful it was that the prison had arranged this courtyard ceremony. Only from Javier's tone did Vic understand that no ceremony had taken place.

"I don't understand what's happening to my body," he says now to Javier, because Vic can't rise from his cot. There's a machine making his heart tick and a numb ellipsis occupying the nib where his stomach used to be; the ellipsis makes it hard to rise. He speaks to the fifteen by fifteen sound tiles in the ceiling.

15+15=30, as he knows well. Also 5+25. Also 9+21. Much better to count these than the click and screech of gates locking and unlocking.

Javier stands on the other side of the food slot. "Didn't take your meds yet? Took the vitamins at least?"

"I'm not that optimistic."

Javier sees the untouched tray. "Señor Legend, maybe it's time for us to call Doctor K?"

"No. Interference would be problematic. Who's Doctor K?"

"You'll see him tomorrow. Maybe later today."

Such concern emanates from the guard, for a second Vic knows Javier to be one of the thirty-six righteous people walking the face of the earth, if not already an angel.

Vic waits. "Could you please come in?" He clears his throat before repeating himself.

Javier looks behind and then unlocks, making the choice to reach upward and slant the cell's camera a few centimeters away. Someone might see them but in so many ways his prisoner is right: who's looking?

"I'm here," says Javier. In the protocol book, one exemption gets its own page: once the Bureau of Prisons finalizes the sentence and only the slimmest chance of gubernatorial intervention remains, humane and dignified treatment beyond the scope of protocol becomes permissible. How can anyone define the slimness of a chance?

"Would you mind lying with your head right there to give me some of your body warmth?"

Javier gets down on his knees next to Vic, ginger in laying his head down on the bony prisoner chest, an emptied birdcage. "This is crazy, man."

"Your warmth is kindness," says Vic. "I feel it entering me. In your hand too. But you could lose your job."

"Also my pension."

"No man ever laid his head on me."

"Well, they don't give out teddy bears around here, right?"

"True. No one ever gave me a teddy bear."

Javier stands up quickly. "You okay? You're talking strange."

"How do I talk?"

"Your tongue, like it's heavy."

In mock joust, Vic sticks out his tongue at Javier, a proof of how manly and battle-ready he remains. He tries straightening the wayward vertebrae in his spine. "The rain in Spain falls mainly on the plain."

"You'll be okay, boss. I'm going to ask for another blanket. Maybe I can get you another Mahler recording."

"You know he's a distant ancestor."

"I know, Legend."

"What do you live for?" asks Vic, desperate to keep him near.

"My kid. Or grandchildren." Then Javier stops.

"But that's for them. What keeps you going?"

"I don't know." The guard waits. "Maybe your daughter will visit today?"

"Now you're lying," says Vic. "You never lied before." His eyes betray and don't stop betraying. Since the time when he was small and someone shot a wolf cub in front of him, he had never cried, at least not in front of a living person. Today his eyes happen to let tears slide out.

"I'm saying maybe."

"Maybe," echoes Vic, already turning away as Javier leaves the cell, showing the humanity of a good host: flouting regulations, removing the tray.

PART

ONE

On a road leading from California to the flagship Wal-Mart in Bentonville, Arkansas, they come across the sign.

Deceptively simple: MALTEDS, in the rickety orange handwriting you still find in the American south, usually advertising sunbeds or churches. The girls notice that there must be some agreement between sunbeds and churches because find a church and down the road two bends you find a sunbed. Vic speaks an English that still curls odd words: "These places of worship promise to clean whatever they call your soul. Then the town offers you a sunbed to help you become a tanned god. The sunbed does what it can to antidote the tabernacles."

"Right," says Lana, the torch in her gut generally more alive than anything sparking on the outside.

"It's a Lebensraum of flesh."

"What?" Rose knows Lana doesn't like when she talks too much to her dad but can't help asking.

"The space a nation needs in order to live. In this case, a nation of flesh. The sunbeds say American flesh matters in this moment but you can transform it to find a better, higher love. The churches might be native or imported but they all say it's the past of our flesh that counts. To find a higher love, you thrive if you turn sinful dependence on the body into memory."

Within this fry-or-fly context, the orange handwriting is a cool surprise: MALTEDS.

And then Vic begins talking about malteds: "So why do people say you can't get a good malted anymore?"

Lana laughs and Rose shrugs, pretending not to care because Lana doesn't, both half-listening and with the other half making faces at the boys in the car behind. By now the girls know that Vic is warming to his subject.

"Is the malted a marker of some perfect American childhood?" Vic had come to America in late adolescence as a scrawny immigrant. Once, mid-argument, Lana had accused him of having old-world Transylvanian vampire blood that could suck the life out of any room he entered, saying he never got anything about America right. He'd smiled back so coolly anyone could have mistaken him for a vampire: *you may understand America better, Lana, but my blood is also your blood.*

In the car, driving in Arkansas, Lana whispers something to Rose that Vic ignores, staying in pursuit. "So if you can't recapture childhood perfection, what then? You spend the rest of life trying to get back your ideal? Or you turn pragmatic and say no one gets great malteds anymore? You resign yourself to loss?"

Rose answers in the idiom of teen muddle. People have called her knowledgeable but it will be years before people say she speaks with a silky tongue and before she starts thinking silk might free a person. Now she just practices. "Maybe they keep trying to return to the crime scene."

"To the moment of their first bad malted?"

She mumbles.

"Well," says Vic, off on a riff. "There's your problem, Rose! Somewhere in your foster group homes or wherever you lived, someone fed you bad ideology. Twelve steps, crypto-Californian, pseudo-Buddhist, something. Your ideals blind you. There's your paradox."

"What paradox?" Rose dares to say. Even if the foster comment was gratuitous, even when she doesn't understand all the crypto-pseudo parts of his speech, she loves when Vic ribs her.

"You have passion but don't know for what, Rose. Makes you think that to find goodness you must push past where others stop."

"That's a problem?"

"A custom that could thicken a person's skin. You lose the possibility that lives in porosity. Your passion," says Vic.

"You know a lot about Rose," Lana interjects.

"A little. She's a real Californian. She has that sunny appearance of hope rubbed up against some arid inner plan. Who really knows what she cares about?"

Lana shoots a look at the rearview. She may be Rose's best friend but she is still Vic's daughter. Just the three of them in the car. Everyone knows that if Lana's mother had traveled with them, Vic wouldn't have snuck in any comments about passion or rubbing. Lana snorts. "What are you talking about?"

The girls have been stretching into the luxury of high-school summer between sophomore and junior years. Only they accompany Vic on a road trip from California to some conference. When in the car's mobile temple, they dedicate themselves to hedonism or exhibitionism, busy tanning their legs out the car window. When in a motel, they go giggling in polka-dot bikinis to soak up chlorine in motel pools while Vic, on various shaded lounge chairs, wears reading glasses and peruses journals, rolling them up only to kill mosquitoes drawn to the tight cordons of his professor legs.

With Vic they trip through a catalogue of dining moments: BLTs, Cobb salad, Reubens, Spanish omelets, Waldorf salad, pit stops in diners filled with evangelicals, golfers, Hells Angels. Lana and Vic serve as amnesiacs while Rose is trip historian, saving every single napkin and matchbook for a journal that for years will be a prized possession until the day she tries to give it away.

Vic's parables about perfection on this trip do leave Rose feeling as if he turns her into some kind of clumsy Goofus against Lana's elegant Gallant, given that he makes it seem she will have little choice left but to impale herself on perfectionist ideals if she doesn't first founder in some vale of passion. Of course he leaves her dumbstruck, because who ever refutes Vic Mahler—*Mahler the lawless maker of laws!* as one of his followers always salutes him.

With no one volleying, between new tangents, Vic's hand bangs a polyrhythm on the roof of the car. "People say nothing distinguishes our time. Big deal, this hundred ninety-ninth decade. So what, they say, we bridge the age of petrochemical industry and the age of information. I say big stuff! Because we just moved from the age of collective accident into the era of individual control." His bang gets louder. "Who doesn't think consumer control leads to happiness? But we end up lost in some new Middle Ages. People found greater collective meaning during the hula-hoop era. Nowadays we're as starved for absolute connection as any peasant during the Crusades. I'm talking about that famous god-shaped hole we're supposed to have—you have that too, girls? What's the difference between one of your chain stores and ye old cathedral?"

Rose stops making faces out the rear, at core unbothered by anything Vic says, loving how this important man talks with her. "Maybe people feel that if they make the right consumer choice, they find a perfect mother, you know, someone who will meet every need."

Imitating her father without meaning to, Lana beats an off-rhythm on her bare thigh, the tactic falling short, as not much will ever keep her friend from talking with Vic, who now looks over his shoulder.

"Rose, what you need is a love golem. I mean it. Wish I could give you that. Someone who would meet your needs. Some little woman who'd stick with you for about three months. She'd tend your every need. Unpaid. Plug up your holes. That would really help. After that, you'd be mothered enough. You'd be healed."

"Please, papa," says Lana, arriving late to Rose's defense but still arriving.

"I'm just asking Rose whether she believes no one gets a real parent anymore?"

"I said that?" asks Rose, wishing to sound steadier. "Or what do you mean?"

"What he always means," Lana says. "Everything is relative."

As reward for the unintended pun, which happens to silence Rose, she gets from her father's rearview face a lifted eyebrow and wry grin.

Everything is relative, the easiest of insults to a foster kid whose thin skin is no secret to the Mahlers.

The conversation sinks, enough that Vic decides to spin around on the two-laner: they are speeding back to where the handwritten sign commanded with its promise of MALTEDS.

Rose, still scrabbling out of conversational quicksand, wants to ask Vic a question that will mark one of her first disappointments in him, because until Arkansas, she had mistaken his exuberance and thumb-worn bedside stack of *Playboys* as signs of an idealist: "But you were saying you don't think you can find a good malted anywhere?"

"Forgive me," he says to Rose, "but I must take you as an example. You romanticize the pain of your childhood. Right? Think you're stronger for it? While I see you living around some central lack. If you could just acknowledge that things won't ever get much better than this moment, you'd be better off."

"Please," says Lana, truly meaning it this time.

"You're going to tell me I'm a buzzkill again? I'm giving you girls a gift. It's called the reality principle."

They get out of the car to walk toward the MALTEDS sign, overseen by a toad-eyed woman seated on a lawn chair beneath a trailer's flamingo awning. With time to spare, she watches, a lady of impressive girth wearing an apron and little else over sweaty flesh. Somewhere in that face you might find remnants of a heart-shaped chin. With method, she has pulled back strands of carmine hair. And now the lady says nothing, one minute of life dispensed into watching their approach.

For a second, Rose is free to see her fellow companions as strangers, Lana a tawny jungle cat in cowboy boots, a shaft of effortless cool around her, eyes hazel and obscenely glamorous: almonds, delusions, foreign shores. Earrings jiggling, a shiny brown ponytail bouncing, a tall girl walking with a man her height but made of rougher stuff, shoulders a skewed shipwreck, his face dark-browed and rumpled, this man called a lapsed Yves Montand by his wife, walking toward the malted lady with a stride both serious and bandaged.

And what does Rose look like to anyone, their mesmerized chameleon, hard to place, flip-flopping along with them, never quite on the ground? A fistful of strawberry blond, the drifting heir of fair-skinned, freckled Cossacks or Vikings, ancestors dribbled across the globe and unknowable. What Rose sees in her own eyes is the thirst of a blue sky and in her skin the porosity Vic calls out, all this haziness partly why the unimpeachable brown of others' skin or eyes holds such beauty, the certainty of brownness shared by her friend and father. Warm, unbruisable earth, impervious.

A few paces off, Vic, never pulling punches, asks, "These malteds any good?" to which the malted lady grunts, taking them for what they are, namely, people whose insolence warrants little notice, even if nonetheless the lady's sales instinct remains vital and bubbling: the teeth she does have glint a near-smile. With a confidence worthy of a screen deity or lizard, moving mainly her tongue, flicked sideways before she speaks, she asks: "How many you'd like?"

A shared article in deference to the car conversation: none of the passengers can commit.

Vic seems dumbstruck but finally says, "One, we'll share."

Curiosity thrills the girls: stakes are involved.

The woman's heavy tread levies her up into the trailer. There she busies herself blending up the single malted. A biplane could not have sliced the air with a greater knife of nostalgia: the three customers hang wordless, awaiting the seller and her unrushable rites. Once done, she pours the concoction into a paper cup marqueed with the face of a silent-screen idol before passing it through the trailer's window.

Vic avoids her eyes. He tastes the potion, considers, and then points to the cup, handing it on to Lana who sips before Rose. "Wow," says Vic finally. Of course Rose, with her tic of echoing, answers. "Wow is right."

"It's thick," says Lana right away, beaming up at her father, not yet wholly disobedient to the regime of Vic.

They take turns sipping and savoring while the seller glints, confirmed. From the trailer's window she waits for them to pay, unsurprised when Vic tells her to keep the change.

Back in the car, they barely talk the whole way to Bentonville: the perfection of the moment has stripped them clean.

Years later, Rose, unsmiling, will show the scrapbook from the trip to a man named Hogan just as if she were an emissary revealing a relic lifted from the last days of Christ. Matchbooks, napkins, the spoon from the malted place.

Usually people say you can't go home but that day the three of them arrived at a taste no one else shared. When Rose tells the story, she says every now and then the world trickles down some grace.

Hogan will say that what Rose calls grace has to do with a more testable physical principle, like the conservation of matter. "You like thinking everything recirculates. Like what Mahler called the metaphysical law of thermodynamics. That everything is basically permanent." Whatever Hogan says, Rose will not agree, because given what everyone has lost or gained, she might never stop craving mystery but can never again believe in permanence.

SIXTEENTH OF MARCH, 1982

marks the first and last time Lana will attend one of her father's events. She comes so she can bring Rose: sophomore year of high school and second year into their friendship, already at a peak. When Lana's father reads at Berkeley, she has heard, the scene defines chaos, and though Lana knows about the legion of fans, she still finds herself surprised by the number of people splayed out. The loudspeaker on the lower floor plays a segment of an old interview with Vic, one she has heard quoted too many times to count. Still it is disconcerting to have her father's disembodied recorded voice following her; he didn't know she was coming to hear him talk tonight.

"I am hardly the neo-Freudian some take me for, nor, as others have said, the latest town crier of Californian existentialism. Not a classicist in neurobiologist clothes nor a latterday William James, not some Jungian new ager in tattered philosopher's rags, nor a lapsed scientist come to the softer realm of words, but rather someone who believes that if we dwell deep in the physical center of our own motivation, aiming to understand how, when and why our neurons fire, we receive the truest gift of Prometheus. Boil all my life's work down to this one idea, if you must—we have not been created to be machines of genetic input. All recent brain research supports me in this. My claim is that we do best when we articulate our own foundational myths, deeper than psychology itself, the very intersection of our will with physical matter's reality principle. In this way we locate, dare I say, not just the efficiency of our neurons but their endless possibility, which should give us hope when we turn toward fashioning a life of meaning."

She and Rose make their way through followers breathing patchouli and body ripeness, heads lifted, kenning their Vic, the actual oracle himself soon to speak in the flesh. The girls climb past those hanging kamikaze off stairway edges and those who take cues from the piling of books by stacking themselves up toward the store's second floor where Lana's mother had promised to save seats. Before Rose had met Vic and Mary, way back, all Lana had said about her mother was that she was half Yokut and half Japanese and that strangers always act as if they compliment Mary by telling her how fucking exotic she is, how she could pass as Andean, white, Slavic. Whenever Lana hears this, she has to roll her eyes with no little theater. What Rose will never tell Lana is the magic in Mary's untraceable, unmistakable poise. A girl feels she has stumbled into the presence of royalty.

And paired to such poise, up on the mezzanine, in a corner like a veteran bullfighter sizing up his opponent, stands Lana's progenitor: Vic Mahler rumpled in a business suit, eyes burning under the heavy brow, profile sharp. The corduroy patches at his elbows and wrinkles in his suit form cuts of vortex, all lines of energy pointing at him. Nearby hovers the bouncer, his mutton-chop sideburns furious as he yabbers left and right, hands anchored on a huge belt buckle signifying the tail-biting snake of kundalini. "A failed local poet," her mother whispers to Lana about the bouncer, the merest eyebrow lifted toward the man, a comment at odds with her nun posture, unperturbed by the girls sliding in.

At the podium, Mahler too may appear calm but his voice is oracular, booming once he starts to read from his latest, *Firing the Love Hole*:

"What I both advocate and long for is symmetry, an ideal of absolute reciprocity, a perfect task-and-reward system. At moments in history we have thought the productions of the frontal brain define the outermost contours of human potential but what we seem to have ignored is this: Aristotle's final and material causes correspond to mechanisms in our entire animal being. Let us consider for a second the breadth of this proposition. We can already sight leeway in the burgeoning science of neuroplasticity. If our brains are made of movable parts, how do we take heed? This is not to say that, in the terms of the pop psychologist, you are condemned like a slave to serve your bliss, or that like some child despot you alone create your reality, but rather that endless hope remains for those of us who believe they have been locked into some dusty Freudian legerdemain. Similarly, we may also free those who find themselves locked into that other tale, the one suggesting some collectively orgasmic socioeconomic release. Let us consign such talk to poets. Instead, consider taking as a first principle the following: there is no time like the present to understand all the selves feasible in your one lifetime, not to mention the vestigial selves locked in your metaphysical DNA."

Until, afterward, he tells the masses: "I'm ready for your questions."

And a woman stands to say:

"For years I have been interested in extraterrestrial visitations. We think it's a fairytale, the relation between holes in certain cheeses and craters on the moon, and the way all of it could resemble how the drain in your bathtub might make faces from your own past appear— it's true! go look it up sometime!—but what I'm asking is whether you feel there's some biomorphic resonance at work in the culture at large. You know how counterculture forms the larger culture. Basically, do you think it's centrifugal or centripetal? Maybe I'm asking because originally I come from a Wisconsin dairy farm so you can understand what Berkeley means to me. Anyway, that's my way of saying I really enjoy your book. Plus that whole idea of wormholes and portals in one's brain through which all sorts of things can enter."

And Mahler nods, genially, an old European courtesy in his nod. A costumed man, whom Lana hadn't seen, pushes forward. Rose tries to hold back her giggles but still Lana pinches her, trying to get her to quit what Vic has already called Rose's hebephrenic gift, her unstoppable laughter.

Now the man, in a polar-bear outfit, holding a transistor and a giant cream-colored velour phallus, speaks, his voice throttled by anger:

"Excuse me. I appear today in costume as a manifestation of Hermes, the messenger, and just want to say, Mahler, you urge us to follow one kind of life. You preach biological birthright versus choice and self-creation, self-mythologization beyond the determinism of neurons and then Mahler! Man! You live the most predetermined life. A tenure-track bourgeois professor's life! I mean how cliché does it get? You have your lovely wife and rollerskating kid and vintage Porsche, your ivy-covered North Berkeley house, which, if these are not received icons, right, if they are not about choice but about perpetuating the bourgeois status quo, I'm Hermes, so what gives, man, what's with that?"

A speech enough to make the bouncer-poet with the belt buckle start toward the polar-bear Hermes with the clear plan of ejecting the offender from the ingathering of Mahlerites.

And yet Mahler raises a cordial, slow hand, an emperor emerging from a long sleep to say: don't worry, I know this man. Mahler pauses before beginning again, this time with greater care:

"No one knows with greater pain than I do the disparity between what my work suggests and the way I lead my actual life."

Which fills Lana with a passion for her father. Honest, not thrown by criticism, a father who knows how to handle everything. Distant, maybe, but capable of inspiring such outlandish loyalty among his fans. *If only they knew about his rage.*

Still, for a second she can see her father as he is loved, reflected in the cracked-marble eyes of his followers. How could his calm not make her love him more? She is his Mopsy, his good-mood moniker for her, her name when he is smoking a Cuban cigar. For a second she loves him more than she can contain.

Two women up front start waving their arms in genial paroxysm.

"Yes?" he says, pointing.

One begins:

"I just want to say, in response to whatever the Hermes guy said, that your first book really gave me great permission to follow my muse all these years. It gave us all sorts of freedom. And we both really want to thank you for it."

Which is when Lana realizes the two milkmaids on the metal chairs—but for the pansies bedecking their long hair—sit naked, their butt-flesh spread in luxury.

She nudges her mother. "What's *that?*" she asks.

Next to her, Rose still giggles, unstoppable.

"It's okay," says her mother, lower lip trembling. "A new sort of shaggy. You know your father's work—it attracts certain followers."

Lana studies her mother Mary: the way she lingers on the idea of work, their family's holy flag, while the nervous brown hands stay crossed like the well-bred schoolgirl she remains, an optimistic product of the twentieth century, a leftover from Catholic-school-near-the-rez upbringing, Mary's nunnishness her continued trait despite the reams of essays she may have written on the lexicographic, neutering failures of Western thought in its depictions of othered women—

—and again Lana makes her favorite vow: *better to die than grow up to become her.*

marks the bracelet of nights during which the dance, in so many ways, creates the friends: one boy says some invisible goddess moves their limbs. Using their false names, Lola One and Two, they most often call their dance the Lola flow, though the name matters less than the span of time during which they close their eyes so that arms climb unseen ladders. And who cares if hips shimmy or whether knees bend since the rules stay simple: you close your eyes and life will toss up what it wants. Risk, salvation, seduction. You cannot do the dance alone, you do it with a friend, your flesh almost commingled in order to surrender control. If a person could x-ray the thought above the dance, the hope for early death or glory would be clear while below the two girls stay teenage fish indefinitely, blind and riding currents that say all will be smooth, sweet, a fantasy of selfhood.

To this flow there is background, the electric guitars against a drumbeat that Vic calls the idiot snare, and if sometimes the girls call their dance the electric sugar glide or the beauty of choice sway, it is always flow, hands climbing, eyes closed.

To only one of their followers do they teach the dance: Jane Polsby, a girl who sticks around, forever alert to the idea of Lola squared—Lana^{Rose}, Rose^{Lana}—the two friends never admitting they need Jane as glue, her outsider's zeal coupling them all the more, while poor Jane never realizes the Lolas could never become LanaRose^{Jane} as it would undo a central tenet. If the Lolas do teach Jane the dance, which Rose does one day, the act marks a confidence that the universe will never budge, no one else will ever enter their rhythm.

Because their flow depends on silly vigils of twoness, on cutting the corners of pillowcases to make them tunics. They go to school sporting such tunics or pajamas with no underwear. When people ask, the girls start calling themselves Lola One and Two since a song about a British transvestite is Rose's favorite, one that can move her to tears.

The Lolas think they stay impermeable in their Berkeley of the eighties, a town inhaling during the corset of the Reagan years. Conspicuous consumption lives in the gourmet ghetto and beyond, a future of blandness and money awaiting the girls like a gaping dragon's maw. On the streets the Lolas ignore the bland spermatic yuppies spilling out of new zinc bars, the men in candy-hued shirts emblazoned with alligators, mouths half open, caught in yet another moment of consumption, so much foreplay taking place a beat away in a cleft valley of computers. If the bar-studded streets possessed subtitles, they would say *I am hungry and nothing will stop me.*

The Lolas live beyond all that.

They first meet in a market near school, when Lana calls out gleefully from a neighboring checkout to borrow money she will never return to Rose, Lana's gangly self clumping around in boots terribly attractive.

For all sorts of reasons, Rose had been told she was one of those textbook foster kids, one of those resilient kids who patch together a parent out of cornflake-box commentary or the few fleeting adult connections they make. Patchworking, she had lived in orphanages and group homes, awaiting placement. After second grade had ended up in Berkeley with a wealthy older single mother named Joan, a therapist who'd always wanted a girl to complement her ten-year-old birth-son. It didn't take a genius to know to call any future mother Ma almost immediately, because doing so had seemed to increase Rose's chances of staying longer in a good situation. When Rose had first seen Joan speaking to the social worker in the office, Rose had sidled up, clutching her little teddy bear and saying: *are you the rich lady who is going to save us?* And Joan's smile had been so warm, Rose thought she had done something right for once, so she had added quickly, speaking for herself and her doll: *will you be our Ma?*

In this case, Ma soon felt right. Kind as she was benign in her negligence, nest-filling, Joan aimed to supply. Rose would never again want for anything material and whenever tenderness flooded Joan, most often on holidays, she would pull Rose toward her muskmelon breast and call her saved little daughter her egg.

Stationed in that grand house with Joan and her caustic son, Rose went to public school in Berkeley and Oakland during the height of busing, happy in hallways led by that first principal named Big Daddy. Respectful toward every part of her new social order, Rose learned how to perform, eyes closed, the Black Panther handshake, to dance Miriam Makeba's Pata Pata and the Robot, to make her dancing body mechanical in strict enough a way to outperform any machine crafted on the backs of industrial-revolution slavery. With awe Rose listened to *Free to Be . . . You and Me* and sang Japanese kite songs. She would never learn what states neighbor Oklahoma or what happened in 1816. Instead she learned how to hula and incubate chicks, and in third grade started carrying around a big pad and pencil as transcriber for her own yearlong project, *Say Something*. Its highlights:

Rose: "Say something."
Local Informant #241: "Something."
Rose: "Something else."
LI #241: "Something else."

As a pale girl who looked ready to cry, always a minority, Rose kept getting beaten up at school. Her acquaintances rescued her about as often as they also showed great talents for disappearing. Once Rose managed to escape from spelling-bee whizdom, shy dorkhood and *Say Something*, all of which had delighted Ma, once she came to the small scruffy private high school that was to be her own personal incubator, she sighted her future best friend in the halls like a flash, already laughing—long neck, round earrings, formidable bones— and later talked to this tall girl at the market while simultaneously handing over all her money.

It may be Berkeley of the eighties but it remains the Berkeley where no household lacks its bedside copy of Gibran's *The Prophet*, the western equivalent of *The Bell Jar* that lives on every east coast home's bookshelf. The prophet matters in Berkeley, a place where no one has breakdowns because the idea of a breakdown simply does not exist. Instead people go into periods of healing and newly outfitted jargon. Adults visit others' homes and speak a psychological code Rose learns to decipher. They do not say *I'm thirsty* but rather *I find myself feeling the need for a glass of water.* They lock themselves in lecture halls to have speakers accept confessions, forbid urination and destroy egos, or they follow leaders who demand that all possessions be placed on a pyre made up of the leaders' bank accounts. Some massage therapist friend of her mother will end up living with Rose's family for a spell. His first week with the family he will sit on the backyard's divan, touching points on Rose's adolescent neck so as to better connect her interior polarity. The next week the therapist will rub off the lipsticked lyrics scrawled on her bedroom mirror because a young girl should see herself clearly. *Mirrors are important.* The next week, one morning before school, the therapist will lean back on a pile of clean clothes in the darkened laundry room and beckon Rose into a hug she will run away from, as she has run away from other adult hugs composed with similar theme and scope. That afternoon she will have the good fortune of meeting her future best friend in the market and hand over her money with great good cheer, the massage guy at home immediately not mattering as much during his last few weeks at their house until he too will slip out of her mother's life like all the other passing-in, passed-out therapists and humble gurus, French psychic ministers, Tibetan explorers, Israeli bakers or midwestern secretaries who have paraded through the stained-glass light of Rose's living room and ended up staying a spell.

None of this perturbs the onset of the Lolas. The week they meet, Lana and Rose—not yet Lola One and Two—will take a bus together to the avenue where grizzly war veterans lean against storefronts, everyone reassured by the open-air market of entrepreneurs trafficking in items bohemia calls useful, all the T-shirts tie-dyed and jewelry beaded, silver or turquoise in homage to conquered indigenous nations, all the incense handmade and quartzes magical in honor of eternal spiritual quest. A friendly, nonconformist orthodoxy pulses around all this and its consistency cocoons the girls. On the street, the black-bereted Bubble Lady will be selling books of her own poetry, blowing bubbles their way as if to salute her own girlhood.

The Lolas, forming, buy a stick of sandalwood incense from a passing man, burning it as they walk, getting to feel happily outré since they wield the secret sincerity of mobile, satirical youth, feeling richer for passing by the dying world of the hippies. It will take only a few weeks after their first outing for the Lolas to become a bubble unto themselves, Lana being a prankster possessing a certain oblivion to the feelings of others and a welcome spirit of invention.

Lana's humor can be cruel. From the start Rose is so besotted, she cannot be a conscientious objector. One confident sophomore girl has a limp that makes her lift her right toe, pointed like a ballerina doing a parallel pas de chat, and whenever the Lolas see her, they too indiscernibly point their toes. To do so feels to Rose less like cruelty and more like crafting a bridge between their solipsism and every element of the external world, connecting to the world in a fit of girlishness, like a Giacometti drawing from art history class in which the potentially isolated figure bears a wild network of lines between the self and the surrounding room, the lines those drawn by the girls and their weekend night rituals.

Latchkey kids for different reasons, the Lolas walk between Rose's house—in the south flatlands of Berkeley—through wooded campus, rape-oblivious, to the highlands of Lana's house in the hills swathed in the mist and oleander of north Berkeley. Along the way they stop to climb plum trees or enter the fluorescence of the convenience store for bubble gum. Or they eat cereal in the aisles of a supermarket, walking up and down using spoons, bowls, cereal and milk borrowed from the store. Often enough, they walk past Frat Row and dip into its endless party swoon.

Into one of these party houses the Lolas saunter and make themselves at home, helping each other to a pot of yogurt pilaf while speaking in foreign accents. They go onto one of the many streetside redwood decks where frat boys barbecue while pretending to be their conservative fathers around sorority girls who mimic some unguessable sort of mothers. The Lolas stay eternal tourists, scooting around aliens who mingle with a drink in one hand and the other plunged into the inevitable khaki pocket. Everything is useful. The Lolas run across the soundstage of the parties while serving each other the college kids' punch and pineapple barbecue skewers. Or else they spray water pistols into a strobed crowd of sweaty dancers sincere about mating rituals. In a sock-scented dorm, they nod their heads while yet another frat boy confesses his need to find athletic girls and then spend at least an hour in the mildewed gilt of someone's bathroom, laughing.

After school, they watch pickup soccer games, tanning their legs and cracking sunflower seeds, later running around inside one player's apartment—poor Savaso—until he gets annoyed with their endless giggle and throws them out. Once two mocked boys from a night-time party throw them into the Bancroft fountain. No one hurts the girls and no one takes advantage, since the sharing of adventure forms their amulet, the Lolas two against any one.

Their absurdist biographies change daily, the one constant being that their names stay Lola One and Lola Two. Sometimes they are sorority girls in Delta Delta Delta. Or they topless-sunbathe at a local lake and when the lifeguard catches them, they become foreign students, quibbling back in fake French or Swedish. Sometimes they are sisters or cousins, sometimes long-lost twins, sometimes they may as well inhabit the same skin.

Whoever they are, they barely blink. They attend upperclassmen parties wearing period-stained sheets they have fashioned into tunics held up by one of Vic's broad leather belts but instead of entering sit inside some improvised tent—and who had brought along the extra sheet? and why?—smoking oregano cigarettes they roll themselves. Or, unwitting in their bad timing, locked into a room at a party, they must pee out a second-story window, potential crushes walking on the street seconds away from sighting their bare rear ends, shameful windowsill teenage moons.

Their reprieve is the giggle, the one forever there to catch them: they fall upon each other giggling to stitch back a world where all is as forgiving as their fun-seeking selves. Because making themselves at home in a fraternity house or anyone's dorm does not mean they ever kiss or sleep with any boy. What is fun is unilateral power, one the Lolas don't understand, the bubble of oblivion keeping them content, the boys as boys never mattering. What is fun is disguise and age transvestism, the two-headed revolution of the Lolas, their statutory taboo entry into any place that would forbid them. Their religion is movement, their sacrament choice, their enemy everyone else's sincerity, their savior the giggle that lets any wound of their own stay unspoken.

Perhaps inevitably, they befriend a guy who may be in his twenties but could be crawling toward fifty, a genial bearded bear of a man who works in a used-record store and goes by the name Big George. On the sly he hands them old records so they each amass a collection, a departure from the lesbian songwriters whose work Rose memorized in her earlier years. *Go back into the darkness like the wild thing that you are; sing out a song of the soul; I would go through the desert for you.* By some implicit agreement, the Lolas divvy up bands. They love obscure songs but once they go to a concert by a London garage band they are smitten and start using the band as a mood regulator while getting dressed in their most frequent uniform, tank tops and plaid shirts, readying themselves for the serendipity of a nighttime walkabout.

Behind these travels in best-friendship play not just a soundtrack but a couple of movies, both from swinging London of the sixties: one features a band in pill-addled, bonking high spirits while the other shows actors from another band as gangsters living it up, rousting about in leopard-print velvet pads with various actresses to whom, in their tease mode, the Lolas have been occasionally referenced. Both signify their mischievous future, the ability to hold power among danger without either element mastering them. Their soundtrack is mainly composed of songs that describe a She who Rose believes she should become, an elusive, mysterious, charismatic and slightly cruel girl driving the singer wild with desire or nostalgia while performing acts as simple as bending to tie the lace of the singer's shoe. Three songs in particular have chord changes and lyrics that master Rose's marrow. The first song, about a relationship gone sour, begins like this:

(lucid, sad guitar riff) *Angie, when will those clouds all disappear?*

During the peak of the Lolas, Lana likes to twiddle Rose by playing "Angie" at her like an instrument of war, since its A-minor sentiment can make Rose cry. What does Rose hear in the song? A future terminus? The malaise of adult relationships? The second song comes from Rose's adopted brother's domain: yearning, a cold spring rain, a smile from a veil, trading heroes for ghosts, wishing someone were closer.

But the last song plays seed to their budding selves, beginning so deceptively bubble gum and danger-free. The song is by the band that Rose gets to implicitly claim, given both affinity and prior acquaintance. The song has an intro that goes like this: C (repeated many times), D, E, after which the majority of the song takes place in the I-IV-V realm of A-D-E. The stuttered insistence of the C is the first foreshadowing of the danger zones into which the song will slip later, the C only a temporary illusion of ease, and Rose feels that if she listens closely enough to the song, she will find her future.

But I know what I am and I'm glad I'm a man
And so is Lola.

Somewhere around *so is Lola*, a potent danger chord enters: the return of the C, which undoes the sharps of the A-D-E system, presenting more of a stealth danger than the going-out-on-a-falsetto-limb of the G#7-C#m at *I got down on my knees*.

In the song that loans them their nighttime names, Rose hears at least some of her future with Lana, who, by letting her live as an outlaw, makes her whole.

On the day squeamish Rose is to dissect fetal pigs in biology lab, Lana covertly places thick slabs of ham between the pages of the lab book so that, on opening the book, Rose almost faints before falling back into the giggle. Or Lana fills Rose's locker with water balloons so that when she opens the metal door, a cascade of balloons splashes her homework. Later that day Lana convinces Rose to steal the keys to her mother's car for some stammering neighbor boy to instruct them in how to start the Volvo so that two girls can drive underage in 1950s missile-breast bikinis they have pilfered from one of those mysterious mother drawers filled with layered silk scarves and well-perfumed earring boxes.

Nothing is not useful. They drive poorly to a eucalyptus clearing where they lie on their backs wearing cardboard-tipped swimsuits, letting rain drum the flat of their bellies, their viewers not just each other but the imaginary, slightly shocked audience they always tote around to cheer them on. They have come to this clearing as if rain-spattered beatnik exhilaration had been their mission back at alpha, drugged without drugs, beatitude theirs to find even if their own chivalric code means that the next day they can never talk about the previous day's hijinks.

Instead they return to their usual sport, running the halls of their school with its organized topography. On the roof, stoners sit between classes, listening to country-inflected rock, ushering in dense, eloquent silences while future alligator lawyers circumnavigate the school's lower levels, nearly indistinguishable to the girls from unmoored oddities like the bearded Trotskyite who will become a deacon, a boy navigating adolescence by carrying a small black briefcase around everywhere, using a ruler from it to measure the straight nose of any potential future wife. Lana and Rose belong to no group but travel in and out of many, still a possibility in a small high school. Because Lana has an older soccer-playing neighbor at the school who is friendly with Rose's adopted brother, the girls hear megaphoned the older kids' gossip. Certain boys who, according to Rose's brother, may have a crush on the Lolas become just silly background. Whenever such boys turn a corner in the halls, following Lana's lead, Rose squeals some non sequitur and runs away.

According to these older boys, the Lolas are cruel. And if this repute has not deterred them in the slightest, if they go on squeaking names and dancing away, perhaps it is because they know they get to stay basically good girls whose friendship keeps them safe, riding every rule on the outskirts of respectability.

Really, they might as well be Catholic-school girls rather than girls whose parents have no idea where they are: their friendship keeps them chaste. Another era surely would call them teases. Yet being a tease suggests manipulation while the Lolas stay virgins, dancing on the brink of understanding the power that Rose will later think America—and especially California but most particularly Berkeley—gives girls too early. The Lolas never look directly into the flame, preferring to use it without possessing it. Instead they act as enlightened despots of pubescent sexuality, willing to listen to their peasants' complaints without ever taking any charge of burnt barns, stolen cows or pilfered land as seriously as the workers might like.

Why take anything seriously? All along they stay physical with each other in some sort of jokey nipple-tweaking way, nicknaming each other Buxom, their love less sexual than total, Californian in its appreciation of the other's physical being, an annexation of identity. They give each other long oil massages in invented steam rooms powered by blow-dryers under a hanging sheet, seeming to horrify Lana's father Vic when he catches them engaged in their sport. But the actual sexual act is inconceivable: music lubricates them, Lana's long-limbed beauty soothes Rose, and what they really mate with is the accretion of all their moments into one brilliant future.

Lying in one of their beds after another nighttime walkabout, adults vanished, what Rose always says to Lana is *can I hug you from behind?* since behind demands nothing. *Can I hug you from behind*, which makes Lana automatically turn and Rose's hand flop over that waist, casual in touching a human screen that lets the world's eye of grace stare back.

Grace—because she is learning something, especially having been let into Lana's house, an abode with two married parents and her bathroom a tiled nave perfumed by kitty litter and the banana-peel warmth of Lana's sweat. Rose seethes with curiosity, feeling as if she has been let into the sanctum of a fellow novitiate who has managed, so far, to navigate girlhood with an admirably simple diffidence.

While Rose will later think that the interior of any woman's medicine cabinet reveals all attendant fantasy life, Lana's cabinet secrets are so simple: scissors, an eye pencil, a medieval French amulet of two fish swallowing one bird. Cloaking all anthropological tendencies, Rose will be studious and make no comment, given the formality that descends on them in the daytime in either girl's house, making them exquisitely sensitive to the invisible rites of family, the girls turning boyish as they grab apples from the kitchen so they can scoot by, usually, Mary cooking, their haunt most often Lana's house. The girls grab their apples before hitting an outside world that returns the liberty of disguise.

One of the things the girls do, and Rose is both proud and ashamed of it, is linger in skinny jeans around one of the pizza joints near the university, the one with its bathroom scented as if with hyperchemical bubble gum, the one with jukebox music loud enough that everyone upon entry ascends into soundtrack nirvana, each person starring in a pizza movie. If the girls are famished, which is always, and have no money in their coats, which is often, it is easy enough to be a bad guy and, when someone else's slice is ready at the pick-up counter, to take it, to calmly slide into a booth and eat it. No one suspects two teenage girls with big smeared eyes and smooth legs of minor crime since it would insult the grace the girls bank on, the impunity granted by the other. Free, the pizza tastes better, though taste matters less than the confirmation of each other, the mobile law of two. And while Rose looks away from the customers' consternation, Lana never seems to notice. Just once she says they are Robin Hood, taking from the pizza joint and giving to the poor. But what makes them so poor? What deficit lives in their hearts?

Sometimes their parents and onlookers want to tell them something to the effect that their gazes will exhaust each other and they should let others in more. Once Vic quotes to them some C. S. Lewis idea about true friendship dwelling not in those who stare into each other's eyes but rather in those who hold hands and look ahead at the road. This quote is what makes Rose, at least, relent and teach the Lola flow to their most die-hard tagalong, Jane Polsby whom they tolerate because she never reproaches them, her bit lip adding only more energy to the Lolas. It doesn't matter. Jane learns the dance and nothing changes. If the dazzle is too great and the Lolas do get exhausted, no one knows: they probably just go off giggling in one more frenzy of activity.

When Rose goes away for a summer after junior year, she returns to find new music forms Lana's soundtrack. If they both once liked certain British bands with bleary morning-after tenderness, mumbled lyrics and fluted nasalities over insistent guitar lines, Rose finds, after her return, that there are zones to which she does not wish to follow Lana: bland overproduced bands, for one, or Lana's new routine of not showing up for a walkabout. Or Lana's new hair-gelled friend who goes out with Lana's neighbor and whose disyllabic name, whenever Rose hears it, acts as a gut punch. It is during the Lolas' last year of high school that, firing against loss, they both take on serious older boyfriends.

And still, half understanding their bereavement, based on the choice of a single upper-class girl they both glamorize, they apply to the same Manhattan college and get in. If it hadn't happened, in a solo move, Rose had considered joining some touring all-women's band for which she had auditioned as a keyboardist.

Instead, aiming for togetherness, their last-ditch attempt, that summer before college, the Lolas travel together, not admitting how apishly they mimic Kerouac or Hemingway. Together they budget-travel in Europe, stay with heroin addicts in Paris, sleep in rosebeds in Cannes, on parkgrounds in Pamplona, at a surfer's home in Biarritz, under fishing boats on the beach in Greece before the policemen come, wielding flashlights. Along the way, bad things happen to both of them, separate and together, their connection faltering, their fuses disconnected.

Rose thinks the main problem is that Lana takes men too seriously, including the budding rock star she left back in San Francisco. In *On the Road*, Dean Moriarty and Sal hadn't let conquests stir up their friendship, had they? On a Greek island beach, Lana reads Rose's diary, the latest version of *Say Something*, and, dismayed by her friend's dismay, Lana finally shows a trace of the female tenderness that four years of ironic teasing and manic listmaking have veiled. For a second, Lana looks upon Rose with a maternal tilt to her head, the unfamiliarity of her attitude a final sundering to the Lolas, Lana leaning toward Rose, sweet as a mother. How much Rose wants to lean away from that tilt, reject any stranger tenderness.

In their era, an unwritten curriculum comes with college: perform a certain kind of lesbian experimention and feel the act to be political, one more strike against the patriarchy! Girls from Boise, the South Side, Rockland County or Berkeley go to college, join the women's center and after meetings tangle limbs, finding a way to bring all those heavy breathers from French lit or feminist film theory down to earth, even if after college many of these same limb-tanglers end up growing their hair long and seeking conventional marriages to brokers.

If Rose does believe that everyone lives on a spectrum of orientation, she also thinks her Lola experience makes her different. She holds the credo that college girls who have never known the kind of friendship she has, a female camaraderie embracing the whole of a person, will be more likely to take their college flings seriously, as cartoon-flipped signposts for their future rather than as some sort of theory-driven gangway. Rose sees the girls entwining and thinks: all these flings let girls undergoing their first homelessness find mother. They just want some breasts to bury themselves between. Either that, or they try hard to reconcile the contradictions of American mating rituals. While Rose will be like a battle-burnt soldier refusing to touch guns: she barely wishes to admit that girls could desire other girls, mourns her Lola days and rarely sees Lana in New York, sensing ahead a wasteland of compromise and more sundering. What had been sacred for her about the Lola bubble was how unconsumed by sexuality it had been, the Lolas a vessel for all those odd hormonal energies, endlessly self-replenishing and never subsumed by anything coarse. Is there a name for the complete love one teenage girl has for another?

For a Women and Love class, Rose writes an essay to ask:

"Is there a place defended against the onslaught of precocious American heterosexist socializing or adulthood's torrid-water echo in homosexist theory? This indefinability makes me understand why a pop song about being initiated by a British transvestite became the high-school song that mattered most to me.

"My best friend and I did a dance we called the Lola flow, one that let pleasure come to the brim. We must have known our getting to live in a bubble, so oblivious and playful, was precious, undefinable, fleeting, cruel and foolish, a song of innocence. To do our dance, you had to close your eyes. Within that spotted darkness we belonged to a league of girls, to rules beginning and dying within thousands of pairs of teenage girls across the world who, at that exact moment, were inventing their own variation.

"Only recently, I had a dream that some big-spanned bird of endings flies over all us girls, spotting our hunger and still granting the illusion that we will get to do the dance undyingly or at least until a whole hopeful universe gets pecked away speck by speck."

Early in their friendship, the girls go with Lana's father to San Francisco, the first of many outings in which Vic becomes not just conduit but charger of the Lolas, a crucial component making their electricity crackle. On this outing he takes them to a department store where he grows impatient with the salesgirls, fingering each sweater or shirt brought him before dismissing it as trashy, his edginess enough to reel the clerks in, making them turn amazed eyes on Vic and ignore other customers, instead hoisting shirts, sweaters and dresses Vic's way, seeking to meet such high standards for this father that he becomes the last in a line of kings to understand garments, capable of turning an overcast Saturday in San Francisco into a medieval Michaelmas: the clothes brought for his consumption suckling pigs on trays, the Lolas mere mannequins for the king's whim. When, too, the truth of Vic is that he cares not a jot about clothes, that his wife Mary tends to every detail of his personal appearance, and only by her ministrations does he approximate a put-together, tweed-patch professor.

Toward the end of the shopping trip, vocal in disgust at the poor quality of today's tailoring, Vic does surrender, asking the girls to try on two overpriced fuzzy blue angora sweaters, a designer name stitched at the waistband. Outside the dressing room he sits, a book on ethics in his lap, smiling at first when the girls emerge and twirl before the mirror. "I like it, papa," says Lana: shy for once, breasts ripe, posture stiff in the blue sweater in order to keep some interior hourglass silt from rushing down.

This pleasure in her appearance swings him toward disdain. Before paying, Vic talks with scorn of female vanity, flipping another switch in Lana: she now preens with ostentation, erect in her sweater's blue fuzz.

"Let's leave this place," he snarls.

"Why?"

"Too much titivation and tergiversation."

"What?"

"Too many crowds."

After which, in a mood, he takes them to the city's edge where he rolls up his pants, emptying his pockets into Lana's purse before wading into the water and leaving them as his onshore watchers. No longer the tweed professor, he enters his body just by walking through water. For the first time Rose can't ignore his appeal. The barrel-breadth of his shoulders, the naked waist. When the ocean shelf drops, he begins swimming out.

Vic had told the girls that in his days as a young immigrant student, fresh from Liechtenstein in the fifties, hopeless and uncool, he had come to community college in Los Angeles, where he had started working in a board shop by the beach and there learned to surf, waiting hours in the waves for the right ride with a philosophical Bolivian friend, a great mentor to his later thinking. Those hours on his board he counted as among his best, the negative ions around the ocean acting on the brain, leaving the temporal lobe more capable of embracing the present. Within this blankness, his best and first ideas had grown: *I'll never recapture the inspiration of those first moments.* Like many young American boys, he'd found the ocean complete as a mother, baseball or rock and roll in how it granted tribe and hope.

"You're making it up." Lana had laughed. "What are you talking about?"

Watching him swim out from the San Francisco shore, Rose wonders how far he will go, because even after she had stopped living in group homes and been adopted by Joan, she has seen that adults in the outside world are prone to freakish displays of will. She also remembers the scene in a movie Joan had taken her to when Rose had been too young, the movie with the proud and stiff Vietnam-vet husband leaving his wife because she had been unfaithful with a hippie paraplegic at home, after which the vet goes into the waves to kill himself.

But eventually Lana's father returns, bobbing up and down in the waves. No one mentions his swim or the dragon of fear raised in the girls. Instead they lean back, hands planted on the beach, mock casual, seeing him so alive. Hair wet, profile rugged, attitude impatient, handsome and grilling them as if he must make an important decision.

He wants to know. "Which do you like more, girls? Mountains or ocean? Mountains or ocean?" When riled, he speaks in pairs, a metaphysical weight hinging on their response.

"Mountains with ocean," says Rose, hedging bets.

"What about you, Mopsy?"

"Neither," says Lana, smirking.

He wants to get at them somehow, riddle their teenage confidence. "Do you two believe God made man before woman?"

When they don't know, his answer is this: he scoops up a handful of sand, leaving a pit and making a small mound. "You see? Tell this to people who accuse me of being antifeminist. You see who really came first?"

"I don't," says Lana. "I have no idea what you're saying."

And he looks at her perplexed, dark child in her new sweater, his girl offspring, shaking his head as if he has fallen into some unfortunate spell that he should have gotten rid of at least fifteen years earlier. And then wants to wear his wet clothes back to the car, puddling the driver's seat, hurrying everyone home to Berkeley, cautioning them not to wear the blue sweaters around either of their mothers, a condition they accept, just one part of an eccentric day with a man whose odd self, like his daughter's, doesn't make it easy for people to fall in love and so most of them can't help but go ahead and fall.

All you must do is connect with prison mind.

Vic's beloved guard Javier loves telling him this. "Prison mind means you get to choose the terms of your imprisonment. Also you got to try to understand connection." Javier happens to be a third-rate philosopher who could have awoken to find himself in a two-bit coffeehouse rather than a grade-one prison. He does not belong in a world made up of contraband tattoo guns, shanks sharpened from seat-release levers stolen from admin chairs, drug-sniffing German shepherds and a super who makes up for his short height by walking the hallways daily around four o'clock with razor nose aloft, squinting into the bike-repair shop where Vic worked in the beginning before he'd tried the child's toy factory until he finally gave up on finding any meaning through the prison's idea of work. Vic actually likes the pompous superintendent and his predictability, his childish bliss when ordering the masked, hooded, armor-plated cell-extraction team to come, the super's obvious enjoyment in rippling safety measures through the institution at the slightest encounter of defiance in an offender. On his walkie-talkie, the super becomes ecstatically terse: we found a kite, he mutters, a kite and a tool besides.

Of course, Vic knows the officials have long considered him a docile offender and as such he has often been granted special status. During smaller earthquakes or fire drills, even the occasional bright-light, midnight lockdown after evidence of gang activity on the grounds, the guards apologize when binding plastic cuffs to his wrists behind his back. From his earliest days, all the guards have called him Legend and the name has stuck. All these years, but for his time with Javier, Vic has done what he can to spiral in upon himself and keep apart from others in the institution. Mainly simple desires plague him. To see Mary asleep in a window seat, head resting on her hand. To breathe ocean air again. Vic has made friends with no one but for one jocular, well-tattooed offender nicknamed Fatback who'd landed in Old Parcel for two counts of murder on a bad Wednesday, as Fatback told Vic in their first meeting in the showers. Two notable years later, on another Wednesday, Fatback's execution date, Vic had been unable to eat, sleep, speak a word to anyone.

Vic knows his luck. He knows, too, about shanks slid under light-bulbs or along elevator shafts; he has always tried to avoid staring at the offenders inking gang tattoos in the yard corner. Being stationed in a cell block with no bad offenders nearby, in a final station of the cross these last three months being administered by a CO named Javier, a real gentleman of a guard, all this should spell luck, if highly metered, for Vic.

Because unlike the other COs Vic has known, Javier early on started confiding in Vic, making Vic feel whole slices of himself dragged out of deep freeze. About Javier, Vic knows plenty: not only that Javier is alone in raising his daughter but also that his first child, a son, had been born in Mérida with cerebral palsy. And that after the family had crossed into California, right after Javier's young daughter's third birthday, the son had died.

At night I mothered that boy, Javier said, he could do nothing for himself. I had to neglect his baby sister. You know the boy was an angel, but I'm glad he found some peace. After the boy died, the kids' mother was diagnosed with such severe depression that some American flag-flying, beer-drinking neighbors called child protection services while Javier was trying to live the American dream best he could. At that time Javier worked two jobs, one in a filling station and the other in a convenience store, while also taking night classes in criminal justice because he was the one in his family everyone knew would get out, the husband who had promised the mother of his kids he would never yell, having seen what bottles and fists do to a family as well as the sadness stretched like a crowbar across his own mother's shoulders so that at age fifty she ended up with an actual dowager's hump. He tells all this to Vic, Vic thirsty for others' confessions. While another CO had once squawked on the intercom *what, is this place a library?* when Vic had asked to get some new books, Javier makes it a practice to bring Vic any new book available from the library two whole cell blocks away.

Anyone can see Javier is a good sort, which is why Vic fails to understand his life story: though Javier had been good at promise-keeping, working around the clock to support his damaged son and perfect baby daughter, the child protection people had, some years ago, taken his daughter away just because the girl's mother refused to take antidepressants and had one day let little Deisi sit for hours in a dirty diaper, playing with dirt in the yard. Javier's entire life could have fallen like the house of cards it was had his wife not chosen to return to Mérida, a decision best for everyone given that Javier now gets to play both mother and father to his sixteen-year-old girl now entering the difficult teen years. His main wish is to keep the girl under tight lock and key so she can stay an honor student. His luck has changed and the raffle had granted him a green card, making citizenship hot in his heart, the name of the twenty-sixth president the kind of fact he can summon quickly. And Javier never, not even in traffic, speaks on a cell phone, a recent outside-world custom, one of many about which Vic knows nothing.

"Isn't it nice sometimes to not be on the phone?" Vic asks, to which Javier just shrugs. He tells Vic that at times he is getting out of his car while staying on the phone with his daughter who stands at the door watching him tell her he is getting out of the car.

"That's how things are on the outside," says Javier, "we need tons of connection."

Since the best pay in the area comes from the local prison and since a neighbor helps him supervise Deisi, Javier recently started working night shift, moonlighting two jobs to keep proving to the child protection people, who have never let him out of their sights, that a lone Mexican can make enough money to play both mother and father.

"Believe me, I do it all for my daughter," he tells Vic. "Funny, right? I work for the state so I can keep the feds away?"

It is clear to see why everyone trusts Javier: he can speak others' lingo. Vic especially appreciates the way Javier manages to rally, always ready to squeeze a philosophical frame onto experience and in not just this way, Javier reminds him of one of his old-time students, trying to impress. Despite his cologne, Javier puts on few other airs, happy to entertain Vic's talk of anything, even of vigilantism and lynching history as strong predictors of the density of a state's inmates who reach capital punishment. And if the CO knows Vic's crime, he instead chooses to talk of issues like prison mind.

Javier has said that the people in charge of the Bureau of Prisons want more than anything to connect: to taxpayers, bureaucrats, offenders.

"You're one of the few appreciates the guards," Javier tells Vic, also seeming to think that by sharing protocol with Vic, he will free at least part of Vic's mind.

Because Javier had loaned him the execution protocol manual, Vic knows every step that will lead to his own death. Beyond the choice of electricity over poison, few other choices exist, the supreme joke of a humane age.

Lunchtime, doing a double shift, Javier shows up outside the slats, hair glossy, gaze muted.

Vic senses that something embarrassing and unmanly may have transpired the day before—had the men hugged each other?—and that it might be advisable to seek restitution. "You know, prisoners want connection too," says Vic. He senses, speaking what he meant as an apology, a thump. His terminology sounds vulnerable as a come-on; a tongue that used to be able to turn anything into glissando is now too thick to spin a riddle.

Another piece of prison must be this loss of control. Sentences slip away with unmanageable echo, even as Vic would like to make a joke about one of Javier's stories, the one about the dimwit doomed to be executed. He'd been condemned the year before Vic showed up in Old Parcel, when Javier had been assigned to another unit. "That cheeseburger guy?" Vic manages this half-sentence in Javier's general direction.

During his last meal, the guy had eaten half his cheeseburger. He had then carefully wrapped the other half in a Bureau of Prisons linen, saying to Javier: *I'll save the rest for later.*

"Dimwits on the taxpayer's dime," Javier says now, having delivered the lunch tray, readying himself for disappearance. No one has yet mentioned what now comes back clear as a heart attack: that Vic had asked Javier to lay his head on his chest, the memory a nail hammered through Vic's sternum.

"Sir, actually? Take your meds before lunch? Stay sitting up." Javier turns back, remembering, waiting to watch as Vic chokes down the rainbow of horse pellets since this happens to be the week that finds Javier and Vic between nursing assistants. The Bureau of Prisons, one of those rare institutions suffering from a budget surplus, still has a hard time finding RNs willing to work in any capacity within the broad field of capital punishment. Given the extra medical and forensic credits Javier had taken during recertification, until the BOP finds a solution for Vic's cell block, Javier has been asked, in the interim, to sign on for additional duty, including checking on the functioning of Vic's pacemaker, that little electronic disc only the slightest little bulge out from his chest. "Keep going," murmurs the guard. When Vic is done with the big-pharm golden-calf veneration, swallowing down the last of the water, his guard asks: "You okay for the afternoon, Legend?"

Left to his own devices, sometimes Vic organizes what is happening in his case. He sits up again to write out facts in a spidery handwriting, one skittering toward the edges of the paper, claiming corners in a penmanship no longer his own:

1st—

he writes,

I tried to get a mistrial called because that first defense attorney remained a drunk, despite protestations of sobriety, and had been thrown off many other cases. The judge failed to call a mistrial because it would have marred her unblemished record of completed trials.

2nd—I am waiting for a stay on compassionate, medical grounds. That is: a cancer eats me from the inside out, no one ever fully sur-

vives brain cancer and I am on the tail end of some chemothera-
peutic protocol which is not working, so why should the state go to
the bother, expense and political capital involved in execution? The
new lawyer says the question forms the answer, but also that given
the imminent California statute, the answer could work in my favor. Too much interest by the state at this juncture could prove
dangerous.

His handwriting foils him: it fails to provide the satisfaction of
ordering chaos, and in this way as well, Vic sympathizes with the short
super and his love of control.

On good days, Vic likes to call it impulse rather than choice that
led him to prison: but do distinctions matter? Whatever it is, at this
point Vic's choice would have graduated from college, and now those
who rule far above the razor-nosed super of Old Parcel wish to do
exactly this, graduate Vic.

At least he still has his mind or most of it, usually, and for this
greater portion the officials have sustained their illusions, offering new
college degrees and a choice of chaplains, the opportunity to create a
prisoners' Web site, throngs of pen pals. The only good thing about his
cell block, this final row before execution, is its relative quiet, a boon
for Vic's sensitive ears for years bombarded by inmates shouting out
chess moves through iron grilles at one another, each inmate with a
board in parallel, moving queens, pawns and bishops made of com-
pressed toilet paper. Vic, too, used to engage in cage chess as well as
all the other desperate games, cage Monopoly, checkers, bridge, but
now the people in charge have rendered upon him this balm of quiet
and soon the BOP will offer its final fur-lined coat: the last meal and
statement.

Would any pharaoh not have been stymied by the idea of making
a last statement?

I am clear-sighted, pragmatic, prepared. Does one wait for the elev-
enth hour to write last thoughts on a subject?

Cynics in the fourth century suggested that parents who outlive their usefulness might become food for their children. First night in prison, Vic decided that every word he would write would be not for his dead wife but his absentee daughter, though sometimes the women he has known and what he imagines as their poisonous sac of rage against him merge and in this way his wife and daughter appear to be one. *It's about correcting behavior, not being,* his wife used to caution whenever he mentioned using some harsh, old-world child-rearing technique on their daughter Lana. He used to say back: *she has been spared the switch and probably spoiled.*

Though in truth, given his background, he had never been that vigorous a believer in any kind of corporal discipline. If Mary could have lived and just known her wrongness, lived with wrongness at the base of her self, clearly Vic would have chosen that she still be alive. No man wants a dead wife. Not divorced, not separated but dead when a man can't talk back to death. The ultimate gag. In fact everything in these last few years, everything but his luck in being assigned such a supreme, excellent correctional officer as Javier a few months ago, seems to have been designed to lead Vic toward mutism or at least superior control of his mouth.

Ever since those first days in prison, Vic has given up protesting his innocence. As the first of the guards had told him during intake, people never say what they're in for and, besides, no one will believe you anyway.

That first guard, avuncular Kevin Barraco with his long jaw scar, had taken chewing gum from Vic because gum of all flavors can jam a lock after a guard leaves, and had also tossed the highlighter pen Vic used to keep compulsively in his chest pocket, telling prisoner #4267 that highlighters make marks that the surveillance camera regards as identical to the invisible-ink numbers stamped onto visitors' hands. Kevin Barraco had been so casual in surrendering prison secrets that Vic could not help but be fascinated by what seemed like the tubercular hotel he was entering for a little R and R. The guard had said: look, you'll thrive if you assume everyone has maximum guilt. People pass in the halls and who cares what they stink of, disinfectant or damp wool blankets, you got to turn your eyes inside, play the game, smell only mood. You'll never get to pretend you have a pressing arrangement someplace else.

Based on the optimism of the first of a phalanx of forgettable, incompetent lawyers, that first year Vic still believed he would get out. *Self-defense, mistrial*: the ideas had floated like happy unpopped balloons at one of his daughter's old-time birthday parties. Back in the child balloon era, he used to think that actually all he needed was the equivalent of a hotel, some anonymous place functioning on its own rules, plus a few good years alone without family to think. You get what you wish for, he'd preached to the followers his family called his shaggies, and here for years he has tasted the bad news: prison lets him think. The special cruelty being that, whatever liberal ideals anyone has about rehabilitation, redirection, recidivism, no way in hell can the officials fill your moments, the machine so much huger than anyone's ideals, knowing that around every corner, second-guessing awaits you. *What might I have done differently?* And the state knows this second-guessing will kill you better than any state-devised torture, your time like taffy, uncountably palpable. The key is that you must stretch into time, not let it stretch you.

Sometimes Vic uses the bones they throw, time-killers like the frat-like movie nights with glazed donuts, or even the computer room, filled with the banter of all offenders deemed mid-risk by the super. Some leftist billionaire had gold-rushed the commodity of blue-green algae and in a similar onrush of do-gooder spirit had granted the prison its computers, each branded with his company's name in letters the exact hue of the green-lace mildew spilling down the room's corners.

Though Vic got iron-barred before people started using the Internet for everything, he quickly understood the idea of a web connecting people's brains—his earliest work had rotated around this idea—and so he became among the first in his cell block to apply for privileges. In the computer room, using this new web to catch old flies, sometimes he almost finds that former thrill of freedom. Only occasionally does he stoop to looking up the sites everyone else looks up: the best way to pick padlocks or the lurid history of some surly CO.

Part of the problem is that the computer room is so dank and subterranean: whatever bones the officials throw your way, they also make sure you never forget that above lives the law with its memory of your act, and this act means you have become unremarkable muck flowing below others' surface gratings. Sometimes in their special cruelty the officials of the machine open a slat in the computer room so offenders catch a surprise whiff, not cafeteria-fried chicken but rather wet daisies reaching up.

During intake, Vic had failed to guess at the machine's vastness, not understanding that some force had it in for him, one that would find maximum excitation if the rest of his life became one long bridge of sighs, and that also there would be little he could do against any chunk of the machine without getting written up as some hapless revolutionary.

After he turned himself in, a foolish believer in the blindness of justice, he had no idea how reciprocal his act would become, how terrifyingly symmetric. His faith had claimed that a justice that wished to hear both sides existed and that such justice would let him live, the delusion clinging even after they slapped him with a date and an end that bore the thousand plumes of all those ridiculous inmate nicknames, the product of the bastard creativity that flourishes only inside a machine like state-sponsored execution. At first he finds the names for execution so optimistically witty: the necktie party and meat-fryer, the crown of thorns, the reverse toilet, the Rosenberg hug, the sociable, names letting a person both belittle and cozy up to a cranky patriarch. Later Vic will revile the poverty of nicknames:

whatever its tribe members call execution, the thing still will beat them.

What Vic pores over and cannot help but revisit is less his bad act and more his failure in facing off against the jury, composed of bland western faces who surely lived in their own glass Sacramento houses and yet dared throw such stones, convicting him before going home to sleep just as if Vic Mahler—he had to think of his case as belonging to an entity named Vic Mahler—lacked extenuating circumstances. For all that Vic had tried, he had not been able to talk them out of their smugness.

After twenty-plus years, the actual jury faces had faded enough to let other demons take their place: the parade of lawyers breathless in explaining the shifting winds of constitutionality, the governor's fickle finger allowing some offenders to live and others go the way of the chair, Vic witness to it all, to the rising popularity of lethal injection, the trails of campaign promises made and rescinded, the referenda and ballot initiatives, the need to build new prisons to satisfy communities, the state's debates over fear versus finances unending. It is clear that the machine undergoes its convulsions, the machine with its need to keep him in a place evil enough to boil the princeliness off any frog. Truly, the slowness of the boil is most ingenious, one that makes Vic's current address the obverse of Eden, a sadist's ultimate expulsion. So why had his overmasters not gone and offed Vic years ago? Instead they want him to second-guess and suffer, to choke on the hemlock of memory, to sight his own Gomorrah. They like him less as a man and more as their own personal pillar of salt.

One day someone will take his tray.

One day, unseen, people he has never met, members of the community benefiting from the prison's placement in a boom-and-bust agricultural valley, workers trained and registered for the job, will emerge from the arteries and move toward the heart, knowledgeable about oxygen. Everyone will file into an execution room the color of gray fingernails. The workers' goal will be to guarantee that the air-conditioning works and lighting functions. Their chief concern will be that all inside, witnesses and condemned alike, remain comfortable. To the warden, at some point, they will give a thumbs-up.

A man or woman, because at this point it might still be a woman, will press a switch. Down the hall a blue light will blink its jealous eye, a sign for the strip search in his cell, a mild indignity Vic likes, the laying-on of hands a rite good enough to ease a backache made chronic after years on a cot, the hands better than a visit from the doctor, and this when, in life outside, he had never known as good a doctor as you find inside, feeling himself lucky to have encountered so many wonderful doctors, with names he has forgotten, all dedicated to promoting his health.

After the strip search will come the reverse promenade.

Somewhere between the opening and closing of curtains, he will make his last statement, noted by the Bureau of Prisons official recorder. He will have five minutes to speak before select witnesses, numbering exactly zero, an empathetic and beautiful figure to contemplate, zero, a gift from the Arabs, an icon comprehending the existential abyss. If he will not have managed to summon his daughter to see him while he lives, why would he invite his heir to be with him, buffering him from zero at the moment of death? So he will be alone, out of the cradle forever alone, and yet he will have five minutes to speak, this allowance a humanistic vestige from the Greeks and Romans: he will speak before the Warden, the Executioner and the Recorder. He could call these officials' mandate to inscribe his utterance a gift of the Enlightenment, and, as if Vic were truly a pharaoh or at least a Christ, he will become their burnt offering, reminding them of the worth of their own survival as well as their bourgeois pieties, allowing them to feel sober and practical in considering how many gifts they have given him on the path deathward.

At the right moment, 1:15 p.m. on December 26, 2008, drapes will be pulled so that the witnesses won't view suffering. The drapes, he notes, are a gift of the Americas: he may know the history of execution but the morphology still confounds him. In one of his books, which exactly he can't remember, he had called suffering *the dramatic interpretation that life performs on pain*. He had told Javier that the drapes must deprive the officials of theater, though the drapes must also act as a covered mirror for their own conscience.

And no one will care whether all memory of him dies right there or if his memory is resuscitated and finds new life.

Thus, until now, he has left the crumpled form on which he could write a final statement elegantly empty. Any script or utterance will be released to the media and his living heir.

Now, pen poised, given the equivalent of a fairytale's final wish, he considers what a lifetime of speech might free him to set down.

I would like to be given one last choice, he writes before immediately striking it out.

TWO

Rose could begin with superstition and the way all commonplaces
have turned into a command. All signs have been speaking to her in
the imperative. WASTE reads a trashcan and she wishes to chant back:
I refuse, I will not waste away. THE UNIVERSAL SIGN FOR CHOKING,
showing someone gagging, makes her say: I am no one's universal,
I will not sign for choking. When she reaches for an alarm clock in the
dark, her fingers close on a penknife and not because of the bloody cut
she gets but because she reached for the wrong thing, her day falters.

For years she has been sending letters to someone on death row
who used to write back letters funny and deep and these had been
good omens, but during these same years this man has refused to list
her as someone who could visit. He keeps his daughter's name lonely
on the list, Lana Mahler, and this when he lives behind bars 108
miles north, a number with enough mystical overtones to have invited Rose up from the apartment she calls her little rabbit hutch in
Ellay.

Thirteen days before his date, no stay in sight, she tells herself she
must have struck the wrong note. Plus she has failed to procure his
absentee daughter for him.

Zero letters from him in the last three months. A freak heat wave
demolishing a town that makes it an article of faith to scorn air

conditioners as a sign of imperfection. She leans over the kitchen sink and dyes her hair with sixteen ounces of black potion, breaking with a recent spell of bad luck. The chemicals she inhales with greed, the friendly tang of a foreign body piercing her solitude.

Hair dripping black, she gets on the phone to her assistant to cancel every object-loving, death-obsessed client. Mainly she wishes to cancel the march of time, what others call her business: she works part-time as an estate planner, helping people with loads of cookies or crumbs decide who gets what after they pass.

It's all about planning, she always says in her first meeting with clients. Being able to control the ultimate unknowable. Plan your passage well and no one loses, no one gets upset.

While to her boyfriend, not long ago, she had said that fulfilling appointments often makes her feel as if she too were swallowing cookies. As if everyone considers her, in the face of the uncomfortable topic of death, heroic for helping control what after all is just one more display of the hoarding and manipulation of crumbs, the sale of whatever someone held dear. In law school, she'd had a classmate, admirable if not friend material, with abundant dark hair and a glow Rose had admired, the classmate flouncing around and saving people, ending up a specialist on the problem of snitching in low-income communities and its impact on death-row cases. An exemplary road. Rose could have chosen a field of law where she really changed people's lives for the better, child custody or capital punishment, but she had been repelled by, on the one hand, the rise of vigilance about sexual abuse, and on the other, the use of DNA testing, finding both too exact in their methodology, allowing for little nuance, and without planning, she had ended up in the cul-de-sac of estate law which was nothing if not about exactitude.

Only a couple of months earlier, she had followed in the news the case of Dondi Watson, a boy from her elementary school who had grown up to face the death penalty for Oakland gang killings but who had one of those popular moralizing lawyers able to exonerate Dondi via DNA testing. Now that too seemed laudable: Dondi free to live. Years ago Rose had won a spelling bee, her face in the paper, and Dondi had biked up afterward, hair shiny, mouth happy and jeering, solely to let her know her chest was just as flat as her picture had promised. Back then she also could tell he was impressed and they had exchanged something of value and unknown valence so that years later, feverish in reading an interview with Dondi, just prior to his exoneration, she felt called to be less useless, as if the two of them had left invisible ash thumbprints on each other that only now became visible. She had thrust down the paper, lack of purpose heaped up, venting to her boyfriend all the reasons she felt so meaningless practicing something as petty as estate law. Maybe this uselessness had kept her barren, hope mislaid in her womb.

Don't be so hard on yourself, her boyfriend had said, *want to go walk on the beach?*

In the welcome chill of the corner diner, awaiting an omelet of two whites, she lays down fork, knife and spoon with care, as ever trying not to feel the hole in her stomach, the one that makes her, right now, see the utensils as signs of the devil, ending and lost hope.

Twenty-eight days prior, the city starting to cook, Gan, potential father of her future children, had left.

Twenty-nine days prior, they had gone to a Dutch movie about a woman vanishing. In the movie theater, Rose had sat between Gan and some dreadlocked latecomer. At first she had not realized the hand running up her thighs belonged not to Gan but rather to the dreadlocked guy. Once aware, she vacated herself and let the stranger do whatever he wanted, his eyes on Gan the whole time. If this wasn't the first time she had gone so passive, she now reached some new peak of dissociation. The movie unspooled before her, unheedable. Once the lights came up, in the aisle she did confide at least one portion of the extracinematic activity to Gan, leaving out her own awareness, finding herself pleased that Gan flushed. For the first time her fiancé showed his caveman side by saying: *I want to go find that guy and smack him.* Though clearly the dreadlocked guy specialized in covert ops, having long since fled the theater, who cared about that, Rose was thrilled to find herself smack in the middle of a freedom stolen from her Lola days, the movie moment parachuted down into one of her bleakest epochs yet, studded with uselessness and the bad news of fertility appointments. Between Gan's anger and the dreadlocked guy's disappearance, she got to feel criminal, heedless of usual laws, and at this joy, Rose had needed to hug Gan close, after which she was good at faking a knowledgeable, reviews-based discussion of the movie.

Gan's caveman side was what made her, the next day, all the more surprised. In the same tone a person would use to cancel an order of burritos, Gan chose to say—while driving to yet another doctor who would advise them on the odds of sticking six human eggs into Rose's forty-one-year-old womb so she might gestate nine months and have at least one baby—that he thought it best they take a break.

Take a break. She didn't understand at first. Hadn't they been getting along? They used to kid about her unknown Viking genes and the fanfold held by a foster kid's endowment. He liked telling her she could be a product of royal incest, the heir of Lars the explorer and Birgit the queen. And when they had flipped through catalogues of potential egg donors, they had talked about Rose as a reverse chicken with someone's new eggs laid inside. Hadn't the whole thing really been one big copulative joke linking them? The odd-numbered dark rooms to which prim nurses sent Gan so he could scan magazines boasting trios of semi-naked Russian cheerleaders in order to ejaculate and save such strangely loved vital fluids in a test tube. And if their jokes faltered, hadn't they anyway been doing their best? Hadn't they been trying to produce something viable, the miracle of an organism with divisible heart and brain cells, a child and carrier of exquisite voltage, not triplets, not twins, no need to get greedy, just a singleton. *Something viable*, the voice of a newscaster broadcasting into her skull. Just one viable fertilized egg. She got it as she listened to Gan explaining his reasons for leaving: the punchline to all their attempts. Rose might end up one of those child-craving people who never got even one baby to cuddle.

In the diner, she counted and realized it had been exactly twenty-seven days since her last conversation with Gan and that this moment had augured her month of bad news. Clearly, the universe was not exactly voting in her favor. Was she being punished? For what? For having let some guy with incomparable hair touch her during *The Vanishing*?

Fourteen days before the diner breakfast, Rose had received a call from her adopted brother saying her adoptive mother had died. Nine days earlier, trying to understand how she fit into anyone's planetary scheme, Rose had rocket-launched herself out of Ellay to go find the gravesite of her birth-mother.

So this morning, after breakfast, still recovering from the bloat of all her recent egg-stimulating drugs, it makes sense that a flashing lightbulb in a diner's bathroom could be the sole sign suggesting escape, one that Rose interprets this way: she should go visit a section of Ellay she never frequents just to find a little something, and, while driving, she finds the boulevard's green lights confirm her choice. Having arrived at a freezing store, Rose fingers clothes undulating on a rack under five racks of recessed blue light, the beauty she has wished for serenading her down to the last wistful detail, to the sales-girl with her brown skin and a tattoo on her lower back: two tiger eyes, one of them winking.

"Your name's Rose?" says the salesgirl. "I love that. An old-fashioned name. You never hear it anymore. You barely belong in this modern period with a name like that, almost like Phyllis? I say don't go to that rack, Rose, you'll get lost over there, let me find you something amazing, like your name."

The salesgirl climbs high on a ladder to scavenge through boxes, working hard to earn her commission, *here you go, Phyllis*, when a voice enters the store, cutting through years.

At first, when the woman enters the store, Rose doesn't recognize her, since all women in Ellay look familiar, given that in Ellay women fashion themselves into recognizable icons so others may sight their potential as quickly as the eye processes a film frame, one sixteenth of a second. Yet if this woman in her long purple dress is disguised, her laugh gives her away, ripping through the store as she asks about park-ing, the laugh unmistakable, given that her former classmates used to say only a mother could love that kind of voice. Still Rose must squint, fast-shuttering past the purple muumuu over espadrilles to find pale-skinned Jane who back in high school did have the kind of mother unusual back in that era, so attentive and keen on expanding everyone's horizons that she hosted foreign students, a mother showing up early to every teacher meeting who made it seem that caring equated socially with throwing a smiling albatross around your kid's neck.

"Jane?"

"Rose! God. Can't believe it. Yesterday guess where I was? Remember that nudist colony up Five? Where we went years ago with Lana and her dad?"

"And her mom." Almost whispering.

"Yeah. Anyway. Guess who I saw? Lana. I'm not kidding. She didn't tell you she was going up there? But she looks great, of course, you too, right? But isn't that a coincidinky, like we used to say?"

"You saw Lana."

"I mean she barely had a grip on the fact we were all there together once. I'm not saying my memory's great either. But you guys must be in touch."

"Sure." The first voiced lie of the conversation.

"It's crazy she's moving to that place. I mean permanently?"

"Crazy."

"Not like I met her new boyfriend, but I'm sure he's, you know, or I can imagine. She's already been there a week. Different, right?"

"Totally."

"I always admired her free spirit, I mean yours too, but wouldn't you get sick of being in a place like that constantly? Her boyfriend's going to be guru. I'm not that groovy."

"No, no, you are but what's the name of the place again?"

"Hope Springs."

Rose smiles as if someone had just emerged from all life's inconsequential merchants to say now she could go dissolve herself in honey.

"You're too young to get senior moments, right, Rose? I mean we're in our prime. You know, speaking of, did the spa special up there. The best. If you're going up to visit Lana, got to try that, if you like seaweed—"

Hope Springs! For years Rose had been looking. She had stopped with the detective and computer services, had almost given up looking for Lana altogether.

Yet outside, after enduring much talk of seaweed facials and restorative wraps, there waits for Rose, on the Santa Monica curb, a perfect wheat-embossed penny, so rare these days.

Continue long enough in life, you find that what you call hope, some call amnesia and others call nostalgia. A woman enters a sulfurous open-air spa just south of California's navel. The place happens to be called Hope Springs and its clocks lag at least ten minutes behind any other clock on the Pacific coast. The woman will learn that the name, Hope, does not come from the misunderstood name of some native tribe, since, if once there had been prayer grounds, they now lie beneath the place where feet—brown red black white—pad toward one of three pools.

In her head she hears the refrain *Kansas, she says, is the name of the star.*

The hot pool, as the sign notes, is kept at 116 degrees Fahrenheit so that it scalds the skin, a way of saying that purification has begun and all prior selves will be scalped.

The woman—Lana Wagner, born California Fukuji Guzman Mahler— tells herself she is glad not to meet anyone's eyes, though secretly she cannot help her seduction habit.

The pamphlet says the warm pool is kept at a decent 96 degrees. Most people stand neck-deep, leaning against walls, showing a clear religion about the avoidance of gazes. Others float on backs, toes hooked under the guardrail, absorbing healing minerals, a whalelike breast or groin occasionally surfacing. Some help others float so they may deprive the senses. A few sit in dead seriousness facing each other, whispering, still enough to be having a sex at least tantric. The goals of this chosen gaol: push the senses forward or back, be in the body or float out of it in dead-man's pose.

As the catalogue states: this is a retreat center+site for soul expansion.

The cold pool is at 30 nipple-hardening degrees Fahrenheit. You are to plunge into this immediately before or after the hot pool. In a zone partitioned away from the adults' reconnection attempts, two small kidney-shaped baths await phantom kids.

I am dying, the woman is thinking, as many have thought before her, heat working at least ninety-nine strands of her past out into the waters, since, like many others in the spa, she is making vows about future behavior. Her hair waves, swirls upon itself. She pulls it up, ties it in a knot.

Tomorrow the Thirty-third Year birthday celebration of this place is due to start, a month of activities attracting all sorts of people wanting to let go, let it out, let God. According to rumor, there will be gatherings, rehearsals, reunions, a performance.

Nearby, a man in a railroad cap sweeps mulberries off the path. Does he also study the back of her neck?

Rules are posted everywhere around Hope Springs, taking on a tone familial or punitive, sometimes both.

NO BREAKABLES OR ROOM TOWELS IN THE POOL AREA.
NO CELL PHONES, DRUGS, PETS, OR CHILDREN IN THE ADULT
    POOLS.
NO TALKING IN THE POOL AREA, ONLY WHI$_M$PERING.
CHECK-OUT IS AT TWELVE.

NO MEAT, FISH, POULTRY OR NUDITY ALLOWED IN THE COOK-IT-
YOURSELF KITCHEN AREA.
UNLABELED FOOD WILL BE THROWN AWAY. ROUND-TOP COOLERS
IN THE FRIDGE ARE PROHIBITED.
NO USE OF RESIDENTS' SHELVES.
NO TARDINESS TO YOGA CLASSES.
NO STAYING PAST YOUR PARKING PERMIT'S EJECTION POINT.

If people want utopia, they need rules, she keeps hearing her father's voice. People come from everywhere with every bastard breed
of idea so rules become both their linkage and religion.

Uptight, she thinks, one of the few words her father had borrowed
from the argot of his day, believing it an apt neologism. Uptight, Lana,
is a useful idiom. But groovy, no. Radical as bland ubiquitous praise, no.

The idea of *uptight* floats in her as the pool does its job, heating her
up without fully undoing her. From other sectors that she has been
in, she knows some people, radically groovy or uptight, giddily vol-
unteer themselves to be enforcers, while others find delight in breaking rules, and that the signs bear witness to this essential division in
human nature.

NO UNINVITED SEXUAL ADVANCES OR ACTIVITY IN THE POOLS.
NO SEXUAL ACTIVITY IN THE SAUNA—SECURITY WILL BE CALLED.
IF YOU'RE IN A HURRY, YOU'RE IN THE WRONG PLACE.

She reads it all, relieved by the explicit. The sum total of these signs
is innocence: nothing can be covered. All can be if not regulated at
least washed away.

This is fertile valley in what would otherwise be unbroken desert
along Highway Five, south of Bakersfield and north of Los Angeles,
just below the Grapevine. Apart from the fields, the prison some miles
north remains the main institution in the greater underpopulated
county, one tip of the golden gulag, and having seen the signs while
driving down, she can't help knowing this, or that, by historic quirk,
the current governor's personal residence is planted only some twenty
miles south of the prison, since one of the things the desert does well

is maintain mileage signs. Along the interstate, no matter how isolated you might feel among tumbleweed, broken barbed-wire posts and dead-dream paralytic oil pumps, at least you know where you are—in your car, free in the USA, speeding north or south.

She leaves the hot pool for the warm, in which an older man says to a younger girl: "Today is the first day of the rest of your life," the girl laughing as if the cliché breaks anew upon the dawn of her consciousness. Does this exchange count as an uninvited sexual advance or would it be considered merely affable?

Lana can't help but be perturbed by the familiarity of certain details. The mulberries, for one. Why do the mulberries seem so familiar? Somewhere once she had learned about these dark fruit, about their short lives and need for little tending, here ending up smashed into the pavement next to the pools so the concrete bears a splotched map of regret, not even the squirrels hungry for them.

The ethos of the group dance night at Hope Springs, according to the catalogue, was: LOVE LIKE YOU HAVE NO FEAR, DANCE LIKE NO-BODY'S WATCHING, LIVE LIKE YOU HAVE DIED A MILLION TIMES.
 The folksy but peremptory signs go along with the free Q-tips, cotton balls, lavender lotion and soap, all of it sharing the noblesse you find in utopia. Then again, there's no blaming the place if something goes wrong and you get lost on one of the 1,600 acres of hiking trails or a mountain lion snags you because you crouched and didn't throw rocks and spoke in a high voice or you end up getting Lyme disease from a tick bite since you did sign that liability release when you entered oblivious and hopeful through the big metal griffin gate: palsy, depression or memory loss being just a few of the unshakable symptoms you could get from a minuscule bug.

That afternoon Lana had checked into the room that would belong to them, to her and her beau Dirk, the new resident guru of Hope

Springs. Like a honeymoon suite: ruffled swag, floral bedprint, angel-shaped soap, towels well fluffed, next to the room for her nine-year-old twins and just down the path from the Moroccan-styled scarlet yurt in which Dirk would receive supplicants under a canopy, where he would seat himself on zabutons before a mirror shaped like a louse or maybe was it a scarab?

Sometimes you open a suitcase and glimpse a ghost leaving: your hopes for this journey or your past journeys, all the beings you have traveled with. In much the same way that driving down here with the boys, the telephone poles had bounded like colts into her rear-view and then stayed, impassive, sentinels passing judgment. She'd been so caffeinated she'd jumped each time a pole appeared like a judgment from on high there in the desert plain heading toward the Grapevine. The boys hadn't noticed her jumps because to distract them from their loss—leaving the north coast of Yalina and the house they'd known since they were tiny, their grandparents' land, the whole bit—she had plugged them into watching movies like *The Wizard of Oz*, a fantasia for backseat animals.

A horse of a different color! she heard the taximan in Emerald City saying and then later I am the great and mighty Wizard of Oz, followed soon after by the response: I am Dorothy, the small and meek. And finally, her favorite line: pay no attention to the man behind the curtain.

This maybe shone as the most important idea: paying no attention when you were starting an adventure, keeping an open mind. She is trying hard to ignore certain features lining the chute toward the adventure she wanted to have.

For one, the extent to which her boys have been skeptical about this new man Dirk, whom they call the Dirkster. In their meetings with the Dirkster up in Yalina, they had not been able to see how different he was from the few other conquests she had known after their father's death. Dirk was, she had decided not to tell them, a bouquet of firsts. First time she is with such an older man, in his early fifties, a man wishing to achieve something beyond his own brute survival, and this means something to her given how many times she has heard her father complain about the limitations of his followers who thought their bliss could magically release others. Really, isn't it one of the first times she gets to be with someone who, she thinks, is no hypocrite?

Dirk wants to create what he calls an efficient methodology so that others' bliss may come to full release and he bears this intention as if it were a proud burning torch. *Lana Mahler, you get to be my age, you start wanting to have a last shot at something, really make a difference in people's lives. I want to do nothing short of helping transform world consciousness or at least create seeds of change.* In this vein, he has been invited to Hope for an indefinite residency, to be its resident guru, helping heal masses drawn to this Kurort, as her father liked calling any water spa.

The other sneakier truth is that for long enough she had accepted the liberty of confinement as a new mother in Yalina and now she requires this adventure with Dirk. She must uncover her old self and shake things up enough to remember what freedom tastes like even if the twins think this move spells one bad idea. True, she had given up her job at the Yalina market and at first they would have to depend on Dirk's gig. He himself had said to her: *Lana Mahler, find your trust, don't worry, all will be taken care of.* (Though depending on anyone for too long always makes her itchy.) Don't worry, she had echoed for the boys, we can always turn to your grandparents if you really need something special. Though of course she would never let it happen, would never go running back upstate to her would-be inlaws Jennie and BJ. No, she wants to make of trust a lilypad and just float on Dirk's gig, supposing that at Hope, she too might latch on to a credible gig.

First on the list is to see about the school for the twins. She had told the twins' grandparents that schooling was her priority, saying this both for them and to remind herself. The grandparents should have stopped wringing their hands in trips between her car and their home that cold morning when they helped pack up her old brown undercover sedan, what their son Kip had called the *pimpmobile.* She had told Kip's parents, in so many ways, that it would be good for the grandkids to have a break from studying up north among all Yalina's fresh-faced but secretive children of potgrowers with their well-rehearsed scripts about daddy's job, this being her last jab at her in-laws, one last hook at Indiana grandparents who had been the ones to choose Northern California and yet made no secret of blaming her for their precious, wild son's pot-harvesting ways and unlikely death. He had driven his car into the ocean right at the point where their property had an easement into the ocean, namely

Tract Two:

A non-exclusive right of way to the existing stairway, and down the stairway to the ocean over a ten-foot strip of land lying along the Westerly side of the following described property: Commencing at the ¼ section corner common; to Sections 21 and 28, Township 11 North, Range 15 West, Mount Diablo Base and Meridian, said ¼ section corner being the NW corner of the property previously vested in the name of Tobiack; thence from said ¼ section corner South 73^(degree sign) 14'40" West, a distance of 562.08 feet to a point marking the corner of that particular piece of land conveyed from Riverside Townhouse, a corporation, to Walter B. Carr and Jane L. Carr in that instrument dated March 12, 1963, and recorded in Book 621 of Official Records at page 338, Mendocino County Records, State of California on March 19, 1963; thence North 44'48'20" West, a distance of 107.22 feet; thence Easterly in a meandering line that follows the mean high water line to a point which bears North more or less to the true point of beginning

as her father-in-law had waved this section of the title at her, you made Kip do it right here, Lana! You drove him crazy! Right here!

Anyone would have had to escape that. The blame and being a she-devil in that place with Kip's family: all a little too tight, familiar and foreign. And yes, she hadn't known what kind of school her boys would find at Hope, only that it was *accredited*, a jawbreaker she likes rolling over her tongue, capable of soothing guilt. Her fantasy had been that at Hope her sons would find themselves playing and studying with California's other grandsons and granddaughters, the spawn of Indians and ranchers, Mexicans and migrants and cowboys, those who had stayed put and those who moved through, all workers and heirs half-settled into a valley riven by the great highway. A person can dream; a person hurts no one by dreaming.

Back in her room after the hot baths, Lana wonders if mulberries are edible or poisonous, slow while stripping her robe before the cheval mirror, the yellow-rose wallpaper reminding her of someone's eyes on her in a room like this, whose or where she cannot say.

Lana not unhappy, sitting on the patio near the warm pool, outside the main dining hall of Hope Springs. Sitting with her sons, dawdling over fleshlike apricot-flavored tofu that her sons think is shaped like ears. Sedge says the stuff looks like it has been ripped from a troll who might grant endless life if you just answered the riddle correctly. The thirty-third anniversary of this place must be starting already, thirty-three in honor of Christ's age at death: hordes of arrivistes come, towing expensive backpacks and battered suitcases, people clean-faced or hirsute engaging in long, decade-erasing hugs. Something about it makes her want to laugh.

"What, mama?"

She asks her boys: "Does this feel right or what?"

"I dunno," says Tee, blowing a strawpaper onto the pile of those he'd already jetted toward the general vicinity of a recycling bin.

Sedge looks up from where he has returned to having a private talk with his space robot Lestrion, who to the outside world is no more than a tongue depressor and Q-tips, a crucifix with pentacle dreams stranded on legs, the robot's head bound with rubber bands, his gamma-ray deflectors swaddled by well-crudified masking tape: the hidden nature of Lestrion aids his appeal. Sedge whispers "Q forty-one" before saying louder: "I guess. Mountains in the middle of the desert are pretty."

"Look, ma, why doesn't that man have a face?"

She looks before shushing her son. "Tee! He just doesn't have a nose. Let's not stare, boys."

"But the man doesn't have a mouth either. It's all sewn together or something. Just two dots for eyes, two dots for nostrils and barely a mouth. Like Michael Jackson!"

"You want a time-out, Tee?"

"I'm just saying."

"You're on warning. That's a one." Lana quotes from yet another recent book on parenting. "Two."

In the warm pool, a man laughs, big, extending his arms like a bear. "The colonies have been good to me," he says loudly to another.

"Nathan Hale," the other agrees, nonsensically. Two large seals in a zoo, dunking heads, splashing up. "So you call this a colony? Hey, had a good time last night?"

"The calories have not been so good."

A trio of women who in garb alone could be escapees from a hula troupe ensconce themselves in a hug between the warm pool and the dining patio. Lana recognizes them from Dirk's grief workshop during which, this morning, all supplicants had been asked to wear straw skirts, though Lana, as Dirk's primary aide, had not participated much beyond handing out name-tags, a task he had called of course fully her choice.

"Are there lions here, mama?" asks Tee.

"Probably," says Lana, remembering a sign warning what to do if one came too close to a mountain lion. You back away and scream, you raise your arms to look bigger than you are, you don't lean down to pick up a child, you throw stones. So what do you do? Leave your children as bait while you run off and get help? How clear is it at which point you intervene, lean down, hoist the kid high, get away from danger? She would ignore all of it, get her kids on her shoulders, probably ruin everything—it would be too hard, like the instructions they give on a plane, one of those biologically impossible imperatives. *You're supposed to ignore the hindbrain and fasten the oxygen mask on your own face before making sure your own kid's okay?* her father once had asked as they flew toward Nevada for some conference of his, just before using the safety manual to slap the top of her head. How much she loved exactly this kind of moment with him. Later she had paraded around the conference, watching his hale greeting of people—the names he could remember!—while she twirled some transparent adult drink. Only once in the hotel room had she felt uncomfortable, in her pajamas reading a Jim Morrison biography, not liking the way he ran a finger down her spine a little too low before asking what it was about ole Jim that interested her so. Psychic incest—as one of her friends in Yalina had termed it—almost worse than the real deal because it's way foggier.

"Shh," she says.

"What?" her sons ask at the same time, twin habit making them synchronous only sometimes, boys who talk to mirrors as much as to each other.

At the next table, a woman in a purplish dress studies menu choices, an older woman with reading glasses who shakes her head, scanning the menu again before turning straight toward Lana.

"Lana?" she says. "Incredible. Lana Mahler? That you?"

Lana doesn't remember the woman but shudders at the evocation of her old last name. Only Dirk knows her whole moniker. Years ago she'd gone through the whole bother of changing it, one of many feeble tactics, though she could not help but be inconsistent about the bandying about of names, and of course had checked in here not as Lana Mahler or Lana Fukuji but as Lana Wagner, her own made-up and not wholly necessary confection, at this point more tic than need.

"Jane Polsby. High school, remember?" The woman chews bubble gum, her butter-blond hair a librarian bob over tetragonal horn-rim glasses, a substantial line incised between the brows, only one eye fixed by the snake-glaze of middle age.

"Of course," says Lana, bits and pieces floating up from whatever still remained of her neocortex.

Back then it had been easy to consider Jane a blowhard burdened with the desire to be a model, a girl who'd gotten shots done and posed herself on her senior page in a manner meant to invoke celebrity. Hips thrust forward, knock-kneed, elbows akimbo, Jane gazed up from the yearbook, dark head tousled and lowered, Jane splayed out in twenty-five letters of the alphabet of seduction without ever having quite located some crucial twenty-sixth.

Lana once had told Rose that she thought Jane was emotionally tone-deaf despite the sensitivity you'd think would be hers, given the small, minkish eyes and pallid skin. And still Rose and Lana had spent certain kinds of time with Jane Polsby, eating jam-slathered scones at the local bakery and acting polite whenever Jane quoted her aphorisms, so poorly remembered. Only later would the Lolas giggle in imitation. *Be there then! What doesn't make me stronger won't kill me either!*

Vic had said he liked their third wheel's vitality, calling Jane the kind of girl overendowed with life. "She's the opposite of neurasthenic and the opposite of cool, true, but look, girls, she also makes no secret of craving the unction of cool! You've got to admire the honesty. You'd do well if you had the smallest ant-bite of her sincerity." He had even said something approaching this idea to Jane's actual face during the one dinner Jane had ever attended before a sleepover at Lana's with Rose. Whenever Vic addressed her, Jane had acted flattered, kicking Rose under the table. Later she whispered to both girls that maybe Vic liked her a little. That night, in punishment, the Lolas joked about Jane, saying they could imagine her having both the sprinting ability and morning breath of a racehorse.

"Jane Polsby," Lana sighs, marveling at the rejuvenating magic of memory. She doesn't stand because she is not yet ready for a hug or any precocious admission of anything: her hands are bloated, useless paws. And the boys can tell something odd is happening, their mouths hanging open with food.

"I know. I changed. My hair for one. Screams midlife, right? Like a neon sign. I don't care, blond hair makes me happy. Reminds me of my inner princess. Hey, you look great."

"Thanks," Lana demurs, wiping yogurt off Sedge's shirt because he still lets her do this.

"Oh." In full solemnity. "Sorry about your dad."

Here's where Lana tunes out, crumbling some tofu between her fingers, only coming back at this: "Can't believe someone would be that famous and get put on death row for just one slip-up. Crazy. That must be hard."

Lana goes lifeless herself, her shiver taken as a nod. If she could, she would just jam the signal.

"I mean, brain cancer on top of dementia? But the law's changing, right? The governor should let him have that last stay, not like it's skin off anyone's back. I'm sorry, must be rough. You know my mom had dementia, called me Caesar's daughter, but god, two weeks? Are you going to be in the room when—? You'd think there'd be some medical place where someone could just live out his days. Sorry, no. I understand. My dad, I wouldn't want to talk either."

Lana aims for a shrug. If there existed a term for both horror and numbness hitting the windshield, this would be its moment. Most people don't know Lana Wagner is linked to Vic Mahler, and Lana has been conscientious in avoiding details of the Mahler case. So this aged version of Jane delivers the news: brain cancer and a last stay? Dementia? Lana had not known. But she has found that the more she avoids the news, the more it chases her. In a highway coffee shop a television plays the tail end of Vic's name, letting her know his time is coming. In a waiting room, from a tabloid's headline, the Mahler name blares forth. Now Lana has run into Jane Polsby and gets the full slam-dunk.

Clearly this Vic Mahler case is having its fifteen minutes of infamy. The thing had been caught forever in what Vic used to call the strobe of attention. Once he'd yelled at a tribe of reporters: stop playing the mommy-and-daddy's-rolodex game of mediocrats! Her mother had later told her, lips pressed, eyes rolling, that papa was resting because after his lecture he had apparently needed to start ranting at the reporters: *what, you people all did J-school together at Berkeley? You're into conformity? Or what, you all got hazed together at some tony Upper East Side academy?* Mary could imitate him so well Lana used to find it spooky, but back in those days, no one, especially not his wife, dared say the great Vic Mahler might have been, as people were just starting to say back then, *losing it*, which in his case would have meant that Vic Mahler had lost some central moral hub. None of them, whether family, follower or rival, saw his outbursts as anything more than flicked-off sparks of brilliance: inscrutable, irresponsible, the byproduct of inspiration.

Later the day of his reporters' rant, Vic had come downstairs, puffy-eyed, to slice a piece of French bread for himself. While studiously avoiding Mary, he told Lana that what had bugged him was how reporters kept marring the purity of the shaggies' circle, being bottom-feeders who like nibbling at any frond that appears before them, just nibbling away until there's nothing left for their appetites. And they do it without real intention. At the end of the day, Mopsy, what a person *intends* is what matters most, tell me I'm wrong?

Sure, papa. Once Lana had been walking with him on campus when he was trying to outstride some young reporter asking about the controversy surrounding a recent book. Finally Vic had turned to the poor boy to hiss: *you're imagining some famous actor playing you as a young cub? Or you're one of those kids with a last name on some old stone buildings around here? If a bomb fell on your parents' home, would certain newspapers and TV shows close? Tell me I'm wrong about this guy, Mopsy.*

Sure, papa. This second, he probably does some similar second act in prison, busying himself making pronouncements against the power structure. All too easily Lana can see her father rabble-rousing, ranting about guards who should cease invading the prisoners' right to freedom in the showers, or something about the cafeteria—but this is not a good path. She has kept herself from Vic being a live and screaming presence before her. Had she not worked overtime to lobotomize all memory of Vic?

She comes to with a start. Again she has been a bad mom, again faltering, abandoning her boys by teleporting, letting herself seem present and yet spiraling off into Vic-land while Jane spoke. A good mother would have done more to protect her sons from hearing about the bequest of such a bad granddad, grandpa, grandfather, all the names the boys will never call Vic. She will never let them meet.

Belatedly, Lana tries glaring but Jane is too awesome a force to silence. "The governor must have to throw bones to some big pockets in order to have to—"

What Lana can't accept is that her old schoolmate is so oblivious. Vic had once told Lana that Jane's prodigious lifestream must keep her insulated. If you happen to believe in the idea of a soul—he had said, taunting Lana—you could say your little friend has a little too much blubber around hers.

And Jane kept going, making Lana mock-slit her own throat and eye her sons significantly.

"What's she saying, ma?" asks Tee, perking up.

"I'll explain, honey," says Lana. "One second."

Finally Jane does attempt to change the subject. "Hey, remember freshman year? Your mom and dad came up here. You and Rose let me come? I don't bear grudges, I know I was a tagalong. We came for a weekend?" Lana does not recall a single bit of this, still in the glacier flow following the mention of Vic. "You don't remember? We were the NoCal girls. That weekend you guys let me be Lola Three because remember how you were Lola One and Two—" assuming a mask of mock childish hurt.

Tee tugs at her hand. "Ma! Can we go to the kiddie pool already?"

Jane's last factoid penetrates. Lana had been at Hope Springs before? Enough to explain why the place feels familiar. The mulberries, the wallpaper.

"In a second," she says to Tee.

But how could Lana not have remembered? She had been here with Rose and with this Jane Polsby standing before her. Her mother and father had taken the three classmates on a trip. Memory is mischievous but bits return. Lana had thought that spa had been north, not south of San Francisco.

What Lana remembers from that trip anyway has little to do with what her old classmate prattles forth, something about making art by gluing stones on redwood slats or how the girls kept their two-pieces on even among all the naked older men bubbling away in the cauldrons. While she cannot fully sight a younger version of Jane Polsby, the person she really sees for the first time in years is Rose, the spoken name enough to act as a lance through ice, making Rose palpable, puppyish in her love for Lana but also trying to get her back for something. Pulling off Lana's bikini top. Or standing atop the rocks behind the sauna trying to appear smooth while instructing Lana about blow jobs or tampons. Vic had always said how knowledgeable Rose was. And then Lana could say one wrong word or another, enough to make sensitive Rose cry, enough that Lana always had to end up apologizing in what Rose called too casual a voice.

But easiest to remember Rose laughing. They had given up finally and nude-sunbathed among all the lechers made ludicrous because of desire, males rendered beta because of the inherent weakness of statutory lechery. She could see Rose again, how primal she had been cannonballing into the cold water, strong in water just as Lana was more balanced when climbing rocks, and in water was probably where

Lana loved Rose most because in water Rose fled adolescence and Lana, who had never learned how to swim well, got to follow.

"Anyway, god, Lana, you look fantastic! You know ever since college I come here every year. Love the place. I'm leaving today but it's great to see you. Going back to L.A. Basically, I had to declare a mini-sabbatical. My husband?" Jane grimaces. "Hates when I do these solo trips. Guilt-trips, you know, but got to do it. For sanity. Because my kids are three, six, seven, can you imagine? Left them with the nanny and instructions but no matter what, it's hard, right?" She pats her cell with delicate attention as if it were the still-twitching end of an umbilicus. "Can't get reception here. Your boys are twins? They're eight?"

"Nine," says Tee, unable to let a slight pass.

"Adorable. Hey, got to get together sometime. My kids love older kids. Let me see if I can dig up a card."

Tee smirks, Sedge manages a half-smile, Lana nearly chokes.

Mainly she is surprised by a sneaky self, some part greedy to be recognized by anyone from the past. This greed fits with nothing and should be excised immediately. But while she says goodbye, while the boys finish their tofu before heading off to the kiddie pool, while she watches Jane take a latte and rolling suitcase and toddle off toward the griffin gate, Lana still pinches Jane's card between her fingers, hard, as if she'd been thrown a rope from a leaky lifeboat.

"I don't get it," Rose is saying. Outside, steam rises from the motel's asphalt, calcium striping the hills. Chalk lines her lungs. "Not like it's a holiday. It's still mid-December."

The motel owner tugs her sari and peers through glasses at her pad. "We're overbooked, ma'am. Perhaps that place up the road? The spa?"

The dust on the windowsills suggests to Rose that nowhere else will she approach her quarry with such lovely concealment.

"But I called. I arranged for a place here," says Rose. Here is where she came, here where she must find a room, in this motel off an interstate for which she still uses Vic's names: Five or Highway Five. "Sorry, but I just drove all the way up. I can't pay extra? There must be some room. Just a place with a phone?"

"Not permissible, ma'am." The syllables start a carnival whir behind the phrase, a rattle like the woman's bangles.

"But I called. Made a reservation."

"Sorry, ma'am. No record of you. If not in the books, you are not entitled."

"No one said entitled. Just said—"

"You have no receipt, ma'am?"

"No. I called in the reservation. If they charge me—"

"You will be paid. On your statement."

"I don't care about payment. I just want a place."

"Of course." The motel owner now answers a phone, asking with deathly calm if ma'am wants three nights, repeating a name back before hanging up to examine Rose, her glasses reflecting the parking lot and the hills beyond. "People do stay one exit north, ma'am. One exit up you find the coffee shop. You go, ask about a room. People like those baths. Hot, you know? Not expensive."

"I said money's not a problem."

"You will be okay. Come. No need to get upset. A tissue?"

Rose leaves, trying to ignore the unignorably bad signs: no record of her and no room at the inn.

To remind her of earlier times, she has put on a short red cotton skirt covered with black swirls which lets the carseat stick to the back of her legs. She opens her computer to the unsent letter she had written the day before to Lana's father:

December 13, 2008
Dear Vic,
Hope you're well. Haven't heard from you since they set the date for the hearing. Forgive me, this is not an attack but weren't we on something of a roll in our correspondence? Maybe you were getting something from it? Now I'm wondering if you don't understand the offer of help I've tried sending your way. I understand your feelings about lawyers but at this point wouldn't it be helpful to have someone who actually cares about your case on your side? Don't you think the others have bungled things a bit?

Let me speak more directly. I have a small break from work and I understand you might not have gotten my last message. Thought I could come to the hearing next week and see if I could in any way be helpful. What I understood online is that your case is being presented to a federal judge north of Old Parcel.

My plans are to be in Buttonwillow as of Monday the 15th and then continue north. What I wanted to ask is if you might reconsider putting me on the Permission-to-Visit list. I ask outright because it seems important. Of course I understand if you don't want anyone you really know to see you in what must be a difficult state but after our years of letters, and given the current situation, don't you think having a lawyer on your side would help? (I really have no motive other than trying to help.)

And, too, let me err on the side of being too clear: receiving the sentence of a medical stay would mean not just your life continuing as it is, which I understand might feel a bit intolerable, but an actual improvement in your conditions. Maybe you'd be held in a different facility. I feel silly pushing it on you but must ask again: given how delicate your case is and that I don't qualify as kin (and since you have no kin visiting at least for now, as I understand it), why not put Rose Lemm (I'm going back to my birthname) on the list for approval?

The letter will live as pixels unsent. Unlike her other letters it will never cross prison walls, instead going brittle in a metal box that Rose will keep until she is old enough that her own force has ebbed and she has neighborly customs, walking a dog every morning with another old lady down a dahlia-lined street. The box and its data will be bequeathed to an heir who uses pop-up electromagnetic holographs requiring only gloves to communicate so that Rose's box will collect dust rime in a cellar until the day her legatee's grandchild pulls it from an old-fashioned recycling bin to find its quaint computer backboard perfect for a bowling rink made of baby bottles.

Lana fails to appreciate how slowly her boys are taking to her new beau Dirk. She can hear them through the thin stucco talking about the guy.

"He's creepy. That laugh of his is super-fake," says Tee. And then attempts a machine-gun facsimile, a rat-a-tat-tat piercing through.

"Almost as creepy as that guy who runs this place."

"Hogan? His eyes cross. Like this."

"Yeah but Hogan has a terrarium," says Sedge, slow to laugh. "Anyway, Hogan doesn't run the place, he manages it."

"Big diff," says Tee.

"You know Hogan doesn't have any hair on his arms," says Sedge. "Probably burned off."

"He said he'd let us see the tarantula."

"No way."

Tee has severe arachnophobia and Lana wonders that her sweet, sensitive Sedge would bring up tarantulas. Since they came to Hope, Sedge has been acting out.

"Ouch!" moans Sedge.

"C'mon, that was not a hard pinch. Don't fake it."

"I'm not."

"How long is mama going to be with this guy? The Dirkster?" asks Tee, apparently unafraid to grant Sedge this tribute: his twin's social periscope is capable of wider angles.

"I don't know—" stretching it into at least three syllables. *Kno-oh-oh.*

"Just asking."

She doesn't want to hear their mock-casual twin prattle. How easily the boys cope by faking not pain but adulthood, using this mortar to patch up their days.

Were she to write a book about life as a mother, she would put a giant fluorescent-orange earplug on the cover. This is the cost of being with kids: to breathe any inner music, at times you must tune things out. No one, let alone her own mother, had ever told her about this trivia of motherhood, the comic battle of present self versus past. For nine-odd years she has buried herself in two boys, in stocking and waste-management issues arising from refrigerators, diaper pails, hampers, toychests containing objects wooden or plastic: this toy question had engaged her until she had just surrendered to the tsunami of petrochemical industry that is American upbringing in the early twenty-first century. She had found it easier to engage in talk of bisphenol-free mouthables with other mothers and superspy space robots with her sensitive son, all this much easier than trying to remember what kind of fruity wine she once liked or how she used to like taking hills, her legs avid for a quick climb. And then, as if surprised by an uninvited guest, she sometimes catches a glimmer of her old self when it comes around knocking, a sheer exile showing up in dreams, saying: excuse me, did you mean to abort me? Tell me you didn't mean it.

She had wanted a normal life for herself, for her boys, but is flailing.

For example, they have arrived at a nudist resort.

Could be someone else's idea of normal, she says in defense.

She has asked the twins to do the unheard-of, to hang in their rooms before breakfast because what she really needs is sleep and instead they must start piping in their twin prattle past stucco walls that must be super-thin for her to hear them so clearly.

Across a pillow her hand crawls. Just one soft orange and yellow earplug that her hand finds with as much ardor as it used to find another's hand, yet when she squeezes the plug in, the twins' melody still pipes in. Imagining their discussion can be worse than hearing it.

I give up, she tells her unmuscled pillow. Forget sleeping in today.

Dirk is already out convening with the people who run the place. It's true she knows the guy none too well but early signs have been promising. *Normal, normal,* this is her song. She does wonder if, during their courtship, she may have blinded herself, banking too much on her past, using the past profit of other men's appreciation to bring Dirk into the black. Her swains have tended to be of the passionate and jealous ilk and it turns out there may be no such appreciative streak in Dirk: he appears to cherish little beyond his own ambition.

Can she help it if she likes him anyway? Or likes him enough. For one thing, he makes a big show of talking equally to the bald groundskeeper Hogan and the owners of the spa, Doreen and Albert, DorAlba as they are called around here, two nudists in their seventies, hot-tub sitters proud of their intelligence who, in their first sentence to anyone, let it be known they are key members of a society for smart people but will never hold this fact against all the world's non-members.

And though the terrarium has endeared that head groundskeeper Hogan to her boys, Dirk confesses how unsettling he finds the guy. *Even if some of our future survival here depends on him,* Dirk says. *That guy Hogan is in tight with the owners.*

Still, Dirk tries to show an egalitarian streak, one she appreciates, especially since his vision is to turn this residency into something more than a residency. Allowing him this bit of male vanity, she hadn't pressured him to tell her his age but guessed he must be somewhere in his fifties. He says that after all his years in the trenches—a transcendental meditator leading groups in dance and emotional management while maintaining a strict focus on dance continuum and contact improv—he had realized the time was ripe for him to find a following for a movement that had come as a flashing epiphany. Now, he says, he has moved beyond movement to form an all-encompassing theory/praxis.

"It's about the slash," he had intoned, his smile serious and then—this is half his charm—quickly sexy, almost self-deprecating, ready for fun. "Whaaaat?" he says, never quitting the smile, as if he could join in the prospect of someone laughing at him.

Which makes her hear her father's edict on Jane, that a person's SELF-REGARD MAKES FOR A BLUBBER OF THE SOUL, though whenever Vic's phrases flood her synapses, inevitable and urgent, Lana cannot help but cringe. And yet her situation has to do with exactly that, the blubber of self-regard in new beau Dirk, one offering the strangely appealing outcome of making her own goals haze.

In coming here, Lana had thought it might be great to get back to songwriting and had brought along her guitar. Or maybe she would paint a bit, though Dirk had been concerned when she'd asked where she might set up a painting studio. He'd pointed out the ecological mission of Hope and that pigment carried in toxic media might not be great for the local watershed if they hoped to make a good impression, given that he was coming with a family *entourage*, one that, if you thought about it, hadn't been in the original *ecology* of his arrangement with DorAlba.

Which makes her wonder: when had she signed on to be part of an entourage, a blight on the ecology, an addition to someone's roadshow? But hadn't it been fun to release into Dirk's master plan, even if the plan does start to seem birthed from the head of a narcissist? Because it is relieving to be stripped of choice, here in the desert, and she is unhappy as ever to hear her father's voice still pinging about, Vic's ideas keeping a manic, eternal pinball game alive in her head's backroom. THE DESERT MAKES MOST HUMAN ENTERPRISE START TO SEEM FOOLISH OR, CONVERSELY, ALL TOO NECESSARY FOR SURVIVAL.

In bed, Lana tries remembering what foolish or survivalist hunch had led her toward Dirk when she'd met him four months before during a dance seminar in that rain-spattered Catholic church up north with its exquisite name—Mary, Star of the Sea.

Hadn't a sign come? The sign being that her womb had softened, a cell with doors flung open. Even the church's all-windowed walls had fallen away. When Dirk had walked afterward with her on the cliffs, she chose to follow this sign, deciding to tell him stories that, with inarticulable instinct, she knows function like a universal Turing machine of mating, stories good as patterned stockings and tall boots in that they kick open certain responses, enough to make certain men surrender fear and allow them to make a move if said move is up for question. Concerning:

1. Times you have been raped or almost raped;
2. Times you have worked as a gogo dancer;
3. To certain men, you could tell the story about using heroin in Paris.

Hearing such stories seemed to send electric impulses direct into the reptilian brain. But did she want Dirk to make a move? After one of her mother's stories about a colleague experiencing sexual harassment on the job, her father had said: "Mary, you believe your friend? She says that once she announced her engagement, she became prey for constant sexual predation? But we've talked about this too many times, please, let me finish. Your friend's experience has nothing to do with societal unfairness and everything to do with the testosterone-driven neural loop. A clear case of the norepinephrine circle jerk of aggression, one more case of the bride laid bare by other bachelors. One man's claim paves the way for others. No, this is a friendly discussion. Where are you going?"

The bride laid what? little Lana had asked, making Vic stare a frozen second before he too left the room.

Lying in bed at Hope, Lana recalls her favorite scene in a movie, where the girl gets raped before the guy kills himself, the one Lana had watched so many times with her lost fiancé she still feels guilty. Could the scene have caused his death? Had her Kip thought of *Last Exit to Brooklyn* before choosing to drive over a cliff below his parents' house? His reptilian brain had opposed evolution, Vic would have said. Or he had made a decision about the calculus of sadness, believing it easier to bear on the other side.

She returned to these questions, south of that suicidal cliff, during her walk with Dirk in the first moments of courtship, trying hard to zone into what he was saying.

Years ago, Dirk had been in costume because of Vic Mahler. Starting in 1960, Vic Mahler had written about neuroethology and the bioethics of possibility within the brain in such a visionary way that a whole generation woke to feverish new thoughts about the mind and perception, a generation happy to scramble his message into acts undertaken on behalf of their own drive toward free love and pharmacology. Eventually the scrambling of his message swayed

Vic, too, who started issuing what most readers took as edicts, statutes, challenges: if a scientist replaced every one of your neurons with a micromachine replica, would you then feel any less your own self?

On the coastal walk she listens to this potential beau Dirk, the way he sucks ocean air deep into his lungs talking of Vic, and she gets that no matter what she tells, if she ends up with this guy, she will essentially be uploading another bit of Vic Mahler karma onto her truck. Had she ever asked for such karma? *Nosirreebob*, as she'd trained the twins to say. And it wasn't that everyone these days knew about Vic: his consignment to the past shocks her, one example being that the ostensible father to her children seems never to have heard about the groundbreaking work of Vic Mahler in creating one of those disciplines credible only in a state with its rocks constantly on the move.

In Yalina, her woolly north coast, before she met Dirk, she had been trying to keep it simple. You could hole up for years, stabbing toward normalcy by using kid-feeding rituals and odd jobs, everything to keep you from the existential brink. About this brink she could have written a user's manual, knowing that her life and its mainstay job at the government-cheese supermarket, where she loved the happy numbness of passing food stamps over a scanner, had become one easy *beep!*

True that after her fiancé left—that was how she had to think of it, that he left, that he had not killed himself—she had hated living with her inlaws. Nor had she ever been a fan of the hardship of making ends meet: she would not have signed up willingly for the fun of being a single mom supporting two sons. She had done what she could to survive and stay away from all brinks, using sacraments such as the spectacular hygiene of her boys' teeth and the wearing of her hair in two penitential braids. According to Vic, however, any brain with holes—he had accused her, too, of having such holes, due to brain trauma after a bad crib fall when she was a baby—could correct itself only so much, and was doomed to pathology, nymphomania, borderline sociopathy, aggression, psychosis, who knew what else?

If Vic was right and her seedbed or fate were that dire, she thought she had been doing pretty well.

I'm a regular success story, she tells this pleased fellow Dirk as they continue to wind their way along the Yalina cliffs. She halfway means it: by her own lights she is a success. She then chooses to tell Dirk the stories that open the portal, hers a generous act, a recognition that the drumroll of intimacy has begun, the stories that serve as opening ceremonies in the potlatch of love. Someone must be the first to start giving up stories.

And to match, his tone a thick fruity soup, he starts speaking of his past as a follower. He'd spent an era of his life in costume and she cannot tell if he speaks with endearing embarrassment or in ancient, rebellious identification with a cult figure.

Until finally she gets the relevance.

"No way!" she shouts. "You were the guy in white?" She must stop walking the cliffs: disbelief makes her savor the weirdness. "You're the polar-bear guy!"

"I was." But he grants her an autograph: his smile.

If not the weirdest shaggy, certainly Dirk in his prior mutation dwelled toward the weirder end of the spectrum, barred from the title of weirdest only by the rasta whose Hindu self-mutilation—long steel spike through scanty shoulder flesh—failed to impair a tai chi practice requiring the rasta, sunrise and sunset, to perform his martial art wearing a leather loincloth on the Mahler driveway. The neighbors had protested all the gutterside urination, begging Mary for an electric fence or at least lawnside cayenne-sprinkling.

One hundred and fifty miles north of her old Berkeley home, only one mile south of the dead-daisy-chain spot marking where her fiancé's car had caromed off the cliffs, Dirk divulges that he had been Hermes. The fact redoubles before her.

Hermes-Dirk had been one more character whose primary purpose seemed to come from stalking her father. Thus Dirk must be older than he looked. During preliminary intake, first seconds of courtship, Lana had gotten him wrong, mistaking Dirk for one of those California men who, burdened by too much motherlove, gets confounded by life extension and ends up some kind of exercise-nut, a user of embalming sunscreens, the kind who can never wash mama or their yen for eternity off their faces.

This is the kind of puer—as Vic liked to call such a man—whose primary vow is to undergo only slight erosion, men focused on out-witting actuarial odds by their faithfulness to California protocols: ease, cheekbones, the low glycemic index of their diet, fire-trail hikes, cardiovascular gestures, wealth, Tuscan vegetables, phytonutrients, heart-benefiting and cancer-fighting volunteerism, the kind who into their fifties remain manboys, pursuing life-risking activities without ever wiping off that constant smile. If misfortune happens to such men, a hemorrhaging bank account or loss of an actual limb, such men call it *process* or *a learning experience*, ready to die before admitting failure, failure bad as a hairweave, a condition practically requiring surrender of the state's driving license.

What matters to such men—and despite having heard her father preach so often against these puers, Lana has known a Cecil B. DeMille legion of them, as they tend to like her long legs—is the smile. The manboys' smile advertises their soft-pocket hedonism, suggesting that riches and goodness have flowed toward all luminaries elected by grace.

So this man courting her, this smiling Dirk, used to be phallus-carrying polar-bear Hermes! Part puer, part shaggy, part something unguessable, this man grins, far from the province of guessing he speaks with the actual daughter of Victor Mahler.

Lana may have stories to tell but in all the years since she heard the news about her parents, she had never told anyone who her dad was. True, foolish as the gesture was, she has kept her first name; the name forms her being. And at times she has grown sloppy, occasionally needing to revivify her mother and so letting herself use one of her mother's last names, Fukuji or Guzman, instead of the alias of Lana Wagner.

Yet once Lana realizes Dirk had been the polar-bear Hermes, she wonders how wise it would be to unclothe herself and blind him with patrimony. It is clear to her that if Dirk knows he is talking to Lana Mahler, daughter of famous Vic, all that synchronicity will just about swing the vote.

Along evening cliffs they walk to where the most historic hotel in the region had burned down, to where you still smell ash, like a friendly hint of campfires gone by. Three spindly stone monoliths rise in judgment upon the landlocked, hundreds of feet below in the surf. In such a place, the ocean borrows land and returns nothing, leaving only craggy monoliths staring like stern church fathers. The whole moment's spareness could dare two walkers to throw themselves into the Pacific because who would care?

Since Lana's first arrival in Yalina, she has seen how the wildness of the northern ocean sharpens memory even as it renders it irrelevant. The individual takes on risk as an easy substitute for the social: you walk and the sandstone would happily let you crumble hundreds of feet down. She never wishes to recall Vic—he colonizes whole unwilling swaths of her brain—but all too easy up in Yalina to remember Vic's frequent citation of what he called the danger/beauty study in which experimenters showed men pictures of female subjects. Half the men, made to walk a tightrope before seeing the picture, found the post-tightrope pictures more attractive than those in the control group who had walked on an open road. Danger increases appreciation, as Vic liked telling her, citing this study all the time, once using it to warn her away from going hang-gliding with a beau, to which she tried telling her father that riskloving itself might be attractive though she knew, she always knew, that anytime she bothered stating an opinion she baited his usual response, which was to scoff at her teen grasp on knowledge.

Either a risklover or else just deeply invested in appearing gallant, Dirk makes a big show about walking the ocean side of the path, keeping Lana inland as if chivalry alone could protect a woman from sandstone, missteps, earthquakes.

"I used to love doomlovers," she says.

He looks up out of his derring-do. "Some women do," says Dirk, voice uncertain about where this might lead, jolted out of being a knight into something less savory.

"Could be evolution." She wants to explain further, get him into the exact precinct from which she speaks, but he is too busy now trying to bushwhack toward an inland fork.

"How's that." He beams at her, face broad under the lantern-light near the burnt jaws of the hotel, intent on his mission of listening.

"Say you're female, right?"

He smiles, sucking in another breath; his generation would say he was *grokking* the idea of being female, taking it deep past the pores.

"You avoid female rivals if you couple intensely for a short period with a male doomlover," she says. "Only your eggs get the seed of someone with enough aggression to, I don't know, die spearing the bison."

She may as well have performed an elaborate mating dance, a dance of the spider queen. He stops still.

"I did love a certain type of doomlover when I was growing up," she persists, realizing he could be one of those men who insists on hearing everything as a come-hither. While she may want him—not sure yet—she does know that the only way to overcome this lothario tendency in a listener is to barrel through and keep talking. Meanwhile, the urge to confess rises like a thirst, as if she wants to take him into her throat. Instead she tells Dirk that as a teenager, she had certain doomlovers' posters on her walls and that she had a girlfriend with whom she had celebrated doomlovers. "But then the problem is you end up living with doom as your wallpaper."

"It has a certain half-life," he says, "girlish romanticism, right? Drives a lot of women off the deep end." Whether Dirk means to be telepathic or not, he may as well have gone sea-diving and emerged with the right pearl. His prize being that he gets her full smile, not the bitten one she'd turned on him before.

The ostensible father of her children, Kip, had done that, deep-ended her: this is the phrase she likes using. *I was deep-ended.* Lana still has not told Dirk how in so many countless ways she is a survivor. Nor has she said that she thinks she deserves her widow karma or that she has most recently described herself, to a Pomo fisherman from the rez, as *your original black widow mom.* But mainly she is not yet answering the what's-your-name, who's-your-daddy question just so she and Dirk may linger a bit longer in unspoiled vales of curiosity without having to scale any peaks of confession. For the moment, he probably stays simple in his plans, concocting some idea about bedtime, and guessing this concoction fills her with reciprocal fantasy. She imagines Dirk dandling her boys and the flash comes as it has come with other men: she will move toward him because to move toward Dirk would be like walking on a spit of land toward the light.

Light, she tells herself as he talks, *keep it simple.* He could be a flush card.

In and out of this flushness he returns to mentioning life choices he has made—a student in Berkeley, a beloved professor, his time in Chiapas, a recanting of such ways.

"Wow," she repeats herself. Dirk faces inland toward her. "I still can't believe it. You were the polar-bear guy."

"Hermes," he corrects. "Call it a phase. I carried a message to people. I stalked Mahler, basically." Dirk's grin a wrinkle of embarrassment. Of course he stalked Vic.

"People need their heroes," she says, taking cover in blandness.

Now he realizes that Lana had said *the* polar-bear guy, and that she must have seen him in the Hermes guise. "You were, what, in high school in Berkeley? A beloved cheerleader?"

"So what was it about—that professor, Mahler?"

"I was one of his first real followers."

"I don't even get that part. Why so many followed him," she says with unusual heat.

A reciprocal flare. "They called him the Pied Piper."

Her expression stays fixed, something he might recall, but she avoids his gaze, watching her feet tamp down seagrass.

Really, what little girl could forget the shaggies camped out on her front lawn? Who could forget her own mother putting out Sunday scones and jam for the followers? Their hippie gratitude for such humane touches, smitten by mother Mary as coeval of the Mahler myth, a transubstantiation for the shaggies since motherly hands that had touched Vic's privacy had also kneaded and baked scones now offered to dirt-thick fingers.

Back when Lana had been ten or so, suffused with the desire to be a nun in order to heal the world, a quick phase, she had asked Mary: can't we have the shaggies come and live in our wine cellar? This was a hard request to explain, harder to win. Later Lana saw how absurd her idea had been: the shaggies living in her parents' house? Flanked by sociological tomes advocating pluralistic societies, her parents would nibble postprandial French cheese above the wine cellar in which a bunch of shaggies knocked heads?

"I studied with Mahler in undergrad," Dirk is telling her. "Went to find him in his office, waited with everyone else slumped in the halls. Then I got my shot at the king. Look, I said, I'm starting far behind, because that was my delusion back then, that reading books made you a better person? So I asked how do I get ahead, you know, I'm so far behind? And I swear the guy looked through me. I'm not kidding, hazel eyes like yours."

"You're the first to call them hazel."

"Well, gray, whatever, they're beautiful. So Mahler told me someone like you, you shouldn't be in school. He called me a maverick. Said I should just go and live in Mexico cheaply, that I'd learn more." He waits as if this should be enough but then gets it is not. "He put his hand on mine for a second at the end, way professors used to do, but thing is, it was different, swear it was like getting an electric jolt. The guy could see into me. Anyone would feel naked before that gaze. So you see," says Dirk, "right, how Mahler set me on a different path?"

She can see. Too easily. Or rather, whether or not Dirk is one more puer, she smells eucalyptus.

In one week men of any Northern Californian denomination can regress and conflate. They turn from studying the bioactivity of mercury to probing the biodynamics of Hacky Sack or start wearing full-tilt training gear to ride high-performance bikes into hills flanked by eucalyptus imported by the British from Australia a long time ago, the tree that had become a quick weed, feathering Northern California's landscape with long peeling bark, scenting the hills with its aromatic sap, all of it putting everyone at greater risk of fire.

Vic had hated Berkeley's eucalyptus for many reasons, not least of which was that, to his nose, it smelled like both cat pee and colonialism. Whenever he wished to insult someone who gave no heed to the natural rise and outgrowth of tradition, who believed he was inventing his own traditions, he called his target Eucalyptus Man.

What emerges, as Dirk continues to talk, is not just eucalyptus but also the hurt boy who had been lurking behind his mantle of preternatural enlightenment: she sees that Dirk's habit of rhapsodizing is how he has survived, a masking of any wound, and this disparity between his superficial and genuine faces does not bother her. In fact, she welcomes it, as such contradiction had lived in her lost fiancé and many other men before him. Her empirical findings have shown that a man whose front—stoic, surly, rapturous—hides a great wound means that inside lives a boy arguing with a grown man. Which means that in bed, the boy and man turn passionate, making her body into a ladder so they can meet in the middle: by this means, she gets to be a healing nun of sex.

"You know, my background?" says Dirk. "I was one of those guys with a trucker dad."

"No way." This guy had his own breed of surprises.

"Almost a pedigree. From a family of truckers. They thought higher education was the biggest privilege you could get. Both hated it and wanted it. I was supposed to be the one who'd get out. My dad told me you got to make better choices than anyone else. And my mom was one of those Bible-thumping Christians who worked for the church all the time and never told me I was adopted."

"Wow."

"It screws with your head. You don't know where you come from. One day I was mowing the lawn and my father blurted it. He said he was shocked that, for a jewboy, I was good with lawns."

She likes him more. Maybe the potlatch of intimacy is happening faster than she thought. He is offering up good stories, maybe his best. "How old were you?"

"A teenager. We lived near the Nevada border, one of those two-bit towns. My first baby bottle was filled with chocolate milk. After the lawnmowing moment, I came down to sin city. Basically, I got to Berkeley and Mahler stepped into what he kept calling the Jesus-hole in my psyche. I thought the guy saw me."

She says nothing for a bit. "You followed his advice?"

"Look, he was Vic Mahler. What can you do when someone really knows you?"

He lets the remark stay in the air, seeing the unpremeditated reward, his comment gathering romantic grit he hadn't intended. In his experience, this kind of woman likes a little slamming; he could crush her bones. She might even let him brand her with his initials mid-thigh, as one girl had, a long time ago, a moment he had never fully recovered from: the scent of burnt human flesh. *What can you do when someone really knows you.*

"Not much." She shrugs the grit away.

"It's a gift," he says. "Can't take that away from the guy, even if people like to revile him. I ended up in San Miguel de Allende with all these painters and liberation people but when the '68 uprising was crushed, that's when I went to Chiapas, you know, wanting to resist the main party. We started our own small group there, built houses in the jungle. Then it all fizzled. Too much infighting. I spent years there, don't get me wrong, we had high hopes."

It's hard when people get older. So much life history to share. Dirk has to use shorthand for entire decades.

"So Vic Mahler—?" she says slowly, drawing it out. It's odd to say the name, entangling and liberating. She has never said it aloud so casually.

"You know, news travels slowly. Still in my Hermes phase but even before I heard what he did to his wife, I got a sign, gave up everything, cut my hair, went straight. I wanted some answers. I'd spent years under a spell, being a student, Chiapas, drug trips, coming back to stalk Vic as Hermes. Finally I cleaned up. In San Francisco I found contact improv."

"You started it?"

"No, it was waiting for me, that whole discipline of contact. I refined it."

"I still don't get why Mahler was such a big deal in your life."

"I mean, the guy was my hero. I used to memorize every one of his declarations. Before I went to Mexico, I did meet his wife once. In person, at a faculty party."

"—Mary?"

"He invited me and then I was a brute, I tried cornering her. Who wouldn't? Mary Fukuji Guzman Mahler." He tastes each syllable, making Lana quiver. "Tall, in red silk, you know, like a samurai's wife? She was part Japanese or something. And always laughing. Who wouldn't have liked her?" His eyes closed. "Of course she wasn't interested in some young protégé. Not the kind for real talk. She was used to Vic's acolytes."

"You were in your Hermes costume," she points out.

"Not then. I met her before Mexico. After Mexico I became Hermes. Anyway, I only did that for a while. It's hard for people to understand but I needed to stalk him. Just a phase. Something I needed to do after I felt he had betrayed me."

"Oh." She can't keep his life straight. "Can we talk about dance?"

By now they have circled the ruins of the burnt hotel enough times. "Hey," he says, his face bright in the gathering dark. "You were so great on the floor today. Your spirit was wide open. What just happened?"

"Can we not talk about it?"

"Like a shadow."

It's not a choice. Not like choosing whether to tell a rape story, a gogo story. How can you live a long life without letting on who you are?

Especially when you can tell your story to someone who will, to speak Dirk's lexicon, grok what helped make you. He compels it: she wants him to grok her. "You know what?" she says.

Smiling, he leans in, ready for the kiss.

"I'm Mahler's daughter," she says.

He steps back. "The missing daughter of Mahler?"

"I'm Lana Mahler."

"That explains it!" The grokking triumphant. "California! You changed your name from California or Callie—right?"

She nods, recognizing Dirk's subtype. An ex-shaggy with depth, no shallow surfer over the family mythology but a researcher, a porer over kitchen scraps and paper waste, a savant. Clearly one who had shadowed Mahler enough to know at least one of her parents' romantic whims. *Let's name her California!* On this point, her father had relaxed, letting Mary have her way, giving the little baby the name of the state that had hosted Mary's parents and Vic and later their own courtship.

What kind of straight-edge parents give their child the name California, a birth-certificate moniker requiring her to endure first-day teasing every year of school? *Hey, California! Join my fifty states?* Lana had glowered until the students stopped but it took too much effort: she chose to change her name to Lana right before she met Rose, first year of high school.

"But Cal-lie Mahler! Man," Dirk is saying, sky-rocketed back into that other jargon, exulting in the glory of return.

"You know I've been Lana for years."

"Lana fuckin Mahler," he says.

She doesn't really remember what else they talked about that night. Only his face: a riffled pack of cards, calibrating, some cards glowing. He returns to it, the justice of finding Mahler's daughter here in this nowhere coast town of Yalina. How amazing was that?

EDIE MEIDAV

All signs fit. Dirk had fallen in with a whole Mexican group of liberationists because of Victor Mahler and then the corrections system never would let Dirk visit his hero, but here they are in Nowhere-lina, Ya-whatever-lina and Dirk gets to meet Mahler's daughter. It must be preordained. But this is mainly coincidence for him, not for her, and as Vic loved saying, people always fail to notice the gross statistical frequency of non-coincidence, noting only the rarer appearance of coincidence. "Today on the dance floor I must have recognized you. That's it!" He drops her hand, claps his own. "I remember. I tried not watching, you guys were too young, but you and some friend used to rollerskate outside your dad's office, right?"

"Rose," says Lana, reluctant to say the name. "Then you saw me when I was about fourteen. Maybe fifteen."

"You guys wore white shorts," he says. "That was the thing. You guys were so wholesome. Like bursting fruit. Or a geometric proof."

"What?"

He starts to irritate her. She wishes she could undo the whole subject.

"You were proof of all Vic Mahler had said."

"What, that he could pork my mother?" This comes out more scornful than she means. Still, she wants him to quit.

"Wow. You're angry. Makes sense. Sorry. I can see your parents in your face. For sure. But you ever, you know, go and visit him?"

Her *no* is a head locked in a shaky elevator.

Nothing fazes him. "You know it's only your name he keeps on the Permissions list, right? I actually tried getting some higher-up at the Bureau of Prisons to let me override that list but even if I were a lawyer, they wouldn't let me. Because he's a special case. A celebrity. No one gets to see him."

"Probably not."

"You never went? He must write you, though, right?"

"Want to see my painting studio?" she asks. Mainly because Dirk had been the white-phallus Hermes guy, but also to change the subject. Also because she is tired of semi-caution: she wants to slip down the rabbithole.

"Hey, if I can't be inside you—" he says, scenting his chance, changing his hunt, incautious in using a line that could boomerang if she happened to be a woman annoyed by directness. "At least I can be inside your mind."

Later, to her chagrin, she learns Dirk is no fool, he is an empiricist. On many previous occasions, with the right kind of woman, this exact line has worked wonders.

He says it again, this thing about her mind and what he calls pussy: the word dates him while also speaking for some envy of tougher men, becoming almost sexy for its bold weirdness.

By this point, she has brought him to the porch swing, outside the house of her children's grandparents. "I'm not in touch with Vic," she says. "Look, my kids are going to wake up."

He barely digests the fact that she is a mother to kids. "I'll whisper," he says. "Anyway."

Later on her studio futon he sticks fingers in every possible place and it is impossible to ignore the guy's focus because it feels as if a million slave Lilliputians have gathered around a core, worshipping it, having tied a string around it and only now starting to push a giant stone attached to the string away—slow, tiny but resolute struggles toward freedom—so that when the stone breaks free of the string, it boomerangs enough to liberate all the little slaves. They ramble out in luxurious slowness, spreading through her limbs, ready to enjoy the summer night.

Yet only the previous week, after a few months of less than optimal hookups—one alcoholic logger, one clubfoot crab-potter from the rez, one unkempt computer billionaire—she had made some resolve that she wouldn't be vulnerable with someone for a while, wouldn't give herself over to the love craving.

When she makes the decision to go south on Highway Five with Dirk to the Hope Springs oasis, they have known each other a total of four months. *Je t'aime jusqu'à la mort* plays on the tinny local radio station. Dirk entertains the idea that they will be one of those modern couples beaming out from the advertisement of an alternative-living journal, shiny and smug with connubial delight: *we can teach you our relationship secrets. Self-actualize our way!*

What he says to convince her to head south is that he'd read somewhere that everyone needed in life three things:

1. Someone to love
2. Something to do (right action/meaningful work)
3. Something to look forward to

or else only two

1. Belonging
2. A sense of meaning

She knows he has cribbed most of this from Vic and others but lacks the guts to say so since upon such ideas Dirk is trying to build his own fortress of ideation.

He thinks that at Hope he and Lana might be an exemplary couple. He rhapsodizes: not siblings repulsed by each other in the Freudian house of matrimony, not merely passionate couplers, but a couple above all rise and fall, welt and schmerz, zero and sum.

Half sold, Lana decides to uproot her sons from their beloved scorched earth of Yalina to head south. She will help in Dirk's role as resident guru and will play her own role, as he says, of pastor's wife, rebbetzin, an avatar of thriving.

After her decision, she still has to sell the plan big-time to her kids, because those kids know to stay loyal to the myth of their great lost dad Kip, a bursting brilliant flower too great for Lana, according to at least one of the myths sown by their grandparents. For the moment she decides you never fully escape other people's stories, but you can at least sidestep a few of the nastier ones.

Dirk hadn't told Lana the exact truth. He had streamlined, as that is how history works, all thirty-year movements cresting into baroque effusion before clarity can emerge, as Mahler once theorized. Dirk had also streamlined because, as Dirk too liked to tell his followers, long before your deathbed it becomes important to think your one life has sprouted more than the merely banal.

One part is true: Dirk had been one of those guys arising with gumption from dust and muck, in his case, Truckee and its mountains and their charismatic cartography, the lure for city drivers who come to peek at snow, all the I-5 offrampers wielding maps like compasses at the convenience store and eyeing him. Dirk had been one more local runt drinking chocolate milk, wearing misbuttoned logger's shirts and flooding pants, Dirk squeezing by to hang up front, coughing on stubs with other wedlock or shotgun Truckee kids smirking with rotting teeth. His entourage was inbred or, more often, devoid of parents. Those few with both parents probably would have been better off with neither, Dirk and his milieu forming a quaint footnote to the vacationers' satisfaction of all rustic urges. Having shown promise in high-school chess, after his bad adopted-son lawn-mower incident, Dirk had escaped being another rich person's local color by throwing chess trophies into a duffel bag and lobbing himself southwest, becoming a student in Berkeley of the seventies.

In the town's city-country microcosm, one that transforms dwellers into lifers, he had found the noblesse oblige of high ideals. He'd been of a piece with the men's tanned oiled muscles, what he called *chicken-grease legs*, liking the simple entitlement of boys and girls who wore both river-guide sandals and floppy mountaineering hats. It was easy for him to understand their embrace of liberal ideals, yurts and hill-climbing, the headiness of a college education studded with wholesome sex and orthodontial perfection. You could conserve and consume simultaneously, all of it subtly evangelical like the barley potash flecked with international greens you were supposed to bring to potlucks.

In his co-op with the other guys, on their day for cooking a late lunch, they would burn cumin lentils and then race shirtless to play congas outside in Sproul Plaza, their chicken-grease legs in happy communion under the sun, good as bronze castings of eternity, honored by at least a few Africans in attendance: at such moments, Dirk felt united in a grand purpose. But what was that purpose exactly?

All the people I know who dedicated themselves to hedonism now are having a bad time, they have health problems or don't have houses or children or paying jobs you could hear skinny sparky women with hair dyed blue-black confiding to sincere younger suitors in the cafés, women who'd survived heroin habits and pimps and worse. Dirk could have followed this track, becoming one of the overgrown hedonism-loving boys in river-guide sandals the traveler sees upon arrival in the Oakland airport. Instead Dirk caught fire. He would lay aside Frisbee and tai chi, would change the world.

Because he'd had the good fortune of crossing paths with the great Vic Mahler. First, he'd taken every course the teacher had offered, namely, two: Neuroethology and the World, and Motivation on the Level of the Cell.

In their first and last office meeting, the teacher had looked straight into Dirk and had said: I don't know what you're doing in school. You have the temperament of a maverick. Where you really belong is on a cooperative in Mexico. Take this book by Freire. Why waste your time with orthodoxy?

Who had ever given Dirk such a name? *Maverick*, a cattle-wrassler, a Logos capable of branding his soul, making him study the carmine paperback of Paolo Freire only to see the maverick face of God and his own future. He took Mahler's diktat, surrendered the prospect of a B.A. and made himself into the maverick bachelor of possibility, the next day hitchhiking south along Five until San Miguel. Sure, it did take a few months before he could dislodge himself from its expat comforts and head toward Chiapas, knowing little but his wish to avoid his Truckee past and truckdriver father, but he was earnest and fire-powered enough that he could create a school, nightly reading Freire as if a new covenant upon his doorposts while working daily to follow its commandments, doing what he could to enter into a dialogue with his students without snubbing himself.

At first Chiapas had seemed fruitful: he brought education to the people. Leeches sucked his blood dry in a jungle from which he'd learned to cut whole swaths, swinging his machete while traveling forward on the back of an ass but Dirk was good, trained well in the local ways. Give him a flat stone and masa flour and in less than a minute he could slam together a tortilla. Plus he kept himself away from women local or foreign, letting the pure autoerotic beauty of monkhood fill his skin when he wasn't in the outhouse bloating or deflating from dysentery and its own autoerotic fascination. The system had been sustainable until the thing had collapsed in some horrible Zeno's paradox, the peasants so close to achieving the dream of collective empowerment that they turned against the gringo in their midst, calling him inescapably elitist in exactly the lingo he had taught them. He had given them a fishing rod only to become their first fish. Couldn't you call this a sort of success?

Dirk read Freire—*the man cannot give others a sense of their own liberation*—and ashamed, he decided to go inward. After a bad aya-huasca trip during which the shaman had gone nasty, incanting *you are a gringo, you are a gringo*, some wires in his brain had crossed. Dirk saw that his romantic gesture (coming to Mexico) and his overactive brain (distinctions he had learned in Mahler's classroom) and his mistakes (trying to pretend he wasn't acting like one more white messiah) came from central fissures in Vic Mahler's thought.

In Dirk's post-hallucinogenic clarity, it became imperative to bring the message home to daddy. He would retrace the trail of tears and return to the safety of Berkeley, keeping himself far from the chicken-grease fellows of yore, instead he would turn the town into his own theater, a place to consolidate fragments Vic Mahler had strewn, a theater in which to stage a necessary act and intervention, urgent to his identity. He would take whiteness to the nth degree.

In an era of discourse about Sun People and Ice People, Dirk manifested himself as a white polar bear, a means of showing that if a man fully embraced his identity, he most powerfully could subvert others. In this guise, Dirk started stalking Victor Mahler. Mahler would sight the polar-bear Hermes on the street and duck into boutiques or homes. While Hermes knew he was being avoided, it didn't impede his addled purpose, as his brain had ricocheted and he needed to dog the man. Sitting outside the professor's house in the predawn, Dirk/Hermes hoped to eavesdrop on moments of domestic dispute to prove that Mahler was guilty of whatever rhetorical term tracks the lack of consistency between someone's being and actions. Ad hominem but also ad absurdum, a necessary gesture, a moment of Theater of the Real, of the Oppressed, of Life, of consistency being the hobgoblin of great beings. His eavesdropping never yielded much but the gesture meant something, since in those days, theater still trumped biology, hands down. Only later would come the triumph of chemistry.

Sometimes Dirk/Hermes ran into one of the chicken-grease guys from the other era, and it was like, okay, they couldn't understand what he was doing, but that was fine, let everyone coexist, one planet and how long did we have, the earth was at its midlife and we were its crisis, and anyway we'd all soon be blown up by those fuckers in government if we didn't first get incinerated by some communal death-penalty pact.

In this period he abstained from eating meat and upon awaking every morning performed a ten-minute headstand until his neck gave out.

What really brought him back was when he had read about a special event for Those Coming Home from the Sixties, an event at a place called Hope Springs, just past the abandoned nuclear reactor, in which great musicians from the sixties and seventies and even the eighties were going to play—

—naked!—

—just down Highway Five, a highway for which he felt obscure gratitude, given what it had so copiously given and taken. With its migrant workers and unreconstructed cowboys, red-jawed religious families and blue-collared car salesmen, broad-haunched Italian ranchers and thin-lipped diner waitresses, the highway served as an artery of his future and past. Add music and bodies, better than a nude beach! His sign had come; Dirk was ready to shed Hermes.

Plus a friend from the old co-op days owed him a favor and let him take a skanky truck down Five. He was happy to be wearing his old plaid shirt and same old chicken-grease legs, tanned and oiled, lead-footing it past every speed limit so he could make it down in about four hours of driving. And okay, so the truck broke down a few times along the road but his mood changed: he felt restored to a vision of human goodness.

A cop even forgave him for speeding, letting him off with *Do better next time.*

I will, man, said Dirk with great solemnity, I am trying.

Many times he almost didn't arrive. Who needed the concert at Hope Springs?

Because along Five, one Mexican family took him into their camper-trailer, kids' legs wiggling from sleeping ledges up near the ceiling, frying up for him the best chilaquiles he'd ever had, pimento-spotted, tasty, larded with goodwill and non-gringoness, loving Dirk's good Spanish and laughing when he used his idioms in trade, his best the like-father-like-son *el hijo de la gata ratones mata.* Dirk could have stayed on with them, they offered something that huge: a whole fantasy of acceptance, crossbridging and quinceañeras, an educated amnesia, something he'd never found in Chiapas. Easy for him to have stayed with them and followed the garlic harvest in Gilroy, the oranges near Valencia and the wine grapes in Sonoma and Napa, just moving up and down the state picking crops in order to fall dead asleep in their camper-trailer.

But something ticked his skull. A person could call it destiny, not superstition at all, given that Mahler had once said that superstition was the name people used to describe religions they were afraid of.

He could have mislaid his destiny along Five but something about this place Hope Springs just itched. The name sounded right.

Plus, the subtitle—Hope Springs, The Temple of Coming Home—made him feel he'd finally find the place where everything could be embraced, the Truckee chocolate-milk past, the cumin lentil potash, Mahler's fissures, the masa and the outhouse, the bad trip, the polar-bear outfit and his time in the Single Resident Occupancy in downtown Berkeley where everyone in his cagelike room along the corridor had stories not so different from his own. All those failed café philosophers were still having afternoons of flea-ridden herpetic sex in the embrace of amiable slumming patchouoli-scented college girls after having spent caffeinated mornings filling random notebooks with block-lettered sentences dependent on chiasmic axioms and islands of nouns like WORLD CONSPIRACY and U.S. TOTALITARIAN GOVERNMENT. If they didn't have a willing sex partner and moneyloaner, the SRO residents played chess in the afternoon. Or lined up for the gourmet, local-produce homeless dinner served in the church near the famous coffeehouse.

Dirk was pondering it as he drove toward Buttonwillow, the riddle of identity as the millennium approached: to each individual an orthodox routine as predictable as it was self-invented. You could jog your parcourse or sleep in an SRO, but everyone hungered for a buffet of choice, namely, the Emersonian invention of a religion that made sense to the individual, as Mahler had said.

In such spirit Dirk had come into Hope Springs, the buzzkill of the early nineties bearing hard on his neck. After his first hours there, Dirk had gone to the communal bathroom, and after shaving off his long beard and mustache, his dream of playing Paolo Freire preaching revolution to peasants had drawn its last breath.

The place—was it the negative ions released by the bubbling waters?—made him want to be part of something more egoless. Almost. Because everyone walked around naked, and, bucking the trend, he would be clothed. Everyone came to this place in order to free himself while he came for binding, ready to serve. He found a better place to camp out in the main field. As he set up his tent, building on knowledge he'd gleaned in Chiapas, he noted structural difficulties in the sleeping platform, the warped wood and varieties of lichen growing near the pools, the mulberry tree dripping fruit in liability-luring manner upon the walks.

Soon as he could, he shared his insights with the founders, DorAlba, never to forget the pleasure of their respectful listening.

This is why, years later, in 2008, having formed a new dance liberation praxis, Dirk wrote to DorAlba. Of course they remembered him because, being MENSAites, they remembered everything, their neocortex that refined, and they invited him back, this time as guru-in-residence.

He kept certain quotations up on the wall of their room in Hope Springs, upon which Lana's eyes cross:

There is the need for the interdisciplinary reading of bodies with students, for breaking away from dichotomies, ruptures that are enviable and deforming.

Newness is not the gift of a tabula rasa, but a resurrection; or miraculous pregnancy. A virgin shall conceive, in old age, as in the case of Sarah, or the Roman Empire. Natural innocence is only an image of the real, the supernatural, the second innocence.

If you're dancing physics, you're dancing contact. If you're dancing chemistry, you're doing something else. When an apple fell on his head, Newton was inspired to describe the three laws of motion, that carry his name. . . . In his attempt to be objective, Newton overlooked the question of how it feels to be the apple. When we put our bodymass in motion, we raise above the law of gravity and go toward the swinging, circulating attraction of the centrifugal force. Dancers ride upon and play with these forces.

The phenomenology and aesthetics of human movement have reached theoretical and practical insights about human interaction and embodiment that are closely related to the ones that are found recently in the fields of artificial intelligence (embodied robotics), cognitive science (embodied cognition) and new biology (self-organization and emergence).

The earth is much bigger than you are so you'd better learn to co-ordinate with it.

Lana heads out with the boys and Hogan so he can show the grounds with what seems a scoutleader's pride: she almost expects their guide to start demonstrating rope-knots.

"There's the reptile cemetery," says Hogan, bald head gleaming as if ready for planting, she thinks nonsensically, afternoon sun addling her. A few years earlier, one of her sons had asked why his thingie needed to live at the top of his legs when, if it grew out of the top of his head, it would be more convenient whenever he needed to pee, and she recalls this conversation as Hogan puts a railroad cap on over that off-putting face of his that resembles the famous cross-eyed actor. The gaze pinioned at some central meniscus, the skin so unmarked and eyebrows frozen at such strange peaks that what he resembles most is some albino creature peeking out from a rock. She tries not to laugh at the weird combo dancing before her, the vision of baldness, thing-ies, an albino glare and meniscus. Some sensuality lives in the guy. The skinny-rat, boyish narrowness of certain older men, toolbelt and heavy keys marking turf in their hang, as if all expression had been shunted to the periphery, to everything below that tight waist, or just to the shoulders and hands, these parts twisting and quick, and isn't there great life in Hogan's close-set eyes, the way they hold tight as if trying to slam her into recognition?

———

Admittedly, the encounter a few days earlier with her old schoolmate had rattled her cover, enough that she almost has the urge to natter on about Jane Polsby and her old friend Rose to skinny-rat Hogan, but she must haul herself up short. This guy shouldn't become some newfound confidant, especially when Lana has the bad habit of turning the wrong people into confessors.

"That's because you lack the boundary of trust," a half-friend of hers up in Yalina had said—crossing the same boundary in her appraisal—"it's something that happens to victims of sexual abuse, which, by the way, I'm guessing is part of your background?" to which Lana had just grunted.

When Hogan had learned Dirk could not join their tour, given all the supplicant work lining up, Lana had not been surprised by how apparent Hogan's relief had been. She had guessed Hogan might be the kind of man who, like Dirk, flourishes away from the cynical, rivalrous gaze of other men, no surprise there either, given that the majority of her life has been spent around men who yearn for the undivided flower of female attention, men who when young probably had been scolded more than once for not playing well with others.

"There you have your motel and diner," Hogan is saying, down below. "That next tier above? That's where you're staying. Above you have the kibbutz," he says. "Nothing zionist, just what we call the school for your boys. Experiential learning. Fully accredited," Hogan continues in a brochure voice. "You didn't know about that perk, did you?" She did, since to entice her out of Yalina, Dirk kept using mom porn of the organic-bib, glass-bottle variety, telling her many times of the experiential school that was *accredited*.

Smiling, pleased this fellow Hogan works so hard to please, she lets him continue to throb, climbing behind him on the rutted, lupine-fringed fire trail. Directives fill Hogan: she hadn't seen it before but he comes off as hypomanic, dedicated to guarding against peril, his portable oasis a bota, the leather Spanish-style canteen slung against his dungarees now offered her. "Got to drink. Dehydration isn't pretty, people go crazy. Plus we don't have a lot of yucca here, ma'am."

Ma'am: she is at the age where a man older than her calls her ma'am. Finding herself less pleased, but still wanting to oblige, she lifts the bota to drink water with the tang of leather, metal, someone else's mouth.

"Heat so dry in these hills you don't notice you're losing water. It's like some people lose their thirst. Boys, you too. And stay out of the brush near the arroyo. That's poison oak. See the oil on the triple leaves? Not red this time of year. But that smell? Sumac. We're going to burn most of this down. Too much fire hazard. Here," says Hogan, commands shooting all directions, giving Lana a sprig of wild fennel. "Boys can chew this."

"Yum," says Sedge, agreeable. "Like Wrigley's."

Hogan shoots his puzzled cantilevered glance at Lana. "Must be your poet, right?"

Later she remembers: not long after the poet comment came the lion. At first Lana had thought: how cute, a cat's face, beautiful eyes dark-rimmed, weirdly not unlike her dead Kip. Tail twitching, gaze fastened. Just before it pounced down through the dried brush straight toward Sedge.

A mountain lion.

Time froze in her veins at the realization and at Hogan's voice lowered: go backward NOW. While Hogan stood his ground, managing to spirit Sedge above his head, holding him on his shoulders, already throwing stones at the cat and now shouting to Tee and Lana: keep facing him but get away!

Tee's hand in hers, she staggered backward down the trail only a few paces, stopped by a ravine, watching the cat watching the man throwing rocks, her boy on his shoulders. Hogan heaved miracles, never bending down, but the fear bound her close, her legs so dense she could only grip her boy's wet hand, the two of them stockstill until the cat quivered its nose in distaste, flicking its tail and slinking off into the canyon.

Afterward, Lana glows with gratitude. The moment so swift but Hogan had saved them, risking himself with an exact measure of un-preening gravity you rarely find in California men. "That cat could have mauled us," she says, wanting to grab the boys to her chest yet trying to let them keep their big-kid dignity, Sedge and Tee quaking with the fun of having almost been destroyed. This close to death: their hands mark the distance like gospel singers calibrating nodes of ecstasy against heights of menace until the inevitable squabble rises over the question of who had been closer to danger, Sedge (on Hogan's shoulders) or Tee (because only his mother's hand and the ground had supported him). "We could have been eaten alive," she says to halt their dispute.

"True," says Hogan. "Mountain lions are no joke, ma'am."

"He would have eaten me first," says Tee, happily.

"Cat gave you boys your tongues back?" says Hogan. "Ma'am, you okay?" On her arm, his touch is tender, overstepping nothing, though she sees in the black depth of his pupils two shiny little imprisoned Lanas. "What's that scar?"

Inside her wrist from old self-cutting days: she flicks her hand to flick off the question. "Thorns," she says, unable to stop her post-lion tremble. One doctor in the asylum had told Lana that either she was Californian and her origins left him incapable of fully understanding her terms, some of which sounded mystical, or else that she was an unthinking force of nature and contained too much energy. At least the latter proposition seems to be the case. Lana still shakes, long after the others have stopped. "It's like I could use some leeches to suck off some of this adrenaline," she announces. "I got to sit."

Beside the path, her boys, celebrants of life, fence with dried madrone branches. Her throat gone dry, she'd still rather not ask this Hogan fellow for more of his bad water. He has gained too much advantage too quickly, though she likes his way of saying ma'am: it reminds her of Kip's family and their country speech. "Give me a minute," she begs.

Finally they descend the mountain, adults reticent, Lana's knees wobbly, kids abuzz with glory.

Aiming for solitude, she tells Hogan she wishes she could find a way to thank him.

"Well," he says and already she regrets the words, because the face he turns on her is so dead and thick, mouth barely moving, he could be a raptor ready to snap thorax from abdomen: "Anyone would've stepped forward."

"No," she says, "not anyone, " which for who knows what reason must be exactly the right answer to rip some light through that face.

Rose finds herself explaining some recent signs along with her idea about people being either symbiotes or mavericks to the odd resort manager she has just met in the highway coffee shop with its every inch of wall space fitted out with western kitsch, all the fringed, signed, worn-saddle, cowboy-with-a-whip, days-of-glory paraphernalia any nostalgist would consider decent findings for an afternoon.

Hogan, he'd said his name was, don't call me anyone's hero.

In her booth, she had finished her ice tea and was asking a waitress about the spa up the road when Hogan had entered, setting down a leather canteen and taking off a railroad cap before sliding behind the counter not to attend to customers but to make himself a green-algae power drink labeled on the side of the can with a rainbow-hued globe and the title Elixir. Every flick of his had been economical and when he noted Rose studying him he said: "Each minute of life counts, right?"

He then told the waitress he called Zabelle some anecdote about hikers facing down a mountain lion and had stood lean and straight while measuring powder, eyeballs crossed as he raised the tumbler, a mock toast toward Rose. "To staying young always, right?" His noticing her didn't lift Rose's mood. Nor did his touch on her arm, a cold reptile's before asking *mind if I?* while not awaiting an answer and slipping across from her in the booth, its seats hued the shade of old tongue. "Try some?"

He ignores her demurral. Must be the manager to be so confident, pouring the skeevy slop into an empty coffee cup and waiting for her to sip, clearly not satisfied until she swallows some of the green whey or whatever it is and lies. "Delicious."

"You're here for the protest," he says, not really a question, leading quickly enough into conversational voodoo that gets her to disclose more than she means to, telling him she is not a therapist, as he first guesses, not a teacher or nurse but a freelance columnist. And only when she thinks it might help her cause does she also admit she is a lawyer. "Part-time though."

Perhaps the lawyer thing does the trick or at least it doesn't backfire. Whatever he thinks of Rose, he hints that despite her lack of a reservation, he can get her a room: he says *get* like *git*, his lips almost immobile until he flashes a smile, dark and fissured, his teeth displaying what she cannot decipher, whether lower-class upbringing, the poverty of a large family, in utero chemicals, schoolyard bullies, prison time or maybe just rebellion against a high-class upbringing. His skull is shaved clean, a tiny tattoo at its base a near-indecipherable infinity loop within a Celtic ring, and in a move of old-style flirtation she asks to study it.

Once she has explained her whole symbiote-versus-maverick philosophy, the smile again flashes her way. He relaxes. "What am I then?"

"I'd call you maverick-one," she says.

"I like that. Maverick-one. What does it mean?"

"You take charge, sometimes at others' expense. You like protecting people. But you have enough of a birthright of charisma to let it be okay. Usually. But you find your loneliness hard to take. It forces you to extremes."

"Way to help out!" he says.

"Sorry. I don't mean to—"

"Hey, you're good. Like a cable psychic. Should have a late-night show." Their time must be up. He glances toward the door.

"People probably tell you you're a good listener," she says, a mild flush of abandonment rolling down her fingertips. "I told you a lot about myself. Usually I'm the one asking questions."

He waits. Spits into a handkerchief from his back pocket, sizes her up. Then hands off a flyer showing slicked heads floating atop a pool. "How about stay at the spa," he is saying. "Go on up that dirt road.

Past the griffin gate you'll see the office. Just say Hogan says you get a good place in Venusberg. The women's dorm. Say you're my friend. They'll orient you about the baths and all." He's suggesting she stay at the very spa where her old friend may be, entailing a direct approach when Rose had wanted to arrive crabwise, unseen by Lana until the last moment.

"Geothermal," he says to her hesitation. "Hot springs. That's the ticket. Sorry to speak bluntly. You got to clear your mind for your task."

"Which?"

"The important one."

She shrugs.

"Thought you said you were a lawyer."

"I did."

"Sorry. Usually never get it wrong. I took you to be one of those anti-death-penalty people."

Her chin does a slow wag.

"I've been wrong before." Again that dirty smile comes her way. "You know they call this place the local fry zone. Old Parcel heats up, protestors flock. We call them the anti aunties. I was sure—but you didn't know about the execution?" Now authentically perplexed.

"I came—for vacation."

"But you said you're looking for something? Someone?"

"I mean, I did, but not—"

"See, you can't hide. Vic's people I always spot a mile off." He is triumphant. "Your skirt gave you away. Something about black on red, can't explain. Could write a book on it. Practically a science. Well, want my take, sure, the guy did screwball things in life, none of that gels with his work, whatever, all true, but the guy still deserves a better lawyer. One he has now's famous for having sent off about seven people. Kaputski."

"Seven?" She doesn't will her squeak. "I didn't know. But you know I don't practice that kind of death law."

"You'd be good though. Look like the kind born knowing lots." He gets up suddenly, their colloquy finished. "Well, welcome. Spa's just the ticket. Up the dirt road. Tell them Hogan says you get Venusberg, you'll love it. Great views." The reptilian coolness of his hands stays in her palm, not unwelcome, the hands of a man who knows how to fix things. As she leaves the coffee shop, uncertain, she feels his crooked smile on the swish of her skirt.

Outside, she stops, deciding, not lonely any longer, excited, almost revealed. No place at the inn but a room in Venusberg. She twirls a strand of her hair, surprised to find it black, as if she had managed to forget a whole phase of her recent life. "Lana," she says for no real reason, just reorienting internal magnetic fields, no clear sign having appeared yet. A trucker emerges from his driver's door so all she sees are his square mud-caked toes in flip-flops, his toes waiting while his spit shoots crystalline just past, followed by his pee, an arc sizzling on contact with asphalt. The only literal sign around hangs from the back of his sixteen-wheeler and is addressed to whores: LOT LIZARDS NOT INVITED.

Under a dripping waterpipe lies a child's mechanical alphabet board, gaudy orange against the shop's desert-shale, unable to stop its battery gone wild, its bleat hard to make out at first, but which, when she understands it, becomes enough welcome for Rose to accept, played out in the perfection of threes: a tinny, automated Hello! Hello! Hello!

1983 & 2008

Sink of the tattooed and cockringed, of pierced or natural, Asian African Anglo Latino, bellies tight or multiple, breasts tiny or tripled, red brown yellow pink orange white, buttocks furry or denuded. Some bodies belong more to the fourteenth century's fields, child-bearing and early mortality than our space-age, vitamin-capsule eternity of the twentieth, the twenty-first, but no matter, a representative from every niche has shown up at this roll call.

Vic's commentary about the place still echoes, a bombardment making Mary say: "You think the rest of us lack eyes?" To which his response had been to talk, much of the time, to his daughter's little friend Rose, a parlay advertising his ideal of genteel discussion.

Long-testicled, long-clitorised, siliconed or liposuctioned. Those of skin pocked or clear and multitufted, the puffy littoral, the cluster-nutted. Exercise-addicted, lenient or unfetishized, all bodies here testify to denial or indulgence, to their treatment of time and time's treatment of them. Bodies parading, rushed through college and meals, cars and bars, through lunchtime walks and ischemia risk, bodies coddled into rock-climbing or Sufi-dancing, into Mommy & Me classes. Bodies displaying tree rings or invisible-ink actuarial charts: when will the angel of death visit?

Not to mention men with penises that are tiny surprises resting on crepuscular sacks. Or those of corporate girth who follow bellies around in bewilderment, their heads distinguished and well groomed, or the older women with eyes glittery, noses narrow, buttocks smooth and self-aware, labia Brazilian, rucked, speaking to young men with honest eyes and handlebar mustaches. Pierced noses and equipment everywhere. The hermaphroditic, paganist, or transgendered, the hunched and erect, males or females with friendly clumps of beard, hair afloat, bodies scarred or blemish-free, all crying out the story to anyone who will listen: leisurely self-fulfillment or slow martyrdom.

Every breed of homo sapiens comes to Hope to be shed of shields like coffee-cup sleeves, kids' doctor appointments, making a living. They reject ailments, annoying colleagues, portable music players, chamber music subscriptions, aging parents, the new black or the old gray, free themselves from nepotism, cronyism, bad politics. They come to abandon their helplessness in the claws of syndromes, carpal tunnel, overworked mother, acquired immunity, finally liberated from powerful housemates and gauche, controlling neighbors. Ostensibly free from race and class, from absentee mates or alcoholic parents, but never fully from gender: gender stands alone.

Mary saying: "Vic, let's just be together somewhere? Or next time I pack duct tape for our mouths?"

"Someone's mouth, maybe." Vic shooting back his most winsome grin.

"You know some people seem to have taped up their hearing."

"But I'm listening, my dear," pulling his lobes long, turning on her his most wolfish smile. "Whatever you want to say. I'm all ears."

Cowboy heritage continues in the Hope Springs oasis in that peek-aboo showers with swinging saloon doors tease the viewer, revealing shampooed heads and, below, bare legs, while more contemporary plein-air showers let you see everything. Mirrors in warm light reflect back loveliness but in starker light make people shrink. Everything gets seen. Between pools, some people wear towels or bathrobes, naïfs taking on the sophisticate's effacement. Usually, however, big, small, fat, thin or thinner yet, people wear nudity covered over by bliss or focus, two useful veils over intermediate layers of solipsism or narcissism. Some people, younger women and older men, tend to wear shame or its cousin brazenness as a cloak over all other affects. Some stare at everyone else, a preemptive strike against being looked *at*.

But nothing really hides. People may pretend not to look but bodies—a rainbow, a cornucopia—are seen that beg surveillance, bodies never depicted in any magazine or Renaissance painting or African sculpture or specialist porn.

Mary saying: "Honestly. You said we'd have a getaway. You think I care that much what you think about other people's bodies? How you're acting, you just made me turn 360 degrees in the space of twenty-four hours."

Vic turning his most charming look on her: "So that gets us back where we started?" Clearly hearing some inaudible knell, sensing his charm waning, he rises from his lounge chair then, sacrificially upsetting all papers to go kneel by her chair, to be a good husband embracing his wife in a bear hug, to muffle her qualms. "Come on, Mary," says Vic, "Mary honey," and after that, Rose is embarrassed to keep lying nearby, unsure as usual whether any Mahler cares if she hangs about, their little noiseless mothgirl Rose, or if in some secret way they need her, as if the presence of Rose helps them keep the peace, their daughterlike moth making up their best audience yet.

Beyond how to manage grief (Witnessing Your Emotions, Hope Springs workshop #89, led by Omkari Rigatonne), there is no perfect evacuation scenario at Hope and no convincing earthquake survival scenario either. December thirteenth, 2008, the plan is to account for this soon and post more signs.

Liquid lavender-scented soap (made from flowers grown in the surrounding meadows and crushed near the cob-bale temple) flows out from opaque teats stationed at the sinks and showers around Hope Springs and because of this, everyone starts to smell the same, a combination of lavender and the earthgut sulfur and iron piped into the hot pool where the pyroxene filter keeps the whole thing clean, fifteen hundred gallons of water pumped through daily, catching any inorganic material, allowing only H_2O, Na, S, Pb, Fe.

Lavender interestingly brings out the low notes of sulfur and the high of iron, while also efficiently tranquilizing the amygdala, the brain's efficient center for both trauma and pleasure. Water flows from the hot pool into the warm pool so a special hot oasis happens near the stairs, an arsenic footbath near the entry to the warm pool, though the catalogue promises that the arsenic flows in trace amounts, not at all poisonous.

Sometimes white flakes of calcium precipitate form on the surface of the warm pool, alarming pilgrims whose imaginations and self-awareness already tend toward hypochondriacal arousal. Yet such flakes just mean that many humans have crowded the pool and that the spa works its wonders, each person having acted as a human ice cube, cooling the earth's magma-warmed waters: the calcium is sugar condensing in cooled tea.

"You manage to see everything but me," Mary hissing to Vic, their hug having spanned the mere second-long blaze of noon.

This sameness of nudity and scent makes sex a greater plausibility. How many veils are there between your floating member and someone else's hole, your wet hole and someone else's member? Thus, people's faces work to hold up new veils by the minute: the all-time favorite is dignity, as is the visage of sex-transcending enlightenment, a new kind of spiritual chastity armature. Bliss always works. A naked couple will seem clothed by virtue of a pride in the mate's naked body when displayed to cold air and hot water, faces singing out a courtship story and continued attraction, making the discrete nature of their bodies evanesce.

The men's dormitory flanks the women's dormitory. You can get private rooms with shared or half or full bath, you can try dorm life or even tent-camp, out in the meadow past the half-constructed cob-bale temple still awaiting the right nudist or aquaphilic donor to complete Hope's most ambitious project yet.

There is also the sauna. No matter the lavender soap used as a disinfectant, the sauna never stops smelling of the sweat of thirty-five years of wet and prone bodies. Oak soaked with a sweat gone archival, a legion of Finns and Swedes and everyone else having shed toxins so deep into the wood that no one's new sweat has a fighting chance. One breathes in the heated old sweat and at the same time history, the Hope Springs into which one humbly enters one's own body as a worldly petitioner, a stressed-out nutcake, a beggar for the rite of cleansing and healing, as close to immortality as one can get in this life, longing for youth and renewal sans mildew.

Some song plays on the radio in the guard station: *dream of Cal-i-for-ni-cation.*

Statistics would state that clever conversation doesn't occur much at Hope Springs and that political conversation is barely tolerated. What does unfold, no matter the residents, is a curatorial discussion re: choices and the consumption of regimes ecological, psychological, moral or digestive, career-minded or habitat-specific. A parade of bruises brings on a parade of cures. Sacred sexuality as a weekend practice combined with being a Web site manager and renovating condos? The conversation consumes all: ways to overcome trauma by holding versus selling. The benefits of Pilates versus yoga versus NIA or Gestalt versus transpersonal versus meditation, or zen versus Vipassana versus Mahayana versus surfing. Stay in the relationship or leave? Twelve steps versus transcending the literalism of the step? Committing to Amerikkka instead of leaving for Asia or Europe or Latin America? No matter their ostensible import, all conversations can be reduced to this: the attainment of greater health whether in one's muscles, mood, karmic plane or colonic hygiene.

From the brochure:

Get over grief.
Get over loss.
Find yourself anew.
Be not the root, digging deep toward the molten magma center of the earth.
Be the high branches.
Better yet, the leaf, free to wave in the wind, reaching high up toward the sun.

December fourteenth, 2008, day four of the anniversary, day one of the Surrendering Grief workshop and the beginning of the EnlightenBreath experience. At the break between these last two, a clump of men sunbathe on the cramped spot of sun on the deck. They lie on their sides, of womanish hip, their stomachs sliding a bit, reading, not lazy, doing leg lifts and abdominals, their sex falling this way and that way, Peter Rabbit and Jemima Puddle-duck, childishly vulnerable, pierceable, blushing, a confession of boyhood. Some may be ex-felons or even feds—but who cares? One innocence under the sun. To each individual let there be all over again the simple birthright of body.

At the tail end of a Yoga of the Heart class, Rose listens to the female instructor—every inch of her revealed belly self-aware, its notches a form of invested capital—as she has students finish the last stretch so they can lie like corpses or napping kindergartners awaiting the fairy-wand that will wake them into a better future. Rose lies prone and breathing, knowing some weepy stage of life has gathered her up. Everyone else is lost in trance while she fights tears: the dorm had given her one lonely night.

So easily Rose could tap someone's wrist and just confess what she is seeking.

"Let thoughts come and go," says the instructor. "Don't chase. Your breath is the wind, your thoughts clouds blowing away. Call your practice a ladder up and your detachment the ability to pull the ladder after yourself."

But detachment proves ornery: why must one person always be designated to become the vessel of memory?

Lana running in front of her on one of the paths. The hushed arguments Mary and Vic had. The married pair seated at a table—they always kept their bathing suits on—in the shade, lost in journals or arguing, interrupted when Lana came asking for lemonade money. Jane Polsby had started saying to Lana and Rose: "Let's not bother

Lana's parents. Let's just use money my mom gave me. Let's leave them alone." The friends accepted Jane's money with false promises of repayment, one more example of the bad faith they showed others' deficits and the tenderness showed only each other.

On first talking with that odd Hogan, Rose had kept much of her goal in coming to Hope concealed. Later that evening, she had leaned onto a fence made of rickety desert sticks, strung with Christmas lights, listening to Johnny Cash blasting from the loudspeakers, the bass line a low itch, finding herself dangerous and unbounded, lips full, throat parched, so restless she felt ready for any random man who might press up behind. She had looked out at the valley falling into dusk, watching preparations for the anniversary theater presentation about the founding of Hope. How humid the actors became, returned to play-acting their former selves or heroes, only rarely breaking into hilarity.

Hogan had come by then, surprising her by asking in his flat tone if everything had been to her satisfaction so far, and Rose had pinched the flesh between her thumb and index finger to keep herself from begging him to locate one person among the three hundred milling about. Only when he left did she let herself exhale, again, the name she has for years tried not voicing: Lana!

In the yoga class this morning following, breathing in rosemary burning from a smudge stick, Rose is being undone and tries not to cry. "Identify with your potential to change. Not with the old self you keep toting around. Identify with the harmony that could be yours," says the instructor. "Because you are spirit in body form! Consider the expanse of this! Your body is on loan. Everything you believe to be solid will be taken away. Everything you believe is you will vanish. Think how free that makes your choices right now." Rose must have made some pact with a devil to end up here alone; she won't find Lana; or she will and it will make her hunger greater. Somewhere she had made a wrong decision if at the right fork or had mislaid her life, since everyone else seemed to know better how to live. As a kid, Rose had worried that if she voiced certain words in the wrong sequence or even said *murder*, unknown to her, someone across the world could die. You could do wrong without ever knowing it, not to mention all the wrong you had already done and could not forget.

"Rise up slowly. We have time for a little sharing," says the yoga instructor. "Feel your body. We're going around the room to share which characters inhabit you. I'm asking you to name parts of your body where these characters are most alive."

The spa crowd has come to unload and needs little prodding: one man with a smooth face confesses that a girlie dancer lives in his chest. One large freckled woman with frank, fleshy arms admits she has a mother and kittens frolicking around her knee area. A Hawaiian woman wearing a lei says an aboriginal goddess lives at each wrist.

Finally, the instructor points a long beringed finger at Rose while gazing down an aquiline nose, her slight accent presumably real as she repeats her question with grave patronization before Rose truly hears. "And who are the characters in your body?"

To which Rose manages a stammer.

"Too hard to talk right now?" the instructor asks.

"A wizard holds my throat tight."

The instructor acts interested. "What's the wizard doing?"

"Cackling. Holding a whip. Down my throat, there's a scared beaten-down hamster."

"What's the message of the wizard?"

"If you want to survive, figure out what other people want."

"Can the hamster change?" the yoga instructor asks.

"No, it's too guilty, too beaten down." The words speak her. "It always has to strategize and pretend. It works for the wizard. It survives by working." There can be no looking around as she says any of this. "The hamster has no voice. But it does have invisible antennae that help it know what others need."

Acting pleased, the teacher weaves the blurt into a story about the monkey-god Hanuman who straddles the islands. "Any other comments on who else might be living in you?"

Then rises the sweet heat of a voice from the back, someone who must have come in late, and who would not have craned around to find the source of that mellifluity? Vic had once said WE DEEM VOICES PLEASANT THAT COME FROM SYMMETRICAL BODIES.

A woman shushing two young boys who must be hers.

Lana. Lana in full symmetry.

"Mine isn't a hamster. I think I have a toad sitting on my chest," Lana says, joking, not meeting any eyes. Her sons get excited by this response and interrupt each other. One says loudly he has a superspy magic robot in his gut while the other explains that an ice-cream cone sits at his forehead in torpedo position.

If the yoga mat had turned into a thousand-volt landing dock, Rose could not have jolted more alive. She turns back to the instructor, away from Lana, a smile bursting her body: no prior rehearsal told her how to handle this second.

The last she had really talked with her friend, they had been hugging goodbye outside a strip joint, a green magnetic flash between them, before a final non-moment in a New York apartment. After that, their wave had broken, leaving them the wash of separate destinies.

Rose turns around again, unable to stop her goon smile, unmet and probably unnoticed but who cares when she gets to hear again that old knock-knock joke at her heart.

Outside, Lana is cordial and well-defended, friendly and abstract, as if two former passengers bump into each other and in a feint at politesse try figuring out which bus they had once taken together. What she fails to show in the slightest is that—despite two decades of silence, unilaterally willed—once the Lolas had needed each other for survival.

"Amazing to find each other at a nudist colony, right?" says Rose.

"Instead of, what, a convent?" Lana squints, irradiated by a private sun. "So your inner child's a hamster?" After so many years Rose welcomes Lana's mockery, a promise of some return.

"How old are your boys?"

"How old are you, Sedge? Tee? Seven?" Clearly Lana has her father's habit of ribbing offspring.

"Nine and two sixths," the smaller one protests, caramel eyes big. "Almost nine and three quarters."

The larger one twists her hand behind a hip. "Who's she, mama?" he asks.

"An old friend. Amazing to run into her."

"What's her name?"

"Lola One!" Lana snorts.

"I thought I was usually Lola Two."

"O yeah. Where do you live these days?"

"You know, Ellay."

"Right, right," says Lana, as if Los Angeles makes sense, offering no apology for having ignored those letters. Which scenario is worse? That Lana had received all Rose's letters but hadn't wanted to read them? Or that she'd read and had chosen not to answer?

"You didn't get my letters?" Rose unable to stop herself.

"No." And Lana's head does shake somewhat credibly. "That's nice. You wrote? To which address?"

"Maybe I had the wrong one." Cheered enough to meet in some communal alibi. "Hey, I have a room here. You guys too?"

"Sort of. That hotel manager helped—"

"Hogan? He's funny." Which gives them plateau enough to share a first real glance. "What are you guys up to now?"

Lana shakes her head at the boys. "We were—actually, no big plans today."

"Want to take a walk or I don't know?" Rose as embarrassed as if offering a prom invite, her interest too alarmingly genuine.

"I'd love it," says Lana. "We should. Hey, boys, want to go check out what Hogan's doing with that burn?" a concept evidently calculated to a nanometer of precision on impact, enough to set her boys off running, leaving two old friends suddenly alone and facing each other with Lana the first to break the awkwardness. "Actually, Rosie, I'm so shocked to see you," says Lana, giving Rose a sharp little hug, her shoulder striking Rose's sternum, "shocked! Hey, you're still wearing that same china musk perfume."

"Yeah, it's crazy." Rose's face burns. "Maybe let's go meet in one of the pools instead?"

"Because you love the freaks here that much?"

And between them escapes another little smile, almost enough to acknowledge everything. The country club hot tubs they had snuck into, climbing over redwood fences at night, and the boys they had teased into those hot tubs before running away, eternally retreating back into the safety of Lola One and Two.

Or maybe this had just been Lana's version of the polite smile.

But as Rose walks back to her room, Venusberg 9, Lana's touch still vibrates her shoulders. An old song hums inside, one she used to play badly on guitar: *keeps me searching for a heart of gold.*

Lana breathing sulfur, dangling her legs in the tub called the elf cave, struck by two impulses. Of course one route suggests it is only right to stay and wait for Rose. She could trust and tell her everything, girlishly tear the skin off the years. But then again, maybe something is closing in: it might be prudent to gather the boys up and, what, head back to Yalina, tail between legs, after only a few days here, because did she have any other choice?

An alertness pours through, suggesting the nearness of escape. Instead she summons a rain of commands: don't be a coward. You came here. Even if Rose has shown up, it's not right to drag the kids north again. Just because you haven't hooked into a gig here yet. Stay the course, Lana, she tells herself, in what is actually her mother's voice, quiet and stern, just as Mary could coax even the most wayward dog to stay.

On the deck, guests whom Lana has started to understand are the usual suspects start to gather. On the concrete nearest the elf cave tub, two girls—one dark-haired, one reddish—start talking, oblivious to any eavesdroppers:

"So what happened? I was with that guy the rest of the night?" the redhead asks.

"No! You left and then I don't know."

"So tell me what I did?"

"You drove to that place."

"No!" More giggling.

"That was fun," says the dark-haired girl, acting as historian. "You saw them."

"I don't remember any of it."

"Those guys in Kim's room, they asked who you were?"

"Who are these people?"

"The guy with the ears."

"I met all of them?"

"You were in Ray's room."

"Ray?"

"As we were leaving—"

"They said they wanted to go somewhere with me, right?"

"I wouldn't have let you."

"Oh, I was with John!"

"Yeah! You looked happy. Or happy enough."

The amnesiac ignores an incoming call on her cell, preferring to drink water and green tea with her friend, a way of plumping herself up from whatever nighttime ghost marauders had gnawed out of her.

"Could you be more out of control?" says the historian. "Or what's gotten into you?"

"I don't know. Maybe I haven't worked for a while?"

Watching each other, a moment, a stalemate.

"You're crazy."

"I don't need any more meds."

"You know how I told you about my friend who's schizophrenic, back at home?"

"Nope," says the amnesiac, a giddy, flirtatious tone entering, clearly relieved to be out of the historian's spotlight. "You forgot that one."

"He went to Swarthmore but then they put him in a hospital and he sent me an email saying it was all useful because now he understood how the stock market worked."

"That's so sad."

"He also said something like I want to be inside your freaking mind. Come visit me in my workplace and that he was a little prince in the world of the undipped dipped."

"You have such a good memory."

"Because it was hilarious. I saved it. Come on, lie on this towel with me."

"Could you scoot over?"

Lana cannot pull away from her eavesdropping. The girls find each other, soak up sun in parallel, make others' suffering disposable, create an opalescent fizz around: the world is unknown so they flip-flop the important and secure solace, good at drawing the magic circle around themselves. As reward for their labors, they get to enjoy the unguarded hedonism of melting together, the pure prolepsis of sun-bathing on concrete.

Rose comes walking across the deck then, carrying a tray bearing two tall smoothies with straws and umbrellas. Pink, fruity, forgiving. A bluesy song plays on the palm-camouflaged loudspeakers—*keep shining, baby, keep shining*—and the smile Lana blasts on her friend must look so sincere that Rose almost drops their drinks.

"Don't let me make you trip," Lana tells her.

"Too late," says Rose. "But you have no idea. It's great to see you looking so good. I can't even tell you how great."

"Hey, did you hear that thing on public radio today? About people who die and come back?" Lana doesn't wait for the answer. "They say after the tunnel and the figure of light and all, people have this moment where they experience the suffering of everyone they were ever connected to?"

Rose peers at her curiously, seeming to take this in exactly the way it was not meant: as a global apology. "That's great."

"Why?"

"I love you choosing to tell me that."

"But why?"

In that acre of California, under the sun, Rose flashes a huge smile her way. "You always loved bluffing and you're still the same," and Lana, her pinkie furious in scratching an itch in her eye, lets this go.

"O yeah, and remember that time that we answered that job ad—"

"Between freshman and sophomore years in college?" Lana enters the game slowly.

"I guess, our first summer home, wasn't it—"

"That was weird. Getting flown to Florida. What did the ad say?"

"That we'd be international couriers. What was that guy's name?"

"Zander?"

"I'm so bad with names. But remember you saying he looked like Gerald Ford off a golf course?"

"He did." A man on Lana's left, a bearded older guy, slips into the hot tub, intoning *ventilate, ventilate* before sliding below the surface of the water.

"And then remember that limo out of the airport with a wet bar in the car and we were singing 'joy to the world' with that girl—"

So much depends on recalling the girl's name and Lana is pleased when it shoots up. "Angel."

"Then they were trying to fix you up with some war vet named Shooter, right—"

"Scary."

"And you turned him away, remember, at your hotel room."

Lana rubs her wrists against each other as if manacled, looking into the forest of naked legs walking by, but Rose keeps going.

"Remember—they loved some cheeseball hotel singer singing push it to the left—"

"Yeah." For the first time ever, Lana notices how Rose's face is something like a pink teddy bear's but keeps herself from blurting this. "And then you kept saying when are you going to interview us for the job?"

"And that guy Zander kept saying well, hey, you need it, we'll rig up a boardroom and be in suits, that's what you want?"

"We're a fun company."

Rose lets out a little titter. "Fun."

"I liked those caipirinhas at those dog races in Orlando."

"But you felt bad. Remember the visitors were all white?"

"I hated that. The way those dog-trainers held the dogs up so these jowly white men could look at their you know." Lana shivers. The man in the pool, finished with his long submersion, pops out, still exhorting himself to ventilate.

"Remember you said the company probably had no job for us anyway right before the plane's wing caught on fire? And we had to land in Houston?"

"O, thought that was Dallas." Lana starts laughing, can't stop.

"What?"

"Remember the guy in a ten-gallon hat at the airport telling us his crystal pendant had kept us aloft, saved all of us?"

"And then Zander. He called you once we got back in New York."

"But I started asking questions—"

"He stopped right?"

"And a month later I got this call from the FBI saying it was all a scam, we were just one of some bunch of girls those guys had tried ensnaring. And I pretended to be a reporter who needed more details but they wouldn't tell me any more."

"You're so good." Rose starts laughing now. "What do you think that was? Like prostitution? Drugs? Your dad thought it was the white slave trade."

Lana shakes her head, savoring the weirdness, unexpectedly smiling at a hairy young couple two deck chairs away; the pair smiles back.

"Remember Zander telling us the job was explaining contracts to various divisions of a holding company?"

Lana decides not to tell Rose she had slept with Zander. Sometimes Lana had needed to use men like a yardstick to reach whatever she couldn't reach and sometimes it had almost worked. "Right."

"And remember that millionaire we met in the airport who gave us a ride? The guy with a lisp?"

"What was his job again?" Lana can tell Rose tries to jolly her into one long seamless slide, a slip into happy memory, but now feels as if she is getting one-two-three punched: first with the mention of her dad, continuing with Zander, ending with the millionaire.

"Whatever, that guy was crazy. He liked talking about all the girls he'd been with."

"He served mushy macaroni." No one has Lana's back. With too much material on this one, she wants to cut it short.

"I kept wanting to prove we weren't hanging around just because we liked his technology."

"Like when he showed us the house the first time and said *party-size video room, girls?*"

Rose slaps Lana's arm, the tremor of her laugh almost a cry.

Lana won't tell Rose about the first night. Because Rose was working shifts at her dance store that summer, Lana started sleeping with that first of the millionaires, or rather, she let him worship her. The fact of his wealth did nothing but double his homage. She remembers he had a gogo pole in his living room and wanted to teach her how to use it and she'd felt so magisterial laughing him off, her girl-laughter a divine mantle. But after the first time, leaving his place at midnight, she also felt as if she had a pearl rolling down her spine, exploding into a tiger-orange flower and had the thought: that guy just gave me a tiger flame.

She started seeing him every now and then, that foggy summer before second year of college, beginning a practice of lying to Rose in earnest, feeling she was making an important deposit into her later life by telling Rose that the reason she didn't want to go again to his remote-control bachelor pad overlooking Coit Tower was because she was afraid of drinking too much. Really she didn't go with Rose because she liked the guy's intense solitary worship and the half-life of pleasure, her destiny already rotating away from Rose. In the beginning, of course Lana didn't know the first of her abortions would come from this guy, *one more casual upper-class white abortion* as she over-heard the nurse saying in the hall before the first of the operations to lodges a bone of grief in her throat for weeks after, tethering her so. And if she had glided through freshman year of college in something of a dream, if she had not seen much of Rose in their New York dorms, before overhearing the nurse in that waiting room, Lana still felt pearly opportunity at the base of her spine, still believed that be-ing a girl among men could stake a claim on a credible future. When she had started letting herself go to his Coit Tower apartment, climb-ing the tiny sidewalk stairs, she had jumped when she'd realized the millionaire could have had a goat's face, an orangutan's torso, a mos-quito's hum, it didn't matter, since what really mattered was an inside voice instructing her to see the guy and follow this particular path of service toward glory.

Until she had to cut off seeing him, after the operation, just slic-ing it off without a single word to the guy. This decision she had also liked for its pure power and cleanliness though for some reason right now the question comes: if a figure of light did exist, would it under-stand or instead force her to feel everything the millionaire or Rose or anyone had ever felt? Basically, would she be punished? Lana needs some retort, and lying there on the deck while Rose goes on recall-ing moments Lana prefers to suppress, she considers what she would ask the figure: did everything always have to be her fault?

Rose stealing into Lana's room at Hope, hand on the creases of Lana's pillow, finding one of Lana's long dark hairs, its end a curled question mark. Of course Lana wouldn't have bothered locking her door. Rose had wanted to alphabetize some inner turbulence and so had stolen in with no clear purpose. One of the Mahlers or Wagners or whatever Lana's little family calls itself these days could just burst in after lunch. Someone, having forgotten something, could just show up and Rose doesn't know why but she had needed to take the chance. The boys having left the room, she seized the moment. Now she picks up some of Lana's huge silver earrings and puts them on, for a second, puncturing unused holes in her earlobes. Just for a second so she can duck her head and smile in weary apology back up at herself in the bathroom's bright stage mirror, her hair also newly black, her mind shut down, admiring mainly her backdrop, the geodesic toiletry kit, the room's fig scent, the magazine from which Lana's new mate smiles back under the caption YOU TOO CAN LIVE A BETTER LIFE.

She has not yet met this guy Dirk but he looks as if he holds no candle to Lana's first boyfriend, the first real one, a boy who sang into a mike, so inconquerable, the appeal of a kinetic body torqued around a point. For a second Rose stretches the back of her neck long and sings, a wistful mute in the mirror. Often she has this vision, Rose in a dead-hot spotlight with men pressed up against glass windows, peeking in at her while finding their need insatiable and intolerable. They want her bad. Secretly she would like to scoop up everything in this room, all of it, the Indian scarves and toiletry kit. With time enough, she would hunt for a journal or anything to emit more clues. Already she can tell Lana is keeping too much from her but, heart a gallop, Rose leaves, gentle in closing the door behind herself.

Not having intended any direct theft, Rose is halfway down the stairs when she feels the earrings, such big triangles they graze her neck like a lover's tickle. She must yank them off, pocket the booty, pull her fake dark hair back over her ears.

FIFTEENTH OF DECEMBER, 2008   4:41 P.M.

Lana accepts Rose rubbing her back with sunscreen. Why not relax into other people's devotions? She could just seize the prospect of calm. Her boys play bingo one lounge chair over while the afternoon appears benevolent, acting on her behalf, lenient enough that she gets to glide off.

What they find at their room: the door completely ajar. Was someone here—? Lana looks at the boys.

"I didn't do anything," says Sedge. "I didn't mean to. Anyway, I won't do it again." This happens to be the last line from the Oogie-Poogie stories she makes up for them. She notes his attempt to get mama to smile, using the stories as their bond: tales about two misbehaving boys named Oogie and Poogie, the caught miscreant always using his tripartite weak excuse as the story's moral.

I didn't do it, I didn't mean it, anyway I'll never do it again.

While Tee's face broadcasts the pure and absolute absence of guile.

"Stay here," she tells them. For all Sedge's floundering, a real animal might have gotten in. She goes in to perform a check of all dark corners, making a show for the boys' benefit that there is no beast, nothing to harm them, and then signals an okay. They can enter, return to calm, a family indivisible in the clean shaded happiness of someone's idea of a room. On the couch, the boys eat saltines and play cards peaceably enough; she gets to shower. No one mentions Rose or Dirk or any other outsider. The idea of the animal and the fact of the open door have united them. For this moment, they are family and nothing will disturb them.

———

Until Tee strings up Lestrion by a noose and approaches with kiddie scissors in his left hand, ready for the cut. "Lestrion's dyinggg!" he sings in tones half mournful, half gleeful.

"Mom, he's doing it."

"Tee, stop killing Lestrion!" Lana, post-shower, doesn't look up from her magazine. 101 WAYS TO ENJOY YOUR CHILDREN MORE. She's onto RAINY-DAY ACTIVITIES. The idea appeals: things one *could* do.

"Lestrion has to die though."

"Why?" their mother half-asks.

"He committed halitosis."

"Aw man, you don't even know what you're saying," says Sedge, scissor-kicking back onto the bed so Lana's magazine jumps out of her hand.

"You just failed the code of the holy knights!" Tee shrieks.

This room has shrunk, too small to contain three. "You guys want to go see what's going on outside now?"

"A lot of naked people walking," says Tee.

"Tee, I don't like how you're talking." Lana sits up, slaps the magazine shut, her hair falling out of its towel turban. "Did I say no whining? How about you guys going on a walk before dinner? Not on the trails though please."

The boys calculate the degrees of her mood and snap alert, Sedge snipping the cord holding Lestrion so the space robot falls, his swaddled body almost indestructible, Sedge unworried about her doldrums or the robot's physical intactness because he and Lestrion had struck a deal about the supermagic superspy powers the robot grants only Sedge. This deal happens to be necessary as Lestrion is the last of the robots to survive while Sedge is the second of the twins and as such he and the robot possess a perfect understanding or what their mother always goes on about, empathy.

"Later," says Tee, halfway out the door, Sedge and Lestrion following, with Lana already back to RAINY-DAY ACTIVITIES, fending off the moment in which she will have to face Rose again. She does not want to let her mind run ahead of herself when everything is fine enough, when it is okay to release the boys to walk by themselves, especially after they have already seen the lion and will thus both stay on the safe side of statistics and off the trails. Part of her latest tactic as a mother is to err on the side of the super-casual, trying to downplay not just the rare encounter with a mountain lion but also a foolish story she had once mistakenly told them about Bad Scary Strangers. This fable had scared Sedge more than she had meant it to, devised to get the boys to stay good in public and never run away but it had spawned the ultimate monster stranger, namely, the beginning of Sedge's parallel life, his epic serial anthology hinging on a supersonic spy robot named Lestrion.

Whenever Lana asks about Lestrion, Sedge says, eyelashes long, cheek smooth and impenetrable: "Sorry, mommy, can't tell you. Grown-ups can't know supersonic secrets. If I keep the code, Lestrion will protect me." She looks at him, understanding he needs more protection than mama can give, certainly more than she had ever received given that the most safety she had ever gotten from staying close to her parents had been the chance to spy on the wreckage of adult life.

So let Sedge have Lestrion, god bless, let the boys be sent to go forage for dinner at the communal dining hall despite whatever Dirk or Hogan or Rose may think about boys set loose in a place still new to them. She doesn't care what others think. Let them deem her a bad mother. She will defend herself to no one especially since she had not asked for Rose to show up like some ghoul of remembrance telling her in so many ways that a person cannot hide forever.

THREE

Vic jutting forward, saying: you know, you can will yourself to die.

So handsome and jutting toward Mary. This is how she will re-member him for years, the memory central as if fronting an album bound with ribbon around a button. Unwind the ribbon and every picture stays in place, radiant with sentiment, illuminating this fel-low leaning into her.

All she had done was ask about his research but part of his jut means no answer he gives can ever be weak. They sit on a pocket of sand at Fisherman's Wharf, a beach littered on one edge by masts and on the other by soggy sourdough crusts from tourists unsuccessful at luring gulls, crusts rippled like tiny breasts of a half-buried band of fairies.

Years later when she returns to this spot, a spot you could wade out from, gone ugly and tar-balled, she finds it hard to believe how relatively pristine it had once been, untrashed, sand white, driftwood unsplotched, the little romantic fairy boats plying the water. Or did memory play a trick?

The sand seeps through his fingers and onto her arm where she lies, belly down, propping herself up to look at this man with his slight foreign accent, the one she met last week in the university library. In seconds on a tourist beach, this man Victor Mahler could lie atop her, just press himself on top when the majority of her life has been dedi-cated to the thousand and one open and covert methods permissible in the protection of virginity which she feels deep down is a beautiful word, letting a maiden recall the beautiful inviolability of staying *one.*

What she has done is ask about Vic's research and the intensity of his answer chills: she finally understands the phrase *to the bone.* Bones cold, she watches him head into the water, rolling up his pants, begging her to enter, to rhyme with his daredevil ways. She won't because she has a secret female reason not to go in water. Not to mention that she isn't wearing a bathing suit and dampness will reveal her form too much.

But before he goes wading, they talk of willing yourself to death. What could that mean? He elaborates: the mind, conscious of itself, knowing itself as motor, can be trained to stop, as the yogis promise in their talk of spontaneous combustion. This is the forefront of neurological research! Look at me, he says, then see if you can let part of your mind detach from the skull. Can you, Mary, can you?

What does that mean, her mind detach from the skull? What is he trying to prove? Is he being a showman? She doesn't care: what a jolt when he says skull and her name, and then later as she watches the ocean swallow his life force until he emerges, triumphant and golden as one of her childhood's spelling trophies. Can you, Mary?

She can. Tall girl, hope of her people, she'd found her future husband magnetic in his abrupt, cryptic manner. For their first date he rang her doorbell many times, impatient already, and couldn't she have known something from that insistence, a man who had left other girls for reasons obscured, thus bearing the aura of someone she could actually save, especially given the sad hint about his orphanhood? You could love someone for lesser reasons. She appreciates how he carves for the two of them an elite, exalted sphere, rendering dismissive comments about whole tribes of intellectuals—and this when he had never even finished high school! The mischief stuns. Whenever wine-softened in all the years to come, Vic will boast of his autodidacticism, so happy to be found with his fist full of academic cookies: honors and tenure, for god's sake, when he had never even put his hand in the cookie jar. And still higher-ups kept handing him awards, all prizes for how well he had followed his instinct and its superior fibers, his bold, American self-made spunk and grit, pure anti-intellectualism housed in a European body.

Many of these later years, awards flowing his way, will fill her with disgust at her choice, the worst moments like phantasms almost ignorable if not enough to avoid the gallantries of Gallagher, someone her husband had always deemed a decent colleague. Through those years, Vic's phrase will echo. *Will yourself to die*: the brash authority alone would make the hardest schoolgirl fall in love.

I will, I will myself to you, I can, Victor Mahler.

Back in their early days, she refuses none of the roles he believes contiguous with the connubial because she is his bedmate, initially wondering what link their sticky moments at bedtime have with her swoon during that first talk with Vic, or even before, when she had slow-danced at her senior prom with random foot-stomping swains, listening to adenoidal singers croon about hearts and flowers and trying to decipher her future from lyrics about spooning under June moons. She begins to type Vic's papers and notes and one day they are married. At one point, pecking at the typewriter, over her shoulder she tries telling her new husband some point about clarity, this marking the first moment etched into memory that she sees the royalty of his disdain turned for the first time not just on others but on her.

In this way, as if two scientists unearthing a treasure, they stumble upon the one argument that will never let them go: he will never grant her the intellectual respect she deserves and she will never be enough. Because she craves clarity, always, he finds his excuse and, from this time forward, in slow increments, will start treating her as if she has a small mind.

Thus begins her curdle away. For years she will keep typing, typing as if the act alone might peck away enough to reveal the better future that awaits them, the act a form of trust: she will be released from the bad sentence of her marriage into a better one. Because somewhere in her schooling the nuns had given her the idea that her mind could be, if not brilliant, at least able to seize on facts, a mind good at lining them into neat cause, correlation and affinity. Such talent could spell salvation and escape, the equivalent of an arranged marriage between herself and brilliance.

What she was all too happy to leave behind: the star-crossed oddness of her own mother's legacy. She will tell Vic the story only once, early in their courtship. The Japanese internment camp had been erected some hundred miles away from the reservation and Mary's mother Zora had fallen in love with a father Mary would never know, Kenji a Japanese greenhouse worker in an illegal squat behind the council house. "Less trouble," she had tried joking to Vic. "No inlaws for you. But at least my father was brave." The tribal council had wanted to throw Zora out for illicit behavior, while the American feds had managed to throw Kenji into the camp at Manzanar.

In these juices of fear, from a short, taboo-charged, impermanent liaison, near where the reservation stored rusted hoes, the two had conceived baby Mary, a girl illegitimate everywhere, Mary Fukuji Guzman born in the fall of 1942 to an inspection of her eyelids by tribal elders. Her telltale ipecanthus fold made it hard for her to pass as Yokut Indian. Yet in a fluke of gentleness, liking Zora's entreaties and downcast eyes, the elders decided to let baby Mary stay on the reservation with her mother and aunts.

When Mary goes flat in her recounting, Vic teases the story out. Could it have been shame that made Zora turn inward and away from the lovechild to whom she gave the immaculate name Mary, Zora who gave the child her father's last name but forbade any truck with him? Mary's chance at love came not so much from Zora. Instead Mary leaned toward the attention from nuns who looked kindly on tall Mary's deference, Mary a student who quickly learned to say *I'm sorry* for others' mistakes, thrilling to the peaks of the catechism and working overtime to earn the nuns' confidence. Mary only eight at her mother's funeral, after which she had been deposited into the harsh hair-combing and collar-pulling of a trio of aunts sterner than any nun, this part of the story that Vic, years later, jealous of her commiseration with her girl assistant, will use against her. "Mary, don't you think it's time to stop looking for a mother already?" he will say.

In their early days, she loves how Vic holds her hands and listens as she tells him of the tiled schools, their echoing corridors and shadowed naves bearing the imprint of Spanish missionaries. Her sharpened pencils and spelling trophies. How Mary shone. "That's why you became an intellectual?" Vic sings out, and she is not sure, even then, whether he has come to mock or praise.

There is so much to like about him. The way he rushes her, for one, into a wedding that offers the comfort of mischievous conformity. Naughty not just because they go to city hall but because she is marrying a grad student she has met on her own in the library, a white man foreign and older by some tantalizing years, this Vic Mahler who favors loud Hawaiian shirts from a thrift store, who keeps saying he loves her schoolgirl self, her shy candor and sensibility. Under the light of his attention, she finds herself as he seems to, laughable, endearing, reassuring. And despite his later scoffing that the university must be one of the world's most goitered of free-thinking zones, she continues forward on the promise of all her trophies, managing to both follow and ignore the zeitgeist enough to become someone mostly free-thinking, a feminist ethnographer.

When California Fukuji Guzman Mahler is born, the girl who will one day ask to be called just Lana, the baby with a shock of brown hair, Mary tells Vic: *I don't recognize her yet.* The infant California sleeps away from them at the hospital, cleaned up, mouth pursed with a tiny O between rosebud lips, the very center of a fishbowl room guarded by nurses, as Vic sees when he leaves Mary in her recovery room to get a first gander at his legacy through the nursery window. Of course he does not think it right that tears usurp his gaze, that he is unable to watch the peaceful little brown-haired creature straight, but it helps to have heard that some similar sentiment has overcome a gaggle of other stiff-necked fathers and so finds himself laughing with embarrassment at the joy of being united with an imagined league of lachrymose Jimmy Stewart types sharing his moment, finally appreciating why a man would want to pass out cigars to his fellows—until some bandy-legged nurse comes up to tap his elbow, telling him he stares at the wrong baby, that his own girl was too waterlogged after the difficult birth and is in a different room for lung-pumping: little California happens not to be viewable at the present time.

Cast out of the league, enraged, Vic storms back to the room to shoot Mary a sidelong glance: "What did you mean about not recognizing your baby?" Mary's womb had been barren until fifteen years after their first congress and Vic still does not claim complete understanding of his wife. When Mary stays mute, muffled by drugs the doctor had shot deep into her spine, he speaks more loudly. "Don't worry," he says, enunciating as if she had just turned foreign, this being the tone of many of their worst discussions. "Once we get the right one, you'll recognize her. You just weathered a big storm."

And he can't explain why Mary starts bawling. He must resort to a favorite epithet. "Women," he sighs. None of this is playing out as it should but theoretically he believes in nuance so he tries reorienting by a grayer moon. Once she quiets herself, he takes Mary's hands in his, believing someone invisible, watching him, could expect him to do this. Really he would like to run. Most truly he is scared; his wife looks pallid and unrecognizable, beyond death.

"Remember you said you wanted a child?" he tells her. He knows this is useless but what else can a man say?

His wife points her chin toward the door. Their baby lies swaddled somewhere, lungs being pumped. Mary manages to say, out of her morphine haze: "I feel we started a fire."

He chalks her nonsense up to some cause like painful breasts or the postpartum female brain addled by oxytocin. "You'll be fine," he says, pumping her hand in unconscious echo of the mechanical vacuum working their baby's lungs a few rooms away. "She's a baby. Go back to sleep. We always survive, don't we," and then stutters over the idea of their family as a new trio, "so we can survive this."

This survives: parents in the backyard hammock with the little girl swinging between them, eating a chunk of pineapple, a first. Her father's eyes crinkle down. "Tongue burning, Mopsy?" he asks.

"I like it," reports the girl called Mopsy by her father and Jinga by her mother, her father's profile sharp, her mother's nose squishy.

"I'll make your nose into hers!" the girl tells them. First she swallows the last of the yellow burning fruit and then turns to pressing his nose down with sticky fingers. Her father lets her do this forever, before she tries pulling her mother's nose long. "Like clay!" she reports, making them laugh. Her mother buries her squishy nose in the top of her girl's hair. "You smell like flowers, Jinga," says her mother. "Or like our first kitten Roly. You smell like Roly."

"I am Roly," sings the girl over and over, as they swing back and forth, legs bare to the sun, her feet white-sandaled. "Look, I'm making us go!" she says until they agree that most locomotion comes from her.

"A child is potential energy," says her father. "A child wants to believe her parents will always possess a perfect equivalent response."

This moment of swinging goes until it stops. Her mother kisses her father over the girl's head, an arc like a rainbow.

"Why do you kiss papa?"

"To show I love him," says her mother.

"That's good," sings their daughter.

"Why?" Her mother laughs, taking her hand like a small pat of dough before it gets thrown into boiling water to make dumplings.

"Loveisgoodgoodgood," their daughter chants, liking the unimpeachable response from her parents, charmed beyond words.

One time, not yet five, she goes on a parade around the house, singing a different tune: "You're a bad mommy! I want a better mommy! Go to work and bring back a better mommy!"

"Is it that you want me not to go to work?" her mother asks gently. "Or why do you say that? How would you feel if someone called you a bad kid?"

"Happy," says their daughter, already a contrarian.

Mary will notate the whole discussion in a book of their daughter's pronouncements, one Lana will come across one day with her friend Rose as they poke through Mary's belongings, an endless cabinet of curiosities. Rose will think that Mary having written down the discussion proves at least some maternal caring. Not really, Lana will say, my mother's an anthropologist and I was just one of her objects for study. Rose will scrutinize her for a second. You're so mad. You really think your parents stole something from you.

Lana will laugh, changing the subject by putting on one of Mary's big flouncy hats. At least she gave me some fashion sense, right?

Once, daughter a little older, father gets sick.

Her pale papa unable to keep anything down, left to tend himself with only a six-year-old wisp of a girl in a nightdress trying to soothe her father. Again and again she scoops up a rag to press to his fevered brow. Did anyone ever tell you you're an angel? he murmurs, pressing cloth to his face, water dripping down.

Later that night he gets better, enough to descend stairs in his rumpled half-open striped bathrobe and share vegetable bouillon, their concord perfect. He has passed the hump. They are united.

When her mother enters the kitchen shortly after, breathless from outside, bearing a scent of fall leaves and busyness, appointments and lectures, people seen and the perfume of impatience, their little daughter announces proudly, Mommy, I cured papa.

Nice, says her mother, not paying attention, how'd you do it?

And the girl, sincerely wishing to teach her mother how to help Vic—but even then, one tiny bit lording it over her—explains how she has washed Vic's head.

"I dip the cloth like this. Then I squeeze it out in the hall. Then I place it on his head."

It takes the parents a second to realize where their daughter got the water, a second that offers no little girl a chance to finish, because soon as Vic realizes a ministering angel cooled his fever with water from the toilet, he bellows: *what's wrong with you?* making his girl stand stricken, hands open, palming a low and invisible muzzle so that Vic's only recourse is to stomp upstairs.

You did seem to cure him, her mother remarks, turning a weak smile her way, the one that later will make her daughter hate rabidly, continually offered the cherry poison syrup of martyrdom. Mary tries again, calling the girl Mopsy.

The girl shouts back *Mopsy's not even your name for me.*

Livid, their daughter goes to lie in the cool alcove where the fine glass is stored. Years later this glass will be broken systematically, plate by plate, during one of Mary's arguments with Vic but now the glass stacks intact in such a lovely hutch next to where the mobile made by the girl in kindergarten spins overhead, a paper lemon lined with red-glitter veins. Lying on her back, the girl stares at the ceiling where her dusty art twirls, its laze soothing, until she feels restored enough to emerge out into the kitchen. She finds her mother making sandwiches out of marshmallow and peanut butter, a concession toward America, one of Lana's many ignored requests. Though the girl may be hungry, her mother's effort sickens because it reminds her that Mary had taken away Lana's role: ministering angel.

No thanks, says the daughter, happy at the burn of refusal, I'm not hungry. Meaning: not hungry for you, mommy, for your body and its appetites, which means the daughter already acts as if her first fall was the mistake of popping out from the wrong body.

1970–1979

What Lana can save may not be their fevers but their arguments. When her parents start to fight, she does a little frantic jig from one foot to the other. She has become good at the dance, raising her voice louder and louder in nonsense syllables so they have to raise their voices too. She makes a sign, cardboard pasted to two paper-towel rolls, that says NO ARGUING OR ELSE I WILL BE VERY MAD and parades between them. They keep ignoring her, too caught in their song with its decibels and glares. One day she is clever, devising the joke that makes them stop, running to the pantry to get out cereal boxes, lining them up like a wall between. They are forced to stop and laugh, calling her creation the Berlin Wall: this becomes her routine, her last-ditch bulwark and it usually works. As she gets older, she abandons the jig and just heads straight for the cereal, this tactic good until it stops working, until the decibels and glares, slammed doors and car driving away become as unstoppable as a runaway train.

Finally a mother, she tells her boys, pining for any story from her childhood, about the cereal wall, telling the tale as if her strategy had always worked. The first time Sedge starts building a wall between her and Kip, mid-argument, Tee thinks his twin has gone nuts. But when the cereal boxes actually get their mother to stop speaking in what Tee thinks of as her tightrope voice, when the boxes make her crack a smile, he sees his twin's wisdom.

The next time Tee is the first to head for the boxes. The third time, however, the wall stops working; both boys are told to go outside and check on the garden, an answer like an abyss, their only resort to burn flywings with magnifying lenses or throw acorns at squirrels. If the boys never make the wall again, years later when both try to remember their father's face, they at least remember the bright yellow cheer of cereal boxes and how it marked one of the last times you could do a simple thing and think it big enough to stop calamity.

A great peace seems to be found by at least one of the father-daughter pair when Vic drives his daughter to her violin teacher, a woman who herself happens to be the daughter of a famous musician, requiring a drive of ninety minutes over bridges and mountains both ways, but Vic is committed to the drive because the teacher claims Lana has a talent for composition and improvisation. During the lesson, Vic sits in the next room, reading his book, happy to be released from other claims, looking forward to afterward when they go as pilgrims to his favorite mecca, a pink-stuccoed restaurant called Me & Me, a place to sip cumin-tinged soup with a loyal daughter.

"These are the best times in my life," he says each time they station themselves at Me & Me, making her ache inward and proud, tongue heavy from the burden of having failed to improve the rest of his life and her constant betrayal of her mother. One time he goes further. "Did you ever guess how much of a salmon I am, Mopsy?"

"What?"

"I spawned and am good to go."

"What does that mean?"

"I'm not afraid of death. Never have been. Not when I surfed, not now. But when I'm here with you, Mopsy, you make me feel so alive. These moments with you make me think if I go on living I at least serve some higher purpose." Casually he makes her his sharer, the one to keep away life's dismalness, offering her the cinderblock responsibility that lies heavy on her breathing. His words make clear how much she must aim to be all the more amusing and interesting, a good listener, his daughter the perfect granter of life. Nodding toward an older woman at a nearby table, deep in some fog of dementia or sedation as she speaks a vortical codex to her crumpled napkin, he goes on: "Promise me you'll make sure I keep my independence, my intelligence, dignity. An older woman I knew well didn't recognize me when I went back to Liechtenstein and I had the horrible thought that it wasn't worth it to live. Later I felt so guilty about my thought, I didn't go to her funeral. You get my point? I never want to burden anyone. To be like that. So promise already?" His palm grasps her loose fist. He takes her unwilling shiver to be assent. "I knew I could count on you."

During one of these Me & Me retreats, a psychiatrist at a neighboring table leans over to ask Vic: "What is your secret to such successful father-daughter interaction?"

"Well," says Vic, "the paradox is I always listen. I find my daughter so interesting."

"Would you like to share your secrets on a panel I'm organizing about parents and children?" asks the psychiatrist, and though Vic is usually a loud pundit against shrinks and their apothecaries, anyone who dispenses neuroactive chemicals too easily, he accepts.

Some weeks later, after fussing over whether or not Lana should wear a frilly dress or can go in her usual overalls, Vic and Lana head to a panel where they sit onstage with a mother-and-son pair and speak to a professional audience and answer questions about how they get along.

Vic speaks while Lana smiles shyly out: he talks about the great longing he had as a young adult for a perfect task-reward system. He says that having a child has proven such a symmetrical reward for all life's prior tasks. Nothing could be a cleaner fit to all life's yearnings than a fulfilling dialogue with one's own child.

The last question aims at Lana: "What does your father do that helps you get along with him?"

She falters before saying, "I admire him. It sounds corny but I want to be just like him when I'm older."

This answer stirs a ripple of oohs in the crowd, palpable desire.

After the father and daughter depart their anointing, after they run a gauntlet of hands possessed by beaming people who scrutinize them—seeking what exactly?—Vic chooses not to explain the title of the conference to her, Oedipus/Electra, saying certain topics can be understood in the course of time. While of course, the missing partner in all this anointing is Mary: where is Mary on their day?

After the panel, they eat again at Me & Me. "Not such bad apothecaries after all," says her father, "what did you think?"

"Fun," she says, getting only now for the first time that few other answers are available, that he is a little blind, choosing to hide this new awareness by slurping her smoothie in what she feels is his fairytale hall of mirrors.

In some remote nook of herself she guesses that for years, anytime Vic's pride in her flickers, he will choose to remind her that of all the denizens of Berkeley, one shrink-apothecary had singled father and daughter out. They have been elected for Vic's special way of talking at her and in her prediction she is not wrong.

At the breakfast table they read the paper together, the kettle whistling for his coffee a Pavlovian signal of closeness: Mary is a late riser and they alone share these mornings. To Lana, Vic will say of certain photos that this woman is beautiful but that one's chin is too sharp, this one's legs make her look like a giraffe while that one has eyes too deep-set and wide apart, far too brazen. He does this as if he must work overtime to inculcate in Lana his connoisseur's eye for female beauty. She will never be able to see any woman, including herself, without also simultaneously regarding her through Vic's prism of appraisal.

Later about this fairytale pre-adolescence of Lana, Vic will marvel: I never had problems with you. He will regard her teenage self as if she had, at the end of their pink-stucco era, fallen from the moon and now, sadly, bears spores of unknowably foreign and potentially lethal origin.

Soon after the panel, Lana will meet her new friend Rose and, almost simultaneously, tell her father she wants to quit violin, a wish he will take as a blow to his heart, her perfect arrow meeting its target.

In those last years before the advent of Lana's best friend, Vic still takes his daughter to school, deep into an era when you find few other fathers at drop-off. This is part of a concession to Mary during the mid-to-late throes of feminism, that Vic will be a grand husband, enspirited with noblesse oblige, supporting his wife's work. Hence, in addition to the violin lesson, he drives Lana to school one morning a week. He and Mary are professors and have, if not leisure, flexibility. Though he admits it to no one, though he cannot say why he would not wish to admit it, he looks forward to Thursdays and has said, mock sighing, many times to his Wednesday-afternoon students in his office: you have no idea what a twentieth-century man I am. Out of many grapes, one wine! You have no idea how domestic ritual shapes my week.

One Thursday morning finds him sitting outside the house in his Citroën, motor running, waiting while items are flung or discarded from Lana's backpack inside. Every so often he sees, through the paneled glass of the front door, a dark panel, a form moving or zippered, a picky silhouette casting off her mother's choice of jacket. He stays in the driver's seat while interior commotion swirls because he tries to find the right frequency for the classical music station but gets buggered by the hills they live on. He needs it: sometimes just one sweet strain of violins can set his day aright and if he doesn't hear that sweetness, something to let his soul surf high on a crescendo, things go a bit awry. While he knows the need is illogic, he can't help it.

In his most recent book, he tipped his hat to the site for illogic in the forebrain as well as the hind: forget Freud, it is not just atavistic, superstitions have their place.

Superstition is the name for other people's religions, he postulates, wondering if he unwittingly swipes someone else's idea.

On the grass between him and his ivy-covered stone house, a shaggy in a sleeping bag fancier than he should own stirs. The mottled mass arises and shakes its mat of hair before offering a bedroom smile to the professor in the car awaiting his daughter. Out of professional habit more than intention, Vic nods. The shaggy proffers a slow peace salute.

Finally the door belches open to show Mary in her blue-and-white men's pajamas, the cast of her face before caffeine, mussed in sorrow. Lana ducks out from behind, waving her backpack at her father, a victory salute, this their collective morning tarantella, a dance with steps known in blood. As their daughter descends the first step, Mary continues to stand, a statue peering over her glasses and ruing their haste, as if she had signed on for worry, as if worry alone could stitch a family together. Or, as Vic has accused her, as if Mary doesn't know what to do with the freedom he grants.

Out of the house Lana runs, backpack half-open, her forward lip impish. She could be a French schoolgirl from Vic's private adolescent hall of fame, a young colt with hair in barrettes, a ponytail. When she falls, which she often does, she doesn't so much stumble as fly, falling on one knee so that her backpack's contents spray over the grass.

Through his dirt, the shaggy cracks a grin; at the door, Mary shakes her head.

I'll come, mouths Mary but Vic gets out of the car. He finds himself by the yawning pack, kneeling so he can stuff Lana's belongings back in with more force than is necessary. He can't help his force. He pounds more than stuffs notebook and sweater and pencil case in, electing to ignore the yogurt leak from the bottom of the brown lunch bag. In this moment he is focused, a man of action and not observation. He does not need to look to know Lana in her recoil, shocked into watching him. And yet he cannot stop punching inside her bag because the punch is meant to teach a lesson: how important for people to try to be careful, thoughtful, more considerate of him. A more insidious subtext snakes under—the genetic material of mother and daughter remain inferior, mixed, and it is their haste that has brought them to this sorry pass, the mother mainly to blame. Beneath that message, he is also telling them what a self-made man he is, Vic an orphan who has triumphed on the strength of all his superior innate qualities. This is a point about genes and also about how genes have nothing to do with your success. The will can triumph. And all these points beat together in a crescendo about how these two women have stolen seconds of life from him, seconds of ambition otherwise lived.

Because he never, but never, asked Mary to make him a parent.

Done with the punching, he zips the backpack closed, its rip like a tiger's teeth.

Mary has retreated inside, her form still visible through the glass panels. She may be trembling but he doesn't bother noticing. Years ago she stopped crying in any outright way.

Onto his shoulder he slings the backpack and strides back to the car, knowing that Lana will enter a telltale second later. Lana is still curious, wishing to be near, her quietness meaning she has not yet arrived at the fully sullen age. He knows her well enough to know her love for sitting in the front but today he will let no small talk sugarcoat anger's purity. That she sits in the front means she at least accepts him. Anyway, if he were to speak, he guesses he might be, at best, dismissed. Instead, a form of apology, he hums to Ravel poking through radio static. Once they get to her elementary school, they will get out, he will escort her in.

He breaks their quiet only to point out, far away on the hill, some women on horseback: where do you think they come from? he asks. From her tiny shrug, he sees she has not wholly shut him out.

Yet at the school she undoes their routine. She says no goodbye, just pulls the backpack from the tiny backseat to run up the ramp to the schooldoor and is immediately consumed by the institution. Gone so quickly, leaving him empty-handed and, though he will not name it, with a sinking heart. She must be happy for the order of school, he realizes. School must provide an order higher than that of the Mahler household. In that dim moment a future chapter begins to form on how society disrupts blame, how its schools, sanitaria and jails always trump the innate disorder of the nuclear family. His daughter won't give her angry father a moment more than he deserves and for one unfortunate second he almost regrets his vigor.

"This is how it works with a kid," Vic tells someone at one of their end-of-the-semester parties. In the next breath he asks teenage Lana in tank top and plaid shirt to go around and check on everyone's drink but she cannot fulfill the request as someone must have sunk her boots into unseen cement blocks, forcing her to stay and watch him talk to the young coed whose wildly fertile horizontal hair already looks as if it argues with Vic's gray peaks. "The kid becomes your libido, yes. Something messy on the boulevards of life. Then you do what you can to contain libido. You wipe the kid's drool. Your swipes and smiles act as a tissue over their libido." He takes a sip of champagne, swishing it before swallowing and then nodding at Lana politely as if she were the stranger she has become. Yet she can't leave, afraid he will spill some childhood secrets. "The tissue marks the thinness of civilization. Meanwhile your kid grabs her crotch or her mother's breasts." The coed laughs, starting a reciprocal whirlpool in her drink. "Your kid wiggles her bare derrière poolside before strangers. Wipes her nose on someone's heirloom silk. Crushes berries and crayons into carpets. Essentially the kid does whatever she can to make all your wipes and smiles—which are probably your form of the death instinct—ineffectual."

"I'm not planning on having kids," says the female student.

Vic arches one gray eyebrow. "No?"

"Too many things I want to do first."

And it is as Lana finds power enough to leave that she hears him say: "Good woman! The plan's great! I'll drink to it! Semper iuvenis! What's your name anyway?"

No one knows, Lana thinks. No one knows the big things and the little things. How the night before, needing a pencil, she had burst into his office and found him on his belly, on the carpet, marveling at the dance of carpenter ants parading under his bookcase. She was not sure which Vic she was finding. On seeing her, her father had laughed like a wild beast. "Look, Lana, these ants only eat books by Apuleius. They have comic proclivities!"

"Oh."

"And then they eat only the sexual pages. It's the strangest thing. At least they know their taste, right?"

Right. Later at that party Lana remembers bringing red wine to Gallagher, the flame-haired friend of the family with his freckled butcher arms, her father's colleague, a bachelor with *money to burn* whom she likes because every summer they stay at his beach house but as she hands him the glass, her father says: "Hey! Gallagher deserves only wine coolers. Guy's a lout. No burgundy for him."

To which Gallagher lets out a jovial belch and her father jumps back, recoiling as if burnt, Vic with his delicacy affronted, Vic who raises an invisible flag of higher civilization atop his pinkie each morning while slurping his morning au lait from a bowl à la française. "See his manners, Mopsy?" Vic says to Lana.

That teenage night, ashamed for many reasons, she considers what Vic said about kids playing out the libido of the parents—Lana knowing mainly that libido means something bad and eager, an idea her father uses whenever he wants to tweak a conversation—and if in fact Vic's words are true, whose libido does she play out?

"Lana's diffident," her mother had said at the same party, drink-loosened and ignorant of the keenness of Lana's hearing from across the cheese table, Lana only pretending to fold napkins.

"Charismatic though, right?" Mary's assistant answered and for this defense, Lana half-forgave the assistant her theft of Mary.

"Despite herself. People do gravitate to her. For all I say about nurture, she definitely has her own strong nature. Funny, what I just said refutes all my cultural work, right?" Mary tossed back her drink more quickly than usual. Only Sherry cast an anxious look across the table. "All I mean is my daughter could do more with what she has. But she's not the kind to stick her neck out into the world. She always shrinks back."

"Maybe she's one of those empaths. A kid who can't let too much enter her pores?"

"Is someone empathetic just because she spends hours in her room?"

"Reading?"

"Trying on outfits. In black. Or making little charcoal scritchie-scratchies on paper."

"Maybe she's an artist."

"But it may sound harsh, I'm sorry, no real talent, at least as far as I've seen? And not exactly the reader you'd think would come from two professors."

"Maybe she's a late bloomer?" to which Mary had demurred. Sherry persisted: "You'd be a hard act to follow. If I were your daughter I might hide in my room too."

"Thank god you're my assistant then!" The women laughed, ending as always in one of those loose, knowing embraces that Lana both hates and covets.

If no one cares to know exactly what Lana has been doing in her room's seclusion it is this: ordering. To this task of ordering a girl could lose herself. Some secret meaning, occult even to Lana, dwells in her methodology for organizing horses, dolls, saints, snails, banana slugs, potato bugs and pebbles into hierophantic combinations held in shoe boxes or jars, sometimes on banana leaves, traveling over a Mao-green bedspread toward individual eucharists. Most commonly she spreads out creatures of two and four legs, amassing them into random families, each with its own distinct flavor, a sensibility, each clan happy that she alone serves as its capricious creator and destroyer.

Though it is also true that soon after meeting her friend Rose, some months earlier, Lana had started to put away childish things and has slowly surrendered some of her passion for ordering.

One foggy day when Rose complains that Lana always seems to be half turning away, for once Lana lets her friend's grievance pierce her, realizing with a start that she probably had not left her shoe-box-and-jar solitude so far behind. "You're right," says Lana, "maybe that's what my mom calls my diffidence."

Rose gasps. "I love how you can admit things. Such a great quality."

Lana cuts the flattery short, saying whatever, she can know something but that doesn't mean she can change it. What she is unable to tell Rose is that turning away might always stay one of her greatest pleasures. She doesn't elaborate but what better joy is there, really, than knowing you are not quite of the family of man but not shut out either, that rather you have your own niche, in parallel? What Lana loves most is when others breathe nearby, accessible, making noise yet not about to make an incursion or cross any border, keeping themselves from burdening her with all their messy insides.

What starts it may be the wine but it is the unbelievable light that continues it. The girls have set up a wine bar culled from Lana's parents' collection and the Lolas are busy sampling not just dessert wines but also those that should have stayed corked a few more years. This venture is the logical aftermath of their jaunt a month or so before when the girls had concocted a French bistro to which they had invited random boys from school.

For the bistro, on Lana's veranda the girls had served oysters to a couple of crackly-voiced skulkers, mere rehearsal for the fantastic restaurant the girls imagine they will open up in Paris one day, Lana and Rose murky in their giggle and their shared French-waitress personae while serving mystifying hors d'oeuvres that their teenage customers, dutifully enough, swallow.

The bistro started it, a halfway success, and a month later the wine bar continues it. Vic is the one who ends it.

Why Vic did whatever he did seems less relevant than the how of it: an amber afternoon, the girls solo and raiding the liquor cabinet, one more lark as Lola One and Two. First they had pretended to be wine snobs uncorking various pedigrees for each other, sniffing and swishing and spitting, only sometimes swilling, girls together in the golden afternoon light spilling forth from the arched windows. Soon for some reason they found themselves down to their underwear, wearing only Mardi Gras beads they'd discovered secreted away in Mary's wicker cache-tout. Swilling more and now aiming for the very perfection of wine snobbery, Lana has some torn white sheet scrap wrapped around her head while Rose sings old Cuban revolutionary songs her adoptive mother had used as lullabies when, in one single ear-splitting moment, the front door creaks and in Vic walks, early from work. He stands in the entry, half-solid, bathed in that honeyed afternoon glow.

The girls too must stare. "We were just—" before falling upon each other in a topple of girl laughter.

"This light is unbelievable," he says then, ultra-slow, "unbelievable," and then, as if this were logical. "I'll just go upstairs and get my camera to capture it."

So that what remains captured so many unbelievable years later are these tawny photos of one girl staring into the camera or lying, laughing, shoulders against the other's, torso arched over another rib-cage, arm, nipple. Entwined so it is hard to know where one begins and the other ends. Each of the girls will keep one set of photos until Lana in college will lose hers. What Rose will wonder later is what Vic said to himself, standing with straight face after having them developed, in line waiting to pick up triplicate sets at the film counter, paying, saying thank you and then what later to the girls while handing over each amber set? If neither friend remembers the exact steps down into that afternoon, each knows she stared at least once—a teenager deep-eyed and naked—into the lens of a Vic whose thoughts on the subject remain forever guarded, a victim of history.

This will stay one more thing Rose would like to ask, a question upon a humpback multitude of others: what was he thinking?

Which really fronts a deeper question. Had he liked her? And to what extent might he go because of his liking? Who was she to be so liked?

With all the questions demanding, most broadly: what hunger had crossed him?

Years later, because of such questions, she will not be able to say whether her justice-minded efforts to meet with Vic are her way to bring back Lana or at times more truly the reverse.

A Saturday night and the girls head to a dance club on the far side of town. They are fifteen and a half, reveling in driving. Lana has learned to drive her father's French car with its stick shift but Rose finds it too difficult to learn more than automatic; it is just too hard. At the club a mediocre band samples zydeco. A bunch of mostly whiteys jump around in off-time. Two bearded men in their mid-twenties start circling the girls, a move the girls are used to: some birthright makes them think such circling natural prologue to a night's adventure, Kerouac-tinged. You hitch a ride onto someone else's story, someone hitches onto yours and this hitching shoots everyone out at some undisclosed starry locale that much farther toward knowledge, with the thing that guards each girl being the other.

But because these are men with important jobs, men who say they work at a Renaissance fair to recreate Shakespeare, not just skulking boys, Lana and Rose end up in separate rooms in a house where each suitor has his own carpeted floor. In the context of their fuzzy house and shiny objects, the bearded men seem impossibly mature. Rose is talking with the full-chested fellow, pleased to tell her all about the boat he works on: he gives her a picture of himself tying knots, masts and ocean behind. To forfend anything else she tries exchanging a massage, all energy coalesced two inches before her throat, a fearful ball of what might be said, wishing to push that power into her hands kneading his neck. It is not that she feels an ounce of desire but rather that she is nervously curious about what will happen behind each successive door in the night and what someone might be drawn to do. Now she massages his back.

You're like a concubine, he tells her, you're only fifteen, how do you have such a mature touch? This is meant as a compliment: she could be good as a boat, belonging to a world of shiny kept things. Downstairs Lana plays games with her fellow and Rose finds these games reassuring, Lana doing her usual skitter away from anything too direct. The girls have some understanding that there is no need to tell either set of parents where they are, since each set—if they did think of their girls—assumes their daughter of Berkeley spends the night at the other's house.

In the gray morning, they walk back toward the French car over sidewalks littered with the tiny yellow flowers that fall into Indian summer.

Rose says to Lana: "Well at least we didn't sleep with them."

To which Lana fires a look. The look says Lana had gone and slipped over the brink alone.

The last semester of high school, Lana finds herself a tall rock-star boyfriend. To be exact, not a rock star but almost, down to being skinny and fickle in black leather pants during the last breath of punk, right when punk starts hiding in the mainstream. It is true you hear the beau's songs on the radio and see him perform in San Francisco, but he is biggest not in self-regard, which is considerable, but as he looms in the imagination of two teenage girls. He loves to make them cringe, saying things Rose remembers and Lana forgets like *playing guitar strings is like playing a clitoris.*

Rose works after school in a dance-clothes store and doesn't know it but she is preparing to meet someone. The dance-clothes manager walks her down Telegraph Avenue and there Rose meets her object: ten years older, like Lana's boyfriend, an equivalently tall man in overalls who knows the manager. Everything falls away and stops. Rose will always remember what she is wearing that day, a plaid pajama dress disguised as streetclothes under which she is bare.

Something kindles a light in this man's dark eyes and she cannot help but be excited by such sheen.

One day after school she walks to his bare apartment with its mattress on the floor. For an art-class project she winds plaster strips around his thick fingers: the cast dries, she pulls it off and leaves. A week later she rides her bike around Berkeley and bumps into him; he walks her home. At the foot of her twenty-three stairs he says: you want to go out? The phrase is anathema to her. She says she doesn't believe in going out but then calls him later. It is not long after that she skips her prom to take this new tall man to see Lana's on-again, off-again beau perform in a San Francisco club.

After, near where the earthquake swallowed early-century bathers in the coastal rocks, they go to a beach. Her first sex is wordless and brutish and interesting for this exact reason. He is half-child, half-man, mourning the death of his father and living in an apartment in Berkeley, not really clear on any purpose other than his interest in art and philosophy books. She says to him why don't you come live in my house? She is sure her mother won't mind. Ma will barely notice. Or if she minds it would be hypocritical. Rose tells her ma that her new friend has landlord troubles and would it be hard if he stayed awhile in the unused guest room? When Joan lets this slide, Rose has her boyfriend living in her house, a coup.

Off Rose goes for her last days as a senior at high school, feeling unbearably young and filled with potential, walking with her laden backpack and enshrined in someone's affections, happy that when she comes home she finds him standing atop the sunny garage, gently brushing pollen from a tomato plant. She is sixteen and he is twenty-six: if they lived in a different kingdom, they would have exchanged cowrie shells and be married already.

They spend hours driving up and down Highway One, the cliché road of California, its cliffs and coast: she does not know its interior roads yet, Five and all the others. Their silence she considers deep and philosophical. He talks of an old girlfriend who ate little—she liked to make herself disappear—and then Rose doesn't want to hear anymore. One time he tells Rose he loves Lana as well because of the goofy smile she had once when her purse got stuck in a car door and this is also not such a fruitful subject. When Rose gets into a bad mood he calls her Murk. They hold hands all night, drinking coffee in a mah-jongg donut store in North Beach. As if all the philosophers flank their romantic passage, he says Kant says but Kierkegaard says. They sit under a tree in Golden Gate Park. He tells her she has the body he had always dreamed about. She shoots out of that same body to see herself, pleased, from above. Now everything will work; any button she presses will open whatever she wants. She seems to have ascended into being that mysterious, courted girl of every song she has ever liked.

The great tragedy of this time is that despite whatever romantic flowering each girl finds alone, the Lolas' life together gets smothered and their experience heaps dirt for the grave. At times they confide in each other but the confessions turn compulsive, spears into a body already struggling for breath.

Enter a lion's cave sooner than meet with an angry teenage daughter.

One of many subjects Mary has learned to discuss with Vic in a roundabout way: the ways in which all the beneficial tinctures that had flowed into Lana are seeping away. There is no real way to conjugate parental control: she is not yet lost, she could be lost, we cannot lose her.

Of course the hope had been that Lana might grow with the beauty and strength of a black-eyed susan in rich imported soil: the best from everywhere. This being the myth of the Berkeley microcosm, with the special myth of the Mahler household being that it dwelled at the acme of same. Guests at their dinners often heard that Berkeley alone could raise a child to be tolerant and strong, and if anyone ever dared confront their bubble by calling it smug, the Mahlers would share a look. "It's not as if a person can spoon-feed tolerance into a system," Vic liked to say, his smile and meaning a mystification.

And of course, a parent knows ahead of time that a girl will push hard against any wall formed by her mother. Mary hardly wants to be that cliché, a mother trying to restrain pubescence. On this account she has been quite vocal, trying to free her daughter into the embrace of awaiting womanhood, one she cannot help personifying as some kind of bare ivory goddess standing beyond the door, clutching cloth to chest. Mary has done what she could. In the wane of the twentieth century, when Lana was all of eleven, Mary had written the first of her treatises on fraught mother-daughter relations, *The Corset of Anxiety*. In the front she thanked Lana, part of her attempt to release her daughter, as important a token as the pink conch-shelled razor Mary had given as a gift for Lana's thirteenth birthday, a day on which Mary found herself studious in avoiding the discussion of womanhood she had intended, speaking instead of leg-hairs' directional growth, hoping to leave tougher jobs of explication to her daughter's new friend Rose.

For all Mary's ability to chart anything from dinnertime discussion to larger social structures, she believes in the alleyways of her childhood Catholicism, and a dire vision long ago visited itself upon her, occasionally returning at night to steal her sleep: she thinks a sad fate might swallow Lana's future. She has a vision of Lana lying on a bed while opaque needles from thousands of directions fly toward her prone body, the exact opposite of the light radiating from the immaculate virgin of Byzantine paintings. In Lana's last year of high school, adolescence having bored through whatever recognizable tissue remains, Mary wishes to label no one but does find herself wondering if her daughter might not be exhibiting at least a few of the traits of a sociopath?

From Mary's field-notes book:

- Impulsivity
- Lack of remorse
- No tone of contrition
- Not much guilt
- An animal-like course of self-pleasuring

And if Mary's line of work asks its faithful to abandon many beliefs about innate lineage, to consider all influence cultural, even without Vic's phrases humming in the background, she also cannot avoid the genetic and god-given. Just look at her own family, for god's sake: hadn't her own parents crafted, in the fields of Californian possibility, a golden calf out of impulse? Hadn't they behaved like rutting animals? And hadn't Mary followed her own animal nature in seeking out a force large and impulsive as Vic? While it is also true that in this era of dinner parties Mary cannot find a trace of whatever had made her beeline toward Vic: his voice too loud, his gestures too jerky, his thought too predictably provocative.

Yet it will also be at parties that Mary can still locate whatever intimacy remains. All groups let her recall, if not animal nature, at least her familiarity with her husband, two allied steamships powered by their shared work ethic and skepticism about cultural pieties. The napkins will be laid out, candlesticks glimmering, first guests about to appear and she will find herself also gleaming at Vic. The person she tends to confide in is not Vic, however, but her assistant Sherry to whom Mary tells the fear: Lana represents the return of the repressed. That Lana is already refuting her mother's feminism by starting young to lose herself in animal submission to men. Mary hates to admit how easy it is to see: her mother Zora begat Mary who birthed Lana, three generations of women linked by rebellion masking great inner compliance.

For many years it has been Mary's guilty pleasure to speak with Sherry, such a no-nonsense midwesterner, the kind of daughter—or even mother—Mary might have wished for, with her definite chin, her conscience clear as an empty silo and a wonderful tendency to write flower-trimmed thank-yous. Sherry often says the hatred of an adolescent daughter might shock but it will pass. And will even quote Vic: the hormones endured by women, estrogen and proges-terone, can be called two gloved fingers of the devil.

If Lana had seemed somewhat safe during high school, deep in the sanctity of her girlhood friendship, once Mary had glimpsed her daughter's rock-star boyfriend, who came in and out and in again only to disappear, she had started to fear that Lana, nominally college-bound, had grown too enamored of the edge. Far as Mary can see, her daughter finds only bad seeds interesting, with one particular fel-low named Tumbleweed sticking around longest, Tumbleweed who emerged from the band of bad boys wasting time around the head shops, all the pot paraphernalia boutiques of Telegraph Avenue.

For these latterday derelicts whom she must pass on her way to classes, Mary feels no pity. These boys stink of violence, whether from smoke, skateboards, needles, music or innate cruelty, a violence the shaggies with their world-peace saucercup eyes never exhibited. Mary studies this new breed of boys, the way they hold sarcastic cardboard signs begging not for peace but for coinage to spend on mary jane, boys whose very first fuck-you is their glassy youth followed quickly by the multiple piercings and their over-inked skin, shoes and skateboards, boys who crouch low so as to better whistle tunelessness toward the gutters where they all seem to have already lost some important treasure. The only thing such boys appear ready to consign themselves to is the care of girlfriends, social workers, MRIs and bloodwork, clearly being boys whom any right-thinking parent would stow in a chamber far from the dark porcelain of a daughter's body.

So Mary will not let it happen: she may have messed up, not wishing to ponder how, when or why, but the one thing she will prevent her daughter from doing is falling in line with the laws of men. And because Vic laughs off the concern she does finally voice, she considers enlisting Rose. *Might you talk to Lana?* she imagines asking Lana's friend, though instead she tells Sherry one afternoon, deep into a project of shelving books, the Lolas on the other side of the door, eavesdropping while getting ready to go out to a movie: "The terrible part is you never forget wiping your kid clean on the diaper table. You always remember that little rosebud smile up at you. Of course the kid gets lifelong amnesia. No child remembers her own sweetness." In the epoch of a slogan made popular by a president's well-trained wife, *just say no*, Mary decides that afternoon to do just that. *Just say no to Lana.* She steels herself from getting angry, believing it unhealthful, yet could not be angrier: her girlchild has slipped outside the hall of femaleness in which Mary wants her to live.

Making Mary, the next morning, give no choice, saying to Lana: "Let's meet somewhere."

"Why?" Impudence so much Lana's default mode that Mary almost fails to notice.

"Because we never do that anymore."

"When did we ever do anything?" asks Lana, indefatigable. As it is appointed however, that Sunday in the old neighborhood diner of South Berkeley mother and daughter will meet, Lana saying she will spend the night before at Rose's a few blocks away.

Upon entering, Mary is surprised to find Lana already seated.

When driving down College Avenue in the stationwagon, Mary had passed her daughter, wrists taut and flared, but had shown motherly restraint, not shouting out, showing caution by not interfering with that brown-gazelle stride. Go laissez-faire, she tells herself, first do no harm. And only the direction of Lana's stride reveals the first lie: her daughter had not slept at Rose's house.

The self-lecture had continued while Mary procured a parking spot and then entered the diner masked in briskness, existentially surprised as ever that this particular daughter had burst out of her, this mango of her being, a girl with the quirk, like a mafia don or Tourette's heir, of always needing her back to the wall. Lana has started to be hard to recognize in her temporarily magenta hair, bone holding it aloft, hood topping the entire ensemble, her dark-kohled eyes flickering the warning of a cave-dweller.

A mother could think the girl meant to style herself to look, in yet another clever forfeiture of birthright, as if she'd crawled out of a hangover. Yet as Sherry had suggested, at least a strong daughter could not be pushed around and as Mary's mid-century mission schools suggested, why not accentuate the positive?

1. Lana had shown up;
2. no one needed to wake her;
3. so what if she leaves a diaphragm visible and unashamed in the shower, her daughter is punctual, a trait which might guarantee later success in life, not just with bosses but with others.

When the truth is she cannot imagine her daughter ever having a serious adult job. "What're you having?" Lana asks before Mary sits down. Not even a pre-flood parent would be fooled by this parody of politesse, Lana's forestalling of discussion a feeble tactic.

"Oh. What do you suggest?" Mary smiles back, her fake good humor making Lana cringe so that both beat a retreat into their study of menus. Once the waitress comes, Mary chooses the western special while Lana's enunciated choice—single egg, dry toast—rebukes her mother.

Don't take it personally, Mary tells herself, since, according to Sherry, all girls go through the realm of hell called adolescent mother problems.

Mary does hear this parry: "So what's the big plan?"

"Maybe let's go to that bookstore down the street. Isn't there something you've been wanting?"

"No." Lana rolls her eyes, glances away. "Something you want. You want me to stop seeing Tumbleweed."

Mary could both admire and hate Lana's straight speech, an example of the loss of finesse over generations, the bold crudity of naming all conversational goals, a way of saying *ancients, I lack time to wither away into you.*

Because of course Mary wants to speak of Tumbleweed, whom she has glimpsed hanging around corners. At first she had mistaken him, thinking he was another of Vic's shaggies, but there Tumbleweed had been every morning at 8:15 on the street just below their house's perch on its hill, his battered moped pointing downhill, waiting for Lana whenever she left off her dalliance with the rock star who at least showed courtly manners around Mary. Instead this Tumbleweed came punctually to speed her daughter off to either her last days of high school or some unguessable adolescent hell.

Ma, don't need a ride, thanks, bye, Lana would shout before slamming the door on her way out, heading for this guy whom Lana and her friend must have met during one of their nighttime walkabouts.

When Mary had talked to Vic about this crisis, given how clearly Tumbleweed ranked as one of those vampires who want to suck freshness out of young girls right as such men stand to lose their own, Vic had asked: "Is it a crime to be struck by the beauty of youth?"

"No comment," Mary had said.

Last September, perhaps before Lana had ever met the guy, Mary had started seeing Tumbleweed lying on Telegraph Avenue with some teenage girl or another strewn over his lap. *This is the kind of dog who shoots up girls*—the thought had flared so purely through Mary's head she had known it to be truth.

And now that dogweed waits every morning on a street studded with poinsettias and liberal ideals, ready to give her sixteen-year-old a ride on his motorbike.

Surely Rose would have had more sense. While Mary wants to believe Lana and Rose might still be virgins, she also guesses the girls like collecting ragtag men. Of course there is an appeal to the female hindbrain, as Vic would say, in any man who revolts against established orders. Yes, of course, able to spear more bison. She knows. But that Lana should be in such an antique scenario makes Mary's feminism want to scream. If she could, she would make the weed himself talk with her. Of course the conversation would be doomed: the guy would pretend not to recognize her, scratching his crotch while lathering her off. And if Rose's mother Joan were more available for discussion, perhaps Mary would have a mother-to-mother conference. *What is happening to our daughters?* Yet perhaps some similarity links the two mothers, Mary and Joan, a link greater than either wants to admit, making them, under the guise of delicate respect for their girls' friendship, bristle in each other's presence. No, Mary cannot talk to Joan. There really was no other way than meeting with Lana herself, this conversation in the drugstore diner Mary's only gateway. Her smallest goal had been that Lana would open up and not stomp out.

"You like Tumbleweed?" begins Mary, using a technique drawn from *The Art of War.*

"His parties are okay," offers her daughter, more an admission than Mary can guess, as attending these parties happens to be one of Lana's favorite things to do with Rose, the girls getting to pass as twenty-one, allowed in by one of Tumbleweed's cool bouncerward nods just so the Lolas can spend their time with their arms climbing air ladders, eyes closed, doing their flow.

Rose the viewer, hidden behind marbled glass bricks three tables away in the drugstore, stifles a cough. She will later say that never before had she known so painfully the pretense of family. Here mother and daughter have what could have been a civilized chat—enough that Rose can almost see the floater in Mary's head, *this is something mothers and daughters do when smoothing disputes, they go out for coffee*—but from the looks of it, couldn't the mother have leaned over and just wrung that lovely throat?

How frustrated Mary must be with a daughter who probably never allowed much entry, but what great privilege Lana has, that she can risk barring a mother, that she is so unafraid of losing her mother's goodwill, that she can patronize Mary while explaining Tumbleweed as if the guy belongs to a breed requiring rare sheep husbandry.

Lana's monotone emerges, reading from a parchment of insult. Rose cannot imagine speaking like that to anyone, so dully. *We just want to try and*— Lana keeps saying. *He can't really*—

"It's like, okay," Lana is telling Mary now, managing three microharmonic quavers within the last word. "It's not about the relationship, it's about how natural it feels. Natural," repeats Lana as if the authentic were necessarily foreign to Mary, her mother looking away before excusing herself to the ladies' room.

Lana smirks and in a gamble peeks at Rose, thumbs up, having asked her to come; she needed backing. When Mary finally returns to the table, her face that of a general not ready to concede, it is clear she has pepped herself up with some internal command on how to continue. "Well, let's keep talking, then, see how you feel."

Rose may not be able to hear everything Lana says but sees the scheme of self-enclosure, this girl successful at shunting her mother outside the jewel purse of youth. Rose had tried telling Lana that at least she was lucky. "No, you're the lucky one," Lana had said. "My mom's unreasonable. Not there most of the time and then wants to float in, protect me like the lady in white she's not and I'm like where have you been? Then she gets this wounded face." Rose had loved this moment of confession: if not the Lolas against men, at least the Lolas have mothers. "She'll want me to stop seeing Tumbleweed. I hate how she says relationship."

"You think she's ever been with anyone besides your dad?"

"Don't make me think about that. Yuk." Lana had long ago told Rose that what she had noticed about other mothers with daughters was that there were mothers who could sit across from their daughters and listen with true interest, undistracted and present, not doing some checking-off against an internal list stolen from the playbook of the latest child-rearing expert. "While my mother cannot for a second pay attention. She tries but can't. Everything circles back to her. In my childhood, okay, maybe she was more there in body than your mom was? But really she was off somewhere in the future where she thought all her promise would be redeemed. She cannot listen."

In the diner, Rose believes Lana must be wrong. Mary seems to make every effort to understand Lana. Would Rose ever be that patient?

Several times, Lana overtly teaches her mother. "No, it doesn't work like that, *Mary*," she says. Only occasionally comes a crack in Mary's facade which seems to make Lana want to surrender to impulse and do something like throw ice water on Mary before storming out. How long will this charade last? How much of a masochist is Mary?

Finally the cavalcade of insult clearly fazes Mary. "Honey." She tries taking Lana's hands in hers but fails, her daughter too slippery. "I've been involved in situations like this."

"This doesn't have to do with flipping the pages in some book."

"You remember my friend Juliet?" Mary adopts a soap opera tone as if this might penetrate Lana's cool. "She had to play second woman to some man but just kept hanging on."

Lana turns nasal. "Yeah," she says, dismissing any life knowledge Mary might have as inherently ludicrous.

Rose had heard about Juliet, a friend of Mary's once involved with an inappropriate man. The year before, she had attempted suicide, botching it enough that Juliet continued life in an institution, poring over the oracles of coffee grounds.

Mary musters. "There's something you're not facing. Look at the situation. Talk to his parents."

"Parents?" says Lana, smirking. "Someone like Tumbleweed doesn't have parents, Mary. This is no big deal."

"Well, to me it is," says Mary. "Not until twenty-two is your brain developed enough yet to understand—"

"Risk. I know."

"A person can go over some slope and never get back."

"You have too many books about teenagers on your shelves. Drug addiction."

"That's just one concern."

"You see one side of this but we, we have to make our own decisions."

Her mother shows allergy to this *we* that includes someone named Tumbleweed. With great daintiness, her daughter chews the last of her single egg.

"I want to take the position this isn't entirely over," says Mary.

"Okay." Lana offers up a limpid smile.

"I'm sure you don't want to be selfish," says Mary. "Or maybe you don't want to hurt him. Maybe you don't know how easy it is to cut off from people."

"Like you from dad?"

"I'm saying later in life you'll have plenty of chances to make mistakes without me."

Lana ignores her but when the bill comes makes a big show of paying for her own breakfast, scrabbling for coins from the beaded purse that her mother had once bought at an ethnic fair. Mary waves off the gesture but Lana insists.

If Rose could, she would rush in to protect them from each other but she can't, clandestine behind the nook with its magazine rack, just as Lana had asked her to be.

When they are almost ready to go, Mary leans in. "What about writing a paper with outline and content about how you see this thing proceeding? Just let your mind go there. To the end of the line."

The hatred in Lana's look at Mary, sharp as an icicle, makes Rose turn away. "Mary," says her friend. "Mom." A curse, as if trying to chill her mother into permanent cryogenic suspension. "Can you even get this? This is not a term paper. Not about colleagues. Not soft cheese at some faculty event. I'm talking about life."

"Life?"

"Being natural. It's hard for you to understand. You don't know the first thing about relationships."

"Jinga," says Mary softly. "Jinga."

"You don't even call me that anymore! You cannot just show up and get me to connect like I'm some kind of daughter on tap."

And then Lana storms out the drugstore, leaving Rose alone to see Mary at the table, a goner, slumping as if someone had slid a hanger out from her sweater, a middle-aged mother barely able to keep herself from weeping at whatever barbs she must live with.

Sitting, Rose fights the urge to reveal herself, the urge to be recognized as a sympathetic ear and good daughter. Instead she watches Mary gather herself and finally leave, bells jangling.

Chord progression being an island of a moment in Greece bearing two girls, nurtured on American soil and pieties, hitchhiking to get a boat back to the mainland from which they'll take a bus toward a plane toward home so they can return toward starting the first year of college and all its unknowns. These girls intersect with a native mode: two men of the islands driving a truck on a highway.

The truckers pull over, understanding the girls enough to suggest a destination, asking do the girls mind stopping at a restaurant? Four plates of salad and fish, an afternoon stretching on, a broad continent of arm, a brush of skin, a narrow hand pulled back, continental drift, rough thumbs pressing an apology and offers of endless ouzo. The men drive farther down the road only to pull into another outdoor bar. Drink, dab bread into glistening plates of olive oil, dab hands, a brush of skin, no apology, drink and drive, brush some more, pull into another bar.

We got to get to our boat, says one of the girls, it's getting late. Let's go check the schedule at the train station. One girl looks around outside the truck while one slouches inside, contemplating. The afternoon has slipped through their hands, a wild rodent. One man inside, one outside and, a drink-and-dab earlier, the plan must have been hatched:

without warning, the man in the truck takes off with only the one girl inside, a tectonic plate shifting.

He is driving her up the mountain road toward, ostensibly, the train station. For no reason the girl can see, he pulls over on the side, offering her then that downward arc that will become so familiar: his hand on the back of her neck, pushing her head down toward his lap as if a gentle derrick.

She resists and he pushes farther, deeper toward the core of the earth. Years later another man will explore this similar gravitational potential and she will throw up in his lap, oddly elated. But right now there is the problem of her head's habit of numbness and the bothersome question that lets her go down more easily: had she wanted this overpowering?

Also and not insignificantly she wants to ace the situation, survive intact. Like that heiress, kidnapped, who immediately saw her kidnappers' point of view. Could spinelessness be a surprise tactic of strength?

Ravines and clefts in his forearms, along his neck.

Does he do manual labor on the side? She had liked his looks, the delicacy of the eyes, a femininity against harsher angles. His hand not ungentle but insistent on the back of her neck toward his lap where he is conveniently unsprung. She hadn't chosen to enter this situation but now it has arisen, a pop-up dollhouse. A man's hand warming her neck and is she willing or not? If she doesn't want to be doing this, can this son of this country of mothers' sons tell? How can a man want something not freely given?

Does he tell himself that it is wanted? But maybe she wants. Is it bad if you aren't the first person to know what you want?

And hadn't the lolling tongues and technicolor availability of certain magazines, her mother's creased copies of certain novels, initiated her into some permanent hoarfrost of open-lipped readiness?

In ninth grade, on the pastel carpet in the parental bedroom, the televised cartoon of *Yellow Submarine* playing on the tiny TV set above a pile of tea towels, had she not mouthed for the first time the young and grateful Flynn, seeking to initiate both of them? What was different between her liking for that boy's good nature, his father-less making-the-best-of-it self, and this moment in a Greek truck? Flynn too young and flimsy to bear the weight of her vague fantasy, not desire, really, but an apery of futurity, an ironic paroxysm.

Her head breaks on the thought. She's no virgin but in this truck in Greece she wants to choose, choice everything: she could *choose* rape and then, in a fight with this fellow, wouldn't she win? If she doesn't choose, she'll emit the scent of fear and some unguessed-at contraption might release a lever making the whole moment plummet be-yond danger into irreversibility on a mountain roadside where no one in the world knows the exact coordinates of her body. The mo-ment narrows. She floats above her body, allowing for a certain kind of survival.

After and in the truck's fish-scent, she rifles through the phrase-book. Trying for *let's go back*, though can a person go back? *Epeestro-phe*, she says.

Her rapist, a man of few words, agrees, drawing dignity back into himself. As if something quite normal has transpired, he drives back, fingers tapping out an idle rhythm on the steering wheel, knuckle hair matted by a wedding band shimmering in the last of the day. At the restaurant bar, her friend runs to the car. To stay safe from the other truckdriver, her friend had hidden atop the restaurant roof if in plain sight of diners and cooks, another chicken avoiding the pan.

Stunned, the two girls grab backpacks, running blind in the dusk only to end up lying in a ditch. The girl who'd gone for the ride hugs the one who'd been left behind, crying: I hate men! Falling still when the two men tramp near holding flashlights, muttering as if they've stumbled into an outtake from a war movie, seeking American girls fallen to an earthen trench, parachutes broken. A search party of en-emy soldiers who back away when they find nothing. One girl raped but might as well have happened to both of them.

They will never talk about it. A vessel containing past and future, all the crisp nights when one girl failed to show at the other's house or the moment when one had cried, saying your friendship means more to me, I didn't mean to hurt you with that boy, I didn't know you had a crush on him, he just showed up around my house, throwing rocks at my window at night and I won't see him if it makes you feel better. Or the moment when one visits the other's room at college. A debutante roommate will say—after seeing the girls' shared uniform of messy hair, thrift-store patterned skirts and men's white shirts—to the girl she'd suspected was a witch because of her penchant for standing on her head and burning incense, that, at least, after meeting the girl's friend, she could understand the girl a tiny bit better.

It will contain the night when one of them finishes college and moves to Los Angeles, driving fast at night on Highway Five's hills toward an art school with an old boyfriend who himself had just finished driving across the country to start over and he's offering a bite of moo shu vegetables while her favorite song of the moment plays, a latterday version of Lola which happens to have the name Jane in the refrain.

A truth will pop in her mind: that lost bubble. She lives in a post-girlfriend universe, left entirely alone to experience others. She will hold that boyfriend's hand, drive hard.

What shoots Lana into the asylum?

Her first day there, she makes a list to answer the intake question: what factors in your life may have worked to bring you today to Ulster State?

Lana writes:

the urges of my body

and at first thinks that probably should stand for enough but then decides to vary the theme:

too many abortions—I mean how can a person know what to
   believe when after each one you have a bone that makes it
   impossible to swallow, like something got lodged in your
   throat for weeks after—all this makes it a little hard to know
   who you are
my mother (never really able to see me etc)
my father (thinking he was such a big deal etc)
my habits (solitude, art)
my habits with people (letting too many tramp in)
my parents' hopes (my failure because I was never their star
   student etc)

my inability to speak (can't say the words me or my and really
   know what they mean)
my friends (never really being good to at least the one friend
   who was decent to me, Rose)

before she chokes up and quits, though no one else will, since the
white coats push forward the juggernaut of inquiry that rules this place
and will keep wanting to ask her why she ended up, essentially, a nut.

Here's how it works. Count backward into the ether mask and then start to see numbers fly near the tongue-guard and they soon become dream angels with folded wings, soaring straight into the smoke-box of the room. After that you exit your body. Shock gets administered. Sometimes it takes a few days to come back: this is, at least, the story they will tell you after the days have passed. You get piloted toward various human functions. Eating, sleeping, drinking.

Lana fakes sleep and stops counting backward. Just to know. To not sleep as atrocities get committed. She sees it from inside and then from the ceiling. The lever pulled, her back arched, every muscle contorted, her head someone else's banging back and forth on the table.

This however is better than a lobotomy, her asylum roommate later tells her.

Lana hisses back: "I'm sure even at Ulster they don't do those. Not anymore," though later she will find herself envying that same roommate for the way a partial lobotomy lends a person the patina of spiritual calm.

At least one thing Lana does know: being awake for shock is better than those times she has overheard the psychiatric resident whispering facts about her case.

She is twenty, a time when lots of girls crack, and she is not alone. As the resident says in their opening interview, given who her father is, doesn't Lana have a community of love and respect surrounding her?

1987

One of the two things Lana will never tell anyone is about the time in the hospital because isn't it better to keep certain secrets buried in the trunk of family? Though the bothersome part of this decision is how secrecy makes family all the more important, shame its fierce lock: only her parents know about the hospital time.

She had not gone down easily. Once she woke from sedation, finding herself staring at a Georgia O'Keeffe poster of a weeping purple flower, soft-cuffed to a hospital bed, the room perfumed by an orderly's acrid sweat, she kept saying: there must be a mistake.

But there was none. They showed her the forms signed by mother and father, the signatures no impostors. Once they let her move about, even with someone's arm on hers, she felt as alone as she had ever been, walking halls in which every footfall felt spongy, a deep impress on the linoleum. For a good five minutes she had paused before the door marked ELECTROTHERAPY, eyeing it with dull alarm. Apparently her parents had found the one revanchist place that still believed in electroshock. Ulster State had an advanced program, certified on puce paper by the state: electro*therapy.*

That first evening, having refused a meal made entirely of orange and white mashed items, she started to realize how improbable escape might be. To the resident psych with the kind periwinkle eyes, called in to see about her low-level defiance, Lana had explained: "I was never like this."

I understand—the eyes twinkled, kinder than her mother's—
you don't belong here.

"Does what I'm saying shock you?" Lana asked.

"No. You're more polite than most," the shrink said, her professional spiel not yet watertight.

"Why? What do people usually say?"

"Usually they start by saying f-you!"

"Uphill from there, right?" Lana had said, deciding to aim for
penetration via charm but deciding later that her stink of desperation, undisguised, made the shrink leave soon after.

Who would not be desperate here? It was all too easy to see the
lost and charmless, the drooling chlorpromazine cases, the cardboard
people. It was also disconcerting how at the outset of her stay, she
was a little too happy to surrender the tyranny of getting dressed in
streetclothes, too happy at the prospect of surrendering decisions
about minutiae. No choice of clothes, no choice about which spices
go on food.

Back in New York, temporarily staying at Rose's apartment,
Lana had entertained a bad moment, flummoxed about which spice
goes with oatmeal, cayenne or cinnamon, her head blurring on
the question until next she knew people were strapping her onto a
gurney toward the asylum. The afternoon after being admitted,
during Quiet Time, she decided to locate herself in the Mahler-
sanctioned manner by going to the institution's library, trying to
ignore the young cross-eyed orderly assigned her and thumbing
through grease-tabbed romance novels and textbooks. The quiet
dormer windows pleased her. For a second she let herself pretend
she still marched on an upward path, improving herself in college.

That first day she found herself attracted to reading a single passage from one of her father's books on neuroleptics and systems theory as if—if she could just understand it—this passage could provide
a better answer for her presence here:

Ordinary objects run down unless they are fed energies and repairs
or replacements from the outside. Entire physical systems cut off from
other systems run down in this way too. But there are exceptions to
the rule, and these are found within the closed systems of which the
Second Law—that natural systems maintain themselves in a changing

environment—speaks. The Law is permissive: it does not determine just *how* such a system runs down. It can do so very unevenly. In fact it is quite possible that it should run down on the whole, while in some areas or parts it should actually get wound up. That is, there can be subsidiary systems within the whole system, and these subsystems can get more organized as time goes on, rather than less. Of course, the rest of the system gets correspondingly depleted, and the sum of the energies used up is always positive—more energy is used up than is generated. The system as a whole gets disorganized, whereas some of its parts become increasingly organized at the expense of the rest. It is as though we used the electricity stored in the batteries of our house to produce more batteries. We concentrate our available energies in the new batteries, but use up more energy from the original ones to make them than we preserve. The sum of the electric power available to us has decreased, even if locally it has increased. The whole house runs down even if some parts of it wind up.

She must have appeared so wound up that no one had yet asked if she wished to contact her parents. For this small kindness she was glad; if she even imagined talking to the parental units, rage rose in her throat, a bolus making it hard to imagine the phrases a person would use with such inhuman robots. Wasn't it better for her to punish everyone with mutism?

Yet that didn't mean she didn't hold out hope that her father's name might save her. Once, before a psychiatric session, she asked a different doctor, possessor of a particularly caustic gaze: you don't know who I am? Lana *Mahler*.

Soon after as if in answer, they were strapping her to a gurney all over again. How had her life come to fit Vic's thoughts so perfectly? Her whole life he had talked of the magic of the brain and scoffed at the barbarism of early psychiatry. Back then she had still been asking him questions. Vic loved discussing trephining, the twelfth-century Italian doctor's invention meant to treat psychologically unfit patients, the vise with its screws on the head or its predecessor, evinced in fossil skulls of prehistoric man, a metal spike driven by hammer blows into the skull.

He had explained all this and yet still had managed to make her his puppet, putting her in a box where they could do whatever they wanted. On the gurney she let out a short barking laugh. The lunatic is on the grass. Beg pardon? asked the white coat. Exactly! said Lana, her triumphant tone making the orderly flinch. She had somewhere missed out on certain instructions and from now on was going to have to stop begging pardon from the awesome birthright of the Vic-and-Mary show. I'm done, she therefore explained to no one.

Over three months in the nutcracker she tried explaining to a whole retinue of white coats about the slipping sands that made time not her own: about the abortions and potentially contaminated weed and the streetshow man who stood at Washington Square in gilded paint, barely moving. How whatever Lana called her soul had found its most definite expression in watching that gilded man for hours so that once, her mother visiting, Mary had needed to shake Lana's shoulder to shock her out of a trance. Maybe this moment had birthed Mary's worry, though no, the worry had lingered earlier, back in the era of Tumbleweed or maybe even Rose.

"No antipsychotics," Lana instructed one of the kinder white coats one time, her memories starting to jumble. "No Thorazine. No electroshock."

With the male psychiatrist who became her mainstay—my squeeze, she called him to her roommate—a stooped vulture upset with what life had doled out, Lana stayed defiant, stuck in this mode until she realized she had landed on an alien planet and had failed to heed its rules:

1. The first question to ask when landing should always be who is the leader in charge?

This part she had neglected. The aliens may have already captured her. She had imprinted like a duckling on the blue-eyed woman psych resident, following the wrong person until she realized that resident equaled powerless, that really the male vulture controlled the planet. He must be placated and made to move toward sympathy. Had Lana been just a bit more compliant from the start, she realized, the vulture doctor would not have ordered biweekly electroshock. Finally she clicked to it and stopped wearing a nightgown. Instead she raided her father's unconscious in order to assume the dim smile of a madonna dressed as a fifties girl, hair pulled back and ankles crossed, carrying books prim across the chest, arms slim, breasts full, cribbing her affect from the pages of *The Bell Jar*, a book she had read first semester in college in New York. She would drill deep into the vulture's secret heart, try to come off as milky and compliant.

But would it work? Would they discharge her? And to what? And why would no one visit?

How are treatments going? the vulture always asked.

O really well, she started to say, *doctor*, inside telling herself: *milky, compliant*, sometimes orienting her womb his way to give off the message of *you're a big man, you protect and serve*. Disembodied, she could enter the story they were creating together, see herself as a tall wisp of a girl in a nightgown ready to be snapped around his will, ready to run away and let him spawn monster vulture babies in the seedbed of her compliant womb.

Who was the one who had betrayed her by leaving her to rot, her parents or Rose?

Only once do her mother and father come, pulled from France as if from their own distant bunny planet. They come on a day when Lana is so drugged—or could it have been after a treatment?—that she registers mainly what a silly fuss they make about getting her some fresh air and that her father is weaker than the orderlies when wheeling her out into the garden. The family Mahler sits near black-eyed susans, a flower her mother used to love. And if Lana's tongue is too thick to explain that milky compliance toward the vulture has helped lessen the frequency of electrocution, there are documents in a clear plastic file pasted near her bed, its contents her reading material on lucid days, stating all her parents need to know:

Given that the medical team deems it advisable for electrotherapy to continue for unknown duration

Later Lana will wonder if her parents' visit did help her case since it seems that on a day not long after—was it seven days, a month?—

the vulture's face cracks toward a simulacrum of a smile, asking: "How do you feel about being discharged in a few weeks? If all goes well?"

"O good," she says, milky, compliant, "no, really, super, great." The day arrives and she tells herself all is well, though she feels faint, taking a breath, going through glass revolving doors clutching her purse, following Mary into the parking lot with the childish urge to hold mommy's hand as they pass other cars and head toward a maroon stationwagon chosen by every parent of her generation, a vehicle strong in its frame if poor in its high center of gravity and handling around curves. Lana cannot stop seeing herself from the outside, cannot find a moment of sensation within, and it is only when she imagines telling Rose about her sojourn in bedlam and the pity she would be met with, Rose's sensitive face mirroring how bad it has just been for Lana, that her knees buckle and her eyes well up. With each footfall Lana tells herself ACT NORMAL, willing her voice to stay unquavering while asking Mary: "Where's Vic?" using his first name on purpose and accepting Mary's near-silence as they enter the car to drive to the airport, Lana sly in her role of prim fifties girl throughout, purse on lap all the way, even on the plane back to California, even when flight attendants make her quiver, so much like orderlies in their concern that Lana stay buckled down. Finally Lana dozes off, head on Mary's shoulder, shaken by a dream in which a stewardess takes her to the No Smoking bathroom to administer a shock, small but sexual, so that Lana wakes to the plane's din in which voices scream in code. For a second, Lana looks amazed at the reassurance to be found in the softness of her mother's arm but then pulls back. When Mary asks what the matter is, at first Lana cannot speak through the voices, the high yappy sort that used to teem in her head before a shot of tranquilizer hit the bloodstream and though she tries listening to whatever Mary says next, her mother's mouth opens and closes like a fish flopped onto a beach where someone had asked her to play parent.

The two of them manage.

Crossing the threshold of Spruce Street, some questions return. Is Lana supposed to stay in what never had been a home? A house once refuge with its closets now all reproach, its spiritual life discernible in the fridge hum. And where is her father? Have her parents foundered on unimaginable shoals?

That night Vic does return and Lana, from her room's garrison, hears how grand he makes the front door's initial bluster, cloaking himself within fatherly loudness, a role she readily understands: he is covering the sin of having padlocked his daughter. As she hears him tramp upstairs, she buries her mouth in a musty pillow, mouthing *you believe in freedom?* at the moment he enters without knocking just as if they have shared an unbroken reverie of good nights.

"You're okay now," he instructs, as ever speaking his worst questions in the imperative.

Anything she says could scar and anyway her eyes have nothing left to give. "Yeah," she tells the depths of her pillow, fully deceiptful, "I am."

A month or two since her release and in a major feat of avoidance, the house sustains its hushed rituals, broken only the evening Vic enters her room again to come sit on her bed with intent, telling her that though he has never talked much about his childhood, he needs to explain a little about his life. She leans against the wall, pretending to continue the charcoal sketch she was doing when he entered, wishing instead to hide in the light cast by a jeweled deco lamp he had once bought on an outing. One for Lana, one for Rose. But she cannot hide, the rainbow light filling his eyes with mania, his words orchestral, first a violin's grumble but on a speedy trail toward crescendo and trill. Because of how he speaks, she has to believe what he says: this is no longer Vic of the patient teacherly cadence and hypnotic pause but Vic rushing to exit some maze of his own.

First he must tell her the truth: he had not been an orphan. What is true is that his mother had been a prostitute and he'd had to watch her—how could he have avoided the curiosity?—sleeping with men.

"What are you saying?"

Caught in his moment, he doesn't hear. His mother's legs up around pallid buttocks, animals scuttling together, little Vic caught peeking in. Afterward his mother made him sniff one of the men's leather belts, left behind as if for this exact purpose, before using it to cross-hatch Vic's back and legs. "How people did things in the old days." He cannot shrug away the burn in his eyes. "You got it easy, right?"

That she won't give. "So why," nonetheless delicate around this subject, "did you always tell people you were an orphan?"

"Tell me in what way am I not? This must be one of the reasons I ask people to be so careful when considering choice. Clearly we do receive a bounty of choices in life. That said, choice cannot become some global fiend devouring what is actually given. So much is fixed and immovable."

"Please no lecture. Not right now."

"Let me just finish. To be seen is the ambition of ghosts. Instead I found one of the best ways to be born again. You give up being seen. You rescript your origins."

"That means you lie?"

"You have no idea what my upbringing was like. When my mother was angry, she locked me in a wooden pen. Big enough for a colt." He looks gratified by his daughter's sympathy. They have never talked like this before, have they? He is confiding; he could inspire her.

"I found a way to weaken the latch. Enough to escape to a neighbor's house. I'd get back in an hour without anyone ever knowing."

She keeps scratching charcoal on paper because his eyes are danger. "Wow."

"We tried giving you everything. Probably made a mistake. Too much liberty becomes no choice. Worse than a wooden pen."

"You've said that a million times." She goes back to her paper. "But why wait until now to tell me all this?"

"You're not afraid of much." He says this as if just noticing.

"I'm tired, Vic." She uses his name on purpose, insult and rebuff, suffocated by how he watches. From him she has tried to learn the card-player tactic of giving up little. Nonetheless she thinks this could be the first time he has ever tried looking into her.

"It's hard to be a parent," he says finally. "I'm not talking about the values you exchange with your kid. Really it's all one-sided thievery. One day you'll see." As if about to cry. "You'll see. How to keep a stiff upper lip." Her charcoal furious in scratching the paper because how palpable it becomes that her parents are foolish over-indulged children, the whole mess combining in her as the burden of understanding. "You think you create your reality?" he asks, his tone not letting her go.

This she has also heard a million times: how, if you think you create your reality, you don't have to deal with the fallout of social inequity, you can ignore mass misfortune, environmental catastrophe, class injustice and theodicy because create your reality and you can always say victims choose their reality. To his latterday adherents, trying to set them straight, Vic preaches that Californians, like so much of humanity since the rise of market economics, lack humility. This hubris might be his favorite idea to hate, one he has called the prime misunderstanding the shaggies have about his work.

Create your reality? "No," she says, glowering. "You know I don't believe that. But I'm not in a real mood for talking."

"You know," he says, contemplating his outstretched palm long enough that she looks up. "At first I didn't want to have children. Your mother was the one who said we had the money and her age might be a problem. Back then, you know, she was pushing what we thought were the outer limits so I let us be careless. We had our fun. I let her use Ivory soap as protection." He smiles. "But when she was about three months pregnant, we had some words. I told her I'd never wanted a kid. You understand this was a bad moment. But after that she started bleeding and had to take to bed for a couple of days. And then she always blamed me for the moment and how you turned out. The truth is that once I saw you, I never regretted the decision. Maybe without kids I could have written three more books but—"

"Why are you telling me this?" she asks, this time unable to guard herself. Embarrassed, he jerks up, stammering the usual need to retreat into work, the sham something not even her asylum time could make her parents surrender.

After their moment, he appears to abandon most any desire to talk to her. She comes to regret the conversation. Secretly she had wanted him to say more. She had loved and hated that he had come—to her!—for confession and absolution.

He will never start again. Raped by others' stories, sure, she'd had tons of that in the asylum. Maybe in this case he had offered his stories as a blind man would, a gift for a lame girl, a blanket to sling over all the ways he had failed her. Once she had been just a mere blood spot and in his own clumsy way he was saying he was glad she had been born.

In the following month she almost forgives him, a quiet closeness living between them, something like the understanding she used to have with Rose. Yet the three, Mary, Vic and Lana, shuffle around as if choreographed by a vigilant demon in the wings whose commands make them puppetlike when crossing rooms, unsure of the score. Feeling orphaned too, Lana writes half-finished letters to Rose, all of which end up in her wastebasket, only to have Mary pore over them later as if they were runes.

Also it is true that the electrotherapy seems to have altered her brain. Odd facts arise, quotations from a Chinese revolution class almost in their entirety:

Chang Ch'un-ch'iao handled the task of rebuilding the new power structure with coercion and persuasion. The Chinese notion of justice used the moral concept of good and bad rather than the more familiar legalities of innocent and guilty, though good persons could make mistakes,

but little coheres, nothing sticks. *Cinnamon and cayenne* she tells herself, a little mantram for trying to be a docile shell, trainable, awaiting good influence.

Summer coming on, she wants escape, a job, and so sticks the initials B.A. on her résumé after Studio Art. This fakery doesn't help since in interviews, despite Lana's ostensibly fancy pedigree and qualifications, people sense the hole and no one hires her, not as a film intern, babysitter, waitress, dance-store salesperson, overnight homeless-shelter watcher, pet-shop cashier, editorial assistant, rental-car dispatcher. She quits the search.

Afternoons she avoids the intensity of the Spruce Street manse to walk West Berkeley's windward side, traintracks zippering the bay. To optimistic self-blinded winos she says hello while feeling how easy it would be to fall into a rift, how much pleasure could be found in becoming a hard-lot case who can't even get things together enough to camp out on some scholar's lawn.

Not even a shaggy. She hadn't meant to get on some elevator shooting down but perhaps it's too late. Her parents try acting out normalcy while she cannot. Or maybe what has fled is the prospect of seeing outside herself, while her parents seem flies caught in their belief about the importance of toil. She sees no way to continue living inside their world.

During one dinner, green-flecked sausage and new potatoes, pity overwhelms Lana to the point that she can't breathe, the only one with superhuman vision enough to see, as if plastered to the ceiling, their forks moving like the legs of overturned insects, trained to perform the serene, synchronized dance called family. She barks out a laugh. "What are you looking at, Jinga?" Mary asks and only then Lana realizes her face hovers inches away from her empty plate, staring into its reflection.

Perhaps it is during the next course that they all come to some agreement that it might be a good idea for Lana to get back to what they keep calling her life back east, one that seems made up of brownish placed items from a Morandi painting. Nothing living, nothing that Lana remembers.

Mary says it this way: "Maybe it would be good for you to get back to being an adult in New York."

"Ship out the problem?" Lana asks. "So the problem doesn't crack?"

Their only answer is the scrape of a fork on a plate, redeeming the last of the andouillette.

A few days later Mary drives her to the airport. At the gate, mother presses a bottle of water into daughter's hands while studying molecules somewhere to the left of daughter's face. "What?" asks Lana.

"This time will be good for you," her mother says. "I see it."

"You've always been good at convincing yourself."

"Maybe." Mary cocks her head, quizzical, letting Lana in a second before she remembers herself as mother. "All this will help you return to your other life."

"My other lie?" Low in Lana's throat lives the itch to be like any other traveler around her. Someone who could hug her mother, who could say *I love you* without hearing parodic echoes. For the long journey to reach the place where this particular idiom won't ricochet, Lana lacks stamina. Her mother then offers the most mysterious send-off Lana will ever receive. As if she were parroting Vic. "Parents are never perfect."

"Sure," says Lana, starting to turn. What she means to say is *goodbye* and partly *I forgive you* but also *please get out of my body*, her mother's frail-bird look already starting its haunt.

1987

They will never get over the thing with Lana, which is what they call it, the thing, never the lock-up. How had the thing started, a thing recalled so often, it keeps slipping off the shelf of the past with a hot little sputter. Vic says he is certain the thing began with Mary, as it was definitely Mary who had set it off, Mary who in France had mentioned some kind of therapeutic retreat for their daughter, though later she ended up doubling back, saying she could not have guessed how thorough Vic would be in his follow-up.

But could his followers ever have believed how conservative their Mahler is? Mary knows. At his core, despite all Vic's advice to others, an inconsistency for which the Hermes character had taken him to task, Vic believes in institutions, the university, the nuclear family and the university as one big happy nuclear family, so Mary tells him that she is unsurprised that Vic would think a sanitarium—a nuthouse, an asylum, true bedlam—could have helped Lana.

Sometimes his breed of rage enters her: what is this stink of marriage, to use his axiom, this body-sharing habitation with a demon? She cannot help remaining permeable. Though she had grown up in California's dust plains and hills, she writes in diaries about feeling like a sea creature, someone with edges like oyster-colored frills. And she had chosen this man Vic with his fire that rendered all her nuance irrelevant.

In France before and after the lock-up, she does seem to concur with his demonic energy, letting her rationalizations bloom a full bouquet. For one, when they are leaving France, she tells herself they are merely heading back to New York to check on their Lana, a teenage girl having a breakdown, the breakdown being a phenomenon they have heard about from east-coast friends. Breakdowns out east seem to happen to colleagues' children after they hit adolescence. She cannot help but feel relieved after Vic says Lana's problems are not specific to them or the professoriate in America since it is also the case that in remote village societies across the world, people pray over the blossomed body of a particularly confused or libidinous teenage girl, commanding demons to flee.

What the parents cannot forget is the phone call that came at dawn, their small French landlady summoning them to her mentholated apartment while squinting up at her gargantuan American tenants, now with final evidence that les americains were up to nefarious ends. Over the tinny connection some girl calling herself Debbie, a medical student staying in Rose's apartment, spoke to Mary in an insincere, nasal voice: "Mrs. Mahler? I'm sorry, but—" and in the pause, Mary knew almost all, since fake apology never prefaces good news. "I'm sorry but your daughter has gone over the deep end," Debbie the premed finished.

Having once studied the clichés used to describe both death and insanity, the formulations that help reassure people of their own grip—*it had to be done, sometimes there's no choice, you do what you need to*—Mary is left speechless, with nothing to tell Vic, which will be the case for years whenever they find themselves talking about the end of the mystifying catacomb of decision that led them to lock up their own daughter. They get set on the course that will return Lana to a womb, to someone else's institution, while Mary gets swallowed by the minotaur of clichés. *No choice.*

Because when Mary looks back at it, their plan seems to have begun without root or branches. The two will just hone in on the problem and show up where their daughter seems to be staying alone in Rose's apartment. Their daughter is imploding and anyway doesn't Vic need to research in New York at some specialist archive on manias? On the plane from Paris to New York, Mary berates Vic: why must she be the one to figure out what to do for Lana? Why has she always needed to be both heart and connective tissue of their house? Why must she be the one to consider what is best for their girl? Could the household name beam down to his own household a bit?

The conversation ends where it starts, each hushing the other so that Mary cannot help entering what he calls her martyr mode. To punish her, he returns with what she calls the cold sizzle, a rage manifest in the precise torture of inanimate objects, the quick flip of a magazine, the undoing of a seatbelt with great force, a stewardess call button pressed too often. No ice in his gin and tonic, the coffee acid cold, the pillow insufficient: goddamnit, nothing goes right.

In the airport, the married dance continues. A slam of keys onto a countertop while awaiting baggage, a tight strop to get their luggage bound. This being the tango they know, the dance of martyr and tyrant, continuing in the hotelbound taxi as he pounds the seat hard enough to make the driver, an old-fashioned hard-luck-actor type, turn back toward Mary and Vic to ask: what's with you, friend?

Nothing, this is who he is, Mary whispers to the traffic, *unfortunately*. An elevator rises, their container in a hotel chosen not for its faux marble and creaky balconies but its bargain price. Vic breaks its calm only to ask her if she really wanted a plan.

Before Mary finishes her shower, Vic has arranged it, eye for eye.

At most, Mary later considers, he must have talked five minutes to one of his old colleagues, five minutes in which he had learned from his psychiatrist friend that Ulster State, while a bit old-fashioned in its techniques, would be just the thing, since the colleague had a son who'd also gone off the deep end. He therefore advises Vic that they will have to approach the whole thing like wild game capture with poison darts and name-tagging.

To Mary, Vic leaves only the most insidious details: the medical transit for their daughter upstate and how to gain parental rights of entry with the terse man who calls himself the super for Rose's building, all plans and details arranged so they may burst in on their progeny in some New York abode.

He will later berate Mary that it was she who had asked him to arrange everything.

Arranged, unarranged, they discover their daughter. She has turned
Rose's apartment into the habitat of an adult hamster so that even
Mary, having thought herself inured to varieties of teenage protest,
finds herself shocked by the tiny papers shredded into a nest around
a prone body.

Lana's head twists atop a disjointed neck and torso, a daughter far
too narrow, veins pulsing out, a girl strewn over papers on a sofa not
knowing she is prey for the gray-vested men who burst in with arm-
lacings, needles and gurney, their force so great Mary must look
away, only able to stay in place by imagining nuns' nails holding her
feet, mental stigmata she has not needed to use since schoolgirl days.
All while Vic does what he excels in: absenting himself fully in the
next room, flipping through documents before lifting drawn blinds
to gaze out as if seeing a tugboat for the first time. Mary steels herself,
mouthing platitudes no one listens to. For this willingness to be on
the frontlines she suffers. Before the syringe pierces flesh of Mary's
flesh, meant to dull Lana's electricity, her too-muchness, before
the sedative seeps in, Lana manages to shoot her mother a look with
enough venom to freeze time.

Parents, concerned parents: Mary and Vic try locating themselves in
this role as they ride down the elevator and out into the morning.

A few days later, having been successful at avoiding each other by
various appointments in New York, they take the subway from their
hotel into Grand Central where they transfer to the local up the Hudson. It could not be a more splendid fall day. Together they try not
admiring the showy orange of the leaves, try not uttering phrases
like *peak moment for foliage*. "Such a pretty mask for death," Vic does
say. Mary is not sure whether he means the leaves, train ride or herself
and decides on the first. It is permissible for them to give just a little to
each other in conversation: they will not admit that the Lana troubles
have united them, as one of Lana's long-ago accusations charged.

The wind rushes in at the stations, exhilarated, Vic and Mary having time-traveled to a courtship date from their past. Well-being fills

them. They must struggle to stay somber. They arrive, it is after Lana's first treatment, which, according to the doctor, means their daughter might later recall the visit. The family Mahler sits by black-eyed susans but their daughter cannot eat the sandwich they brought without dribbling it out her mouth and so Mary must dab her chin before Vic wheels her back in, Lana their baby all over, the institution a successful womb in mainly this aspect. Lana's parents share a look that to Vic means their daughter can, after all, be successfully retrained; to Mary the look is a contract meaning the married pair link forever in culpability.

Soon after, to avoid cutting short their sabbatical year, Vic and Mary take train, bus, plane and train again, back to their pastoralia in the town of Foix. In France they go marketing for goat cheese or garden barefoot, continuing with their holy work.

Just once they sleep together, Mary interested mainly in how polite the married pair has become, remembering how the savage in Vic had been so appealing. Now the two seem to have tamed each other. You, no you; please, you.

Afterward Mary broods about who they have been to Lana. Where did we go wrong? Was she this way at birth? And yet she has also managed to break free of some anchor of worry about their girl, having handed over parenting for the first time.

Which is when Mary starts to write about male/female decision-making patterns. In exploring these for the first time she knows the true beatitude of work: throw yourself over a cliff and trust that work alone can act as an elegy, capable of saving and redeeming. Perhaps Lana hates such tendencies but can her parents, captive mates, help their survival instinct?

Soon after Lana leaves the asylum, neat and meek in crossing their Spruce Street doorstep, she returns to one of her several former selves: hiding upstairs, bangs hiding her eyes, face hollow and gaunt, regressing to the loud spiral of a teenager's music.

A month after this return, after the dinner in which Lana shouts that their forks have become the dance of synchronized insect legs, Mary drives her back to the airport.

Lana is supposed to return to school half-time and get a low-stress job but instead will spend the next few months missing all her classes and getting jobs only to immediately lose them, ending up needing finally to cross the threshold of Rose's apartment just to locate herself.

"Going back to my life back east—the doctors didn't think it that great an idea, Mary," Lana will say on the way to the airport, the lie recognizable. "Isn't it just you want to get rid of me?"

"But you'll have things back east to keep yourself busy, right?" Mary says, glancing away from the gouges inside Lana's arm, which might have come after all from some rusty nails on attic boards the day the Mahler family, as it was constituted, had tried to work as a team to help Vic bring down some boxes of papers on narcissism. When Mary was Lana's age, hadn't she already figured out so much? Wasn't she independent? Why had the simple act of growing up become such a difficult endeavor?

After the goodbye between mother and daughter, apart from a few scurrilous letters she sends to Mary, Lana will have nothing to do with either parental unit, as she calls them. She is rageless, Mary will think, spent passion, maybe also a little mean. Lana could have left forwarding numbers but never will.

In that first week post-Lana, to her assistant Sherry, Mary calls it a phase. To herself, unwillingly, she calls it failure, but you can't let failure become a refrain. Instead Mary accentuates the positive. Her daughter needs to find her sea legs again, back in New York, and probably needs time away from her parents. As Sherry promises, it will all work out. Completely expressionless, before the Mahlers' first post-asylum party, Mary stands before a blender, dropping in one cooked potato after another for a vichysoisse, almost ready to lose it herself. For too long she has been the one holding things together. What they could really use around here would be an earthquake.

Lana peruses random newspapers in New York City coffeehouses, perusal being the habit Lana continues from her parents' parallel-world breakfast table. Lana skips class to look for random jobs and finds her mother unavoidable, Mary's book *Wishing for Cordelia* having taken off enough that her face seems a kid's nightmare: everywhere she goes, Mary is quoted, Mary opines, Mary's photo smiles back at her from papers crumpled by others. Does anyone know the ways she has failed?

Lana will not speak of this to Rose, successfully avoiding any café, park or dorm space where Rose might find her since only Rose would be curious enough to pester her about where Lana had sequestered herself these last few months. Instead Lana stays in the single dorm her suitemates call, behind her back, the Crazy Hamster. She registers for classes in psychology, classes she barely attends, and tells herself it will be made up for, that she will still graduate with everyone else given the credits from the fancy high school to which her parents sent her a whole lifetime ago. One morning she realizes she must be depressed but thinks it has nothing to do with her and everything to do with the entire east coast since even when Lana gets on a random train to escape Manhattan for the country she finds not liberty but moldering cemeteries, overcrowded and blatant, pressing forward into village greens, the whole zone infatuated with flags and patriotic rituals as if the country had magically grown older than its two hundred years. The life-span of a single tortoise, as Vic loved saying. Lana tries. She tries to stay open to new people but keeps finding every person in the east hides a strong covert obsession with class and on top of that, she has started to miss the drugstores and billboards of California, the ones highlighting contraceptives, youth creams, exercise tricks, scented pleasures. All the ones here scream in block letters of panacea against hemorrhoids, corns, incontinence, bad weather, bad breath, mood swings.

Against. The operative word on this coast seems to be against. As in the idea of life working against a person. On a few occasions, Lana passes by a television and spots two white-teethed New Yorkers proclaiming against each other regarding the way men and women make decisions. When they agree only on the pioneering work of Mary Guzman Mahler, this whole famous-mother thing fills Lana with nauseating pride, because how obvious that Mary has aced the world of the Mahlers. And how short Lana has fallen, far from Vic's goals, her father of course having wished Lana would have become yet another egghead prized for the egg.

One time the pixels on a morning talk show form into Mary and perhaps for the first time Lana truly sees her mother: Mary with her tapered forehead, an uncaged beast, long and graceful, turquoise earrings dangling. Lana gets it. Her mother is happy after years spent in the cage of Vic's name. She has emerged with her mind speedy, laugh refined, a cough hiding how much she revels in the moment.

> When we say a girl comes of age, we don't mark with sufficient ritual her emergence into what is actually a secret society, its codes, skullduggery, incantations and rituals as intricate as any found by Mead in Samoa.

You could almost discern the immensity of her gratification, her manner in nice contrast to the TV host's crudity. Lana has never seen her mother this way and now feels raped into admiration for the chattering monkey on the screen.

In response, Lana writes the parental units a letter in which she says she wants to blend back into a tribe made up of anyone but her birth family.

And because she leaves no address and moves out of her crazy single and because she needs something beyond their money, which until then has been diplomatically and negligently accessible from any ATM, she does actually call home on April Fools' Day from an untraceable pay phone in the spring of what should have been her final year of college. She asks Mary to avoid coming to her graduation though behind her expression bleats a plea to which her mother might be congenitally deaf: chase me but don't ever lock me up again.

A week later, a note from the college comes to Mary and Vic, copied to their daughter, suggesting Lana has lied, that she will not graduate, that she has done little more than stumble forward from one semester of incompletes and academic probation to the next, having apparently been persuasive in private meetings. An appended note by an unsigned hand says that

> familial trauma has interfered with Ms. Mahler's successful achievement as a student. As such, the committee recommends that she be afforded incompletes and a chance to make up her work for a designated period, while also strongly encouraging medical supervision.

But could Mary have guessed any of that when Lana called on April Fools'? The pearl of their discontent is still well-cultured, a girl for whom finishing college should have been easier than a roll off a hospital bed.

"You don't want to be around all those proud parents," Lana says in that conversation, taunting them from her pay phone, trying to speak their lingo.

"Why not?" Mary asks, entering the trap with presentiment.

"Can't you listen? Please."

"I'm just saying wouldn't it be nice for you if we came to celebrate? Your graduation. It's an accomplishment."

"But Mary. Mom. You really don't want to be one of those parents. You know, double-parked outside the dorm room. I've seen them. They wait in some fuel-efficient rental to whisk everyone home for what?" She waits before the dart. "You think this moment is any different than getting me out of an asylum?"

The logic doesn't track, that much Mary knows.

As they talk, wind whistling near the pay phone by the church with its leering iron gargoyle, Lana hears the strain in Mary's voice and the way she tries to bridge, clearly deciding whether or not to bend down and be submissive, showing her mother's neck to keep Lana on the phone a bit longer. She doesn't. Instead she stays polite, accepting, respectful of Lana's wishes.

"That's all you have to say?" asks Lana, disappointed. "I can listen."

"I'm at a loss," her mother says. "Is there anything else you—?"

To which, in answer, Lana clicks the phone dead.

She stands, hand burning on the phone for a second, staring into the gargoyle's face, unsure why she had hung up. Mary used to say within earshot of Lana that being a mother is a guessing game and that one day Lana would understand: it is easy to imagine Mary saying this now to the receiver in a room gone dark. At least Mary had always tried her hand at the game, never using great rationale to prop up her arrogance as Vic had, Mary never truly slipping away from being a parent. As if her baby's tenancy in her womb had left a permanent stain, as if Mary lacks Vic's methods for freeing himself. And so what if Mary had found her refuges, her absentmindedness and submersion into work, so what if she loves her assistant a little too much, at least she would always stay a mother connected to her daughter, guilt scripting her veins.

That second Lana wonders if she had been too harsh, this second after the phone call beginning a lifetime of feeling worse. Once you act like an ogre, it becomes doubly hard to forgive a mother for her kindness. Hand still on the phone, a regretful Lana imagines Mary as an aged woman on her deathbed, Mary saying to Lana: above all, the person I need forgiveness from is you.

To which her daughter would say, with a queen's nobility: I'm sorry, mom, I was the one who should have said sorry to you.

Years later, Lana will keep creased and folded in her wallet the newspaper article on the death of Mary, the article citing her contributions if shrouding whatever had led up to the terminus. Keeping Mary's obituary in her wallet will be Lana's whisper of an apology.

1988–1989

Right when Rose is thumbing want ads and thinking she will never make a difference, unable to deafen herself to the exhortations of the commencement speaker imploring the seniors to do big generous things in life, Lana shows up a few days after graduation. She just appears at the door, mum about her great disappearing act.

The last Rose knew, some months earlier, before heading off to Roanoke for some useless choreographic internship, she had suggested to Lana she take a vacation from the dorms by staying to oversee Rose's apartment and its real subletter, the itinerant premed Debbie. On Rose's return from Virginia, however, she found a note from Debbie studded with exclamation points, describing how one weekend she had found Lana in a craze. First Lana had turned the whole apartment into one giant recycling bin carpeted with shredded newspaper. Not to mention that Lana had used all Debbie's eyeliner to write formulae for creativity on the walls. What else could the premed do? She had fled the place, not without first summoning Lana's parents from France. Apparently the parents did descend a few days later, scooping their daughter away but failing to clean up Lana's mess, which included not just shredded paper but an empty hypodermic, all that Debbie had to clean up, though she was no reliable witness given her last act—leaving Rose with months of rent unpaid—and her temerity in grousing about Rose's knack for choosing crazy friends.

Rose found the histrionic premed's note incredible. First, the odd unity of the effort was disturbing. Would Mary and Vic have ever united in scooping Lana up? It seemed too unMahlerian to be true. But how else had Lana vanished? Rose preferred to think instead that Lana had entered a new boyfriend or bohemian tunnel, slinking into another dark unreachable place only to emerge with some glittery treasure and a gypsy beau. Maybe the premed was covering her own debt with the story of Lana's craze. Or maybe she was just jealous. Though it was also true that Rose lacked courage to call the Mahlers and find out why Lana had gone AWOL from college, telling herself she didn't want to mistakenly inform on her friend. Also, Rose did not think she could stomach the usual telephonic banter with Vic, a flirt and flutter that used to speed her pulse along through some fidgety tête-à-tête.

Because Vic always won. On the phone, as Lana said, he loved busting people's chops, especially Rose's, in whatever mode suggested itself to him that day. How would the conversation go other than some variation on *hello, Mister Mahler? Oh, sorry, you're right, Vic? Do you happen to know where I could reach Lana? Why do I need to tell you first? Well, okay, I'm studying choreography. Choreography. No, I only dance sometimes. Well, my mom does sort of think it's a waste of my college education. Okay, but why call bodies moving through space any more a useless endeavor than, I don't know, musical notes through time? Thank you, but before college you're saying I wasn't clever? Touché back* in one squirm of a conversation, playing cards in Vic's game with all the rules Rose could never master and now with the added twist that as a college girl, she could not tell whether she wished the old-time Lola-Vic game of her high-school years to intensify or abort.

She would hang up elated and besmirched and despite all that, have no real clue about Lana's whereabouts. Better to wait and trust Lana would surface. Far better. Whatever Lana was going through could not be much worse, Rose felt, than her own genius for getting her heart broken in new unfathomable ways with what seemed to be a flair for finding boyfriends with messy forelocks and merciless talents for fun.

The important thing is that once Lana returns, once Rose sees her old friend, gaunt at the door days after graduation, days after Rose had packed her own mother Joan off into an airport taxi, Lana is love. Lana might be avoiding her eyes, she might be tender-footed in stepping back into the apartment, heading straight for the mustard couch to collapse into it but of course Rose must forgive her the silence, flattered as ever to be back inside whatever holds them together.

"Sorry," says Lana from the couch. "All that stuff."

Whatever was real the second before Lana appeared now turns ghost, Lana studying her twisting hands. Rose wants to wallpaper-strip the sadness right off her. "You were at your parents' house?" is what she lets herself ask.

"For a bit."

"My mom and I looked everywhere for you at graduation. They must have made a mistake, leaving your name off the program or something."

"Yeah. Do I owe you money?"

"Not really. That premed does though."

Lana had plunged so readily onto Rose's couch, clearly making any abode of Rose's her second home that Rose could just launch back. Never mind months of silence or seemingly impermissible questions, Rose would have signed over rights to any future without Lana. "I'm sure whatever happened when you left wasn't your fault," says Rose. "That premed drove me batty too."

All Lana had done was this: she had stood at a door, crossed a threshold, fallen onto a couch. How simple were the ingredients: the raw crudity, the bones and height, the chemical fix of Lana more present than ever.

Vic would have called Rose's question a tautology, but she still had to ask herself later that night how could such ingredients make so painfully clear what their absence had ripped from the rest of life?

Rose uses her mother's favorite Mexican blanket to make a comfortable night bed for Lana on the sofa. Outside the window, on a roof under a water tower, a family cavorts, busy in bringing out plates, beach balls, jump ropes, hammocks for some evening picnic. Lana back, Rose sparkles, their cast-off wryness a lifeline. "Too messy in the kitchen for you to actually bother cleaning, Rosie," says Lana. "Come tell me what you're planning these days."

"Nothing," says Rose, smitten, "or just my next step," realizing Lana is about to become her next step all over again.

During college Rose was supposed to have become a choreographer and Lana meant to become a composer or painter, maybe a biologist. Now at some ostensibly shared crux they bear witness to the snub-nose paper planes of each other's dreams. With Lana having shown up, mainly herself if with a few new eccentricities, such as her smoker's laugh and the way she never parts with the ratty beaded purse she keeps under her pillow at night, the two girls seem ready to make some double-bladed point to each other about how to ignore aspiration. They will slum as a way to get the friendship back and the act will sweep away boyfriends, ignored phone calls, loneliness, parents, disappearance. Only once does Rose ask Lana what has made her so glum. "You maybe don't know about all the abortions?" she says. "After the ones you took me to, I mean. Once I tried throwing myself off the top of a bunk bed just to not have to go through one. Or I don't know. Something seems to have cost me something," and that is as far as the conversation goes. The friendship needs ease and toward this point they unite, taking on the mantle of the bohemian slummer as their best revenge on whatever has cost them both.

What they try to focus on is jobs. As Rose reminds her old friend, doesn't everyone say how important that first post-college job is? Lana mainly wants any job that ignores her dad's connections, waitress, undertaker, she didn't care. Her first week back in New York, Lana acts as the apartment's secretary, hunched over the dining room table, sipping ice coffee and highlighting POSITIONS OFFERED. One job locale sounds insurance-firm solid, upstate, only a half hour north of the city, enough to give up on the list of temp agencies they haven't called yet.

DANCERS! FLEXIBLE SHIFTS.

"It sounds decent," says Lana, "but I'm not super-ready to leave the apartment, just feeling still a little under the weather?"

Instead Rose is sent to audition, and if she likes it, maybe Lana will come along.

Obedient to the renewed law of Lola, Rose auditions in a room in a strip mall for two short guys, Dick-and-Dan, Dan-and-Dick, their names interchangeable as their rapid-fire commodity argot, though one is tall and bald-pated, loose-jointed while the other is a smaller, toupeed version peering with suspicion over glasses, stiff in shirt-sleeves as if someone had just appointed him footman for the queen of Romania. The two Ds say they love that Rose is a coed or what-ever she is, shooting talk back and forth in spy code, their back office discolored by fluorescence, two desks presiding over paper piles and sample cans of diet powder, the men clearly keeping themselves from any existential brink as much as the Lolas used to, using suppressed fiendish mirth to answer phones in a great mimicry of masters of industry. Tell her send three! I'm taking my usual because she won't be bad tonight.

While Rose waits, a minor skirmish occurs when a tabby-cat named Diva refuses to descend from a file cabinet on which is pasted a bulletin board bearing palm-tree postcards from locales to which employees with bubble handwriting and a love of exclamation points have flown for vacation. Sniggering, Dick-and-Dan phone a few people, asking if anyone wishes to take home the kitty. No takers yet! they volley back and forth, no one wants to play daddy to some lost pussy!

And yet exactly which kind of dance the Ds want for Rose's audi-tion is obscured as if some esoteric task until the taller one puts on a song with a chorus about canasta. Mid-song and sans notice, the Ro-manian footman asks her to take her shirt off—just one pic—marking the moment beyond which Rose can no longer pretend naïveté, since the beginning or end of a song matters little to the Ds, the song mere pretext, the moment a fizzle, the nudie photo a minor heist. A girl of twenty-something, with little artistry, her other half awaiting news back in the apartment, finds the ounce of stamina that lets her pivot back toward the men.

On their first day the tall one picks the Lolas up at the train station, fuzzy dice hanging from the front of his car. That he has a bag of laundry to drop off makes the girls share a backseat smile. Someone thinks they are dispensable, equivalent to a laundry errand, and this droll fact makes the girls reenter their delicious paradox: they live again at the smack-dab center of irrelevance.

They drive around that day, Rose having asked if she could bring a friend, the two of them delegated to the care of a stringy scion from a fallen New England family, the scion not clocking a single backseat smile and thus unaware of his utter charity, à la Jane Polsby, in helping them etherize back to another heist as Lola One and Two. No one really matters: they go in and out of dressing rooms while the scion bounces a rubber ball against store walls with a tournament player's dedication.

Because the scion types Rose as babydoll, she tries on foamy confections. "Go white. Lace fishnets, garters, underwear. Men recognize your type plus pervs go ballistic," he says, never stopping the bounce. "Get your hair in curly pigtails. Stick oversize diaper pins on the lace. When you come onstage, suck a lollipop. Because your face has the hunger of a little girl, you got that sadness in your eyes, plus you could bounce dimes off your butt. You'll see, babydoll helps, you'll go like zero to a hundred, make more."

When Rose emerges his Galatea, he seems pleased, ricocheting his ball off the ceiling. In the meantime he has sized up Lana as a savage woman of experience. "You're leopard, jaguar, ruby red. Start at eighty-five then go slow so you don't get to a hundred too quickly. I have a girlfriend, she's a stripper, but I see way too many naked girls so I always say, hey, keep your clothes on, even during lower-case intimacies if you know what I mean. By the way, take off that ratty purse."

When Lana appears as a red-trimmed leopard, she unfortunately seems to have entered a jungle where Rose cannot find her. Rose tries to keep their backseat smile going but finds her friend gone autonomic as if the costume had transfixed her. Back in the old days, no matter the terrain, Lana would have stayed the same impulsive, goofy girl who never took anyone's talismans too seriously. At least her laugh would have stayed joyful instead of this latterday version, a ratcheting cough only hinting at charm. It will be okay, Rose tells herself, we're in this together.

Once they get to the bar, five o'clock with Lana still too serious in her leopard print, a red velvet choker across her neck, the scion asks Bev, an oldtimer with long nails and a lemur's face, to do Lana's hair in a bedtime bun. Rose stands by in her ridiculous babydoll get-up, suddenly wishing to exit the scene, watching as the oldtimer fingers and sprays Lana's hair, keeping up a train of talk during which she states she is bi, swings both ways, and her boyfriend doesn't mind.

"So what's the thing they keep calling getting to one hundred?" Rose asks oldtimer Bev, who shrugs before jutting her chin stageward where a happy-hour welfare mom sneaks onstage with actual safety-pins seaming her skirt.

"There's your dead end right there," says Bev. The welfare mom kneels at the stagelight's greasy rim, allowing some loner guy who five minutes earlier had been scarfing up twenty-five-cent chickenwings to now stick a beer bottle into her. "That lady," says Bev, "don't get me wrong, loves her kids. Does it for all three. Plus you got to admire the Thai stuff she does, tricks of control. You won't see me doing them. She can get a whole chain of safety-pins going in and out."

Overhearing, bouncing his ball against the bar, the scion muses in his Connecticut accent that the birth canal never fails to amaze. Only six o'clock and two friends almost reunite in a smile, ready to rejoin in the deployment of questionable skills, here in a warren just beyond an interstate overpass with a pumping bass driving guhguhguhguhGUH on a collision course toward skull and groin, under lights hazy and gelled red, the scent of spilled beer and smoke in every breath: push it real good.

Bev wants to teach them how to get dollars to slide in more quickly. "Dance together and you'll get more tips. Older guys especially love love love two girls together, you'll see." Lana will dance with Bev the first fifteen minutes, followed by a duet by Lana and Rose for fifteen minutes, finished by solos. "Chat up men at the bar first so they give you quarters to put in the jukebox. There's your soundtrack. Use the pole and I promise you make fifty percent more. Can't learn in a day what a lifetime of hard knocks gives. But you two will do okay. You're the kind has good chemistry."

Chemistry or not, that first time Rose steps onto the stage with Lana, wrapped by smoke but also the worshipful circle of men's gazes, she gets it. She has arrived! This moment is a lovechild created by all those moments of Lola and Vic, Vic and his ironic, confusing attendance to the Lolas, the whole thing spun by the secret code of all billboards and magazines.

Only Rose's new degree twists the coed-a-gogo moment into anything more illogical. B.A., big assumption, bare-faced amour, bitter about-face, she plays with the words while waiting in the dark of the stage, teased, ready, music playing, that driving bass of the song that is everywhere that summer, guhguhguhguhGUH chichichichichi. Rose knows she has arrived at the end of some freeway with the choice being to either jump or turn back. Onstage she and Lana will share one last look before the dance begins, the look containing almost everything, locking up their mobile morality, a flock of everyone outside the Lolas, the policemen who used to sigh and wave them off without writing up tickets. Again the Lolas will get off with another dereliction of duty.

Though after that first second Lana never peeks at Rose or out at the crowd, her diffidence so appealing. She acts as if she needs nothing, her system self-sufficient, running on its own juices, Rose seeing for the first time that Lana's beauty has to do with how she never cops to much, her brown nape forever turning away. While Rose stares out, brazenly curious under the thinnest veil of shyness, her tongue forever inching forward.

At the peak of a certain power, the men's desire becomes a hand persuaded to move. You find a way to convince this hand to uncurl and respond, to come forth with the bill you tuck into your garter. After their first night, on the train ride back, Rose tries speaking of a hand that Lana doesn't want to discuss. Why does she love to hide her titillation? She admits to nothing.

Home in the roach-friendly kitchen over the Hudson, they seem to skulk together, pulling damp bills from a paper bag, each George Washington or Abe Lincoln a mark of a second, an exchange of capital, one favor granted and another withheld. "Really, what's wrong with it," asks Rose, "given that aren't all jobs a form of prostitution?

You keep yourself from following your bliss for some period of time and then capital squirts toward you. At least we're performing our dance authentically. Any other job we could get would serve someone else's system and wouldn't be true anyway to whatever self we want to believe in. Or what do you think?"

"I don't know," says Lana. "Not much. It's a job. Sorry. It's just that these days I do better when I don't think too much."

Later Rose will remember the whole package of Dick, Dan, the scion, Bev, the happy-hour welfare mom and their bar as a loss, another strangled death rite though in the moment, sharing anything with Lana spells adventure all over again. What she likes most is when they start the journey, taking the train ride together out from the grand half-egg of Grand Central. As they get off the train, some blocks still to walk, they travel already in that beer-smeared empire in which the girls become not Lola One and Two but Babydoll and Killer Girl. Rose will also like the way the bartender says with force *get up onstage already* and the sweaty collectivity of shoulder-rubbing near the bar with its customers who have spent their day welding, digging ditches, monitoring accounts or sitting in class but who now link, raising toasts to liquid joy.

When the girls enter from the street they must first walk through the legs of a giant neon girl they nickname Trixie, Trixie whose long eyelashes blink into the New York night until last call, blinking like a person trying to stammer the truth but finding it endlessly hard: only on entering Trixie but never on exiting do they notice her neon flash, the girl giving you the chance to come in but not wanting you to leave.

Though Rose's spare room was long ago vacated by the premed, Lana refuses to sleep there, never budging from her lair on the mustard living room couch, hand thrown over her head, lips half open, dead under an eyemask until noon, playing languorous cat to Rose's anxious mouse. So Lana does not talk as much as she used to and has that new horrible stoner laugh, an unfunny ax stuttering on unyielding wood. Still in that apartment they almost find their old ease, Rose trying not to use any of the college vocabulary to which Lana is allergic, the words she says freeze life, *narrative* or *capital* or *locus* or *agency* or *discourse* or *postcolonial.*

Instead, Lana makes lists for the future

flea market
laundry
needle and thread
instant coffee
cream

to fend off chaos, Rose thinks, saying nothing and going forward with the idea that they surrender conversation and just live inside their bodies, tired or working, drinking sugary ice coffee and on the intensive schedule because the managers believe in working coeds hard since coeds burn out quickly, the girls able to share shifts because Killer and Babydoll will accrue distinct cults, which turns out, by July, to be true enough.

The hardened exes come for Lana. The older ex-music-producer guy like an aged bearded lion, ripped at the edges, shirt buttoned too low. The ex–blues musician, the ex–sports player. Plus grimacing college boys, predictions of exness, whom Rose believes will soon become nervous stockbrokers or lawyers with drug problems, dark images of an eternal spring break dancing in their eyes, their baseball caps tipped toward libidinous gravity, their style drawn in uncasual equal parts from batting practice, the ghetto, jails, boys slumped in solidarity as if they, like the dancers, gun for triumph over society's more standard measuremakers.

Rose meanwhile brings on the manual laborers and immigrants, often the crazies and occasionally the guys who call themselves urban like the Vietnam vet from Canada who wears a duck-hunter's hat pulled low over his pink eyes, the vet who each night brings her a different present: a teddy bear, a daisy bouquet, a candy T-shirt reading DADDY'S LITTLE GIRL.

The only place their followings overlap is among the bland white executives.

One night a man reaches into the halo of the stage toward Rose's crotch and speaks the knotted history of the Americas *just give me some of that white gold, girl, some of that white gold.* Late at night the mirror reflects back to Rose's face a surprised little pilgrim girl in lace and pigtails, one Rose cannot recognize at all. For a second, Rose wishes she could find someone better at the controls.

That night and after, Rose tries using a theme song for solos, a climbing harmonic scale, semi-Eastern with its chorus *I will be your father figure* until Lana forbids the indiscriminate use of the song, saying they should take turns given that the melody mesmerizes customers, bringing on daddy-size tips and since there's a traceable bit of love in Lana's crooked smile, Rose accepts all terms of her confinement.

Though toward the end of their seventh month, neither of them making steps toward any more meaningful employment, it comes to Rose how much they stammer their future, almost as badly as neon Trixie outside the bar. Rose had lost sight of what their plan had been: were they supposed to gogo dance until the novelty wore off or they made big bucks or what was supposed to come first?

She dances with Lana, their dance more slack than electric, and into that hammock of time comes the news. On an unseasonably warm afternoon, a spring day midwinter, they take the train together and enter the club through Trixie to find the smoky regret of the previous night already shading into the next night's dream of sexual blandishment, outside light filtering knifelike through the gash in the velvet drapes. Inside they find Thai Don, the club's round-faced owner, bobbing to some unheard music, the folds between his bald head and neck almost winking. Multitasking, he has told them, multitasking is the way to live and at every moment he lives this credo: twirling take-out noodles from a Styrofoam container with one hand, wiping a barglass with the other, yelling on the phone while also signaling the barboy Manuel to quit raising dust with the vacuum.

When Lana and Rose sit at a bar table, Thai Don twiddles the radio dial up.

As Vic has noted often in his books, adrenaline heightens memory: the amygdala holds trauma better than pleasure, a fact that Vic declares forms an argument for attachment parenting, parenting in which the parent seeks to bind the infant to a sense of security, the delusional faith that all life's needs will be met. Because of such amygdalic retention, Rose believes her memory of the preamble to be accurate. Retrospect, however, as people always say, colors all: look back at such moments and all coherent elements already break into particulate, jelly to powder, each gaining charge, meaning, predestination.

Easily Rose can remember other picturesque moments in the friendship—say, the girls with their legs outstretched on a sun-baked boat to a Greek isle, listening to the song about Lola or later, Rose tight-lipped while driving Lana to yet another abortion appointment, a Buster Keaton gasp as her car catches on the train tracks for a few perilous seconds while far off the girls do see an actual train approaching—all moments that Rose could say, in retrospect, had gunshot the start of their friendship's descent. Instead she ends up believing that in that bar's womb came their first irrevocable loss, the one from which they will never recover.

While her amygdala still hums at a pleasant low-grade buzz, before the moment etches into some unfortunate forever, Rose sits at the bar table and is punctured by love for the place, for the scent of gallons of beer spilled into Astroturf like some ancient peasant sod-seasoning practice, the moment sharp in its dusty column of light and the girls' fake nonchalance, for Lana sewing red and gold jewels onto her costume. What Rose fails to recall, as she later tells the story to Hogan, is whether the girls felt at all flush with their old-time criminal glee or had some sullenness already permeated everyone?

Right before the wormhole, Thai Don doesn't hang up the phone and doesn't turn down the radio but does turn up the TV to an imbecilic loudness because, as he shouts into the phone, he is heading out back to have it out with the cook and doesn't want to miss the chance to see his cousin who sometimes fills in for the afternoon newscast though today it is someone else, a woman discussing in a tone both urgent and unfeeling the Good Life First! policy, some kind of new eye-for-eye justice in the penal system.

This will be the moment the girls first hear mention of Vic, three times in a row, unmistakable.

Vic, Victor Mahler, Mahler.

"What was that?" says Rose half joking, pinching her friend's arm. *Legions of fans. Protest. New judicial policy.*

Already Lana has understood. In that vertical column of light the wormhole opens and she is slipping through. Already Rose won't be able to catch her.

Rose still doesn't get it. "Your dad?" and can't help stuttering. "They said what? Your dad did what?"

To which Lana flashes her deer's look. She touches the beads that are supposed to flash, grabbing the strobes when her hips shimmy. "I'll be back," she says. Rose stays pinioned, craning forward trying to understand the news though she can't, some new topic about a fallen bridge already taking over. When Lana returns, five minutes later, ten, beckoning Rose to the door, her face looks punched. "You come outside?" she squeaks and Rose follows her out. Lana says she had tried calling her parents and when that hadn't worked she had finally reached their Spruce Street neighbor. "The neighbor said it was self-defense. As if Mary," and Lana can't finish. "As if my mom."

Cars may have been shooting by but on that sidewalk the two girls stay safe. The only people who might arrive would be earlybirds like the duck-hunter and it is still too early for him. A few cars slow, mistaking the girls' intention, but move on soon enough.

In the way Rose has waited their whole friendship to hold Lana, beyond their night in a Greek trench, Rose reaches out, understanding only that Mary is gone, for once not asking more. And though their old-time physical connection used to feel like live branches, thorny knots rubbed against each other, a hand flopped over a nighttime waist, now she hugs Lana as if they melt together, a river of bright green molecules flowing between.

"You've always been there for me," Lana tells Rose's shoulder, "from the start. You're the best partner I'll ever have."

Rose shakes her head, guilty. In such a terrible moment, a baby trusts her.

"You know me," says Lana and then her shudder starts. There they stand, joined together for once, Lana quaking, Rose realizing that this moment marks her friend's greatest openness. So that when they finally pull apart, Rose asks what turns out to be the wrong question, since who cares what Lana's next action will be when Rose cares only about the extension of their moment. Her question unfortunately brings Lana back to herself.

"Guess just tell them I'm leaving?" says Lana and what Rose will remember is their fluency at avoiding plans, both telling the other not to worry, they'll see each other later. On that worn road outside Thai Don's bar, Rose imagines Lana showing up at the apartment to sleep on the sofa as usual, believing this roadside moment together will herald some unguessably close era for the Lolas.

All that night Rose covers for Lana, dancing an apology for not being Lana, for not having Lana's rude grace, covering the double shift for both her own hardcore nutcases and Lana's disappointed exes, the cabal of hairy-chest followers. This moment will stick so that the next morning on a scrap, once Lana leaves for good, Rose will write an apology that steals from what Vic said in that long-ago bookstore reading:

> To all the men who were there last night, I am sorry. No one knows
> with greater pain than I do the disparity between Lana and me.

After the shift, the bleary pre-dawn after the revelation, Rose is uncustomarily alone, Lana's bag at her feet at the upstate train station platform, the minute-hand stuck in place at 2:30 in the morning with four bandanna'd gang members shuffling toward her down the platform. One seems to have nodded to the others to start the approach, hands in their pockets, smiling at the girl because time is theirs to play out like the length of a magician's red scarf, smiling as one reaches deep into his back pocket for what could be a knife-handle or gun-barrel.

And Rose could not have prayed for what happened next: Lana's bag overflowing with white goo, pouring out of the bag from some bottle of mousse and exploding into a river as if out of a slapstick Busby Berkeley comedy. Whatever the stuff is, the guys stop and laugh. She hears one of them: *shitload!* The leader punches another guy, the sheer craziness making the two still laugh when, minutes later, the train slides in to the station.

It is the gift of criminal glee all over again, commuted, and Rose can't wait to tell Lana about it though from now on she will have to carry such moments permanently solo. Whatever the news about Mary, riding back to her apartment, Rose exults at life, at Lana, at how no matter what, they will swim through any mess. All the way downstate she hugs her friend's sopping bag. Half turning away, as always, Lana had half saved Rose.

On the next day, right off, Lana betrays whatever their promise had been. She leaves as relics only her books and clothes and necklaces in the apartment so that for years, wherever Rose moves, she ships and stores them, packed boxes of sentiment, LANA'S STUFF traveling with her everywhere.

You can't put gold back in the mine, ore back in stripped earth. The morning after Lana learns of her mom's end, definitively, she stands still as a monument in the light tweaking Rose's apartment. Outside, eleven stories below, the gray Hudson stays a long flat snake. Lana may be unsure but as her father had once told her, no westerner stays east forever. Of all days, an invitation, embossed on pinked ivory, has traveled through boxes and bags and hands, only to land, practically vibrating, on the dwarf entrance table in Rose's apartment.

Lana holds the invite in her hands, her eyes trying to tame the devilish embossed words: the card notes a Berkeley event on the intersection between neuroscience and psychology and that Vic Mahler is to give the keynote speech. The words tug off the paper and start to float.

On a morning when even boats plying their trade on the flat river look like they haul depression, Lana doesn't want to learn more. *Acedia*, her father called it, the depression that even the bacchanalian Greeks had to fight off. Invite between her fingers, Rose still asleep, Lana feels return as a wrench in the genes.

Without considering, *the manic defense* as Vic would say, she starts throwing random items of clothes into a pile, making a mobile nest of her belongings. Even after Rose awakes, Lana keeps going, not listening to Rose say how tired she is, Rose who apparently had stayed up late to watch the news. She only hears Rose ask: "Why leave though?"

The best Lana manages is to say: "Close flanks?"

"Ranks?" says Rose, incorrigible.

Of course Lana can't explain much to Rose who stays loud in speechless judgment, scrambling up eggs for the two of them.

"You have no idea what funny thing happened last night. Before I got on the train," Rose says finally, her back toward Lana.

When Lana doesn't ask, Rose pushes a plate toward her friend. "Here."

Lana ignores the offering, instead rising to pound her nest of stuff into the army satchel from her father's early immigrant years, green and boasting a red-star button she fancies is Communist. She will be happy and not creeped to carry his bag, a talisman meaning some union will be found and that she will be able to shoulder all appropriate burdens.

"You're not hungry?" Rose asks, already knowing that the most she'll get now will be a shrug.

In their goodbye at the door, they stay stiff: no more green-river hug as on the day before, no prickly branches, just two sets of bones, creatures maybe already dead, salt, adipocere, nothing.

Once out that door however, Lana becomes alive as she has ever been, lacking gravity. They—whoever they are—they have finally set her free. How wonderful to escape an old friend's questions and judgment, how free to go in the elevator down to the lobby so out she may walk, anonymous, a woman with a scarf around her neck striding past upper Broadway's laboring and landed gentry, on the same road on which deer once ran from cougar, where according to her father in his one visit to her in college, Indians had sold off an island too quickly, a fact he mentioned in relation to her own atavistic memory and more universal laws of aggression. Now she doesn't care what anyone has said, instead walking as if new in love all the way to Port Authority just to get on the first westbound Greyhound while holding the idea of reunion with Vic as a dim magnetic center.

A bus ride will be the perfect act, granting time to rearrange inner partitions. In line, some businessman asks where she is going but she misunderstands the guy as asking why. She clutches her father's credit card before answering: to figure things out.

"Where you going, miss?" the lantern-jawed station clerk will also ask, making her understand someone must have screwed with the be- fore and after of things: she can tell she keeps giving the wrong an- swer to the wrong people. Instead of her destination, she says, for the last time in years: "Lana—" faltering over the last name "—Mahler." Because it hits: Mahler will now mean belonging not to the small coterie of fame but rather the larger clan of infamy.

When she reaches Berkeley, she goes home because home should still be a place where a person won't have to explain.

Except home is yellow-taped with DO NOT ENTER, a black official car parked in the driveway. And she is beyond tired. From Omaha on, she had sat next to a garrulous addict with a determination to ply her with black beauties but since he reminded her of the days of Tumble- weed and her mother's disappointment, Lana did play a game with him, accepting one hot pill only after every other stop, which meant that by the time they reached Reno's boil all the chafed edges had come alive, making the bus jump into one sloshy mess around the pilgrims, each with a story to be told if time allowed, problem being that time slanted and would end in a crash of earthquakes and doom, horror and history, odd stones jutting up out of the desert, dinosaur bones and worn lassoes, given that all these people seemed to think they were heading somewhere better but the ride would self-combust and seal their fate. The driver, a rotating series of drivers, constituted a multi- headed Hindu savior, the riders and their wizened Dust Bowl faces his multiply condemned. When the skinny pill-proffering passenger got off in Sacramento, Lana entered a mood that didn't lift until she saw the Oakland port and the sexy tiredness of the whores with a dissipation worse than her own, almost good as sea air in their restorative powers because they made the shared faith of the Mahler family return.

Waiting for the luggage hatch to open, she hadn't wished to hear the radio news that pierced her cool.

At one point to the black-beauty man, she must have confessed something revealing because he'd been impressed. He said he knew Vic Mahler's work because his older sister had joined some sort of spiritual commune thanks to the great buckaroo Vic!

Here she is, trying to return to cool, almost laughing at the idea of buckaroo! being used by anyone as a compliment, almost laughing after the bus ride and radio news and another quicker ride to get to Spruce Street, not quite in her body hiking up the hill with its leaf-strewn sidewalks, roots bulging to crack the old sidewalk where shaggies used to stake out bed sites. Here she is almost laughing in the dappled light of her home street, the light a whisper that everything might be okay.

Except it isn't okay at all, she can't enter her home, not according to the bored oil-sheened cop who looks over his sunglasses, telling her that he has orders to prevent driveway ingress. She can't get inside. When he looks over his sunglasses one too many times at her, some fibers start to split.

Worse than the news as it had crackled forth in the gogo place, the spire of coasters toppling as the television had blared forth news of Vic, worse than any end she had imagined is this yellow-taped proscription. No home. She repeats dumbly back to the guy, trying not to cry: "I can't go inside?"

"You have nowhere to go," he states back, bureaucratic tone shading reflective. "No friends? Family?"

Worry tickles her throat, a fringe preventing her from swallowing. She shouldn't have left Rose, she realizes, Rose would have been able to deal. She would have grabbed Lana's hand, brought her somewhere, shaken her back to the best that could be done. While this guy is telling her that, far as he knows, Vic is being held in the famous penitentiary until the trial date. Already she can hear her father's mockery, the way he had mocked Mary, Rose, everyone: what, Lana, you wanted to ride in on a white horse and save me?

Once she had gone, together with Rose and Vic, three dayfarers on the Alcatraz ferry to the island prison just for them to make clever, secretly awed remarks about the graffiti in cells, the scratching of cartoonish naked women, the attempts at bison by latterday cavemen, and as they'd taken the ferry back, the trio had remarked on the desperation of prisoners who had dared escaping in the cold Pacific. "At least those who stayed in prison got time to think," Vic had said.

For the fleetest of seconds, standing on Spruce Street before their old home, Lana does envy Vic his cell, a place to gather the pieces, and while the oily police guy talks, her solution comes. Rather than go to the prison, she will use the credit card of a condemned man, go and book herself into the Montrepose Hotel, the pale hotel with its crenellated walls and fancy pool and tennis club to which her parents, for all their dinner-table socialist ideals, belonged.

Alone at the hotel buffet overlooking the bay, she will stay as Lana Mahler, nibbling on biscotti and crab cakes and signing her name on credit slips as if no one will ever bother following her trail. In the gift shop she will find a fluffy boa to wear as she paces down the halls while eyeing lonely travelers. She will spend a few mornings simmering in the hot tub listening to the lucre-laden gossip of local therapists only to retire in the afternoons to her cell to watch cop shows. How many days can she go on like this?

Third day of exile in the luxury of Montrepose, she gives up and calls a cab, asking the scarred driver to go across the bay and leave her at the gates. On the bridge the driver tries to get her to talk, saying he's only driving while getting his real gig going since what he truly believes in is the future of California, the poetry of real estate. "You know I served time in the pen too once," he tells her, looking disappointed when she makes no inquiry. Only then does he ask who she's going to see, a question she ignores until they get to the gates when she dares stumble over the name: Victor Mahler.

The cabbie whistles an appreciation. "Brave girl!"

"More like stupid girl."

"Want to get the guy's autograph for me?" says the cabbie, probably not meaning it, handing over his night phone number on a card and leaving before she can tip him. She stares at the dollars she meant to offer, damp in her hand. It must be blaringly clear how much she needs everyone's mercy.

Inside prison gates, unless you're a prisoner, there's no possibility of slacking. So go through with it, she wills her legs, walk forward, you got here, go on. As soon as the first gate clicks shut behind, she sees that once officialdom begins, you can't break what you've started without the tracer of your ghost exiting videocams and logbooks, your hand stamped with invisible ink numbers in unwashable memory. At multiple stations, freezing from an air-conditioning system gone supersonic, she tells guards with brilliant eyes, again and again, in total humility, that the person she has come to see, whom she would like to see, her status writ officially, is Victor Mahler.

Lana Mahler, visitor, wishes to see Victor Mahler.

Having to write his name above hers is such a horrible confession of need, far more than she had ever confessed.

One of the many ironies she considers during a wait long enough to make any visitor reconsider intention is how the Mahlers have never been a greeting-card family. Though Mary always kept careful records of her daughter's illnesses, pages tabbed and highlighted—ear infection 1974, strep 1978, mono 1980—she had never taught Lana the protocol of writing happy birthday to anyone. When the officials make Lana wait, she sees the other visitors as if they are a flock of greeting-card homing pigeons, little groups of people thrust into an inhospitable milieu who all appear to be clutching greeting cards, as if these alone could wing them home to the dynasty of happy sentiment, a bubbled and italicized world of births or anniversaries. Kids and tired mothers and girlfriends alike all hold these cards aloft. The proximity of these happy-birthday families and their tiny flags of normalcy makes Lana's skin crawl. She had not asked for intimacy with people unable to help their proclivities toward celebration, people with not just cards but also buckets of fried chicken, fingering messes of tiny bones and amber skin onto white tables, their backdrop a paralyzed line-up of singletons, lone mates or parents, seated against walls as if delegated to hold them up, viewing this pageant of kinfolk with resignation or disgust. Between these two groups, the greeting-card flock or the singletons, Lana does not know where to sit but finds the corridor no better, made up of a bank of pay phones and nicotine-scented girls in tight jeans pacing, skinny from anxiety and dragging infants along for the ride.

Near the fried-chicken gaggle then, Lana finally tries settling onto a plastic chair designed by a mauve-favoring sadist, closing her eyes and willing herself not to think what will happen when her number appears on the screen and shoots her out of her purgatory.

She will say to Vic that now at least she can find him more easily. Or anything to get the dividend of his smile, the one recognizing irony as their shared birthright, scorn being an aspect of her family Lana truly misses, craving it as if you could bite into wit like the pica that makes pregnant women devour mud. Back before Lana lost the promise of her promise, the family's jokes had kept them together, promising a family indivisible against the greater world's banality or lesser intelligence. For one sharp second Lana thinks of Rose, considering that maybe this humor was what Rose had coveted too, a derision promising to redeem tribulation by making all slick, nothing sticky.

The person Lana will not think of is Mary. Cannot and should not, as in the old fairytale her mother used to read about a lost bunny. Cannot and will not, certainly not in this greeting-card territory. She will not admit the desire to know. Though of course a question pulses. Why more than how, though maybe the why acts as an asymptote slouching toward the how. How does a person do this to a loved one? How can a tower of thought justify any part of this badness? The why and how blend while an acid starts to eat out her insides. Why would you do this to any of us? On the ride in, the cabbie prattling on, Lana had sworn silently not to ask Vic: let him come forth.

And when they finally bring her to sit in the chair where he too will be brought in, this trapezoidal visitation room that makes all entrants infants, its interior walls so white they make her caffeinated brain scream, she sees the scene from outside her body, aware of herself as the prisoner's clean-faced fresh-skinned daughter, hair pulled tight. Sometimes Mary used to call Lana a daddy's girl or a papa's girl, the kind of comment that leaves a daughter no exit. Whatever form Lana's refusals have taken, Mary is right in this claim as she has been right in so much, Lana unable to exit being Vic's little girl, even now while waiting for him to appear wishing he will still find her his funny, lucky, pretty, smart or just plain good daughter, the one who at Me & Me was enough to give him reason to live.

When they do lead him in, Vic shaven and in green scrubs, so real and yet also a thousand layers removed, the urge comes over her to bite through layers and kiss his neck, to find papa by actually smelling him.

Though he doesn't take her hands and doesn't lean in for a hug; does intimacy flout regulations? His grin lopsided as if prison has already chomped off half and if it weren't for his eyes she would almost think this oddity an impostor. Already these few days inside have undone some of Vic. "Hey," she says, softly, nothing better at hand.

"Great to see you!" he says, tone a mockery.

She wants to aim for a semblance of a common language. "Mahlers and institutions—" The choke of the thought. Eight days ago there were three Mahlers. Eight days ago her mother was alive and now Lana sits across from a father dressed as a prisoner with a peevish smile and eyes asking why bother? Better to be wholly inside his skin or flee than have to look upon this new intolerable shard of Mahlerdom.

Yet she need take no lead because Vic does what he always does, taking her unawares, continuing as if they had just rounded some turn in a long-standing conversation. "When you were born," he says, leaning forward, hands clasped as if in conclusion, inappropriate as usual. "You had in your body all the eggs of your future kids."

"What's the point of that?"

Just like that they are back to their usual sparring: such return could be almost reassuring and help erase these walls.

I am the one he never—

Never what? *Never had*: the thought is crazy, qualifying as what she in her own institution time never called hallucinations but halloos. She sits motherless in an institution. Until this exact second she had been a child watching the balloon slip out of her grasp and float away, believing it could bounce back.

The guard she hadn't fully noticed, a surly beef hock of a man leaning against the wall behind Vic, informs them that at lunch the inmate must decertify to the refectory with Cell Block A. The visit will have to clock shut in less than ten minutes.

"Fewer," mutters Vic. "Fewer than ten minutes. Not less."

The guard shrugs. Lana has fewer than ten minutes for her to notice for the first time the vertical symmetry of the gouged cleft in Vic's chin and above his lip, her vision blurring so the clefts become two eyes winking vertically. Lacking any other pleasantry, the two of them staring at each other with no map, she tells her father she'd never noticed those marks.

"Cleft in chin, devil within. You never saw it? I always had a deep frenulum. But when you get down to it, no one ever sees anyone truly. Tell me I'm wrong," says her father. Then he whispers: "How'd you get—" tripping and almost saying *home* "—here?"

EDIE MEIDAV

The guard interrupts: less than five minutes before mess.

"Fewer!" Vic barks at him before turning back to Lana. "If you came at the right time, they would have given us an hour," says Vic, for the first time showing desperation, the tensility of a wire about to snap, the most intolerable thing she has seen yet.

Once Vic had opined that need blinds people and hence it is important to love without need. Was it from him that she had inherited the repulsion? Need blinds people and hearing his need she calms the itch in her feet so ready to run, already knowing how good the coastal wind will taste outside, her minutes in an ammoniac room a lifetime too long, her temples starting to pound to the rhythm of I-didn't-ask-for-this, the grandeur of a headache rolling in from the sides.

For want of anything else she asks: "Your room's okay?" immediately tuning out whatever he says next. Lips moving, shorn head angled, he offers a simulacrum of a conversation to which she is deafened, given how the instant bloats into nausea: she has become too important to Vic.

She drums fingers on the soft plastic rimming the edge of the table, seeing grime pressed into its veins along with crescent moons from all the fingernails that have dug in. Signatures of the rueful, angry or hopeless among the visitors and as her milk-and-fish time in the sanitarium had taught her, isn't there something horribly satisfying about what an institution knows? Such places know human need, their intelligent design good at predicting that fingernails will dig into soft polyurethane, showing brilliance in how they soften edges or set up bedtimes, feeding troughs, liquid nourishment, punishments, visiting hours, all with a higher daddy-logic than any daddy can muster. She wants to say some of this but all she can do is drum, things she might say clotting her throat.

"They might move me," he says. "Old Parcel. Who knows."

"You'd rather stay here," she says, gentle as can be, making herself say "Papa?" and taking his shiver as yes. There is little to tell him but if she doesn't click to it, their time together will have sped on with nothing real having left her mouth. True that a why sticks in her throat but there will be no leaning into anyone here as she has done on a few memorable occasions, no crying on papa's stiff wooden shoulder. On the taxi ride in, the driver yammering on, she had worried over Vic, believing in some secret cranny she might come as a savior, the same child to have pressed soothing cloths to papa's fevered forehead.

Now she cannot find the ingenuity of that child. Nor can she, with time ticking down, keep from asking. "I was just wondering," she begins, starting again. "What, I mean—?"

At which he, as always, knows everything. Now he grants the other half of his smile, broad enough to chill. All of him smiles, shrewd, his shorn head and undimmed eyes smiling as if he were the free one coming to see her in a cage. Maybe he can sense the tiger stirring her skin, aching for escape, and though later she will do what she can to forget it, his smile will hover, a hungry ghost in the coffer of her chest.

Smiling, he leans in before bestowing that one curse.

"My dear," he says. "No need to ask why. You already know why."

"Sorry?"

"Ask your little friend Rose. Your sweet Rosie-anna."

"What?" Now Lana can't help but speak stridently since a loud drill has started up, grinding deep but perhaps only into her head.

"Because," he says, tone slow and even, the way he talks to students, unwearied while his listener stumbles over a hard-to-grasp concept. "You too, Lana, are a kind of monster." He takes her hand across the table for the first time, his so cold she flinches. "You can't escape it, Lana. You have charisma but you will stay a child. Your ego is monstrous. You happen to be one of those monsters of charisma. You suck everything into you. You can't help it."

And surely this smiling patient man would have said more but whatever it is gets lost. Her legs are what propel her out into the hallway and into the hope of never seeing Vic again.

Heart thudding, she leaves the visiting area with the guard, tight-laced in the corridor, her leather purse charged on his credit card in the gift shop slamming her hip like a heavy chain. Once she gets out to wait on a bench for the shuttle back to the ferry, she tries to inhale the cigarette smoke of the other visitors standing around her. But his words keep drumming her just as her fingertips had worked the table. And while her head can understand why need had headlocked him enough that he must punish her, and while one day she will forgive him at least the need, she will never forget the greater sin. On this day he became for the first time the kind of parent who wants to lead his child down the most perilous pathway, a parent who wishes to make a child believe herself nothing but a boomerang, doomed to stay flesh of his flesh.

As a teenager, once, angry at her mother, Lana had locked herself in the bathroom so that with a rusted razor she could work at cutting a tiny swastika into her upper thigh.

Outside the bathroom in the corridor her mother had entreated: "Lana, honey, just tell me you're okay," to a girl who wouldn't interrupt her ecstasy of focus but finally did with a blurt of accusation: "Mary, do I seem okay? You want me to say you're a good mother to get yourself off the hook?"

While waiting for the prison shuttle, Lana cannot help but recall this moment, evidence summoned to support Vic's verdict in the kangaroo court playing out in Lana's mind. The judgment against Lana is horrendous.

Vic is right.

What fact can Lana find to prove she is not of Vic, not a monster? What proves she is anything but selfish? Has she ever truly protected anyone? Has she ever shown caring for anyone but Rose? Is she anything but a monster born of a monster?

Later she will think that if Vic's past success had partly to do with how well he could rewire people's associations, his conversation with her stands as the last of his successes. Locked up, Vic finally managed to brand Lana as a dweller in his realm.

A monster can roam anywhere but belongs nowhere. On the way back from the prison, the drumbeat continues: where is Lana supposed to go when there can be no return? You can't go home again when it no longer exists. Uncleansed by the salt air, she gets off the ferry in San Francisco wishing to shed her skin but lacking a way to buy a ticket away from Vic. And how blessed are all the passengers lined up, wanting to call someone at the pay phone. Because who can Lana call? Who will instruct her?

One person. Yet Lana does not want that particular voice brimming with sympathy, Rose her last ally. Much better to slash away all need. What of Rose and the Lolas could help now? What exists that at the last moment does not veer into being just one more decree against Lana? What belongs to any moment not made of fantasy? All a chimera as Vic loved to say. What in her life had ever been more than a whimsical hope?

Only now. Now is what she can count on, as much a creed as a truth.

Now will obscure her in anonymity in some place like Bakersfield or Chico. Thinking of such benign places and their amnesia, she walks several long city blocks to get on the first bus in the San Francisco terminal, finding it her own blessing that the bus heads not where she expected but to Los Angeles, a target she considers almost a sign, since she and Rose used to write the city as Ellay, Lana once marking this onto Rose's sneakers, saying this meant that one day they would end up there singing in a girl band on Sunset Strip, eminently discoverable. Some smidgen of hope—to be seen and discovered—must still live on in her and Ellay can meet it, as much hope as she can summon for any prospect right now.

On the bus ride south, Lana appreciates that each choice she makes appears in retrospect jewel-like and necessary as if crafted by someone unimpeachable far away: she is absent even as she constitutes herself as a person with a small purse whom others could think halfway respectable, a person with purse and satchel who makes choices, a buyer of tickets and a rider of buses, just another humanoid sack of goods getting dropped off in Ellay's nostalgic downtown station.

Inside the station she steals a moment on one of its old-fashioned wooden benches, liking the shaft of sunlight streaming down into the middle of the station and the scent of sawdust, cologne, exhaust. Passengers from all corners are so distinct she believes she will recall them forever. One woman a sun-creased apple doll in a peasant kerchief, another a tall unshaven musician, another a bouncy young college girl in a sweatshirt. So random, she tells herself, so perfectly costumed. Here in this town is where I should stay because here are enough different kinds of people to do what again? What hope is there again for me now?

She recalls a grid of respectability she and Rose had made up on the train from Grand Central in what seems a lifetime ago:

If I walk neatly but dress messily, people will think I am a
    bohemian, privileged girl, or else maybe Brazilian or Israeli.
If I walk messily and dress messily, they think I'm drunk or
    homeless.
If I walk messily but dress neatly, I could be Russian or East
    Asian.
If I walk neatly and dress neatly, I could be anyone.

She walks neatly out into the city, a Khazar, making exactly three visits to various automated teller machines using both of the cards Mary and Vic have bequeathed her. Each time, a serpent of thrill arises: no one knows her. Her passcode is NOWORNEVER. Between each machine she walks, self-conscious in the stupendous heat of Ellay, one that suits her, melting her link to Vic in his climate-controlled haunt. Shadowy and alone she smirks at the ATMs that don't know her secret, since the eye of the state apparently blinks for long enough to let her take out the daily maximum of her parents' money, planning that tomorrow and the next day and the next she will repeat this act, nothing too late, since it seems that no administrator has yet located the totality of Vic and Mary as a legal entity, no state directive has yet frozen anyone's accounts and in this way, standing at a machine and typing in a number, she gets to be linked to the umbilicus of their funds, getting this whit of grace, a benefit of family, another set of twenty-dollar bills tucked into her bag.

In a used-car lot and without too much stammering she buys a former undercover police car, a brown pimpmobile called an Omega, a steal at six hundred dollars, and without too much worry gets it registered and insured using a version of her name, California Fu, with the used-car saleman believing, for the practicalities of the moment, her claim that the rest of her name—California Fukuji Mahler—is some married typo in the process of being changed anyway, an annulment, a legal change. All these steps of adulthood appeal: she uses cash, believing that no one but a sleuth could find her. In this fallow ground new life could start.

That night she sleeps in a rundown motel where the ice machine next to her room sounds as if it moonlights as a training zone for a hatchet murderer and in the morning, paying in cash, bags under her eyes carrying all she has recently seen, she seeks coffee, walking by a line of homeless people who turn out to be part of a film set. This town defies logic. In her new car, she drives toward the fresher air she thinks a person could find near the ocean, onto one-way freeways that become dead-ends, the labyrinth so maddening that she must pull over just to make a list as if a list alone promises a person sanity:

- Rent post office box
- Look at local newspaper
- Find apartment
- Make résumé
- Get a job

What Lana will carry into her new life, she hopes, is nothing. As ever her religion is the gospel of a contrarian. Back in politically aware Berkeley, the only American town with a foreign policy, her religion used to manifest in the way she liked to find those who ignored political correctness. Similarly, back in the groves of ruthless, driven New York, it had been her joy to meet slackers. In Los Angeles, however, she will find it useless to seek people who are unplastic, since the plastic aspect of Ellay is universal, buffering its citizens from awareness of failure, failure here meaning one gets washed out to sea on a wave of mortality or, worse, public apathy and forgetfulness.

Confused, unable to practice her contrarian religion, seeking a tribe, Lana will therefore bed odd men: the underwear model whose career was sidelined when a car accident fractured his knee so that some strange bone sticks out like a knob from the middle of his shin, her bedmate before the bisexual temp but after the limo driver, before the famous bachelor Italian film director but after the millionaire with his steam bath and walnuts, only simultaneous with the hiphop boy who assists the fading disco queen, right before the handlebar-mustached plastic surgeon who claims to have invented liposuction. What the plastic surgeon will ask her at sunset on a beach: who cares, what does real versus plastic mean anyway?

Years later at Hope she and Rose will compare notes about Ellay and will agree: no one in that town ever admits to hardship since everyone wishes to be a recipient of grace.

In considering their last moment together, Rose will find it odd that Lana had been struck more by her father's atrocity than by the loss of her mother. Sitting in the welfare café near the Columbus Avenue crack houses, Rose reads the article in the paper before calling gogo Dick-and-Dan from the outside drug-dealer phone to say sorry, neither girl can continue dancing, Rose having hurt her foot, Lana burdened by some family matters. Too bad, says Dick-or-Dan, regret pure and economic, you two were just getting going, but we did know what we were getting into—you coeds are all the same!

A bit lost, Rose tries reading the article again, wishing to find Mary between the lines, Mary who looms so large it is impossible to erase her. Even if it is also the case that for years Mary has been performing a vanishing act, slipping around corners with her Cheshire grin. On the surface Mary had seemed plausible enough, mother of a friend, a rose-scented feminist professor teaching ethnography to worshipful undergrads, a mother available at dinnertime, half-telling loving jokes about Lana when she was little. *Remember when Jinga ate that pineapple? Remember when you fell out of the tree?*

This being one of Rose's favorite parts about the Mahlers, how Mary acted as repository of memory for all of them, even for Rose as an honorary part of the family: the photo albums lined up, the bemused self-regard and silent applause that followed each Mahler, immortalized by nicknames and Mary's voice so throaty and kind, a cello bow dipped in honey. For all her abstraction, Mary had also been more embodied than Vic, the one to finger favorite recipes on index cards, to keep the house clean and light-filled—and why did the house on Spruce Street seem so still and magical when late-day light collected in the eaves of those interior arches? Mary and her random swipes of cloth over the counter while using careful Spanish with a maid named Dora, the bad idiom Lana had loved to imitate. *Por favor* Dora. For years Rose had studied Mary, half wanting to be her once she got older, tending an herb garden and stag ferns with the help of hopeful ponytailed acolytes, all the female grad students hanging about to decipher clues about their future selves. Late-fall apples crisp in a blue ceramic bowl she herself had potted; Mary turning to Rose after hanging up the phone, having enrolled Lana in a karate class (so Lana wouldn't be gendered too girly) to ask Rose at the table how her school science project was going. On the stove, a sauce forever bubbling. As Rose made up some answer, Mary would be placing cheese in a quatrefoil on a reclaimed wood board. And yet this same mother twinned the other Mary, the one who never stopped abandoning bits of herself, muttering as she sorted through journals or reams of paper.

Both of us must have been half in love with her, Rose thinks, remembering how the Lolas always borrowed Mary's clothes without asking, the old vintage dresses and worn girlish shoes, the paper-covered buckled poodle skirts signaling Mary's past whimsy. Mary must have known the theft and let it go. They'd slide whatever was needful out of the perfumed closet for a nighttime walkabout and Mary never mentioned a thing.

Mary's job as Rose understood it had something to do with feminism and ethnology in communities, willed or forced. Once, Mary had told Rose she was especially interested in modern-day forms of exorcism and self-sacrifice. Yet to Rose the sacrifice Mary seemed most involved in was her own, rituals of fussing over steaming pans in order to avoid Vic's anger about a late dinner. Mary laying sprigs of mint and basil on plates, ensuring the cheese was appropriately moldy and bread correctly sliced, always trying so transparently and with such a nervous laugh, to whisk to the corners Vic's disdain.

All this Rose knew well. She knew something about the courtship story of Vic and Mary and another bit about how Mary's being able to pass as white had let her get a traveling musical theater grant back in high school, something to let smart Indian kids get off the rez, a gift that, long before the era of Sylvia Plath, had let Mary go to Smith and in her junior year come to Berkeley where she met Vic in the library before some oceanic first date. What Rose knew better than Lana was how Mary had entered Vic's Liechtensteinian French-wannabe culture without a ripple since this part Mary had confided in Rose only. And how Mary showed her daring by letting only city hall see them married, trusting their bond would be forged by a private faith. Together they had moved through promotions, sabbaticals, tenure evaluation, only to land near the twenty-first century with that shared faith in work and as Vic liked to proclaim, a daughter whose inner life remained a mystery.

According to unspoken agreement, clearly Vic was the one who got to occupy the position of brilliance in the household, handsome and irascible, a boy despot coarse, refined and erratic, always in a fit about cleanliness, explaining the reason for such fits with blasphemy and profanity, a man not uninterested in body parts, apparently also not unhappy about leaving beetle-colored stripes of shit on the bedsheets which Lana would laughingly point out to Rose.

And according to Mary's murmured hints, later years had changed him: years of teaching others about ranklessness had made him start to rank everyone as if he had struck some bargain with the devil of hierarchy. She was right: at Mahler parties, Rose had seen firsthand how Vic, in his first attempts at socializing with anyone, liked reminding people of any hierarchy intrinsic to their profession:

To someone whose magazine had gone out of business he'd say: what was the profile of your reader?
To a lawyer: how long 'til you become partner?
To a teacher: how much of the day do you actually teach and how much do you spend filling out bureaucratic forms?
To a writer he'd ask: how are your books selling?
To a dentist: how much income goes toward malpractice insurance?
To a surgeon: how many patients have you lost?
To a psychiatrist: how many clients have committed suicide?

Girls in our culture mate too late, he liked telling Lana and Rose as they were hair-brushing before a walkabout, his rant always riffing off the same basic tune:

It's a conspiracy on the part of Madison Avenue and the cosmetics and apparel industries. Young women spend too much time grooming to attract mates. This phenomenon has assumed the vast proportions of an anthropological problem. Think of all the human and creative capital that would be released if young women would just mate younger and then could pursue vocational fulfillment later when they are more mature and actually capable of making choices out of wisdom. No ape ever grooms so much. Greater petrochemical resources could be conserved, mascara wouldn't leach vast elements out of whale and dinosaur bones, and women, who have often been vital forces toward social change, could actually orient themselves toward the kind of revolution we need. Can you imagine Joan of Arc with well-brushed hair?

What revolution did this *we* need? And what qualified him to make these statements? Vic a professor of neurobiology who had slid into philosophy and finally into social punditry and edicts heeded by a swelling mass of followers who had made him the envy of his colleagues. Vic couldn't stop making statements. You know he has his way of engaging, Mary would explain, apologizing. And part of the problem, of course, was how much the girls wished to take him apart, make him a clock whose workings could be understood, the species male proximate and househeld, bearing the bedside drawer innocuous as a pirate's treasurebox, containing what they found from quick survey of other girl classmates was nothing unusual: the same radioactive-hued condom packages, shopworn magazines and sharp nail scissors that many fathers maintained close to the bedside as talismans of their own bodies' ambitions and regrets.

Rose had taken Vic's eccentricities as some wayward bundle of traits that university life induced. Or as Lana had said: "Look, being a professor must mean you can't help getting warped. Each year your students get younger."

"Isn't that true of every teacher?" Rose had asked.

"But it must be hard. At that age, students are deciding whether or not you're what they want to become," said Lana, repeating verbatim what they had both heard Mary say.

Claiming she loved history, Rose teased out from Vic that he missed the way no one kept up ritual, even if blind collective obedience to ritual had also led whole societies off catastrophic cliffs. Vic's daughter in her scruffy T-shirt could irritate him as a visual: the loss of formality had begun with Mary in her plastic garden shoes. Vic's rage came from the desire to restore what once lived, constantly vanquished by the insistence of what is: the made-upness of Berkeley, striving with the microcosm of its garden cafés and epicurean, mix-and-match foods to reinvent elegance, none of it balm for his scarred, riddled heart. He had tried to cut off only certain ties with Europe, California's oceanic amnesia at first perfect, and yet the desire for order had risen, once placated by the planes of Mary's face—you have to admit, the woman's beautiful, he had said to Rose more than once, making her cringe. In Mary he seemed to think he had found something both tamable and recursive, enough to make her his home in the second half of the twentieth century, enough that he too, a young professor, had started to feel that finding the well-lived, unexamined life would not be misbegotten hope.

Rose used to imagine Mary and Vic in their dotage not exactly holding hands but at least content to be digesting in the same room while deliberating the relative perfections of roast beef au jus or pot-au-feu or baby mâche, finding themselves together in a calm French-flavored sanctuary against anyone they considered outside their tribe, happy in pyrrhic victory, and how she wished she could be the heir to such treasure, bearing the pride of her parents' lives together while most of the rest of California scrabbled for significance if not history.

1990–1995

More than a year after the goodbye at the gogo place, finally the legal system leaps to its purpose. In a crowded courtroom in Sacramento, to the town where the venue had been changed to counteract Vic's excessive celebrity in Berkeley, in a room boasting pasty men staring down from huge oil paintings, Lana's father will be tried among legions of patchouli'd fans who have shown up: some in support, some betrayed. Not to count those who have come to rally for Mary: the Japanese-American rights and women's rights people, the faithful grad students, some tenured professors or activists happy to be interviewed outside by ravenous mikes and cameras.

A doubled cloud of notoriety attaches itself to Vic, given that the system, in blind, jackpot manner, will be using Mahler in what keeps getting called a test case, a demo of the tough new Good Life First! protocol unrolled just a few months ago by the governor's office. No one will emerge the winner, one op-ed had declared, no one can emerge untarred.

On a metal chair in the back of the courtroom sits Rose, now in her first year of law school, taught by professors who love to argue about the Good Life First! initiative, called by its proponents a pragmatic economic policy to rid overcrowded prisons of minor offenders, by offering earlier release dates, while also ridding prisons of murderers, by streamlining execution protocol so that death row stays become more efficient. Rose is trembling.

MAHLER IN THE RAGE CAGE! a few signs read, a reference to the title of one of Vic's first published works, on the brain's circuitry of anger: were these signs for or against him?

So far in law school, Rose has been gifted in mock trials, able to find calm: her fellow students have praised her, as Vic had, for her silver tongue. She'd had an especially good mock trial only the week before, arguing that, given the ambiguity of a DNA match, the prosecutors wanted the jury to start at the end of the case and backfill with inference, suspicion and innuendo, applying guesswork when proper evidence still was lacking. With the strength of her argument she had managed to free a defendant facing capital punishment. So that if she lacked wings as a lawyer, without having thought it through, she still believed her presence in the courtroom might prove useful: the extent to which she admits anything.

I will go to Vic's trial and—(here her well-meaning petered out).

She only wishes she might have found Lana and brought her to the courtroom under a protective wing, an invisible cloak. The problem being that, back then, before the Internet starts twiddling everyone's fingertips, it had been hard to track down someone like Lana, so successfully out of sight. It's a shame, Rose keeps saying to herself, her gut sense being that lack of testimony by any member of the family will work against Vic. Sure enough, early in the trial the judge, a square-faced woman with a fixed stare, remarks on the absence. *The court notes that his own daughter doesn't care to come forth.*

Had she been Vic's daughter, just as Lana used to sing teasingly at her, wild horses couldn't have kept her away, no matter what, and it is the refrain of this wild-horse song that scalds Rose as she sits in the back, scenting sandalwood and acid sweat, her mouth dry, eyes hot, the refrain bothersome. Restless, claustrophobic, she moves forward to edge in next to a gray-haired composed woman in the second row.

Only a few people could recognize Rose and she is glad for it: so many wronged, placard-holding groups have gathered that Rose could be a member of any of them. EYE-FOR-EYE LIVES IN GOD'S TESTAMENT FOR A REASON! LIFE CONTINUES EVEN FOR FLAWED HUMANS! LET US NOT CAST THE FIRST STONE! In the front row, Mary's assistant Sherry leans on someone who might have been a sister, now patting Sherry's shoulder down as if she were a new foal.

If Rose hopes that her witnessing the trial will, given the unguent of magical thinking, make the thing go well, while driving up to Sacramento she had accepted that going well might not mean that Vic escapes justice altogether but rather that the trial will restore some Mahler dignity. Rose has come to the trial because not coming would mean she accepted the Mahlers' fall. In coming to hear Vic's explanation, she hopes the family will live intact inside her given that their ideals had fashioned her current life. What they admired had made her.

And selfishly she needs to locate Vic, a lost pharaoh first sighted in a Berkeley bookstore, someone who could spin a full world. He used to like to tease the girls, saying their ontology needed his epistemology in order to keep their teleology if not their eschatology straight.

What? Lana would laugh.

Back then Rose had not just been watching Vic: he had been looking into her when she had been all pullulating potential as he liked to say. He had seen her. He had seen and remarked her, liking something of her mind and questions and promise. She had felt known. On that slim golden ladder she had been able to string up something of a life, his belief in her so luminous with teasing, so teasing in its luminosity, making her still so zealous about the return of that particular Vic that it takes a while once the actual Vic enters the courtroom and starts undoing himself for her to understand how out of control he is, slipping backward. No, he has already slipped. She must fight the urge to get up and stop him. Each game he plays with the jury and prosecutor plays out more outrageously transparent than the previous so that it soon becomes clear that any more from him will hurt his case.

"I just want to say—"

He surveys the jury.

O please, keep your dignity, she begs silently, using her last shred of magical thinking. This will be his final chance to talk and hasn't he done enough damage? First he tried presenting himself as a vulnerable casualty of the system, even as prey of his slain wife, only to spend the rest of his cross-examination ping-ponging between the idea of himself as a victim of impulse and a premeditator of just revenge.

At one especially low point, the prosecutor had sighed. "We cannot exactly claim retardation for you, Mister Mahler." The five-hour-long ceremony, after multiple intermissions, prevarications on both sides and stalling, during which Rose had learned nothing new from either the gossip during intermissions or the bustling parade in court, narrows to his last statement: can Vic reconfigure the case?

Yes. She wants to believe he might. He certainly can do no worse. And given the room's fatigue Rose intuits that Vic might paradoxically manage to patch up the damage he has done.

He scans not just the jury but his fans and the aggrieved as well as the faces of those who have taken him on as an impersonal cause. While he scans, Rose feels the body of the courtroom clench as one person.

"In a sense," he begins, "I am Vic Mahler. In another sense I am whoever you need me to be right now." For the first time in the proceedings he twists toward Rose to point at her. "Take this woman over here. Rose! Rosie-anna!" and she cannot keep from gasping, unmasked, looking behind as if another Rose might be located, spinning back to find his eyes boring into her, fiery with accusation or sentiment. Given her oblique angle, she had been sure he could not sight her but clearly she had been wrong.

"Too late to call new witnesses to the stand Mister Mahler," says the judge.

"Rose. You know this is true. Rose knows me as well as anyone. She was—is—a friend of our family. Of my daughter Lana. Could you please stand up Rose?"

Uncertain, horrified, a moment having arrived, Rose struggles to her feet.

"No temporizing at this juncture. Mister Mahler," the judge says. "I repeat. No time to call in additional witnesses. This courtroom cannot become one of your classrooms."

Rose barely hears the room's subdued titter. All she sees is the brilliance of Vic's eyes. "Rose was a member of our family. A person who could tell you better than anyone how, as you people say, I tried my best. She knows I—"

"Please sit. All respect, Mister Mahler, this status should have been introduced earlier. We stand ready to listen to your final statement."

Vic's lawyer, a famous liberal with gray hair tucked vainly behind his ears, nonetheless turns and looks importantly at Rose, raising an eyebrow, inviting her to ignore the judge. She is being called. They are asking her, in some impromptu last-ditch strategy, to speak.

And she does her best. She tries. Her lips move without sound. She waves an apology. All this happens in the interminable second before her knees give out and she sinks back down.

In the front row Sherry, Mary's assistant, breaks down, sobbing: "This is just wrong!"

"Order!" the judge requests, slamming her gavel. "I have stated the protocol of this courtroom. No one new is being called to the stand."

"This man!" Sherry shouts as if higher decibels invoke higher justice. "This man murdered one of the best women who ever lived. No one asked me to testify because I love women and the prosecution didn't want complications." A significant look at the district attorney.

"Out of order!"

"But what can be lost? Does sexual orientation strip a person of the ability to know the truth? This family I know. I know this beast had a murderer's anger from day one. When you sentence, remember you are sentencing a force of evil."

The judge is distracted, whispering to her aide, and Sherry continues.

"The autopsy shows extreme intemperate murder. This man planned every second of his life."

"Guards?"

"He robbed all of us. Not to mention stealing the only true mother I ever had!"

Later Rose will think that, rather than having gone mute when called to testify, what she wished she could have done would have been the adult equivalent of a childish dream. That she might have spread a net over the whole courtroom capable of turning back time, one that would comfort Sherry, shield Vic and keep the jury from casting stones. She will wish she could have discussed the complexity of justice. Which really would have been her way to question whether anyone ever knows the depth of their own badness and more truly state that Vic's eyes still have a vital force which acts as a kindness in the world. All to finally ask: can't we believe in second chances?

In the moment she fails. She cannot rise again, she does everyone wrong, she is unable to help. The very something that should have helped her speak blocks her throat.

Before the jury returns, Rose excuses herself out of the courtroom, not sure whether or not Vic sees her tiptoe out. A failure, a lapsed Aaron, she walks as if with purpose out glass double doors and into the flat heat of Sacramento streets. For an hour or more she walks nowhere, x-ray vision making her see holes burning through whatever she used to pretend to be. Pure ectoplasm of Rose sees only the faces of passersby who possess enviable destinations. Even an older lady who almost hits her in a crosswalk—pastel car, auburn hair, wrinkled face—seems of an anointed race, belonging to a car and a destination, more of the world than boneless Rose, a pretender belonging to no one. And when the ectoplasm named Rose had been sleeping, everyone else had figured out their lives, everyone else handed a calculus to let them know which appointments to keep and which to cancel, where to live and whom to see, whom to bed so as to lie easily, legs brushing, receiving some share of unmanipulated human concord and touch. All these souls so untroubled, trusting the calmest of sleeps await them, all living a miraculous life outside of which Rose will forever be doomed to live.

If any emotion is boundless, it does not belong solely to you, Vic had once told her, one of their better conversations, turning almost mystical. In it she had been vulnerable, telling him that fatherlessness could feel like a huge Pandora's box: she didn't even want to talk about it. He had stared into her and said: "Someone like you carries not just your grief but the grief of everyone in your line."

"I don't know my line," she had said for the umpteenth time only for him to wave such objections away, his eyes as coruscatingly radiant on that day as on this bad afternoon in court.

Better if I were the one in prison, she tells herself, pacing Sacramento streets. Lucky Vic; he gets a container. She could just drag the hand of any stranger to get answers. Anyone would be better at life than she is. No one can explain how much she had wanted to matter to the Mahlers in the way they still matter to her. Why had she bothered to attend the trial? Was it solely for Lana and Vic and not for Mary? How much has Rose been tainted by the two she has started to think of as complicit culprits?

Stupid, she tells herself, you're a useless savior. Be kind to yourself, she tries following up with all her lame affirmations: I am loved, I am loving, she says, I am lovable.

The next week, unable to finish law school in Berkeley, Rose drives down Five to try to invent a new life for herself in Los Angeles, a place that from the vantage of Northern California looks like a tabula rasa.

By 1995 she finally has her law degree, a few fair-weather jog-buddies and maybe a new lease on life in her small apartment on a palm-flecked boulevard, technicolor blue and sunny whenever copters don't whir overhead. She lives on a boulevard heading west toward the total blank of the ocean and still tries to find her friend, using all the newly accessible but slow computer technology, typing in Lana's name again and again only to come up empty-handed, often having to placate annoyed people who pick up the phone when she reaches the wrong L. Mahler. Mahler is far too common a name for so rare a breed and perhaps Lana had gone far enough to change her name given that Rose can locate no record and not because she is lax. Once she goes so far as to pay a detective service, chalking up the payment as equivalent to the cost of a hundred lottery tickets. No one can help, not even the Mahlers' neighbors from Spruce Street who know only that the state had seized both accounts and house and all was still held in escrow to be refigured. Rose sucks in her breath: how thoroughly into her father's notoriety Lana has vanished.

Nighttimes find Rose in her tiny efficiency in Venice, a former pleasure motel converted to apartments on a road with a few HUD houses good at covering crack addicts from the whirring scopes of the copters, drug-seeking or malathion-spraying, all of which makes her have one sustained two-year dream that she wakes in Iraq with body bits splayed about.

Many nights find her splayed on a floor futon near the long hip-bone stretch of Gan and his oceanic snore, Gan the DJ she had met on the sunset path when unwieldy on skates they had practically skated into each other's arms. In the copter-blast of these early days the couple gets along despite the futon being so thin it could be taken from the moment just after the pea gets placed under the mattress, before mattresses get stacked, before the princess admits to sensitivity.

It is not the flat bed or Gan's snore that makes Rose insomniac, also not the sirens, snores or even alcoholic howls of Sunny, a sound engineer who lives across the courtyard, tan cracking, her lemon convertible undriven for uncountable days of lonely descent. Not even that Rose has finished law school but finds her advice column for a women's magazine more fulfilling than her ostensible vocation, the practice of estate planning. She had ended up not in death law, as it is called, where she had shown what felt like a morbid aptitude, her mind grabbing on to all the cases jamming the courts in those years—the Arizona mother awaiting capital punishment, the date night gone wrong, the pair of hapless friends. Instead she let herself in by a side door by practicing estate law. No matter how exact it all is, the name proclaims the importance of serene, unbroken lines of heritage.

But the main thing she wishes to do, what she can and must do, is write Vic. She writes letters, she tells herself, to make up for her tongue-tied courtroom appearance. Or she does it because Mary had always silently but often asked her to be a good role model. Now Rose believes she might form part of an important overhaul. She will be no one's ectoplasm and will never admit how ravenous she stays for the Mahlers, as if she has left some crucial part of herself back inside their kitchen, she and Lana slipping past Mary, grabbing an apple before heading with or without Vic but always on an escapade.

Rose writes to Vic as rehab for him but recuperation for her.

Her letter-writing becomes so much greater a part of her life than her column clippings flying around her front seat, her advice to the lovelorn:

Dear Clueless,
I suggest you stop beating up trees that no longer bear fruit.

Dear Lost,
High time for you to stop letting other people call the shots. You have a gift for romanticizing others that will lead nowhere.

While Rose ascends as a giver of advice, she finds the letters passing between her prisoner and her brim with enough passion that they filch life out of her own. In one letter Vic accuses Rose of feeling his pain because it is easier than feeling her own. "But can he say that?" Rose asks her intended baby-daddy Gan. "He loves to tease me with clichés. Anyway I'm not feeling his pain, I'm trying to help."

"Maybe Mahler calls helping and pain the same thing? Or what do you think you're doing for him anyway?"

"Nothing," says Rose, trying not to be disappointed by the literalism she finds so unbrilliant and constant in Southern California and maybe in the United States, in everywhere but one cell where a finely honed irony makes do with whatever muscle the pen of Vic Mahler has left.

1990–2008

If Rose cannot say why she keeps sending Vic science magazines and clippings, pretext for the long confessions she also sends, scrawled with her mother's old fountain pen, the inexplicability keeps her sending one bundle after another. A package leaves her hand and a nervous relief steals over Rose.

Vic used to say Rose enjoyed hardship yet whenever she mails him she lacks trust in her stamina. Once she and Lana had been climbing a Berkeley hill together but Rose had needed to run, not trusting the liminal zone, needing to make her desire to get to the top out-pace any bent toward inertia. In similar fashion she mails Vic pack-ages quickly, trying not to overthink them, racing past the sticky threshold where she would have to admit her letters are pure strip-tease. Keeping up a relationship with a condemned man is beautifully asymmetrical as burlesque, an offer of freedom sans future, while also binding her by restoring the past. "O, I don't know, I just feel bad for the guy alone in his cell," she tells Gan, not telling him she also holds herself responsible for Vic's fate. Not just that she should have spoken up and swung the jury's findings; she could have done better, before or after, to reconstitute the freeze-dried family of Mahlers. "I think they're your sea monkeys," says Gan, "those little brine shrimp people used to send away for? Just because the drawings in the ads looked like a frolicking kingdom?"

"I loved those. I sent away for them more times than I want to admit." She almost laughs.

"You never got disappointed?"

At one low point, cycling together, Gan does ask if she prefers her boyfriends caged where at least she can locate them?

"So uncalled for," says Rose. According to Gan before he cycles off down the boulevard, part of her problem is that Rose lives in the past and should dedicate herself more to her current life, not just to future kids. Childhood living is easy to do, Lana used to sing at her, presciently enough. Abandoned temporarily, Rose gets off her bike to sit by the side of the path so she can pull out her ever-present pad and notate her present life, proving she can stay in the moment:

> I am a columnist, a part-time estate lawyer living near the Southern California beach with a boyfriend, trying to have a baby. No one has helped me. I created all this.

She does not wholly believe these parameters of a life. They scarcely resemble the more credible life the Lolas used to hold up for each other, the sparkly crystal ball held inside the other's potential. But she wants to pinpoint at least this moment so as to better inspect it. Rose sits by the path and looks at a butterfly against the sunset, at an animated conversation against far-off waves, a small child confident on skates and tells herself: I am appreciating this moment and who says that can't be enough?

While Vic's occasional silence does nothing but provoke an itch. She works on being good at making herself forget which letters Vic ignores. On a whim, continuing the striptease, she writes a true rape story to send to Vic at Old Parcel, leaving it unclear which girl had been raped. When he queries her later she falls silent, happy to have a nugget he requires: information about his daughter. Dropping the story into the slot of her corner mailbox, she doesn't know how the story will provoke him but still her face prickles with the closest she gets these days to that old-time smile, the wicked joy.

What bothers Rose most is that she'd always thought she would prefer not to have kids, thinking she'd end up inside one of those sleek smooth-thighed childless couples in their fifties who tend to each mate's catalogue of fetish regarding spice preference, coffee strength, waist-girth, animal tolerance, texture, topography.

Because she has long felt illogically enough that her birth-mom's death tainted her own fertility, it has started to seem likely that Rose might never know someone related to her by blood.

As a child carrying her scruffy teddy bear with its welcome scent of spoiled milk into yet another loud living room, maybe her fifth or sixth foster home, Rose had made an oath into the teddy's half-bitten ear that, if she ever did get to have kids, she would die before making any kid feel unwanted. She would make sure everything was squared away and prepared for a kid because she would never wish her fate on another, preferring to die first. The original sin rests in being unwanted, a weight a person never fully casts off.

Yet in some moment when she had been existentially if not biologically asleep, some fiendish maker had on the sly installed that legendary clock: now her sense of purpose seems to come solely from the clock's devil notches laid into her womb's frozen sea which without her agreement has begun its thaw so that every day passes with more audible tick and tock, the exultation and panic of having a baby, someone who would promise that family, her family, known to her by blood, would never leave.

The first anise-fueled night she decides to share the clock idea with Gan he laughs it off: having grown up in a family of strong-minded Armenians, he knows women have their whims and yet part of his beauty rests in his honeyed acceptance of such layers of delicacy. Rose saying she is ready to have kids makes him mug: "The most ecological choice you could make would be to adopt." As if that weren't bad he adds: "But I know how women are. Once they get the baby idea in their head, there's no stopping."

"The hindbrain takes over," says Rose, compulsive in echoing the title of one of Vic's chapters.

"You're forty," Gan tells her. What she listens to is not so much the words but rather the esoteric flute-music of intonation, some hope to be found in the glottal stop and perhaps the way his eyebrow sneaks up, a flag that he might, at the very least, be able to locate the project's gravity.

Long before their anise night she had thought Gan had too much California in him to make any space for fatherhood. A construction worker turned DJ who had glided through the world with little friction, his tectonics had made it easy—a bit too easy—to connect, a man so unmysteriously devoted in first courtship he might as well have rifled through some flower-emblazoned pamphlet on how to get the girl, so easy she had suspected he was not in it for a long sticking-together even as they slid into futon-sharing and all other Californian activities catalogued in local mate-seeking ads, a collective deposit into the state's hedonistic safe filled with all the music-sharing, filmgoing, burrito-biting, mountain-climbing, hill-driving and beach-walking known by other couples.

His easeful Piscean devotion meant that certainly on the baby question her Gan had agreed a bit too quickly, but since her fiendish clock meant she needed male agreement, even if slippery, she chose to ignore Gan's ease, instead welcoming his heedlessness in bed, a quality almost enough to replicate passion. And later when their lack of heed bore no fruit Gan stayed in similar good cheer, his smile well-etched as they trekked to doctors dedicated to helping the Roses of the world reproduce. Until the day they were driving to yet another doctor and they were about to turn left off Mulholland. The luster in his eyes never more alluring, Gan chose to call the whole package of Rose-and-Gan-and-baby-to-be quits.

Into her hangover about this romantic end, ungravid, unhitched, uncertain, Rose had received a morose phone message from her adopted brother on a zen retreat he had masked as yearlong forest service in Alaska.

When Rose reached him at his base camp, her brother spoke with studied plainness: his mother, their ma, had died.

An aneurysm. Happens even when people are young, he said. At least you don't have those bad genes.

Her foster brother did not mean to be unkind by mentioning genes. He spoke of how their mother's brother was arranging all the details of the cremation and that in her aspiration toward simplicity, their mother had explicitly stated she wanted no funeral or commemoration. He droned all this as if reciting headlines without pausing for Rose to insert even silence. Of course she could not help but take the news as a punch to the gut.

She might not have talked with her mother for months. She might have stowed her away in an imagined Berkeley. She might have laughed at her mother flitting about in her puffy blouses and dreaminess. But still and always Rose kept holy a small shrine of gratitude to Joan Batekin, a daughter of Chicago who had airlifted Rose out of what surely would have been a dismal fate uncountenanced by all the world's teddy bears. And in the second after hearing the news of Joan's death, what bothered Rose most was that she could not summon her mother's face: only its glimmering contours surrendering themselves to memory, something of the edge of a blurred second after a joke.

Joan gone. And what kind of ripple would the death cause in her mother's circle of acquaintances? In keeping with her modesty, she wanted no commemoration. But was it not also in keeping with some absolute hole in the center of existence? Would any of Joan's carefully pored-over details of her life matter in the end? Whether she had a rubied fan or a turquoise mala? Whether she had known this concentric circle of clients or that fanfold of admiring friends or any one of her transitory lovers? Whether she had followed her passion in any of her interest groups, squash book groups, peasant blouses, Nigerian children's rights? Her mother had never cleaved to one cause or person. So was it this mosquito-eye affection for the masses that made few people single-minded in how they clung to Joan?

Because while Joan had a flair for drawing people near, enthusiastic applauders who liked her quick smile and sharp nose, she also lacked a more general instinct for keeping friends. She had never believed in any rituals of permanence and loyalty and was it for this reason that her acquaintances tended to fade? This ease of connection—like Gan's!—may have been exactly the quality that had allowed Joan to take on the adopting of a daughter, a foster kid with good report cards but a history of rejection for her involuntary mutism. There Joan had been, no doubt not without some struggle, a single therapist mother raising a son out of wedlock in Berkeley of the seventies, alighting on the decision to swoop Rose up into her life.

Stay true to yourselves, Joan had once told Rose and her brother, that's all that counts. Did the way Joan lived count as staying true?

Maybe two months earlier, Rose had called her mother and they had bandied about talk of a visit. One of them, Rose could not remember who, had needed to cancel, this being their pattern since, after Rose went away to college, by slow degrees the two flowers in the family, as Joan liked calling them, had drifted away from each other on the gentlest of currents with only the briefest bumping up against each other after graduation. It was as if once Joan had succeeded in giving a kid a college education, her contract with parenthood had ceased and now she herself had been trying to graduate into some important second act of life in which she set out to meet loose-hipped men at folk-dance evenings so an expected interlude could follow, the quick pair able to share croissants after talks by ecologically forward-thinking scientists.

Her mother in phone conversation tended to conclude by saying: "I'm proud of you, Rosie," which always preceded "I love you," the signal that it was time to hang up.

On the phone, zen-powered, Rose's brother waits. Better than anyone, he knows Joan had saved Rose. Only once in a moment of adolescent cruelty masquerading as realness had he spelled it out: too easy to see the path that could have been Rose's—left in bad foster care or a series of group homes. "You would've ended up single, without a job, addicted to meth, black-eyed, pregnant."

"Or dead," she had confirmed, the masochistic pleasure adding to their intimacy. For sure she would never have ended up in the private high school where she had found the best friend she had ever known, one with her own methods of salvation.

Rose may have known what Joan had saved her from but still always found it hard to thank her: overt gratitude could open too many gates of vulnerability. At best the saved girl found herself as diffident as Lana, accepting all bouquets from her adopted mother as her due.

Lana had once said of a college beau that she liked to lie there letting him pleasure her because she couldn't be inauthentic by moving one nanometer toward him, preferring to be the object of someone's attempts. "You like being the object?" Rose had squeaked.

"Why not?" Lana smiled back, limpid, incurious, walking along the Hudson toward the George Washington Bridge, the girls sophomores in college. Rose had started a little nattering spiral about how in sex she never wanted to ask for anything because asking makes a person vulnerable especially when no one can ever exactly meet any request, it's like a language game and anyway who wants to be in some kind of Rose 101 mode where she would have to be the teacher, giving up the chance of being surprised by someone's rough hand, hence her rape fantasies and anyway she had a hard time with anyone working on her because she didn't like someone gratifying a sense of accomplishment by laboring toward a goal like arbeit that ends up making a person unfrei. Plus she didn't want a boy thinking himself an expert on Rose. "You're funny," Lana had said. "I have rape fantasies too but honestly, don't you think too much? Maybe let yourself enjoy things more?" Sneaking a hug around Rose's waist, a tardy, quick attack of affection. "You have any idea how bad my life would have been if we'd never met? Seriously, Rosie. My life would have stunk."

Rose had stood, eyes wide, cells stilled, on alert, breath held, Lola revived, a hand imprinted in phosphorescence on her waist.

For some reason Rose thinks of this conversation after her brother relays the news.

This too she gets: there Rose had been lying flat and still—just like Lana with a beau—while her mother had been trying to get Rose to admit to the pleasure of being mothered.

For the first time, the suggestion that Joan might have been disappointed in her adopted daughter raises its head. The idea so clear Rose would have shared it with her brother if she were sure she wouldn't cry. Meanwhile Rose's brother stays dry, saying Joan's most recent boyfriend had called and asked him to come down but what was the point of leaving his Alaska retreat since there was just stuff to sort through and objects are objects—his zenspeak self-conscious—maybe the stuff should just be donated? And then asks if Rose could be the one to go up to Berkeley, go through the house. Has Rose ever felt their camaraderie as strongly as she does now? According to Joan's will, the siblings share a house and given how quickly they discuss a real-estate broker their uncle knows, both are unsentimental in considering how quickly to sell it. If her brother is busy freeing himself of sentimental baggage, Rose will do the same.

"Talk to the executor," he warns. "It'll be a swamp, Rose."

The task is a blessing, a relieving distraction. Into the continental crackle Rose tells her brother: "I don't mind."

"You could say no. No one wants you to become a martyr."

She can say no more. She and her brother tend not to leak hints about the embarrassing weakness found in adult life and she doesn't want him to know how good it will feel to exit purgatory: slamming a door might open another or at least muffle a clock.

Up in Berkeley, going through Joan's oddments from the aspirational life she'd led—matchbooks, wood buttons, pressed flowers, clippings—Rose finds one truth: the grave of her birth-mother.

While Joan liked calling herself a love-mother, here Rose finally holds between her hands the information she'd looked for her whole life, blue mimeograph ink on old-fashioned translucent onionskin: a cemetery in San Diego.

In one of those mysteries that cling to foster kids, the grave does not rest in some overgrown Berkeley burial ground as Joan had hinted, always waving the question away, but in a plot partly deeded to some military camp.

Once Rose finishes packing away Joan's things, having donated most of her detritus to the Brothers of Africa—shoes with insoles pressed by toes that will never again walk, blouses still scented from an evening of self-betterment, funky rosewood furniture loyal to an era—Rose drives in a one-day heat down Five, speeding past the turnoff in Los Angeles, going south until she gets to San Diego an hour before dusk when the cemetery closes.

Along the military camp's barbed wire, Rose stops by a hillock where she sees, hot in mock battle, recruits in camouflage scattering off a green truck and then falling left and right. From a tower a gun-fire sound track blasts, making each soldier appear even more purposeful, vicious in rapture.

Of course a person wants reciprocity. Of course at a cemetery a person secretly hopes the dead could meet one's wish with theirs and that a conversation might start or continue.

"Why do people bother going to graves?" Lana in a mood had once asked Vic. The black-cloaked family-Mahler-plus-Rose had been traipsing to some colleague's memorial.

"Because memory wants embodiment. Because the living want to fix a person beyond the great fix of life."

"Foolish," Rose says back to Vic's voice. Of course, speak at a grave and you get only mouldering bones. Ask for a sign, you get nothing verifiable by outside witness. "What were you hoping for anyway?"

By the time she finds the gate and gets to the alphabetical zone for her birth-mom's gravesite, a tropical wind bows the cypress trees into gnarled hands, the coiled breath of it making name cards and salutations whirl about, lost wraiths.

The paper dampens in her hand, ink blurred: of course she knows her birth-mom's name and could recheck the paper to verify locale but would rather forsake the hunt for serendipity, proving the grave tugs at her genes.

"Say there was a game authored by your so-called forgiving God, what would its rules be?" Vic had gone on after the memorial. She picks up one of the flying notes. I LOVE YOU FOREVER. "People think they love beyond death because the idea banishes death," Vic ostensibly explained to Rose why he'd never bothered seeking out the cemetery of his own mother, though she preferred to think of him not as a lost child but, as he called himself, the world's orphan. He went on: "In the case of a dead public figure, people go to a gravesite because they love history. Maybe to consider greatness forged out of humble origins. Or how the mighty have fallen. Just so they feel better about their lives." He waited. "But when they go to the grave of someone for whom they have only a name and a single fact—as would have been the case between my mother and me—what can they focus on?"

"Lunch?" Lana had said, forever ready to derail her father's talks with Rose.

"A change of fortune? Their own hormonal protest against the senescence of cells? The endless optimism of the life urge?" He accepted their silence. "No. If I had gone to find my mother's grave I would've gotten nothing but worms and some lousy cracked gravestone."

"At least you had children." Lana smiled too hard. "A child."

"At the very least."

In a cemetery in San Diego, Rose comes across the cenotaph of her birth-mother:

EMILY ROBBINS, 1950–1970, RIP

Rose can't read the acronym at first, misreading it as *rip*, as in *a ripping, to be ripped* until she is struck by the lie: while Rose's adoptive mother had always said Rose's natural mother had died in the pangs of labor, here comes contrary evidence:

Rose was born on January 18 in 1967, not in 1970.

Yet in 1970 someone had buried her birth-mother Emily Robbins here. Which means that, for three long years after baby Rose had been given up to the state's dispensations, her birth-mother had lived.

Meaning that while baby Rose had traveled through blankets, cribs, occasional arms, group abodes—contracting hepatitis, ringworm, pneumonia, while she had undergone transfusions and incubations, all those moments still finding eternal life in shards of dreams—her birth-mother had lived. While Rose managed to get good at loss, turning into an infant who became an oddly mute toddler, her birth-mother had lived on for three more mystery years.

Once when Rose had prodded Vic about some inconsistency in something he had said, he had shouted: "You're just wrong, Rose! Your early life made holes in your brain! Later plasticity can correct only so much! You lacked secure attachment." (And then was surprised that Rose didn't stay that night for her usual dinner and veined cheese with the Mahlers.) He had once asked Rose if he could use the story of her life to introduce one of his books—*your homelessness, you know, your difficulties*—and because Rose was unsure which way he'd spin it, because she glimpsed for one swollen second the vulture inside Vic she had said no.

Of course he was right about those holes in her brain or at least Rose couldn't contradict him given that home has always been her lack.

The wind gathers, roiling the Pacific as if a tsunami might soon swallow all those pathetic headstones. When the cypress branches bend close enough to strike her head, Rose ducks and runs, distressed by the notes to loved ones swirling up in such a bunch that she must stop to gather a few:

TO THE MOST BEAUTIFUL WOMAN I WILL EVER KNOW

YOU ARE IN US ALWAYS AS WE REMEMBER YOUR BIRTHDAY

Rose gathers a corsage of notes, holding them close to her chest. When the wind stops, she tries redistributing the notes back to whatever graves seem correct, the act so disturbing she finally submits to the arbitrariness of affection, enough to shove all that flyaway sentiment under one unmarked stone.

One week later she is at Hope, where she wishes she could feel happier about being with Lana and less that she has chased an old friend straight into a gorge.

1993

The last millionaire Lana meets in Los Angeles during her floating time—after the abrupt goodbye with Rose in her apartment, the
bus ride across country from New York with her father's credit card
warm in her hand, the card with which she had bought huge movie-
star sunglasses she'd worn to discourage strangers from conversation—
the last guy in that floating time before Kip wants her to move up to
Northern California.

This millionaire from northern India desires a penthouse overlooking the bay, a sanctuary in a temperate climate. We all want refuge,
he says, chucking her under the chin. He lives in Benedict Canyon and
imports medical supplies from Canada. With the pragmatic disinterest
of the young, Lana believes his biography. Because his ambition forks
toward filmmaking, she spends afternoons before waitressing gigs on
his couch overlooking the ginger canyon. They discuss ideas and in
that late light she tries figuring out what they want from each other.

Each time she visits she makes a point of giving him small inconsequential gifts (a wooden massage roller, a crystal, a smooth blue
pen) to make clear she is not after his millions. In turn he micro-
waves take-out tempura. They met when he asked for coins to feed a
parking meter on Rodeo Drive. He asked to see her fingernails and
supposedly was struck by the lack of vanity in how she kept them,
pronouncing her the first woman since his arrival in Ellay to truly
intrigue him.

He calls Lana by the name she uses as an extra: Trixie Yokut, a waitress, a card-carrying member of the union of film extras, *atmosphere*, Trixie years away from having children of her own and the constant atmosphere children confer, as he says approvingly. Ellay has confirmed her choice of refuge because its daze grants anonymity, everyone sedated by climate, making it easy to cauterize the past and keep encounters in the smooth present.

Is she not like everyone else scrubbing by?

Inhabiting a banal condo in West Hollywood, a girl soothing aches or aspirations, neither murderer's daughter nor the child of a famous philosopher and well-respected feminist but rather a girl with any future or past possible within some millionaire's cool wood-shingled house, sinking into his hot tub on a fog day with the canyon wrinkled silk stretched below. Or else she sits on the redwood deck warming her hands on green tea brought by the Hungarian housekeeper who strives to subdue the disbelief of her penciled eyebrows.

"Why do you love to work so hard, Trixie?" asks the millionaire on the deck. "Let me support you," he says. "Live here! Why glamorize poverty? Only the young can afford such luxury."

Scanning the canyon she thinks this seems halfway true. But always later, drying off, wrapped in a towel, sitting on his couch waiting for god knows what, she hears her mother's grim edict on Tumbleweed: THERE'S NEVER A FREE LUNCH. Each time Lana gets home from the millionaire's house, clean and grimed, Lana has the odd urge to call Mary and tell her everything. The abortions, the weirdness of Los Angeles, this latest millionaire. As if she had ever called to confide, as if mother and daughter had magically become a mother-daughter pair fluent in the trite affairs of a day.

But the purge of their future is so complete. Even the corner psychic cannot convincingly channel Mary though Lana keeps the wish alive, spending hours in the bodega's fringed dark room to pay for a false connection, better than nothing.

Maybe it is inevitable, after enough moments of sitting toweled on the millionaire's couch, moments gathering, a necklace beaded toward final clasping, that Lana will sleep with the millionaire and he will grow addicted to her youth in the way the never-changing weather of Ellay makes old men grasp at the buttery sheen of the young until finally such addiction will distance her. She can see one inch of this rounding the bend but before the moment arrives keeps showing up at the guy's mansion and smiling back at the housekeeper's eyebrows to sit betoweled on his couch. This clinging to habit alone tells her she might be staving off another attack, what sanitarium doctors liked calling her sensitivity toward breakdown.

Before the first time she goes down the rabbithole with the million-aire, it is not that any surge of attraction overcomes her. Rather, she listens to his philosophy, as attentive a student as Rose used to be. The millionaire is saying that he has not yet broached his philosophy of sex.

"Basically," he tells Lana, "if I'm attracted to someone and that person's not attracted to me, we can still do something with the energy that has been generated. This is a Sufi idea. So for example I once met a girl in one of those bootleg video stores in Alexandria and I brought her home and I began touching her like this—and like this—"

"I'm sorry but—" for some reason her voice escapes in tiny bubbles.

One part of her wants to believe the millionaire's thinking because it removes the burden of choice: she knows what it is to surrender responsibility just as if she were an infant, entering the inevitable opening.

He continues: "You are a creature with an open mind. We are adults. We know how to do this. Take my hand."

In a weak moment, all too sensitive, the day before Lana chose to slip down the rabbithole, she had found herself walking the ocean board-walk, lost amid all the neon bathing suits and finger-popping roller-skaters until she ducked into a pay phone. Without planning, her fingers started dialing Rose's old New York apartment. Not to know if Rose was still gogo dancing. Not to talk about Vic. Just to call someone still grabbing a glossy tether toward what Lana was supposed to have become.

But Rose made her usual mistake of answering right away, the hello so hopeful Lana had to hang up. The readiness of that hello terrified, containing the risk of pity, the one insult Lana could not handle since pity rip-cords a person back to gravity and bad choices. Having slammed down the phone, Lana kept her hand on it, breath jagged, while by her glided Los Angelenos, skating or jogging, scented with coconut, pineapple, hydrangea, all exercising toward the youth they wished forever to enjoy. As Vic liked quoting Kinnell: *Here come the runners / they run in a world where brick-laying used to be work / their faces tell there is a hell and they will reach it.*

Lana vowed never again to be so weak as to call Rose.

Better to keep alive the Lolas and their flow than to reencounter Rose in her recent incarnation, pitying or angry, since Lana had no stamina for being triply orphaned. Finally, as she had done with Mary, she pulled her hand from the phone. That evening she saw everywhere she went only two sorts of people: those who had locked themselves into a lifetime of community rich with friends and friendly acquaintances and those solitary types who lived out terms of loneliness, with no other category dwelling between.

Back in New York, Lana had hung up on her mother after what turned out to be their last conversation and had experienced this same brer-rabbit moment in which she could not pull her hand away from the receiver, finding herself forced into the bad type of regret. Not the regret that pillows a person, plumping someone with the possibility of a parallel life continuing on undisturbed by bad choices but rather a truer regret, the double-bladed knife that memory wields.

Take my hand. As Trixie Yokut she sits on the millionaire's couch toweled and floating, the millionaire holding her palm with one hand, his other hand having her stroke him exactly as she had imagined, a dark curl fluted and veined.

"Have an open mind, Trixie," he croons. "We are adults, we know how to do this."

In coming to Ellay, she had wanted to believe she would be free to reinvent herself. That she could hide and be capable of anything, be truly seen, discovered despite herself. Lana as Trixie stares out at the millionaire's canyon and thinks some good must come from learning the extremes. After a friend of hers met and forgotten on the set of a pilot had told her to read the writer Colette she had. With the millionaire's excitement one lap over, she figures she may as well be one of Colette's characters glamorous in Paris, or even like Colette herself because of course the author had experienced what she wrote about, hadn't she?

Amid the millionaire's agitation she cannot keep from crying, which is strange because even when she wants to these days she cannot cry much but nothing stops the guy, a regular steam engine, so different from all those susceptible college boys he must go until he finishes. Afterward he offers walnuts from the tree out back and next morning the wrinkled nuts in a brown bag at her bedside stare back.

To fend off regret, to prove she had willed it all—couch, steam, walnuts—the next day she returns to his mansion and the day after that, making herself available in any way he wants. During various acts, from above she can see their bodies and still manages to float, desire in no inch of her body as he dispatches himself first inside a condom and later onto her belly, admiring his script.

Their routine begins: she affords him their coupling in his spartan bedroom while he intermittently raves about her dark body, always saying later how much he wants to photograph her so he can add her picture to his travel gallery, composed of bare-breasted, bamboo-framed women hanging on his spotless walls. "You could look Polynesian," he says, pulling back her hair. After everything, a responsible citizen, he pats her off with soft tissues and together they step into the steam bath next to the huge bedroom, the bath that makes the sex part of a healthful purifying regime like psyllium, wheatgrass, mantras. They are both acolytes on a trip and their sex is an act beyond, promising everyone a better future.

Until she will begin to avoid him and in response he starts to leave long, stern messages on her phone. "People must have told you before but you're a sociopath. What truth is there to any part of you? You have a predator instinct, there's no consistency to you! You're an animal. You chew off legs. People like you think only about their own beast instincts. You will never succeed."

1993

Equipped at least with social instinct, she goes on as Trixie Yokut long as she can take it, waitressing and working as an extra, dwelling in her condo while shrouding from herself the idea that she counts as one of Ellay's fallen and only the night sky fills with stars. On the boardwalk near an old bohemian bookstore, ducking away from the path of the turbaned rasta who smiles, plays guitar and rollerskates all at the same time, she meets Kip and finds relief in his surfing roughness, his earthbound rituals and buried vulnerability.

Meeting Kip, she stops being Trixie Yokut and calls herself Lana Wagner, close enough to her real name but far enough to surrender Vic. Because Kip reforms her sentence, letting her feel she has served her time and that a new man will release her from her sleeping-beauty float. Both Kip's habit of seeing meaning everywhere and his rage coax her north.

Without knowing the full terms of his offer, she grasps his kite-tail to head up Five, turning left toward the coast to get to his cool foggy nowhereland of Yalina, a cocoon with better geography.

In Yalina she will be able to lose herself in tribal prescriptions and small-town contradictions, a place where her own choices will possess gravity. The town's best escape will be commitment since no one here ever escapes: not surfers who have avoided sharks long enough to chat over morning coffee with potgrowers who steer clear of the feds, not redneck loggers from the woods shunning the publicity that comes from treehuggers who do their best to spurn the loggers' truckwheels, not back-to-the-landers shying away from the week-enders by pulling honey from beehives, not the new computer bil-lionaires shirking desk jobs by driving in with four-wheel-drive conquistadors, desperate to find the city newspaper and evading the rez kids who duck their parents' destiny by hanging with skate punks who dodge everyone in the one town center.

As in Ellay, here everyone obeys the follow-your-own-lifestyle laws of the land with Californian unease, their faces genial and smol-dering, a little scared of personal incursions, keeping self and clan sacred above all. Yet the drama of high cliffs and shark-infested ocean means that those who live here year-round are whether they like it or not connected, unable to avoid the collectivity of geographic fate.

Each night, whole sections of crumbly sandstone cliff fall into the ocean; quakes tremble the mountains; neighbors get eaten by sharks or nabbed by law enforcement. Not to mention that tsunamis could rinse everything away in a second. The single north–south highway gets blocked for weeks on end, surrendered to cows who cross it to get to the better grass on the oceanside cliffs. At many points on the road, no fence separates the highway from the ocean below. Minute by minute you must choose life.

If the scarcity of people gives Kip, a semi-native son, heartburn, it lends Lana new destiny.

Back in the seventies, from what Lana understands, Vic had written a treatise on choice sickness as a contemporary pathology. He'd said that if you made neural plasticity a friend you could paradoxically more quickly find some predetermined bliss and in this way he con-figured the thought of the later pharmacologists, the prophets and wielders of Cymbalta and Lexapro and Welbutrin, the slingers of Zoloft, Lithium, Alvia, Adderall, some of whom Lana had ended up meeting in her life away from the Mahler house, all awed by Vic and his role in having been among the first of the third-wave neurogenic mystics to suggest that one can find self-definition by surrendering prior self-definition and so stumble upon one's highest calling: this is how she understands Vic's thought, which is to say, not fully. And as Lana walks the Yalina cliffs with her head cloudless, feet stumbling only occasionally, she thinks that just because Vic had spoken of choice sickness did not make the idea wrong. Sometimes even Vic spoke the truth. In Ellay she must have suffered from choice sickness, as earlier in life, and now finally, in Yalina, unable to escape its dangerous cliffs and ocean, she is released. Everything here gives little choice.

Another truth being that the job she finds at the market of Yalina—the ungourmet one on the wrong, eastern side of the highway, stocked with powdered drinks and no goat cheese—spits so beautifully in the face of her parents. As hers is the most limited job she has ever had, she gets to feel righteous while collecting customers' government coupons or passing discount boxes of frozen foodstuffs under her hand, each act a breathtaking repudiation of Mary and Vic. And while it is also true that Kip never understands her pleasure in this job, given that his father is the local state trooper, she thrills, telling Kip he can't understand only because if he were the one standing there as market cashier, he would become everyone's sitting duck, absorbing hatred since his father BJ in his prime was notorious for slapping speeding tickets on everyone, never mind if the motor vehicle happened to be driven by BJ's neighbor or son's friend. BJ, so unlike her own father, believed in the idea of a justice single and absolute, a world in which every sinner gets his due.

Both Kip and his father in their homespun absolutisms stay quaintly foreign to her given that Lana had been raised on the elitist exceptionalism of Vic, one that had slipped a skepticism about all orthodoxy into her system. Once she had yelled in self-defense at Vic: you're the one who lives above everyone else's rules! Not me! You have the morality of a rock star who thinks nothing ordinary applies to you!

He had called her his little kitten and said, merely, *touché*.

This then is also part of her inheritance from Vic, a desire for rules so hot in her that she paradoxically as ever cannot believe in any absolute fairness or convention, her oblivion what makes Kip's life easier. For instance, she doesn't care if she stands alone in her job while Kip stays unemployed for most of the year. As she wipes down the conveyor belt inhaling ammonia or deftly prices pudding, pasta and meat byproducts, Lana swells with the thought: all of us are limited but at least we're in this together. Which *we*? What *this*? What *together*? It doesn't matter: in Yalina, on this endlessly shifting coast with only its cows itinerant, she gets to locate herself. Never before has she felt so fully at home.

Only one thought nags.

They have closed her asylum records. When the officials had released her she'd tried obtaining them but an overworked secretary had regarded her request for information as beyond what was prescribed for the post-release period. Will Lana never know what happened to her? Isn't there a Freedom of Information act somewhere? She thinks about hiring a lawyer but doesn't want to stir up too much muck.

During spare moments at her market, she rubs the oddly smooth concavity of her belly with its small scar of unknown provenance, almost sure that at some point when she'd been a zombie under the spell of the doctors and their electricity addictions, the doctors had taken out her womb. Just like that they'd decided they could not take the stink of Lana's femaleness; just like that they'd declared she should not bear fruit and had voted for eugenics. They had guessed how bad Vic was some months before what she calls his atrocity and had punished her, stuffing a chapter of her future history into a glass bottle before throwing it into the ether of forgetfulness.

Mommy: it becomes three syllables, ma—ah—mee. Voiced in the uncanny middle of the night, the middle syllable becomes a love grumble that also locates her.

Ma—she who can put things right—

ah—not coming fast enough

—*mee*. I need you.

The need thrills her. Mommy, as if just like that she had ascended to being the equivalent of a Hindu deity. Maamih. And was any sound more basic? Had she ever been able to call her own mother mommy?

Once Mary had gone a bit nutty, waking up Lana at seven in the morning, on a timetable of her own devising, saying: Lana, I need you to call me mother. This urge arose because one of Mary's aunts had died the week before, too young, an aunt called mother by her ramshackle brood and maybe Mary had realized, standing by as a few oldtimers trotted out to do the Yokut funeral dance, step flat step flat, honoring the spirit of her aunt, that her daughter failed to render upon her any special title. When Mary returned, she explained she wanted at least one remnant of what sounded to Lana like one awful hierarchical childhood made up of nuns and the reservation. As a result, growing up in the Mahler house of slippery nicknames, Lana had never known exactly what name to call her mother.

Lana, from now on I want you to call me mother.

Okay, Lana had said, *mother*, so sardonic her mother had winced.

At least mom, then, okay? Not Mary.

Okay, mom. Up in Yalina, Lana starts to realize that what her mother had missed out on was the full sweetness children could offer. As a daughter, Lana had failed, always teetering in her approach, never sure a lap would stay anywhere long enough for her to crawl into it, her mother always on the move. Her first memory of Mary holds this: a tempting bright-lipped presence across the room, preparing sandwiches for some hike that her baby girl will take up a hill on papa's back. That same baby girl felt she couldn't cross the room toward the pretty lady, lacking an essential right to ask her for anything.

In Yalina, Lana triumphs: I am mommy!

Which means that Lana has become a whole maternal field for her boys. They raise rights of approach to a highly calibrated system all about staking out territory, tummy holdouts, strategic defense of the motherland. Every breath of being a parent comforts her since it undoes what she knows about being mothered. Every small spiky cold toe trying to find the warmth between Lana's calves tells her she is not Mary. She giggles at this: POPsicles! she calls out, your toes are POPsicles! until the boys start to love that word so much, it becomes one of their first.

Later one of the boys learns to write and will start hiding secret love letters to Lana saying he wants to marry her while the other will bury his nose in her hair and emerge to report that it smells like a hundred cones of banana ice cream. All spells confirmation of Lana's choices. To her own mother Lana would never have even known how to start such a love-sentence: to the crash of lightning behind a totem you do not falteringly stutter. Mary had been both household deity and distant force, too removed for Lana ever to do more than smile in her direction. I have come far, Lana tells herself, these tumbling happy boys a bridge over her past.

And Kip snaps to it, no distant god but deep into this fatherhood thing with his boys even if his fingers are too thick to fiddle with snaps on small boys' pajamas. One thumb, the casualty of construction jobs, has been hammered this side of smithereens while one index finger torques south, a ballpeen toward his body's median. Because Sedge's eyes are crossed and Tee's legs bowed, Kip jokes that men in the family turn inward, strong silent manly types, and while she is happy that so much joking goes on in the strong unsilent manliness of this time, on many nights their life up north gets to be too much for Lana. A lonely cabin fever sets upon her so that she must abandon the twins and Kip inside with their loud negotiations over protocol, food, sharing, respect, manners, clothes, bath, sleep and instead go keep a particular stump company on the wet grass near her vegetable garden, alive with the endless quiet optimism of insects and gophers. She sits by her stump breathing in the night and indulging in an old-time furtive habit: smoking a clove cigarette, a small waft of homage to her old friend Rose.

Sometimes on these clove nights Lana feels as if her friend sits and gleams back at her, as if she gets a gentle hand on her shoulder, Rose waiting for Lana in the furrow of pine and sequoia, a muse ready to talk and answer questions. For example, would it be too much to ask that Kip could have a more even temper? Not too much. Lana's loneliness seems to have summoned Rose's most calm voice, one telling her there will be no problem, nature will provide, something greater than that tiny house will swoop down and help if something else doesn't swallow them first. Nature will provide, Lana repeats, meek in the face of a wild beauty that promises all badness can be worn away, absolved by natural cycles the way salmon each year get suctioned up from the vast ocean and come to the same river to spawn.

After Kip's death, once the twins are asleep, Lana surrenders both the garden and the specter of Rose for stronger addictions, smoking hand-rolled nicotine cigarettes in the doorway before pocketing cooled stubs away from the talent for shaming in her inlaws' eyes. New habits pile on others. Lana sleeps late or finds herself organizing her sock drawer in the wee hours before driving to her market job. The moments alone in a car cliffside are worst, making her try to find reasons to live while turning the bad country station up loud.

Nothing fully deafens her to the way Vic keeps his scoffing alive in her head.

Reason to live? The banal name for a simpleton's confection. Reason to live means a bluff against mortality, the one law greater than anyone's capacity to locate meaning.

How had Kip not found a buffer in his sons? How does a father commit suicide? Could she blame it on some new meds?

Smoking at night, those bad first months, she second-guesses the years she spent with Kip, all his stories' warp and weft. For one, the knee. To work the seasonal harvest, during the era of clean sweat, Kip had taken a drug to trick his knee's pain. How much more relieving it was for Lana to think that the painkiller had turned trickster, stripping Kip of free will and making him lose all desire to live, an idea much more warming than believing her mate had chosen death and conned her when she had thought him a vote for stability.

Despite how skittish a widow she is, the neighbors act like heat-seeking missiles in their ability to geolocate. She sees them coming and hides behind curtains, inside locked bathrooms, or, if outside, drops to her knees by the garbage cans. And still they walk around the house: Lana? I brought you something. Blue-haired, bushy-haired, bald, on lawnmowers and scooters, neighbors of all ages keep dropping by to check up on the widow. Perhaps they understand that distractions keep her from some inky well but why can't they let her have the full ecstasy of melancholic dissolution? Both the neighbors and her boys seem determined to keep her from succumbing fully to the urge to never smile again.

Once, to fend off yet another visit, she tells her guest: "Look, Kip and I never married!" This matters little to neighbors who breathe the lawlessness of disaster, understanding it to be as pungent and ubiquitous as salt air. After the donation drive for the funeral and burial, after the memorial fund for the boys, the neighbors still keep bringing their funnel cakes (moldy before she wraps and throws them out at night) and jasmine bouquets (withered before she locates the right vase). She doesn't know what she needs. Outside her inlaws' front door, neighbors mount a birdbath for hummingbirds, Kip's name carved in flowing script. The thing seems to attract not hummingbirds but rather only morbidly obese crows.

Is there a contest for loss? It remains unclear to Lana who needs reparations the most. Would it be Kip's beautiful sons, his suffering parents, or his clearly too edgy widow?

In the local paper, Lana, under her alias of Wagner says of Kip that no one would ever find a better father, her way of making a simple offering, a gift to the twins. One day they will read her statement and, memories dimmed, might know a basically good man had cared for them. "He was ultimately decent. Being a parent made him even more decent," she says.

For this pure immunity of goodness, Lana has often missed the early days of motherhood, boys crawling all over with a touch that would never intentionally hurt, morse-coding with their fingertips that they would grant her entry into the greater family of man, fingers and hot little breath telling her she was trustworthy and good, someone who showed integrity and humanity in every little maternal thing she did. Lana had been so happy to submit to the order of motherhood: the whole apparatus of being a parent gave her a joy greater than doll-playing years had let her imagine. She loved the rapture of doing dishes while thinking solely of dishes or the exaltation of arranging the old-style twins' carriage, Lana's particles humming as she lay her twins down on a sheepskin blanket—her own contribution—in order to spark their intellectual development.

Why so happy, Lana Wagner, Kip asked once and she tried explaining: for the first time in her life, to everything there had been a greater purpose. These kids anchored her, no longer letting her float too freely in the universe.

And because of this, those baby months marked the period when she knew the greatest partnership with anyone other than Rose. Once again she was joined to the greater project of losing herself.

But after the bliss with the boys had started the messy willful period when the boys had spat out food and separated from her ideas about perfection. Only a few months ago the boys had become so fully their own creatures, separate and ill-smelling, that she'd begun again to taste that dull metallic aloneness in her mouth, as fatal as if she'd never known any merge with them or as if the remembered togetherness made the return of isolation that much sharper. And every potential hope—say, any random person she would meet at the market—only dilated her loneliness. Life asked her to labor a stillbirth. Where was the joy? Times like this, she smoked any cigarette she could find and could not believe she had ever been as young as the girl who once found great sufficient pleasure in lying on her back with a girlfriend next to her facing a thunderstorm.

A question to Vic at the one Berkeley reading Lana had attended long ago with Rose: "Why is anger sexy?"

Vic's answer:

Anger is the only strong limbic emotion popularly termed negative—in the way that fright, hate or sadness are considered negative—which is capable of flooding the hypothalamus and making someone go *toward*.

At the government-coupon, welfare-cheese supermarket, on the wrong side of the highway, at the next cashier station over she encounters the world's most civilized man, one Lana thinks of as a neocolonial, a WASP tall and tightly bound, a boy's face on him as she tends to fancy. He makes pedantic comments and then looks out from under his mischievous brow, smiling, eyes blue, seeking concord, handsome in a roué alcoholic way, another man fallen from his intended station in life and wearing a brown tweed jacket to check out groceries. People call him the professor but also say never call the professor after five at night when he gets busy pickling his liver. He could be a smoker's forty-five or a well-preserved seventy-three but what counts is no one can enter the guy.

He sometimes makes little comments to the effect that aging is awful and should be avoided at all costs or that you get gypped when you give to charity but otherwise says little. Once he alludes to a relationship with a woman from the nearby Pomo reservation that went south during a bad drinking era. People try jollying him into revelation but he stays unfailingly civil and closed, tight as his high collar. He eats mostly whitish 1950s foods, brought to work in the same two Tupperware containers every day: macaroni salad, tapioca, tuna, peeled radishes and deviled eggs, making slight concessions toward celery and jicama. Lana never hears about his past, only about his ride to work that morning or what he anticipates watching that evening.

His one bit of public expression is that on weekends he heads toward the municipal beach where he makes giant sculptures out of driftwood. Lana has found she can draw him out only if she gets him to speak about driftwood. He calls it a particularly Californian commodity expressing all those who float here bearing aspirations with short half-lives, turning bone-bleached and waiting for somebody to claim them. On the subject of driftwood he turns eloquent.

But what makes Lana's mind linger on him and why she occasionally imagines him peeking at her has to do with his lunch break. He sits in the fluorescent lunchroom by himself, reading the local paper, apparently unaware of the thinness of the walls so that she alone listens to him saying: cocksucker! Fucking bitch! Cuntlicker! Goddamn the moron! Fools!

Though she never has more than a cordial acquaintance with him, it is this disparity between inner being and outer bearing that makes him almost unbearably attractive. She can't get him out of her mind. Once, they are doing inventory and he brings in a cassette to play, a country singer performing at a prison. Through the night he plays it on loop so she keeps hearing the part about the record company asking the singer not to say hell or shit and also the clanking part when the prison's announcer comes on amid the rumble of chains to make sure all the prisoners stay in their seats until guards come to release them. It is almost enough entry to allow broaching the subject of his lunchtime profanity but she stays mum.

Having heard his fury, she wonders what the professor thinks as he drives to work or sculpts. She alone seems to have witnessed a bound-up volcano let loose. How sexy is that? Such a man needs untying. Such a man needs a magic person not only to unbind him but one who knows how to handle heat.

Once Lana had tried talking with Kip about not swearing in front of the kids.

"Damn is not a swearword," he tells her. "Crap is not."

"You can't blame the kids for your not finding a real job."

"But my job is taking care of them. You're at the market. The kids take a lot of time."

"You're blaming them."

"I'm not—"

"You just said you couldn't find a damn legit job because our fucking kids refuse to put on their jackets and come talk to the logging company with you. You don't want them to spend an hour with your mom?"

Ugly and spiteful, lip bitten down: "Fuck!" Between clenched teeth in the other room, he slams something. The boys look up from their toys to do a nanosecond radar-read of her face, now managing a watery 1950s housewife smile, the kind she has used to navigate airports, bus stations, the incomprehensible: her lips pressed together in that smile bad as the sagged rictus of her own mother when Vic used to rage.

The problem was that Kip's kids were in many ways his sole domain, everything else shot through by his parents. His mother and her ancestry well suppressed; his father whom called that sumbitch white Indiana state trooper moved where he don't belong.

And what do I get from this ball of wax, Lana would think, listening to the fizz of Kip in the other room. A wave of self-contempt for having chosen such an angry mate. How easy to remember exactly this same fizz in her father and how her mother held it together, to consider exactly the cartoon signs that should have made her run from Kip and not straight into this moment: the feeble pressure of top lip against lower, the burlesque of having become a woman eking out a smile, a mother but still an eternal daughter with no escape other than to recall the mocking echo of all the hundreds of interrupted dinnertable conversations back in the Spruce Street house.

One night, a divorced colleague of her parents named Henry had voiced aloud the worry that his son was choosing mean girlfriends, which made Vic discuss the experiment of a scientist named Nambin who in his spare time had knocked the gene for the happy cuddling hormone oxytocin out of a mouse before birth, thereafter finding that such a mouse becomes a social amnesiac bearing no memory of other mice it met.

Hearing this, Lana had thought: poor mouse! And was glad when Henry had asked Vic what the experiment meant.

Vic had sighed. "Well, I'd say it suggests memory depends on the oxytocin-driven love response. That is, your son's choices have to do with some preprogrammed response to affection."

"You're saying he has bad genes?"

"Well, take yourself off the hook a bit?" said Vic, going on to discuss what Nambin had done in another experiment, this time with the prairie vole, Nambin holding a belief about the link between vasopressin and odor, proving that primal exposure to the opposite sex generates nerve cells in olfactory zones of the vole's brain.

"So my son doesn't have vasopressin? Or what, he's smelly?"

"Really that the scent of your wife, his first opposite-sex partner, formed a scent impression which now combines with the emotive track of what he considers necessary traits in the opposite sex."

"So?"

"If your ex was good or unkind, your son is doomed to go on seeking the same scent associated with any allied emotive track your wife provided—say, pleasure—"

"—neglect, misery—"

"—since one scent experience telegraphs opposite sex to his reptilian brain and gets bundled together with whatever emotion he finds most attractive and necessary to replicate with future mates."

"No hope then."

No hope! Lana had listened, tracing a snailshell on her bare knee, at the dinner table but not of it, whorish in what had started to feel like eavesdropping. And also knowing herself to be unlucky: her first scent of the opposite sex had to do with angry Vic and now in some endlessly mitotic fate, it looked as if she would be forever married to the sexiness of anger. She had not laughed, though his guest had. "How can you say nurture creates biological determinism? What can we do with that?"

Vic coughed and then his gaze caught Lana's. "My daughter will tell you, right, Mopsy? What do we parents do? Abandon all faith in our offspring and their prospects?"

And after this parlay but before excusing herself from the table, Lana had for the first time seen herself as a naked slave in the court of the pharaoh. Exactly that: a naked slave. That would be what she would remain, beholden until the day she could figure out how a slave gains intelligence enough to unspell fate.

When she and Kip used to argue, about, say, who got to spend more time with the twins, the fights did offer security. Kip could be as irascible as Vic but unlike Vic, at least Kip noticed what she did. She was not her mother. She was not. Had Vic ever noticed how much Mary managed? All the karate classes for their girlchild, the herb-strewn meals? Kip's rage nonetheless became Lana's pacifier. Where the hell did you put my keys? Why are the boys' shoes on my side of the bed? Who let the gopher into the garden? Who left this shit here? A grit to Kip's voice that made life matter more: Lana could feel her contours knowing she had for a time appeased some local god and would not need to torch anything herself. Plus his wrath meant he would never leave.

But every October into November they both knew the intensity of the pot harvest when Kip had to leave in earnest, able to a year's income from his labors. For three weeks behind three locked gates somewhere on the hot ridge, he worked sixteen-hour days, part of a collective run by a radical faerie named Serenity who presided over his brood with a lordly gaze and made his workers be driven to the harvest site blindfolded.

She knew certain facts about Kip's work. She knew two vegetarian chefs worked overtime to feed the laborers and that ten thousand dollars of pure organic compost from San Francisco had been carefully laid in to the marijuana plants during the year. To earn their keep, workers labored hours in the field to get a half pound of pay each day which, given the ever-rising market price, was anything but tight-fisted. Evenings, the workers had a shiatsu masseur who jumped on their backs to help release the knots of their industry. Nighttimes, the workers heard mountain lions creeping through the jungle around them, staying safe if shivering within tents provided by the entrepreneur of a successful backpacking company whose daughter had died of cancer and who in her last months had depended on the collective for pain relief.

The only stingy part about the harvest was that Kip left Lana alone with the boys, with his father BJ and mother Jennie both on an endless probe about the whereabouts of their son. He's working with a trucking company, Lana was supposed to tell them and she did, holding the fort, loyal and waiting for her fuming Kip to come back with the stories she loved: the helicopters roving the night, search-lighting the tents and coming so close to the plants that the wind almost destroyed all their hard work.

"Not like it's the world's worst substance," Kip once said to his father, stirring up a vodka gimlet for his dad.

"That's right. Show me a man who can't take a drink now and then and I'll show you a lily-livered snot."

"I was talking marijuana, dad, not liquor."

She had stayed to hear this fight, one of the few she did not leave in soundless protest, knowing Kip would never admit to his own harvest connection.

"It's a gateway drug," BJ had said, taking the drink with a grunt. "Leads to worse. Kids die."

"But you know cancer patients get rid of their pain or glaucoma? I mean can anyone argue with glaucoma?"

Kip had told Lana how the trimmers put up little placards regarding doctors' orders for patients along the rows so that if they ever got busted, the feds would see the trimmers had gone a mostly legal route and received certain exemptions.

Okay, so Lana didn't like Kip doing work on the rim of legality, because who needed any extra attention? Not to mention BJ's inter-rogation of her whenever Kip was gone. But it was clean work and she could see after the three harvest weeks that Kip felt restored, back to the land, massaged, strong, his temper more sensible. He'd done it enough times that he was considered an oldtimer. Plus, his collective was a positive entity, he said, not like the armed Mexican cartels up in the hills. You have to be careful, he warned her, don't hike the hills with the boys during this season—too many people accidentally get shot by the cartels.

But once BJ discovered what his son was doing for a living, he'd suffered his heart incident and made Kip's dealings go south.

Kip had been gone a week already, unreachable, since that was the collective's deal, stripping its workers of GPS devices, phones, even watches. The boys were picking cucumbers outside with their grandmother while Lana in the kitchen was trying to make shepherd's pie, the great pastoral orgasm.

The call had come from BJ's close friend, one who used to work in a law alliance against potgrowers. Lana kept stirring butter into the potatoes, halfway listening to the speakerphone BJ liked using, leaned back in his La-Z-Boy, broadcasting all calls as if jetstreamed back to the best of his highway patrol days.

His friend now hinted that BJ must find it hard to have Kip working with marijuana. "But it's lucrative, what do you expect?" the friend said.

Learning what Kip did for a living, BJ had sunk back into the La-Z-Boy, its leg extension springing up. At the thud and cry, Lana stopped stirring to run in, making her the first to see the death mask stretch across BJ's face, his eyes animal and vulnerable. He staggered up but she helped him back into the chair, calling to Jen outside, *Jen, Jen*, like a clicking dolphin.

The grandmother ambled in, the twins after. "Grandpa!" said Sedge, hoisting a cucumber.

All grandpa could say then was winch—wench?—and they understood someone should call the ambulance, Sedge the only one able to get to a phone and dial for help.

Afterward, angel son Kip was not blamed and anyway, he was not coming down from the harvest for a whole nother week.

Instead Lana became the vessel for blame. For a week, Jennie did not grace Lana with a single word, hushing phone conversations whenever this would-be pretender to the family came by holding kids' plates, a load of laundry, anything Lana could do to earn her keep. It was Jennie who created the consensus that Lana should be excluded from the hospital room after they'd performed BJ's bypass, as if the bad daughter-in-law were to blame for what had happened not just to Jennie's son but to Jennie's husband, Lana the prime ingrate who had ripped the fabric of their pure country life.

When Kip returned, tanned and strong, happy, at first he did not realize the house he came back to was not the one he had left: he lifted his head like a perplexed dog trying to hear far-off keening while Lana hovered, puttering with garden tools by the front door.

"Your father," Jen said to Kip.

"Where is he?"

Jen waved her arm off as if in contempt toward BJ, seated in the brown recliner, knees buckled, a pale hand up. They'd put a stent into his heart and BJ had lost quarts of blood; there'd been a few nights of hit-or-miss. Now a pig valve kept the patriarch functioning and it would have to be replaced in ten years. Some of this Jen said to Kip if too quickly.

"Dad!" said the son.

For the first time in his son's life, Trooper Hilson could barely speak so Jen kept speaking for him. Lana only heard parts:

"Your father. His position in the community. She. The boys. You're a father now."

"Aw, ma. Don't put it on Lana. Anyway, dad's half retired."

"Honor. When he goes to the store. People look. Son's a grower?"

"I'm not, ma. Or not exactly. I just helped out." They stopped there, Kip caught in his lie. Jen burst into tears before retreating to the bathroom and locking the door.

"What's going on?" Sedge said. "Here grandpa." He put yet another apple in the lap of BJ, who'd sat a waxwork for days, stunned by the slights family slung on a man.

Then came the afterward: in some kind of hyper-rebellion, Kip went covert. Where before he'd been involved with the natural guys, fledgling hippies concerned about land stewardship and clean crops, the kind to leave their soil better than before, now he slipped around with toters of AK-47s, knives strapped to the thighs leaving dents no one could sleep off. Mercenaries shopped the cross-border economy to truck in any number of famished men with thick necks, usually young Mexicans wanting to provide for their families, people to whom the coyotes had promised employment who found themselves, once over the border, brutalized by the same coyotes, working slave hours and performing in exact fealty with feudal growers' wishes unless they wanted to become mousebait for la migra.

Lana couldn't understand what part Kip played in this. Was he trying to make that much more money? Was he taking too many meds for his bad knee? Or had he become one of the guys strapping a knife to his thigh? Not only could she not tell anymore, she did not care, preferring to lock herself deep away. As Vic would have said, her limbic brain had started telling her to flee but some twist in her neocortex made her hang on, addicted to the house and its rituals, the breakfast hush.

For a year she endured their sham, working long hours at the market but sometimes eyeing the angry neocolonial cashier or the married men who seemed promising, thumbworn in a good way, soft at the waist and possessing portals to vulnerability.

Until Kip, the next September, careened his car into the ocean: that was it.

At his funeral, holding each boy's hand, she had been equivalently dead inside, unable to speak. She could second-guess nothing. Mainly she was unsure whether to stay on in Yalina because of some idea that her boys were so attached to their grandparents or could she just give in to her impulse for flight?

Not to abdicate motherhood. No, instead she could disappear with the boys, take them to find a school where the boys would make friends, all would be better. But days and weeks passed before she could move beyond a few random flings. That last year, in what felt like a final moment of despair, she had signed up for that contact improv seminar at that church—Mary, Star of the Sea—and right after that Dirk had chosen to swoop her up into his life, sweep her down to Hope. So he wasn't the best mate and she seemed to have bad luck choosing men but nothing is permanent, it's all about the slash, her new mate had intoned, it's all about finding temporary connection between any two disparate forces, salsa on ice cream, pineapple on pizza, you and me. And what else so far preached any differently?

FOUR

"You're not eating?" says Rose, picking at a lentil salad. It comes between women sometimes, this thing about hunger and its private rituals. As when once, a teenager, Rose had a beau who had breathed about Lana: she is perfect! Which meant that, unlike other girls whose hips and chests radiated heat, Lana lived in coolness, a promise that if you were with her, you would get to touch that coolness and life would spare you some of its smaller degradations.

They are finishing ice teas when there walks by the rich long-haired man, the fabled computer whiz, deeply tanned, the one who walks everywhere, even the dining hall, with just a string around his waist.

"You know I saw him holding the hand of the yoga instructor after the class," Lana whispers. "Poor guy."

"He didn't hold Dirk's hand though, right?" Rose whispers back. "Anyway, don't call him poor guy. You never knew I had a thing about waist-strings?" which does make Lana laugh until she chokes.

Once she recovers, she waves a hand. "Sorry. I probably haven't laughed like that in forever."

"Your laugh was always your best part."

"Nothing else?"

"I said best."

"That guy though—you used to be so great, you could say exactly who people were."

Rose flushes at their old game being brought up. "You don't think he's just some lonely pathetic boy who wants love?"

"Go on."

"Maybe he had some little sister who was disabled. Maybe he needed to disclaim his heritage and started being nudist to sort of out-physical her."

"Your kind of man!"

After Rose takes it the wrong way, frowning, Lana tries going backward. "You know I've become a real weirdo magnet. I get weirdos everywhere I go."

"Me too," lies Rose. "But now I think insanity is so exhausting. Because it is always just about itself, you know what I mean? It can't listen to anyone else."

Lana has to steel herself, tell herself not to escape, because there is something about Rose—is it her readiness to merge?—that reminds her of Lestrion, her son's space robot.

According to Sedge, on a day when he had dared entrust her with a bit of knowledge about Lestrion, the robot knows holes perforate the skin of the universe and so Lestrion must stay vigilant against the threat of both the holes and also the lightning rods. Holes and rods could mess up Lestrion's job, which is to keep spheres of stealth knowledge safe.

While Lana can't fully follow her boy's cosmology, what she does understand makes sense given that on bad days her anxiety could puncture the universe. Someone like Rose appears friendly enough to take advantage, pretending to be a lightning rod but really coming in sneakily to patch up all exits.

"What did you think when Dirk talked about emotions?" Rose is asking. "You know, during that thing he just did, the benediction or whatever."

Lana imitates him spot-on, droning: "Emotions have their own processes and needs, their beginnings, their ends."

"I was sure you were in a deep trance!"

"At this point, I'm good at pretending."

Rose dares. "You like him a lot?"

After the trance, in the sweaty amber half-light, Lana had seen Dirk's wrist snake, a dark hallucination, round the waist of a pert blonde married to some old Colorado buddy of his, a chi kung master he admired. She decides to tell Rose this. "I mean who ever wants to see a man attracted to someone so plastic?"

The previous night, Dirk had confided to Lana, cracking at least one edifice, that while he doesn't envy what Lana had told him about her old closeness with Rose, he envies the self-satisfaction of his old Colorado buddy.

I understand, Lana had lied, wishing she could find more of an opening in Dirk so she too could confide something: she feels recently as if some kind of lava pushes inside, ready to burst.

With Rose, to change the subject, she says that when she'd seen Dirk's hand at the girl's waist, Lana had felt a masochistic pleasure.

"You think you're a masochist? Really?" Now it is Rose who is good at parroting the guru. "Remember Dirk saying emotions have their birth and death and our job is to respect them—you can't go against flow?"

"You're better than I am at imitating him." Lana scrapes at the skin on her knee, flaking off in bits, wishing to unburden herself. She tells Rose she had overheard a gust of bad news, including the chi-kung buddy talking about Lana on the terrace to Dirk, asking Dirk isn't there more to a mate than six-pack abs?

"What did Dirk say?" Rose leans close, tongue lolling, engaged.

"Dirk said at first it might be hard to see how amazing I was on the inside. Whatever that means!" and in Rose's answer, the way she rolls her eyes with such quick sympathy, Lana feels some magma cool, just a bit, letting her breathe more freely.

For how many years has Lana kept Rose a possibility, patient in the theater of herself? "You are so great to talk to," she tells Rose. "I forgot." Though this isn't really true. On all those nights in the Yalina garden, when the ruckus inside her family's cabin threatened to consume her with insignificance, how many times had Lana, smoking, reminded herself that somewhere, at some point, she had a friend so dedicated that everything Lana did or thought became important?

So karmically cathected, as Vic used to say, a little derisive on the topic of the shaggies. Only now does Lana understand it: once she used to be a Vic to Rose. Once Rose had been her prime shaggy and maybe still is. So who cares about karmic cathection? Isn't the world tough enough that most people just need some kind of friend?

At night in the scented dark of a room Lana had tried to make more about romance and less about Hope, one she has embellished with incense holders, fig perfume and scarves, after a day with Rose in which the old friends had talked in great swooping circles around their lives, good at avoiding any core, Lana cannot help her happiness.

Something shifts under the earth, some small good flows her way, and it helps the nocturnal restlessness of her feet with their endless appetite for new turf.

She turns toward Dirk. His hand, both bearish and tapered, flops over her waist, a lazy claim, just the way Rose used to hold her from behind. And while she and Dirk had made a pact not to talk about past sexual misadventures, to come together as a couple of the future, again she wonders: over how many other women's waists had this hand flopped? Whom has he claimed? How dead is the signifier, as her father loved to say, how debased the currency? Feeling the emptiness of Dirk's hands—unfortunate, because his face is so rough-hewn and a woman would think he would be a different sort of lover, a sculptor with those thick hands—she starts concocting a story about him, one to save and tell Rose in the morning, a story that Rose will find funny or at least interesting.

On another floe, far from Dirk, she cannot quite locate the swoon of their first moments. They've probably cohabited too quickly; this must be the mistake. She had moved in so quickly only with Kip and he had offered truer mooring. To find Dirk, she wants to tell him more about Rose, how just talking with an old friend has reminded her of so much. Yet it is hard for her to speak directly: instead she goes oblique, getting into what Dirk has called her song-and-dance about her boys. That she has been remiss as a mother.

Finally he interrupts. "That's what's keeping you awake?"

"I can't keep those boys from the bad."

She can't explain why this topic is the one she keeps beating Dirk over the head with. Maybe it has something to do with his understanding of who her mother and father are. Were.

"I'm just way too insubstantial as a parent. It's like my body can't ever really stand between the boys and any fate. Like what happened with the mountain lion and Hogan the other day? I just stood there. I couldn't move."

She has already told most of this to Dirk. What she really wants to confide is how Rose's presence makes her feel that old dormant quickstep, the glitter of nighttime city lights and walking sidewalks with a beloved, the only destination being fun.

"I should somehow give more to my boys," she says instead.

Dirk sighs. "They're nine. What would that be? Calculus kits? Lamb's Shakespeare?" He may have tidily kept himself from fathering any kids but still knows his supplicants' shopping lists.

"Other advantages." She tries to explain. If she had been a better mother in their early years, the boys would find themselves striding through life in some better, smarter way. Because her lacks mean theirs and her chips and flaws will keep them unhappy, never doctors or lawyers, never organizers or future leaders of America. These boys have a mother who loves skirting the center, whose best job so far has been at the local market, a mother who tried giving the boys the bushmama community of Yalina and who now plops them down into weird Hope with its naked spa. Once begun, she cannot stop her prophecies.

"Like instead of becoming, I don't know, ecoscientists, they'll end up Scientologists," she says.

Dirk pats her arm before turning on his bedside light so he may read. As if she were half of a worn-slipper, married couple of many years, in slight bitter spoof she returns the act, picking up a copy of an alternative journal in which an ad about Dirk's services beams forth at her. THE LIFE YOU SAVE MAY BE YOUR OWN.

"You know," he finally says, "if you developed more of a spiritual practice—let me finish—you'd feel more linked as a parent. Your pores would be filled. Your nervousness about leadership or whatever American corporate interests couldn't enter. You'd worry less."

"Worry?" she says, ready to mount a self-defense if he hadn't already jumped out of bed to get the phone ringing in the next room.

Watching him cross, she gets something crucial about Dirk. This guy must belong to that breed of older men who lack the patience of the young, the young who can hitchhike across three states and line up overnight, freezing, just to get tickets to hear some band to spike their id. When you're young you have time for hope to find its object, she thinks. And now, instead of being with someone at least youthful in spirit, the way Kip was until the end, she has somehow landed smack into a coupling with one of those older men whose nearness to mortality mimics a surge of testosterone, Dirk the kind of man who must answer telephone calls, inaudible or not, as if they could be last-ditch offers from the angel of life.

A wrong number, apparently, no one on the line. "Actually," says Dirk, putting on a striped robe. "I don't get who you are as a mother. Sometimes, forgive me for saying this, I feel you did sleepwalk into the role. Please, I don't mean it in a bad way, I'm just saying—"

She feels an urgency: SEDUCE HIM. His words slime her.

"For example, tell me if this is okay to say, you never talk about the daddy of your boys. I mean the imprint from daddy is huge, right? You especially know about daddies."

"Didn't we say we weren't going to talk about our romantic past?" A wheedle in her voice she doesn't like. A weak defense but she is not ready to enter the taboo of total confession so fast.

Somewhere in the bottom of her purse is a foil-wrapped wish-sighting pill—the dealer in Yalina had called it Avalokitesvara—that could, right now, if she managed to take it, make her able to handle anything. Without Dirk's noticing, she could just go scrabble in the purse.

No need. He returns to bed, robe on. "Here's a book I've been wanting you to read," he says, handing her *The Lazy Man's Guide to Enlightenment.*

Reading, half-peeking as he lies next to her twisting his spine, she tries to ignore the tornado. She has spent four months with Dirk. Up in Yalina the guy had seemed, like Kip had before him, a vote for stability. To follow him she had sacrificed, confused her ex-inlaws, left her job, left the swearing neocolonial and her vegetable garden and everything, not even saying one goodbye to all the pitying fellow bushmamas she never wanted to see again anyway.

Now because of those burnt bridges she doesn't really want to go back to Yalina. Yet the smallest spotlight reveals Dirk's main flaw: his impatience plus his lust for applause, not exactly attractive traits. Plus had she wanted him or just, to use his term, walked asleep toward the idea that a slash lived between them, some kind of temporary chemistry? What was she thinking anyway being with such an older guy?

Actually, she probably had never cared for his boy-o-boy sexuality. The guy acts as if sex is a rollercoaster ride. It comes to her: the inevitability that she will leave, probably soon, with only the how or when to be worked out. The why, however, does glow. Somewhere, she is sure, a normal life awaits her and the boys.

JUST CONSIDER DIRK A PIT STOP ON THE WAY TOWARD NORMAL

Lana hears it as clearly as if her mother's voice came from across the room. As if her mother sat with legs folded, a person wearing a crocheted sweater, looking up over reading glasses, her mother using one of Rose's favorite phrases, as in *let's make a pit stop for bubble gum?* Lana's spine quivers: never before has she felt her mother speaking so directly or in such strange tones, as if a ghost could speak with a mother's worry through Rose's voice.

"Shhh," says Lana.

"Hmm?" Dirk says, mid-stretch.

New terrain.

Lana will go down Five and then, subtracting her last weird years, cross over to One. She will find a place by the ocean for the boys, somewhere smooth and demilitarized, a beach lifestyle, covert among thousands flocked to the ocean in a place where a person could own a standard slot of normal, a house with a stucco balcony encasing a life no one will question. She will ride her bike to the boardwalk, take pottery classes, paint, study music, have a fireman boyfriend, enough normalcy flowing in her veins to become the mother she was meant to be. Maybe she could finally follow a lifelong dream, take the firefighters' test herself, train to ride the trucks: she'd be a lone woman holding her own among broad-shouldered, capable men.

In the evenings, laughing friends of diverse origins would sit with her to watch kids frolic on sugar-sand beaches in a supreme orgy of normalcy.

But it's too soon to surrender all hope about Dirk. They have not yet arrived at the edge of all that they can do or say to each other. More of a knife needs to twist her gut or some irrevocability to his badness needs to appear, something to let her know that choosing him had been her quest for the edge and the bad choice had at least some meaning.

Alternatively, as Vic liked to say whenever he saw others engaged in whatever they called romantic—tango dancing, Valentine rituals, weddings—the universe is made up of randomness and the copulative dance can be just as meaningful as two ants bumping into each other before signaling each other off.

"Goodnight, sugar. You're the best," says Dirk now. "I love how accepting you are. You really are great at knowing how to give a person space."

"I'd go in the water with those boys but could they just leave their penises out?"—the small girl named Chloe sneaks a sly smile up at her mother, a waif of a woman, seeing if this particular possibility, the omission of penises, could enter the forum. From her safe harbor at the rim of the kiddie pool, Chloe has been watching Sedge and Tee splash about. Anyone watching would think Rose hovering near a lounge chair next to Lana also finds the sight of two small boys captivating.

"Want to lie here?" and Lana is so maternal, placing the towel on the chair next to her, smiling as Rose takes the bait that Rose's old cells reactivate: being asked to be part of two girls lying together in early morning sun. It doesn't hurt that one of their old songs plays the loudspeakers

> Ginger sighs and it's a fogged-up day
> She loves to be part of your whirl
> She lives in a gutter by your Creamsicle hut
> With nothing jeweled you can steal
> O nothing you can feel

Wielding long foam wands hued like carcinogenic food dyes, Lana's sons get happy fast, beating themselves to mock death in the kiddie pool. Little sunhatted Chloe almost falls into the pool with interest. "Hey!" one boy shouts.

"I say stop!" The other's feathery voice. Sedge, Tee, Rose reminds herself, Tee caramel-eyed but sharp as his name, Sedge with straighter hair. Their battle resumes, a serious one heading toward unilateral victory or mutually assured annihilation.

"You believe we're middle-aged?" asks Rose, raising herself on an elbow, the heat of this place almost enough to dissolve the edges, pretext enough to muddle forth. "You like being a mother?"

But she has miscalculated: Lana is not fully ready to talk, eyes guarded. Of course Rose knows there is no way to just appear somewhere and get a person to open like some fast-motion rosebud shedding petals. "It has its days," says Lana, finally mustering as well. "You'd be a great mom, you know. You're so, I don't know, attentive?"

At the breakfast bell they move to the slop area where Lana busies herself tending to her boys' titration of milk and hot chocolate but after all spills and damage control, once there are no more excuses, hungry too for something, Lana slides in next to where Rose nurses a coffee cup at the table facing the valley.

"What I can't believe is we're here together," says Lana. "The Lolas in this kind of place?"

Around them smooth young people with determined hipbones, members of the kitchen crew, surely evolution's most erect spines, show great awareness in how they ladle out leaves from large glass jars before stirring tea within individual mugs. Next to them, two of the kitchen crew melt into each other's arms: a deep hug, pelvis to clavicle pressed as one to exchange silent body agreements.

The manager Hogan veers in, tipping his railroad hat with one hand, grabbing a broom in the other. "You ladies know about the anniversary events today?"

"We do," says Rose, giddy, semi-naked, speaking to someone clothed.

"Great," he says, bowing off to sweep a walkway near the deck, almost out of earshot.

Rose hadn't quite worked out the plan. What she'd thought, after two phone calls yesterday with Vic's lawyer, is that, as she'd guessed, the best bet for an overturn in Vic's verdict might rest in new evidence being introduced. Given that no prior defense team had yet been able to summon any law-abiding, rational person willing to speak in defense of Vic, no one yet offering any substantive character testimony, if the defense could introduce even the merest new deposition in the final hearing, it would not be improbable that sentencing could be delayed. Vic could at least get the chance of a medical stay. This is Rose's thinking and she has impressed it upon his current lawyer.

At least Vic would get the dignity of dying in his own time. Isn't that all anyone wants, Rose had said to the lawyer in the last phone call. Everyone wants a choice about when a thing ends, right? "Sure," the lawyer had said, uncommitted. After the talk, Rose researches the woman and finds Hogan was right after all: this lawyer had served on seven capital cases. One went directly to firing squad, four dawdled toward the electric chair, two ended with lethal injection.

This particular fact means Rose really has no time to beat around the bush with Lana. The hearing comes in a matter of days, before winter recess, and after that there will be only a few more days before the event she does not want to utter. As Rose sips her coffee, the letters glow before her in obsidian.

Lana could just say this one thing: Vic had been prone to a lifelong pattern.

Fits of temporary insanity.

Lana had witnessed these fits, big and small, since childhood. Her testimony would change his fate. Everything had led to this moment, everything was converging. Rose would not fail as she had during the trial. All she had to do now was hand Lana the key.

"Hey. I don't know how to start."

Lana faces her, all interest. "Start what?"

"Well, there's something I wanted to tell you."

"You're a hermaphrodite."

"No, wouldn't you have known by now?"

"Okay. You're pregnant."

"I wish."

"Really?"

"That's a whole different story. But yes. Listen. It's more serious than that."

"Is anything more serious than pregnancy?" Between them flashes another memory, two of the abortion appointments to which Rose had escorted Lana.

"It's you know." Rose stops, wishing to have a perfect mind-meld instead of this clumsy parry. "Your dad. Sorry. Vic's case?"

"Rose." Lana narrow-eyed. "I mean come on."

"I'm sorry. Just let me get this one thing out. At least I should tell you I'm meeting with one of Vic's lawyers today."

"Oh." Lana stirs some invisible poison in her mug. "Why though?" Her squint so mean, Rose must look away.

"Well. Thought I could help—your dad, his case."

"He asked? You saw him?"

"Not since what, our graduation party in high school?"

Lana's stare is unflinching. "So you've been in contact?"

"If some other friend's dad ended up in prison, wouldn't you try to help?"

"What other friends do I have?" Lana barks a laugh, laughs a bark, wishing she could shut Rose down like the Pandora's box she is turning out to be. Only a few hand-spans away from them, one of the kitchen crew nuzzles her boyfriend, splayed across his lap. Lana leans in to Rose, trying for calm, though now she feels owed something. "Whatever. But if you see him, don't tell me about it."

"No, I mean, I'd be upset too. But he's not the one I'm going to see."

"Promise. And don't tell him about the twins."

"Actually, I was wondering if you wouldn't mind coming with me. To the lawyer."

"Well." Lana palms the table, throbbing with rhythm. Things are getting a little out of reach. "Maybe you don't get it? I want nothing to do with him."

"No, of course. We all do what we need to. I'd feel the same." Rose lets the demurral sit only a second. "But just this one thing Lana? Because you know he's sick, right?"

"So I'm trying to figure out what you thought I'd say here. Like wow, that's so great, Rosie, I'm so happy my savior friend is trying to help out my poor murderer father in his last days? Plus she wants to drag me into it?"

"But maybe if I could tell you the exact details—"

"Don't you think I come somewhere like this place so I don't have to know?"

"No, I totally understand."

"Thanks." Lana manages a kinder smile. "But you don't always have to be so sincere."

"I'm not. But he has nine days left."

"Ten." Lana cannot help but correct her.

"You do know then?"

Her face only now starts to burn. "Maybe you don't mean to do what you're doing right now?"

"I just wanted to help. I didn't want to bother you but it does seem as if—"

"Because it's probably hard for you, right?"

"What?"

"I would've hoped, you know, better things for you. That you know—you would have had more of a life by now."

"Actually maybe we shouldn't talk right now."

"Fine." Lana studies her. "I wasn't the one who asked to."

"Fine."

"Fine." Lana steeples her fingers, unsteeples them. "But what is it? The myth of the great family Mahler? Or what, leeching off a great man? Is this about your never having had a real family?"

It takes Rose more than a few seconds to realize how directly Lana wishes to sting. When she does get it, she cringes, hacking her hand like a visor to the side of her eyes and lying viciously: "I'm fine. Really I don't care. It's great seeing you. Let's talk later?"

And against all kitchen protocol, Rose, having blocked herself off somewhere far away, excuses herself, abandoning her flowered mug with its masking tape marked in big block letters ROSE, so that Lana must then wash it herself in communal buckets marked FIRST RINSE, SECOND RINSE, all while muttering to herself, as Mary used to, *where's the tragedy?* only to leave the mug to get lost on the drying rack so that eventually one of the wash crew must strip the cup of Rose's name and set it out to be chosen by some other guest of Hope.

Trying to figure out where the room is, wanting to take comfort anywhere else, Lana navigates what has become a forest of rapists and then the voice comes, a screech from the past ready to scavenge her marrow. As if you could just turn back time and *Wait! Lana?* A voice crackled at the edges. Rose tugs and Lana pats her arm when really what she wants is to burn it, Rose's face so broad in its eagerness, tilting up under that dark hair, blue eyes hesitant but expectant, holding that pink towel around her cleavage. She looks up at Lana as if this could be enough.

"I mean it. I'm sorry," says Rose. "It's a tough subject. I just thought we could—"

"No, I'm sorry too. Lost control. You're right. Let's not talk. I mean I was happy to see you too." But Lana's voice breaks. "So why'd you come? Here."

Rose tilts her head north. "You know."

Maybe Rose means something else. But that particular Rose look after so many years is troublesome. Head ducked, tongue lolling, eyes smeared, hopeful: the look thwarts Lana. "No, actually I don't."

"Please don't give such a mean smile?"

"No, I get it. You're another shaggy." Lana rolls the word with distaste.

"I'm not."

"Finding me was your toy surprise."

"Or more the reverse, Lana? Not like I'm constantly in touch with him." Blue shine. "Only here and there. More recently. Anyway."

Lana has to count backward from ten, because she will not give in to rage. See where rage got Vic or Kip, see where it would get her as a mother of sons. A breath. Eight seven six. "I mean, what gave you the right?" Four three two and she can't be calm.

Rose takes her arm. "Come on. Last time we saw each other was at the gogo place."

"That's not true at all."

"Okay, you're right. The apartment."

"But what is it Vic tells you? You're the daughter he's never had?"

Rose's face puffs up, a big pink teddy-bear face.

"Come on, don't lie to me."

The best Rose can manage, swallowing back the tears. "Maybe let's start over?"

Lana grimaces.

"I mean isn't it sort of amazing we're both here?"

It comes to Lana: in fact Rose had tracked her down and there could be no running from a vampire. Ten nine eight. Start over. Lana could take a breath and try seeing it differently. She would not be so angry if seeing Rose had not brought up her old hungers. Think normal, Lana tells herself. She could be a normal woman on vacation, starting up some new healthy life for her kids. And here appears her devoted friend—but it's too much delusion, Rose the old-time meddler in her family. A huge wave steals over Lana, enough to make her wish for any exit. At the same time couldn't she just give herself over, fall apart on Rose's shoulder? Mary would never had said to trust anyone too much and yet Mary had always called Rose Lana's good influence.

"Well what, you searched for me?"

"I ran into Jane Polsby. In Ellay."

"She told you about the boys?"

"This has nothing to do with the boys." For a second some refuge might be found in Rose's face but then it disappears. This is all ending terribly. Lana can find no bare minimum to get through this, great violence being done to whatever binding she had hoped for. What had made her think she could handle an old friend?

"I can't take it Rosie. This time you really messed up. You don't know a single thing about my life!" All that remains available is her oldtime talent for stomping off. Lana leaves Rose to sink, alone, onto a lounge chair.

It is Hogan who descends from the upper path, cracking a smile at Rose: "So." When that gets no answer, he tries again. "Your buddy?"

Rose just shakes her head. Clumsy, stupid, wrong. Nothing ever comes with a clear label. Dizziness circles her vision: she always tries not to get teary so fast and must do what she can to swallow. Dabbing the edges of her eyes with her towel, she looks up at the manager. "I'm sorry, can I ask you a favor?"

"Anything."

"Could you watch the boys—hers—wherever they are? Got to find her before," she manages. Before what? Before it all blows up. She should have held back, not forced things. Just when the Lolas might have slipped back into the groove all over and naturally Lana would have come with her to testify. Instead Rose had gone and ruined everything.

"Your friend's a hothead, huh?" says Hogan.

Rose's hand rises and flops back onto the towel, only to get smeared with a flaccid spilled curl of sunscreen, a nautilus.

Lana would always know the voice, Rose and her deep-gut shout: "Lana."

She could love that voice fiercely but speaks over her shoulder. "Or what's it, necrophilia? I can't believe you."

"I mean he just thinks of me as some kind of supporter."

Lana in her disappointment cannot finesse the mulberry-strewn ground, the tree roots, an excess of shakti pushing up out of concrete. She trips, splayed out, hands a V before her, a quick knife slicing up the leg.

Now she looks up at Rose's face. "Sheesh," says Lana.

The naked man with the key-string around his waist smiles politely down at Lana, at all female trouble in general, the trouble visited upon the world since the dawn of the akashic record and then elects to step over Lana's shin, staying firm on his course toward the plein-air shower.

"You okay?" Rose kneels down, hand cupping toward the knee as if about to administer a sacrament.

"Don't touch." Last time Lana had done this she had wrenched the leg on some cliffs and it has stayed her weak one, another humiliating affront. It occurs to her that she has just fallen down a new kind of rabbithole.

"Think you twisted your ankle?"

"Please." And whether Lana means please leave or please help, it doesn't matter.

"I'll get ice?" Rose, gearing up toward full savior bliss, tells Lana one of the first complete truths. "Wait for me, I'll be back."

Not a big deal. A little clinic for farmworkers about an hour away where all the signs are in Spanish. NO FUME, NO TIRE EL CHICLE, NO HABLE EN VOZ ALTA, CUIDA LOS NIÑOS CON LA LECHE. Hogan has taken her to the clinic in the cook's stationwagon, the cook riding shotgun: the hooked cook, Lana thinks, a nice vet with a hook for an arm named Antwan who shows her pictures of his bitty girls up in Oakland, Jocasta and Yolanda. Their mother won't let Antwan see them. Lana is almost cheerful talking with Antwan after the doctors wrap a cast on her foot, having giggled at everyone's bad jokes about Viagra and their prescription of bed-rest and lack of weight on the foot, giggling all the way until they tell her about crutches and the rules—

It is her driving foot. She is laid up! And for at least three weeks. She doesn't want to trust her hearing.

"Well, ma'am," Hogan says in the waiting room, a little too merry, having sussed her situation. "Now you guys are here for good."

"Me and Rose?"

"You and your boys. Why not. I'll give you free room and board."

Antwan the cook looks away: something in this parlay makes him need to amble down the hall to study the line-up of WANTED posters.

"I thought Dirk was, you know, already taken care of. At Hope."

"Who said he's not. But this will be on your account, ma'am, not under your guy's name. I'll have to check but I bet I could arrange it so you and your boys could stay at Hope. I'm talking indefinitely."

"Why would any place bother offering that?"

"Because your accident happened on our grounds, number one. You never signed our form. So we have liability issues. Though looks like you don't exactly love lawyers." He studies her. "Also you don't want to depend that much on your man, right?"

"Okay." She's not about to let in any stranger that much.

"And then there's that other thing, you know."

"What's that?"

"Your dad?"

Now she gets it. Either Rose has told him or the guy overheard but who fucking cares when her head clangs, tired of all of them, annoyed, and now there will be no going backward, the rabbit out of the hat, the magic of Vic spitting all over her. "Okay so what, you're another worshipper?"

This Hogan similarly chooses to ignore. "How about let's just call it avoidance of lawsuits, ma'am," his smile hard to read, the guilt of conspiracy the only clear part she sees.

It could be funny. It could be that some force wishes for her never to stray far from Vic or the finger of the law. And just when she thinks she has found some rock to sneak behind, that finger always finds her and diddles her, just like the game of no escape her boys like to play, stuffing each other down under pillows and then tickling each other until one of them says peanut butter.

Back at the ranch, Hogan really does give her a better room. "For your convalescence." He cannot help but add: "Away from your guy. A little bit of breathing room helps any relationship, right?"

Breathing room. Lebensraum on the lowest floor where Lana has no stairs but instead a balcony opening up to the broad mountains and beyond, her curtains marked by horseshoes, ropes, one-eyed dice. This will be her room in which she will try jostling the facts to get some kind of escape, a room from which to spy cars on the freeway, cars trammeled in jams and moving forward like little ants. *My father was the wind in my sails* is the odd phrase that rules her head before she drifts into what might be the most luscious sleep she has had since leaving her childhood bed.

The doctors are beautifully compliant in doubling the dose when Lana asks. She is afloat on a rich cocktail that raises her higher, farther out in the universe than ever, shards pulverized into a fairydust spread over the galaxy as if somewhere she had accepted the fine print of disintegration. If she had only the pills and not her boys, the walls and the deep occasional talk with Elsa, a curvy she-male maid who comes twice a day, showing admirable mastery over duster and vacuum, so much of Lana could just etherize away.

On the first day, Dirk sits by her bed and palpates her hand. The shades are drawn so it must still be early morning. Dirk talks in one stream: he says she should see her mishap as if she were a seed with the earth lying atop her. If she sees the twisted ankle from a materialist standpoint, her situation is in fact terrible and her attitude will be as bad as if she chooses to pour ammonia or beer on that seed. Because can a seed grow with ammonia? If, however, she can see the accident as sparks from a divine plan for herself, she will know to bless the bad ankle—it's a gift, Lana—and her attitude will act as water and light, making the seed grow and blossom into learning and meaning.

"Wait, so does that make me the seed?" she asks, not really following. "Or what, would you bless my ankle? I'm sorry, honey"—
honey what she used to call Kip, her past man and current man doing

a small do-si-do—"could you please pass me one of those purple pills? Just a little water? You mind?"

Dirk does, leaving soon after. Whether she sees the accident from a spiritualist or materialist perspective, whether she has upset him, she can't say, her mind foundering a bit on the question, the fairydust reclumping, earthbound and rimed. Of course she welcomes visits. While she likes the terms of the float, anyone coming through her door does remind her she exists.

Visits are patch-up jobs, she tells the maid Elsa, who turns off the vacuum and takes a break to turn off the smoke detector and go through two cigarettes in the room, telling her about all the operations, her first op presided over by a bad botcher, only interrupting herself to work the air-conditioning so it hums at an arctic chill. Lana feels exultant, listening: she has never met a more fascinating companion than Elsa.

And her boys also continue to function, reporting back to some customary dull spot in their psyche, one cabling forgiveness. Sedge has made a card that says MAMA MAMA, showing her jumping off a cliff into a rainbow. To make him feel she gets the meaning of this loving gesture, she places the card on her bedside table and kisses him for his lie in claiming both twins made the card, since this is Sedge's breed of sensitive, never wanting either brother to suffer from lack of acclaim.

Maybe the next morning, not fully awake, she asks Sedge: "Hey, you just came through the wall?" From his scared face she understands she must have asked something that sounded crazy. "I meant to ask Lestrion," she corrects herself. "I love you. Sorry. Mind if I go back to napping? Do you mind making the room just a bit colder?"

Because cold helps sustain divisions, keeps all from melting into unpalatable fusion, into the endless question on Rose's face or the idea of Vic alone in his cell. Having entered her float through doors called Percocet and Vicodin, names alone that perk her up a bit, now Lana bounces through some cosmic tunnel: but she must focus on choosing the right door at its end. Behind door number one, some optimism awaits. Who was it who misplaced the list on which she is supposed to notate how many pills she has taken so far today?

The worst part being that, come the second day, Hogan or Dirk or someone mischievous seems to have misread the status of her current friendship with Rose. Lana gets the tiger, not the lady, someone having delegated Rose and her inquiring eyes to be in charge of Lana. Instead of her boys or even Dirk, it is Rose who comes bearing gifts, messages, taking over meals, babysitting, reprieve.

Old friends, only stalemated, Rose seems to think, from the way she accepts Lana's rudeness, an ascetic uplifted by self-flogging rites. Lana is almost willing to take comfort in Rose. Their easiest topic is the leg. Does the leg itch? Does Lana need water? Any special books? Should Rose ask Hogan for a movie player? "Don't worry," Lana keeps saying, another of the greater lies. "Could you just fiddle a bit with the air-conditioning?" EVEN REPELLENT LOVE CAN OFFER CHARMING DISTRACTION FROM THE HORRORS OF EXISTENCE, her father had once told Lana, snarling after some gangly would-be swain had hovered around the house. Rose tells her about the thirty-third anniversary activities heating up around Hope but doesn't make clear how she spends her day when not playing nursemaid.

Lana tries making a list of probabilities in her head:

1. Does Rose visit the prison and report to Vic?
2. Does she force-bond with the twins?
3. Is she having an affair with Hogan?

Lana pretends she doesn't want to know.
"Who asked you to do this?" Lana asks finally.
"Wait, you'd rather have Dirk?"
Lana seriously considers. "Not at all."
"I offered," says Rose, simple and efficient, pulling thwarted bridesmaid stems of wildflowers out of a water-glass, the bouquet Lana's boys picked for their mother yesterday.

"They go stale quickly," says Lana, without curiosity, hands interlocked. What she really wants to ask is whether her friend had always been such a martyr. Hard to remember this face of Rose or maybe years curdle a person. Some worse part of her wishes to ask whether Rose ever enjoys herself anymore. Lana weights an elephantine patience onto her tongue. Something about the smooth heft of Rose's loins and black of her hair scares Lana, testifying to some unguessable zone of power in this competent and helpful woman.

But where had Rose stowed her silly exuberant self? Before the accident, Lana had thought she could find her—but now that Rose is nowhere to be found. Only when Lana had slipped into an afternoon dream did she manage to find old-time Rose, so much hilarity in her she had to rise to her tiptoes because she could not contain that delicious laugh, Rose who would squeeze Lana's ribs to get her in on the same joke, who never finished washing dishes, never finished anything, Rose unable to close a bathroom door because she never wanted the fun of connection to end, slipping an arm around Lana's waist at night, losing keys and wallets and sweaters and screaming in happy terror when riding a bike too fast down a steep hill only to urge her up the same hill later.

Lana pines for Lola. Where is the Rose whose story of all life prior to Lana made it seem she had been a precocious sleeping princess awaiting true friendship, Rose who had lived a bad fairytale with a lucky ending, Rose a matchstick girl in a friendless alley who used to fear that voicing the wrong words would make someone across the world die?

Or where, at least, is the Rose who liked telling Lana that a Mahler had nothing to complain about or the Rose who had been such a jaunty survivor, singing sea shanties when the river went dry and they sloshed along holding up a canoe some guy had loaned them?

The only Rose whom Lana can locate awake is the Rose whose vulnerability lives one skewed glance away.

"No bedsores?" asks Rose. As if she is unable to stand the disorder of Lana's room, her gestures are awkward and mechanical replacing the water. Lana's ankle itches. Swollen with white blood cell helpers, as she had explained to the twins. But she won't ask Rose to scratch her, since not too much help should come from this clone sent to tweak Lana's ache for real Rose.

"Remember the doctor said turn every two hours, right?" says nurse-bot Rose, setting the alarm. "Keep the windows open. Maybe stretch a bit. What if you stopped taking some of those pills?"

Lana smiles back. What? If she stopped taking what?

"Painkillers," Rose repeats. Lana cannot help the questions looping her head. An acrid brimstone scent to the moment of this martyr folding a towel, straightening, claiming rights.

Only when Rose leans down to pick up a towel, there in her lower back, two strong tree trunks joined, tanned and knowing, does Lana see more of her old friend, the one who liked climbing plum trees in front of her. In that back is something that makes Lana want to bite.

Rose stares. "Something the matter?"

"What if you stopped making suggestions?" snaps Lana, instantly regretting it. "You know, you look great today," says Lana. "I love that flowered shirt on you."

Rose stops, her smile slow. She sits on what has been claimed as Sedge's metal chair, draping herself over the back of Tee's. "Remember?"

"What?"

"That thing about flowered shirts?"

It takes Lana longer. "That time we convinced some guy to wear your crazy daffodil shirt around his friends?"

"And then his buddies teased him and he tried to get us to explain but instead we took his moped for a ride?"

Lana too wants the layers to peel away. "Then we came home and my mom and dad and—remember Gallagher?—they were fighting about politics in the living room."

"We sat on the stairs and imitated their voices with puppet hands."

"And walked to the park at midnight and went on the swings forever. Then you choked on oregano cigarettes."

"See, you remember stuff, Lana."

"Mainly bad moments. Don't make that face." Lana inspects her nails, says nothing before telling a truth. "I remember thinking that night in the park you had saved me."

"Only that night?" and in Rose beaming at her, Lana gets a vision freed of time, Rose again at fifteen. Then an undercurrent rises, one she would stem if she could. "Hey," says Lana, reaching for more. Rose comes to sit on her bed and pat her shoulder, somewhat motorized but still comforting. It could be so easy to fall apart here with Rose. "I do mean it. You saved me."

"Well," says Rose, "for me, you were—" but some ungovernable meld gets stuck mid-throat, making her cough.

"We had everything. I mean," and they start something of a laugh, cut short.

Rose leans back a bit. "You know. I am really sorry to ask. But tomorrow—this is so hard to say—I'm asking a favor."

"Whatever you want." And Lana means it.

Almost whispering. "Just come? Because one hour, one deposition—"

"O god. You're kidding. My dad again?" Yet because one second ago Lana did feel an old friend was visiting her, she considers. "They told me I couldn't leave this room."

"Don't worry," says Rose. "We'll arrange it. Worst-case scenario, we'll carry you out on a stretcher."

Lestrion buzzes, his message unignorable. Trying to get through to Sedge but the boy can't listen yet. "Please quit," Sedge says. Everyone nearby in the dining room twists to eyeball the curly-headed boy with mediocre manners.

"What?" Tee punches his arm. "We got to be good. Anyway, let's go watch the burn. I swear they're doing it now." He grabs their spaghetti dishes to go push them into a slot where a set of gloved hands seizes them.

"Thanks," says Sedge to the gloved hands. Outside, Sedge can't explain to his twin. What Lestrion's facing is much larger than just being good. Hogan went out on his mission while the boys had gone to eat and once they return to their task of watching, the man stands hillside, watering down remnants of another controlled burn on a slope.

In the early hours, avoiding the risk of hot noon winds and brush-fire, Hogan had conducted the first burn. "You didn't wake us?" Tee had asked, fully betrayed when they'd found out in the morning. Their school hadn't started yet so they'd spent a couple of days here trailing Hogan who clearly lives near the eye of action. But wouldn't the guy have known two boys would have wanted to see a burn? Flames licking brush, an incinerated slope, and Hogan hadn't even bothered to apologize for seeming to forget the boys' existence, but there could be no predicting adults: they always needed stricter guide-lines for their behavior.

"You got to control damage," Hogan says as hello, wearing envi-able thigh-high rubber boots the gray hue of all important uniforms. "Once I'm done watering, we'll light up the next slope."

The twins pay attention to this *we* which bodes well. Next to lopped-off trees they wait, branches bending toward Sedge like friendly gnomes. The day before, Hogan had explained that just behind Hope was a zen monastery called Pol, a place where adults come to sit on cushions so they can imagine their bodies turning into skeletons. "I don't need cushions to imagine my skeleton!" Tee had bragged. But this was how the zen people put what they call detachment from life into action, Hogan had said, they like being thick in this region's dangers because we got plenty to go around, mudslides, quakes, you name it. Mainly, though, it is Hope's fires that lick up these ravines faster than anyone can say Alexander Pfuffelmacher.

Alexander what?

Hogan had explained all this on the way down the path to meet the chief of the monastery, a guy named Abbott Chuck, someone the boys had liked sort of, even if the abbott turned out to laugh at their jokes a little too quickly, one of those adults who act as if some teacher had once told him you could be a better person if you just cherished the humor of little kids more. The boys had stuck around to overhear that, as part of some neighborly venture in fire manage-ment, Abbott Chuck had asked Hogan to clear brush on two Hope hills and that the controlled burn should start today.

Watching Hogan finish watering down the burnt slope, Sedge startles when someone sneaks up on them from behind, doing peeka-boo hands: Zabelle, the waitress from the coffee shop still wearing her apron, the waitress who calls them darlings. Tee likes her more than Sedge does. Her teeth are fake white and fascinating to the boys, remnants of a bad accident on Five, after which, she told them, she'd thought she could live off insurance money for years. She also used to think she could have kids. Now, she told them, she's done thinking, she's a waitress, take it or leave her, still loves kids, darling, and each time the boys visit the coffee shop she gives them a free glazed and goes on a long cigarette break, leaving travelers and cops waiting on their third coffee. "Fig 'em," she tells the boys that first time, acting if they are capable of understanding the sloppiness of adult justice. "Customers don't know what's good. Too much joe and cophearts explode. I'm helping out. Too much caffeine and drivers speed, cops slap more tickets, so it's good people learn about waiting. I'm actually doing them a service."

Zabelle tells the boys about her stillborn kid, how unlike other people in her support group she's the kind stays sweet on other people's kids and then goes and calls her lost kid Pez, which makes Tee laugh so Sedge does mop-up, Sedge's face an apology for his brother, Sedge the kid born to do mop-up, according to what their mother had once said.

On the slope, Tee and Zabelle start commenting on Hogan's new burn, acting as if it is some game's last inning but Sedge can't take the crowd: the fire makes him have to sneak away to a private spot behind the red madrone so he can fist Lestrion out of his pocket. Only the robot's gamma-ray deflectors have gotten bent and so what if everyone else thinks the deflectors are Q-tips, Sedge knows better.

"What?" Sedge is hoarse in whispering down to his friend.

THE MOTHER'S BACK. Lestrion speaks in code. He doesn't always favor Sedge with clear messages. Sometimes static prickles the line, but when Lestrion's instructions are clear, Sedge pays attention. THE MOTHER'S—

"Which mother?" Sedge almost cries; this is his least favorite part of Lestrion, how often the robot talks in secret code.

YOUR MOTHER'S.

"Grandma Jennie?"

THE ONE SHE DOESN'T TALK ABOUT.

Now Lestrion's face turns mute, immovable. Having delivered his piece, he closes back into being a tongue depressor with Q-tips force-bonded into arms, a head wrapped round with ratty rubberbands, a god good at absorbing Sedge's ability to believe.

The blue-and-red striped wallpaper pulses, the lawyer with her pearls pulses and all Lana has to do is let go, speaking some sequence to spin energy in the right direction: it is like being in the first moments of a love affair with all the words tumbling out. She winds up her speech with a final word: "Crazy."

"Wonderful," says the interviewing lawyer, chinless, twisting her pearls before turning off the tape. She then addresses Hogan and Rose, as if they are deaf and yet should know the caliber of a star student. "Won-der-ful."

Rose grimaces. "Why?"

"This kind of deposition will stand up in court. Miss Fukuji-Mahler is articulate. Her recall is specific. Despite the strong feeling she shows."

"It's not just show," mumbles Miss Fukuji-Mahler.

This new pearled lawyer whom Rose has located seems not wholly adept to Lana, fumbling with tape machine and briefs on a desk that, given the rueful thumbprints on its dark wood, Rose had whispered, looked as if it hadn't been cleaned since the sugar-made-me-do-it insanity defense back in the seventies.

Rose chooses to mention more loudly this Twinkie precedent. Apparently the idea that a sugar spike in the blood could prompt uncharacteristic violence in an offender prompts a coughing fit in the lawyer. After she recovers, the lawyer waves off her embarrassment, gathering herself enough to explain. "No, Vic Mahler's defense rests on a far more contemporary concept. The basis for his defense will be, as I understand it, our newer idea of the victim-offender."

"The victim-offender," Hogan repeats, tasting the idea. "I like it. The victim-offender."

After, their group, such as it is, sits in a green room, offstage, Lana with her leg stretched on a dung-colored couch. Sharpened pencils, a tin of mints, a box of tissues on a low table, all detritus of the desire to communicate in a room of bureaucratic hum. Hogan, ill-fit to someone else's blue serge suit, twists a button on his wrist.

"Actually, you were great," Rose tells Lana and turns to Hogan. "Wasn't she convincing?"

"Of course," says Hogan. "That testimony's going straight to the governor. But victim-offender or not, election year's coming up and you don't know what people will buy."

"It's not about buying," says Lana at the same time that Rose says: "He'll buy it."

Lana fades out after that, half listening, the others like schoolchildren prattling the alphabet. "You can't have me be your puppet," Lana had said to Rose that morning, immediately regretting her harshness. "Don't worry. I told you I'll come. I'll testify."

Because most of Lana had been happy to make a choice that morning. Happy to submit to a plan, the subjunctive, some present plinth built on the bedrock of their friendship. To this place she had wanted to skip with Rose and thus rejected the stretcher Rose had gone and arranged.

"How are you though?" Rose asked.

"Don't worry about me," Lana kept saying, "I'm here, right?" her leg serviceable enough to walk to Hogan's truck until the mistake roared in, a thousand needles impaling the shin so that, on the drive, it turned into an electrified stub. She willed herself on, hobbling out into the lawyer's chamber.

Now they wait while the lawyer consults with her underage boy clerk, Lana stretching out her stub. The clerk like some concierge ushering them to a grand meal finally emerges. "You are asked to return for final consultation."

Late on this day, seated in the office, Lana has something close to a hallucination. All these people want to pull a prank on her. The clerk is a poorly paid actor, the lawyer a she-devil, the others reveal arcane machinations. Mainly they have brought her here so they can now draw back the window drapes and reveal her father in some dry potent unreality. And yet she must remind herself he could not possibly be free.

"Given the flickering constitutionality of capital punishment these last twenty years," the lawyer says now, rifling through her folder, papers falling out, "given the odd state and federal challenges and stays that have made the Mahler case so singular, a test case for the death penalty, shifts that have rendered Miss Fukuji-Mahler's father an ambiguous menace to society—" and Lana tunes out, back into the chant of *he will not be let out, cannot be free*. The lawyer finishes by saying that Miss Fukuji-Mahler's father can only now be treated to the best society can offer him.

"Which is?" Rose asks.

"The decency of hospice care."

Hospice! The two old friends share a glance, a code between them, given that Rose used to tease Lana if she slept with an older man: "So what, you're into some new thing, you're into hospice sex?"

Hospice sex. Lana had liked the phrase, ringing in her head for years every time she engaged in it.

Hospice for Vic. Hogan asks some question but Lana has beamed off again, letting them rattle on, peering out one of the windows, arched and Moorish, oddly beautiful, and for the first time in these years, something like empathy tingles Lana: poor Vic has been so long in prison that he has probably forgotten what you do with things like a windowsill or a doorknob. In her wrists she feels the certainty that Vic would stare at a doorknob, unsure how to manipulate it. He would have become a passive defanged Vic whom she would not recognize. The fluorescent light sputters, an orange perfume from the lawyer woman wafts over her, the day ends and still these companions chatter like finches set free.

———

In Hogan's truck on the way back to Hope, Lana sits crunched and uncomfortable between Rose and Hogan, dreamy on the Percocet she had covertly downed in the parking lot, listening while Hogan and Rose discuss heat waves, Santa Ana winds, Ventura fires and the reports that say all fires have been contained. "I did see a burning ember fly into Hope today," says Hogan, "bark chunk big as a baseball. But we'll be okay, we did our burns, this is nothing new."

If neither seatmate would notice, Lana would pop another pill, speed up the medication schedule just a bit, because the drug fails to muffle the burn inside her leg, alternating between being a zipper and a spear thrust inside, a hot sizzle up the ankle through the knee toward an obscure raid on the groin. Of course it had been a mistake to leave her bed and she should have accepted at least a wheelchair, but she'd rather not ask anyone for a doctor since shouldn't the ankle have healed already? Or does getting older mean your body becomes yet another traitor? No matter how many men Lana may have slept with or how much she has tried to abandon stewardship of her body, she has never known a bone out of place, broken or twisted, and as Mary had done before her, Lana has never gone for any physical exam she could miss. Since this most recent accident she has been sure that if she did see the doctor, her ankle would worsen, and yes, this is old-style Mary superstition, one Lana can't help. Vic had always loved to ridicule Mary for having kept her daughter from vaccinations and yet this same medically superstitious Mary had managed to sign, with Vic, a document committing Lana to time in an insane asylum or what they liked to call a sanitarium.

Still, whether a relic of Mary's childhood or some Californian faith-healing package, a flickering superstition formed one part of Mary's bequest to Lana, the wrongness enough to make a person want to cry out. "Now what?" says Lana instead, seeking distraction.

"Our last tactic." Rose, answering, seems to believe Lana still wants to talk about Vic.

"We go full throttle," Hogan says.

Lana cannot help her shudder: they act as triumphant as if they have caught an animal in a trap. She is not wholly sure that the animal in this case is not her. "What does full throttle mean?"

"We ask for the stay for Vic. On compassionate medical grounds," Rose says.

Hogan singsongs. "Ask more, you get more."

"His lawyer didn't already ask for a stay?"

"You weren't paying attention?" Rose elbows her ribs gently.

"Ow." Lana overreacts. "Anyway, they can't release him, right?" She wishes she could tell them the truth, wormed out through the fissures: Lana wants Vic to stay caged. But what kind of sick girl prefers her father—emerging in that afternoon's conversation as an aged, defanged lion—kept in a cage?

Only the talking about Vic had been easy. Everything else about the afternoon had been her own private trial. In the lawyer's room, just before they had left, Lana had imagined Vic so clearly that, for the first time in years, she could see his eyes dazzling with stupendous light, a blare of love, his face in full accusation calling her traitor to the family Mahler.

The rumble of thunder makes Javier remember to turn off the talk radio he loves so much since today the federal inspectors are rumored to be coming on one of their surprise visits. While listening to the radio on state time is no crime, it does not betoken a prison known for spic and span, its satisfied janitor union and its adherence to regulations, a prison that since its construction at the peak of the boom has not seen a single riot.

According to Javier's boss, a good part of this is due to the quality of the guard squad, guards not in the racket for the pension or plump benefits but who bear fealty to the state of California, a republic that has seen fit to provide them and their families with such thoughtful provender.

Ever since the expansion last year, things have gotten better, although there has been just a bit more pressure to use the new solitary cells that were built. Though Old Parcel would get an additional 55,000 a year for each inmate put into solitary, Javier has been stalwart at keeping certain offenders from the solo box.

Old Parcel had even received a citation from the governor because in ten years not one of its offenders had committed suicide. The guards are told that the problem with suicide is that while some crazy types may consider it a civil right, suicide rates smear the state's record, making politicos have to throw billions of dollars at programs and guardrails to prevent self-offing.

Javier flicks off the radio, examining his thumbnail ridges before reminding himself that he must either book an appointment with the manicurist for Victor Mahler or cut the guy's nails himself, nails that have turned hoary blue at the end of distended purple fingers on which already creep signs of necrotic rot, a syndrome among all the other syndromes the poor guy has. Vic's mind might be there much of the time, at least some of the time, but at times of excitement, a fog creeps in from the edges, making Vic argue for ten minutes with Javier over the exact year of his birth, claiming he has been imprisoned for eighty years or that the guard should just let him go downstairs to find his own bedroom. And as such the guard has learned to enter whatever world his charge lives in, whether Javier finds Vic fighting with the Russian army near Cracow or walking bloodied as a small boy away from a wolf cub. Javier turns away from the surveillance camera in order to slide a thread of smoked carp out from his teeth, happy to smell the guards' coffee percolating down the hall.

For the tenth time since his shift began, he reads the day's schedule. Since 4:00 a.m. Javier has had to cover the guard station for a friend. Usually he would have left his condo by seven. In the early morning hours, he'd done the usual checkup on Deisi and had his worst fears confirmed—his daughter had left her princess bed. Who courted her? Was she out flashing her tetas? Worse?

But up until today she had been so successful at making for herself a no-trouble zone that it is hard to think she is not as she seems, Deisi the science student bringing home awards, her future charted and assured given that she had always been a sweet kid who asked what and why. For years, a solo parent who had nailed both his general-ed diploma and a certificate in criminal justice on the kitchen wall, still in his heart an eighth-grade dropout, Javier had tried being clever for his Deisi, and when he had not known how to answer her questions, he always said *mija, I'm not sure but let's go to the encyclopaedia* until a few years ago when she discovered the computer and stopped asking questions, back around the time when he had noted with proud fear a certain jiggling display during her quinceañera.

This is what Javier pities Vic for most. The man so obviously lacks both ritual and family. Tonight Javier will take his daughter to her favorite ice cream stand and get her in a roundabout way to speak about what she is doing when not in school. He tries to be a good example, having told Deisi only part of the story of why he had dropped out: his loathing of Father Xavier's knuckle-raps. Not telling the full story, how he'd taken punishment into his own hands, one day slipping Xavier a laxative that looked like chewing gum, making the old priest spend hours in the lavatory, Xavier gaining from that day the extracanonical name of Father Colon, so that only a year later the poor father retired from the soul-saving of young boys, entering his golden years prematurely. On his ride to work, Javier sometimes spots, like a vision of his own badness, Colon along Five, seated astride a grand pipe-outfitted combo red lawnmower and leaf blower, looking grim while riding over whatever plot of dry land the church had conferred.

And Javier would be damned before his Deisi would emulate his own example: she would graduate high school, go to college, know the bounty of the state, probably not be a civil servant because she would learn that nothing lay out of ambition's reach.

You'll do better than I did, Javier always tells her. *Don't model any of your choices on mine. You could become a teacher or doctor or anything.* And though Deisi's mother had long ago been a victim of diabetes—her delicate foot cut off, her kidneys ruptured—he'd never since fully courted any lady. Those he did in halfway measure were more for an occasional Saturday-night oil-greasing, a stately dance and escort home, a perfumed peck on the cheek and only rarely a bit more because he prides himself on his dignity, a watermark meaning he has surpassed his father's tequila rages, all of it stemming from his belief that Deisi's dead mother stays similarly proud in heaven of how Javier sustains the family, modeling loyalty to memory, a lesson to bless their beautiful normal American daughter whose only flaw so far as Javier can see is that she wears shirts revealing more of her marriageable bounty than he thinks proper.

Pen poised, lips working, Vic trembles on his cot. Today his stomach is a glacier. His knees are bent to make a desktop but unfortunately also let him regard the scare of his horned toenails, ten yellow dragonheads poking up from under a scratchy horse blanket. The meds he is on must be freezing his innards but the only thing he can explore is a final solution to an ingrown nail: he will request a hygiene session.

Today he had received a letter from that girl Rose. She has been asking him to do something and again he tries remembering why it is important but his first hallucination upon waking, maybe due to the new sleeping meds, had been bad, coloring all. A youthful friend had been instructing him how to encapsulate a worm that could destroy all humanity. Though Vic still had one more worm to put into a capsule, his friend had vanished, with Vic lacking final instructions and the worm still writhing in his hand: humanity could be destroyed.

This second, Vic doesn't quite have the strength to get up and go across the cell to where Rose's letter, a distraction, lies on the food tray.

Javier peeks his head sideways in the food slot. "Legend."

"Boss," says Vic, alert to the possibility of repartee. "Do nails continue to grow after death?" His short-term memory might be shot but by now he could have gotten a degree in how to speak to Javier. Perhaps had he known how to speak in such a joking way on the outside, he would never have landed inside. Jocular, he should have been more jocular, his wife would have been kinder, he would have never done what he did and all would be better.

"Don't worry about that stuff. Everything okay?"

"Could use another blanket," says Vic. "But I have good news."

"Don't hold back."

"Hitler committed suicide."

"Glad to hear it."

The silence is awkward even for Vic. "You are a polite man," says Vic finally.

For all that Vic's mind has forgotten and continues to forget, an inconstant friend, sometimes all too present and then completely unfindable, hidden in fog, he does find it easy to remember the basic contours of Javier who said he had acted out the poetry-loving strain from his mother's side and who keeps reminding Vic that, early on, Javier had hit night-class books hard enough to get a scholarship to a fancy school in Southern California. After one of his father's brothers was taken away for graft, he had decided to finish in criminal justice. Poetic justice, Vic had said.

On days he remembers that Javier has a teenage daughter, Vic finds it hard to believe the guy raises her on his own and when he forgets the details of Javier's family, which does happen, he remembers to try to disguise it, because he knows this thing, family, is important to Javier, in many ways still a young boy. Vic likes the way this guard chews his lower lip when discussing the philosophy he'd studied in one survey class, drawing Vic out, asking questions like: "So what do you think is the ultimate in personal freedom?"

Vic sometimes goes with these questions and sometimes must cut to the quick, killing off old-time topics that had interested him by answering with his jailed tongue: "Murder. Murder is the ultimate."

And to compensate for memory loss, Vic thinks he has developed x-ray vision into what—because he had never believed in the idea of the soul—he calls people's intentions. The x-ray vision tells him that however much Javier might use Vic to sharpen his own way-laid promise, something the shaggies used to do, Javier also has pure intentions.

"Worry is a luxury," Vic tells the slot where no one stands now.

He fingers his pen, the kind you can't chew or take apart. He still prefers the medical defense which is to say that, in committing his bad act, his body, rather than his mind, had failed. Yet does this make him wish to plead insanity as one lawyer had insinuated? No, it does not. He will not do what they want. They will not get him to surrender that much hold.

Once he had a self, one with the shadow of repute, proof being the letters he gets from oldtime shaggies. He opens these notes fervently, often wishing he could recall the sender's name. He then reads carelessly before using the letter-paper to sculpt, with slow dabs of water, elaborate figurines, all as if commissioned by some prison Medici. He then sets these figurines on his shelf, beautiful writhing naked paper ladies, bits of handwritten text over them ethereal and veiled. He has even written poems about the ladies he has constructed, lending them names: Medusa, Ophelia, Philomena. Today, however, his ladies leer, their breasts effulgent and impervious and if his pen is in his hand, it has nothing to say, obstinate given that Vic knows the final date is approaching.

In a pique, Vic throws the offender, his pen, to the ground.

Some time later, Javier returns, smiling through the food slot's grille plate, its diamond etchings well memorized. "What happened? You're okay, boss?"

"Hokay," says Vic, speaking prison repartee.

"You look like you just collapsed on the floor," says Javier.

"We're having a party. Does that go against protocol?" says Vic, the unjoke not for his own benefit since, the more he nears his own end, his intermediate goal has become this wish to relieve others of self-condemnation. Such jokiness could be a penance, a small good performed for Javier who still makes it seem the world might care a little about Vic Mahler.

"You and I are symbiotic," says Vic. "No parasites here."

"You need help?" asks Javier.

"Couldn't be happier," says Vic from the floor where the cold on his rear pricks him alive. In this second it is true. He is happy that, for this second, he has delayed the cessation of the fluctuation of the senses.

Once Javier leaves, Vic considers whether it was just an end he had wanted. An end might be the ultimate in freedom. Though perhaps—the fog creeping in, he cannot quite locate the thought—this might contradict everything he had ever said.

"You wanted closure," a banal prison psychologist had once told Vic.

"No!" Vic had corrected the good doctor. "Not closure. I wanted a tunnel. I wanted to know—after a lifetime of writing—what it means to live in existential untenability."

The psychologist had tsked, saying: "Too intellectual, Vic."

Then again, wasn't being a cuckold equivalent to becoming an involuntary mute? No one cares to hear your side as your story undoes their own couplings, sympathy always running secretly toward the adulterer: there must have been a reason for the infidelity, listeners think.

Someone more metaphysical might say that his foundations had been shaken, both ontological and epistemological. Because hadn't he known Mary down to every nervous tic, down to her quick glance around the room after she'd made her own kind of joke? When Mary used to serve dinner, he had liked the shine off her cheekbones, a reassurance that mortality would not make vast inroads. When she had relaxed into clean sheets at night, she let out a little sigh. He knew these things about her. No, he had collected them, an archaeologist of matrimony. Her customs would not change and she would keep him constant. Mornings, she arched into a stretch. This knowledge of her he had gained, a baby jealous for footing, each step a claim over the unknown.

> From the letter to the spirit. The hidden meaning of the body is the spirit; but the spirit is not the ghost but life itself; not the soul or psyche but the breath of life, the creator spirit.

And then it turned out his writing and knowledge was for nothing as none of it helped: her treachery had made him question anything he thought he knew about anything, any person, himself.

Later, in the folds of time he had to reflect, playing chess, reading, staring, crafting paper women, he recalled that his own writings would have said that the neural track toward tribal affiliation and loyalty had been overwritten, in Mary's case, by the illusion of choice, but these words felt hollow, more like archaeological crumblings, relics of another Vic who used to believe himself.

> The crucified body, the crucified mind. The norm is not normality but schizophrenia, the split, broken, crucified mind. "If we throw a crystal to the ground, it breaks but it does not break haphazard: in accordance with the lines of cleavage it falls into fragments where limits were already determined by the structure of the crystal, although they were invisible. Psychotics are fissured and splintered structures such as these. We cannot deny them a measure of that awe which madmen were regarded by the people of ancient times." Split the stick and there is Jesus.

Choice versus birthright: what had he ever had to tell anyone? His enumerations, if you boiled them down, had concerned two ideas. The first had to do with a nuance about the firing threshold in the brain. Vic had been the first to depict choice and birthright as a Krishna and Arjuna doomed to mortal play in the synaptic field, Vic the first to be less deterministic than those who divide the brain into three distinct zones, one of the first to champion neural plasticity and yet also one of the few to have read Freud and Jung as if they were simultaneously folk mythologists and peer scientists, making Vic one of the few scientifically trained citizens of California to speak, in the middle of the twentieth century, of fate, destiny, kismet.

Heroic individualism is identification with ancestors in a new space and a new time: the new space is the public realm; the new time is history.

And here he has stepped out onto the stage, lights on, no longer an announcer of battles but his own combatant. What no one understands is that he had fought for his own light. No one would see him as brave but in his penchant for eye-for-eye justice, hadn't he been trying to grasp some higher truth on the other side of Mary?

Here is the fall: the distinction between "good" and "bad," between "mine" and "thine," between "me" and "thee" (or "it"), come all together—boundaries between persons; boundaries between properties; and the polarity of love and hate.

What he said in that first court appearance did concern his loyalty. He had told them that, simply, the wrong cluster of neurons had fired.

Perforce "he," "Vic," a ramshackle collection of urge and memory, had carried out a command, one dictated fully by his gut, and there had been no choice, this confession buttressed, at least in part, by his lifetime's work. He had made an entire career out of telling people that the neural network was a series of pinball levers but that you could merge archetypal determinism with metaphysical choice via physical intention, which his shaggies chose to read as an edict to follow their bliss, whether straight or circumflex, theirs not wholly an incorrect reading given Vic's contradictory love of neural plasticity, Vic having told them the quest itself could eventually rework the levers and craft new tracks.

Stretch yourself to the breaking point. It is not true unless it hurts; the evidence is martyrdom. "All truths are bloody truths for me." We do not know the truth because we repress it; and we repress it because it is painful.

Make our species wiser, have your choices act as evolutionary selection factors, but never, ever believe you create your reality, the one thought he forever abhorred, calling it a hubristic shame. At least, however, Vic offered this: a person could embrace the reality principle and make strong choices. In his case, the reality principle had appeared one February day as a mixed-up shooting spree of firing neurons.

Chop me up, he told the jury, *throw my gut in prison.* From the frozen masks the panel turned his way, he saw his faux pas. No one liked his forced humor. Worse, no one recognized the part of him that did wish to be chopped up, to have pure revenge visited on his head so that he might join with Mary, a disassembled pharaoh returned to his queen.

No, the faces of the jury would grant no reprieve, their neurons those of rigid absolutists, thrilled to doom anyone daring to challenge their categories.

Self-defense, he said, finally and lamely.

At this point, no one believed the jokester. And anyway, no punishment they could have given him would have cleansed him of her question, the one that had sprayed him as much as her blood, a defilement.

In her last moments, she had asked *have you taken leave of your senses?*

Exactly right. That was it. He had taken leave.

His punishment being, now, that little of his prior self remained. His act had orphaned him all over, leaving him with both no sensibility and a legacy hard to locate.

For years his own self had been up for question and there is little anyone, not even a guard with talents in the field of repartee, can do to shore up a foundering self.

Vic either wakes from a dream that has pulled him as if he were chattel behind a team of wild horses or else returns to a dream in which he is asking a guard named Javier: "What is the meaning of life?"

Javier's face is somber in the half-dark, helping Vic reattach the catheter to his penis. "To appreciate every moment."

"But who is it for? Especially when someone's getting paid to empty my urinal."

Javier must have spent enough time in churchly vales for his answers to carry their scent. Vic loves this about the man: he is good at looking at Vic's eyes before, during and after moments when humiliating security or medical procedures must be followed. He had once told Vic that his training had included a chapter entitled "Preservation of Inmate Dignity," one stressing the importance and use of eye contact. "How can any one of us know the meaning of life?" the guard says to his inmate now, gaze unflinching.

"But you know. Or you have something you tell yourself at any rate."

"Okay, maybe something about not chasing rainbows?"

"Don't get cryptic."

"Well, my priest says everything worldly is an illusion."

"Even more cryptic. You must be some kind of Buddhist Unitarian?"

"Catholic."

"But you're a Californian Catholic. You're throwing religion at me when you know I'm hardly a fan. Plus your priest sounds as if someone mixed him with cornstarch."

"What?"

"Everything gets mixed up here."

"What I'm saying is we get older, right?" Javier is sanitizing Vic's hands with alcohol gel. "Then let's say you were like, let's say, I thought I was some big guy on the block, that's exactly the thing you have to put on the fire. Surrender. My old ideas. Say you thought you were super-dignified. You get older and have to throw your mightiness out the window. Then there's accepting the unknown."

"Now you're feeding me new age treacle."

"No, whatever that is, I'm just saying no one gets to be a war hero all the time. Take my second cousin Daniel. He came home from Iraq and—"

"But who cares if we get more time? Why bother getting more beads on the necklace? Why care if we die at eighty-one instead of at seventy-seven or forty-two? Who cares if you get three moments instead of just one?"

"You think there's no meaning."

"In this moment, talking to you, I say we could say there's meaning. Except for the urinal. But what's the meaning of meaning?"

"You were the one who once told me meaning is doubleness. Remember? You said it's two things rubbing up against each other."

Vic has nothing to retort to his old self who seems to have been able to opine more freely so Javier perseveres. "No one else gives someone reason to live. You got to find it yourself."

"You know you're the first person in my life to talk to me?"

"That can't be true."

"You talk and you have nothing to gain. You're not trying to get anything from me. Not wanting to patch up some hole in your psyche or get me to tell you you're great. Sometimes I think I came to prison just to meet you. Did I tell you our talks are better than what I used to share with my wife?"

Now it is Javier who shivers.

"I'm saying you surprise me."

The guard lets this coast into the deep black next to the cell, a yawning space he always looks toward as if it holds all shreds of conversations not to be followed to their end. "Anything else I can get you?"

"On bookshelves are books I've written. But I have no purpose."

"You have no idea the ripples. You have no idea how your books could help some person. Some lonely kid. Some lady in Idaho. Maybe someone reads something and their life gets a little better." He waits. "I never told you my story." No question comes; Vic must be depressed. Javier glances at the camera that watches them always, making a gamble that the other guard, the noontime guy, has the sound down low, but first he must empty the urinal before he can return, this time outside the bars. "You ready for some singing?"

He begins with the quiet song in Spanish that Vic has told him he likes, the one for which he had once written the words for Vic—de colores, los amores le gustan los colores le gustan a mí—but his charge is in no mood to sing, his breath too weak, throat too sore, only his tongue moving inside that mouth like parrot's gullet. Though Javier knows Vic likes music because he'd once told Javier that even the most banal song has a longing, the one outside noise he really misses, the way he used to feel when he was, say, pressing grapes, the oak handle callousing his hands during some long-ago, suppressed second on a beach with Mary while watching his daughter play violin—

"The chorus. I love it." He looks at Javier with cloudy eyes. "There is no way for you to get me to see my daughter?"

"This is the first time you ask that plainly."

"Well, yes, I do need sleep now. But later, I'm asking, can you see what you can do?"

"It means calling that lawyer you don't like."

"But I could die before they kill me. Would the people in charge call that win-win?" And Vic chokes on the urge to disgorge.

Once he calms, the guard leans forward. "Please, Vic. Sorry to say this. Today you're scaring me a little."

"The only person I scare these days is," and Vic falls asleep on the last word, his cheek skintight and shiny, his mouth open in a death mask.

After they have come back from her deposition on behalf of Vic, Lana is strung out. It is not her fault that she cannot help how cold she must turn toward Dirk. Emotional possum, Rose used to call it, and maybe Rose's presence gets Lana back to former habits but who cares when Dirk, that afternoon, seems to hear the message scrambled? "You're an animal," he tells Lana. "You go lick your wounds."

"I'm not sure I like that." Lana stretches, pretending indifference. In California you can stir away a bad moment by tending to the twisting needs of the spine. She actually hates being called an animal: her mother and one of the millionaires and Rose had all, at different moments, called her an animal. When they used to climb plum trees, Rose liked singing this song, from one of the Oakland lesbian songwriters whose records they'd play, a tease but true:

Go back into the darkness
Like the wild thing that you are
Your teeth are far too sharp, my love
I'm afraid you'll go too far.

One more person with that animal need to call Lana an animal.

Years ago, in a surge, using a phrase she'd picked up from a lisping television psychologist going on about unfulfilling relationships, Lana had shouted at her mother *dependence enrages you*. They had stood in their entry hall at the base of the stairs before the hall mirror. Mary stopped before repeating the exact words back to Lana with such scary sarcasm, one Lana had never guessed could live inside a mother, sounding almost hysterical. A bit later her mother told her not to be such an animal. Lana couldn't understand the statement since she had felt at the height of sophistication in saying dependence could enrage a person.

"I'm not interested in continuing this conversation," Mary had said, putting out a flat hand in her face: "You're rude, you're aggressive and I—" but had cut herself off, fleeing the continuation, controlling it as she always did, already heading back up the stairs, sounding almost tearful. "Never mind."

Lana, lamely, at the base of the stairs, disarmed, had not known what to say. She had yelled up toward her mother: "You're the animal," the echo already unsatisfying.

"I mean an animal in the best sense." Dirk tries softening it, now squeezing her good foot halfheartedly. "Because most other women—"

Hearing of other women does not rank high on Lana's list. Especially not the women inscribed in Dirkian annals as she has understood them, a football field filled with ready happy braless sorts and their lustrous eyes all linking Dirk and Dirkian Dance to the eternity of their issues and salvation.

Dirk can't exit the idea. Lana an animal gifted at self-cure. "You're a starfish—your ankle will grow back stronger than ever."

"Right," she says, wanting to be the kind of person who always believed in fairytales. "Or maybe I'm like a lizard."

"Maybe it's a message?"

"What," she says, unable to relinquish coldness, his hands understanding her tone, lifting as if burned by ice.

"Stop running so much, right?" He says this when he doesn't know half of what she has been doing recently, the lawyer and her pearls and Lana saying for history that Vic had, in fact, been prone to temporary insanity. This morning Rose had promised that, with the boost of Lana's testimony, some kind of petition for a stay is now on its way to the governor. Dirk sighs. "You don't need it warmer here?"

"Not in the least."

At night he comes back to lay hands on both ankles in healing sup-plication all before checking his watch and going on to the next meeting. Because no way can Dirk mess up the Hope Springs en-gagement. Big things could grow at Hope; look how great that she can continue to stay in such a spa; it will help her recuperate. She doesn't tell him that Hogan gave her a room that has nothing to do with Dirk and his gig.

"Sorry, honey," says Dirk, a new phrase for him. He has become her new sorry honey. It seems to serve Dirk's divine ceremonies bet-ter if he sleeps alone, the better to meditate the next day, keeping himself pure like some Sugar Ray Leonard of the spiritualists, a com-parison she cannot keep herself from pointing out, though there was the example of Gandhi sleeping with virgins. When Dirk turns a confused face at her, she says of course she understands.

"So how you guys doing? You okay? Like it here?" Lana asks the two young faces in her room, the two of them a little breathless, worried or pleased at having been summoned so quickly from a duel.

The boys say they are thrilled, a bit too uniform in the response. "We're having the time of our lives," says Tee, imitating some pop hero.

"Why?" asks Lana, the painkiller she had popped once Dirk left the room starting its floatwork, helping ears detach from scalp, head from body, worry from reality: in such a float a person could feel generous and calm and in this calm Lana musses Tee's hair as he warms to his subject, excited about the waterslide Hogan showed them, the reptile cemetery and snakevine labyrinth out back. They like Hogan letting them feed mice to the anaconda and the chain-smoking waitress Zabelle with her cigarette hanging out of her mouth even as she buttons Tee's coat. They try not telling their mother too much about all the free fries and milkshakes and pie they're getting in the diner. Sedge also doesn't tell her what he has already expressed sev-eral times in space-robot talk to the undefensive ears of Lestrion: the best part of this Hope place is how quickly they can find mama.

"You miss anything of our old life?"

Of course Sedge says their grandparents, Jennie and BJ, plus a few of their friends up north. Plus looking for gold at the river or running with their dog Cad on the beach or trying to hide from the loggers in the forest, plus having to wait for cows crossing the highway.

"My leg may be messed up," their mother tells the boys. "But we won't stay forever. This is in-between time." Their faces flicker just a bit. Of course they want permanence and no kid ever really understands the idea of the in-between, especially not her boys with their clear on-off switches. She tries to be clearer. "When mama says it's time to go, you'll say yes, right?"

"Sure," yaps Sedge, always a bad liar.

The loneliness of seeing a Rose who goes in and out of being old-time Rose is what Lana blames for how she has started to add into the mix her popping of stronger pills, all with the cheer of a kid chewing one of those fruit-flavored cuddly-bear vitamins never as good as you imagine. That night, the first in a long time, bruised, tender and floaty, she tries telling her bathed, pajama'd boys a bedtime story but Sedge interrupts, head combed slick on her waist, Tee's head on her hip with the rest of him melting off the bed.

"Mama, this is the best vacation we ever had," says Sedge.

"Plus I love you," says Tee with what Sedge calls his brother's gargly-cheese voice. The words startle her since Tee has never professed love—at least within her hearing—and may be using a phrase inserted into him by the alien masquerading as her old friend Rose.

"I should be more of a mother lion," she says, thinking aloud. She hasn't protected them from foreign influence.

"Why?" Sedge rushes to her defense. "We need you to protect us from lions. Not be one."

"Yeah. We almost got chewed to death!" Tee snaps his jaws.

"And you saved us!" Sedge spins the story to bring her closer.

"Yeah, Maamih!"

In the boys snuggle, damp heads filled with rescripting, the happiness of the obvious lie sutured around the three: she has been enough to protect them, having saved them from imaginable doom, having done right by that strangest of duties which is claiming to be a parent who can protect children from their own worst impulses, not to mention those of others.

"You're telling her?" Tee asks his brother in a screech, resorting to their private language for the last part of the sentence.

"Too freaky," says Sedge. He has found a box of animal crackers in the room and holds them to his chest, not intending any direct theft. From within their tanks, live reptiles stare and maybe it's these savvy captives or the blue fluorescent tubes that make it seem ordinary laws don't intrude much here. "Think Hogan's coming back?" Sedge has climbed onto a sofa tucked against the wall and peeks out.

"He said he was going to get a faucet or something," Tee says. "It's hot in here. I'm dying. I can't breathe. You think there's air-conditioning?"

"Hogan looks weird," Sedge points out, changing topics because he hadn't heard anything about a faucet.

The thought of Hogan's weird face falls into the middle of their diversion.

"Does Hogan shave his head?" Tee asks for the twentieth time. He is trying to tug open curtains different than most, a vertical accordion fold squeezed narrow and wide. He can't see where they attach so he yanks harder.

"You're going to tear that whole thing down. We better go before anyone finds us here?"

Sedge's hand creeps with no real intent into the animal crackers because he is nervous about the way Tee is trying to wrench the curtains open, working with his weight, until a creak out in the hall-way makes them both freeze.

There's the closet, Tee signals with his head so they can make a quick break for it, pulling the door closed to find inside a scary dark.

"No light?" Sedge whispers, claustrophobia crawling up the sides of his throat, especially when Tee scrabbles a finger over the narrow walls. "Maybe it's a pull thing," Sedge keeps whispering, unable to rise from his perch on the ground but trying. "Maybe I should sit on you, try to reach the switch?"

"But he'll see light from under the door!" Tee whispers, at the same second tripping over Sedge's attempt to get up, only by accident slamming his hand into some ball that turns a red light up.

"That is wow," says Sedge.

"Wow."

A closet with clippings pasted to the wall. They have found them-selves inside something like one of those dioramas that always won the blue ribbon each year at Yalina's little dink of a science fair.

"Read it, whizkid."

This being one of the biggest of their mother's worries, that Tee at nine still cannot read, that he gazes with respect at text, seeing tails and twigs with strong personalities but for years, with spectacular feats of memory, has been clever at faking the actual act of reading. Up in Yalina, after Tee's years in a Sudbury school, the special-ed woman had called him dyslexic because of the way letters jump around, making it not worth his bother to get words to march in line or snooze. Now might be one of those times when reading could be worth the bother but Tee can't all of a sudden whip the alphabet beasts and get sentences to behave.

Meanwhile Sedge's lips are moving.

"Read with me!" Tee can't quit how plaintive he sounds.

"See mama's name?" says Sedge.

"That's why we're here?"

"Maybe Hogan put this up after we got here."

"But it's old, right?" Tee scratches at the sepia lacquer over one of the newspaper articles so that tiny amber worms curl off. "We're like Encyclopedia Brown in the middle of a case."

"Should we tell mama?"

They look at each other already knowing what a wrong move that would be.

"Anyway, she probably knows," says Tee, shrugging, offhand and fake.

Out in the room, one of the animals they don't know the name of—the meerkat or hedgehog? an albino dragon?—lets out a weird yelp, an unsettling backward sound, something like a rat swallowing a kitten.

"I'm creeped," Sedge admits, knowing his twin would prefer him to stay more contained, but how can he when a molten lead pit in his stomach could gulp him whole and Lestrion seems busy in some remote galaxy, not coming to anyone's aid. Sometimes Lestrion gets unreachable, heading off to accomplish heroic tasks of rescue and triumph before returning to Sedge.

"Someone's coming," says Tee.

No keys, just rustling. "Come in, ma'am," the guy outside says. "Here's my whole whoop-de-doo."

"Just wanted to locate the kids," their mother says, worry fringing her voice. Did she just stumble over her crutches? "O thanks."

"Boys are okay. They love it here. Probably they're with Rose or Zabelle or Garville."

"Who?"

"You know how people feel when they don't have kids, they get angel dust off them. Garville is one of those guys, friend of Zabelle's down in the diner, the waitress?"

"You're saying decent people?"

"As much as Dirk."

"That was unnecessary."

They hear him laugh for the first time. "But your boys love our playground. They could stay there hours."

"I thought that was a junkyard. That metal stuff out back's a playground?"

They can't hear Hogan's response to this or what their mother says back, something to do with the boys getting hungry or needing some tending. Sedge finds himself grabbing Tee's fingers but for once Tee isn't getting upset.

There is more movement. "This one's a velociraptor," Hogan says.

"Has the weirdest mating habits of the bunch. The female goes into heat, rubs its legs, then eats the first males who dare mating with her. Then it makes this kind of music—"

—he lets out an odd keening sound.

"She's going to be so mad," Sedge hisses. "What if they find us?"

Tee, more pragmatic, quiets Sedge by pinching his arm hard.

"So, ma'am?" Hogan's voice nearby. "There's a guy in the governor's office."

"What are you talking about?"

"La Misión de Nuestro Señor Dolorísimo."

They sense the chill of her silence and in this second, what Sedge wouldn't give for a keyhole.

"Your dad," says Hogan. "In Old Parcel?"

She still says nothing. Then: "What has Rose been talking to you about? Something I don't know?"

Sedge's mind churns over the possibilities. Does this mean they have some new grandpa somewhere? Someone other than grandpa BJ up north? But this new grandpa lives in an old parcel, bound in brown paper, wrapped with twine, waiting for someone to pick him up.

"Your boys, ma'am," Hogan is saying almost as if he knows they are in his closet. He changes the subject in one of those sneaky adult ways. "Amazing. You got one who takes in everything. So observant. I'd hire him to pilot a submarine. And the other's so brave."

"You're saying lawless," she says. "Tee's a rebel. No one could invent a law he wouldn't want to break."

"Let's talk straight—" said by Hogan the morning he stops ma'aming her, the morning he takes Lana by the half-finished, roofless cob-bale temple for a walk, cocking his head at her when she can't stop coughing, though she can't help it, the air burns her throat.

"What's that haze?"

"They're evacuating people two exits down," Hogan says. "We'll be okay. This always happens, it's just feds being cautious since the fire grew overnight."

"Grew?"

"Wind around here's bad as someone throwing a light switch."

Some internal devil had convinced her to leave bed yesterday and this morning she should be trying to sleep off last night's headache, one that continues into today without a pill in sight and Rose gone AWOL and no one around to get her a prescription. Each step Lana takes makes claws hook into her bad shin, the throb unignorable. "You brought me here to shuck corn?" she says.

"You're helping." His smile could not be trickier. "The biggest event of the anniversary's happening tonight. Your Dirk's trance dance thingamajig." When this gets no traction, he stops the pretext. "Look, you and I are practically friends here. I'm not going to pussyfoot. You know your father has, what, five days left? Before he sizzles?"

"Thanks." Seating herself on the stone fence. "I thought you and Rose were supposed to be satisfied."

"I'm not talking about Rose. You didn't ask but I want to give you my take." When she says nothing he goes on. "Basically you're the kind of person who likes mating with the kind of responsibility Rose shows."

"What are you talking about?"

"She may want to be more a wild woman but you want to, I'm sorry, have sex with reliability itself."

"Hey." This guy doesn't know her and dares to talk too straight. "I thought the idea was I'd help out and then everyone would leave me alone. You guys would be satisfied." Shucking corn, silk off shaft, hands well-practiced.

"I'm not talking we guys. Did you hear yesterday Vic asked for a punishment true to what the feds were using at the time of his act?"

"No."

"Guy's asking for electric. Doesn't want injection."

"Okay."

"My theory's a guy's desperate asking for old Tom Ed. Know what I mean? I'm talking about our human capacity for suffering." He watches her hands grabbing one more ear and another from the pile. "It's not like we're animals can chew off bad legs."

"Okay."

"So I'm saying unless you do more," Hogan keeps right at her, "more than your deposition, whatever, your dad's sizzling. Electric chair. Now they got him on suicide watch, you knew that?"

When had she given up the right to be left alone? It would be easier just to exit her skin, exit like the selkie in the stories she tells the boys, the seal-woman who gets to return to the cool friendly seas of childhood and belong to no one. No one's daughter, mother or friend. Yet Hogan's spareness spools her in, the eyes' gloom and dented skull, the blurred tattoo of dots rising from the shirt, a scent of sex or risk making him seem an impatient man holding tight to method. He has stopped shucking to lean forward, eyes stilled. "What I was trying to say before." He mumbles something that sounds like *friends in the governor's office.*

"Look. Sorry." She tries getting up. "Can't you guys give me a break?"

"I said we're not talking we guys."

Below them, two paths below, rises Rose in broad sun-hat, up from the depths of the tepid pool, holding a ball. Should she go tackle Rose and beg her to go get more pills? Rose waves before faking a quick surprising pass back toward Tee, one that ends up straight for Sedge.

"This is about you getting to meet with someone close to the governor." Hogan talks tightly, the words coming out from between his teeth. "Rose doesn't know. Meet with the guy, that's all. Sounds crazy but it's how things work. I can tell who you are. Secretly you want to be good."

"I'm sorry, how do you know this governor person?"

He grins as if this is enough of an answer.

She tries getting up. "It's not like we all get eternal life."

"But we do get opportunities." Getting nothing, he changes tactic. "You have no idea. Your dad did me a favor, ma'am."

"Oh. You were a shaggy."

"Sorry?"

"You read his books once. Or saw him somewhere. Now you feel my dad holds a piece of your young self. Like a preservative. The idea of Vic keeps you young. I understand."

He stands up to help with the crutches. "Way more than that. The guy changed me. It's not like anyone else. He really spoke to me."

"Yeah, right." She looks off toward the hills. "But does that make me responsible for—" finally getting what Vic and his books have spawned, the shaggies like starving little orphan bastards, asymmetrical half-cretins wanting to space-lift her into their custody so they could conduct alien probes. The shaggies. Dirk. Especially Rose. Now Hogan.

"I'm saying, Lana Mahler, I could get you an audience with basically the pope."

"I'm sorry."

"It's called the favor bank. We had a water situation in the county some years back? We managed to help out. Small things we did here and there. But you know, key electoral zones during the campaign? I mean we can't share every detail but it came close."

And she cannot keep from shivering. She doesn't know what Hogan is talking about, the governor, his lackey or her father, water rights, votes, just that someone is owed something and now she stands in line to receive some payback, ostensibly the good kind.

"The guy's a wizard. Works at the governor's office. Behind the scenes like all the best."

She manages to shrug his hand off, get control of the crutches, move toward the first step down and away.

"It won't cost a thing. Just meet the guy, no promises. The guy's a closer. I saw it when we did our desalination." He follows her and unwillingly, as if hypnotized, she raises her hand to meet his high-five. "You'd be doing a good deed."

She does not mean to whisper. "For who?"

"Whom." He smiles as if he himself were some kind of super grammarian so creepy he could have been her very own dad.

TWENTIETH OF DECEMBER, 2008   8:32 P.M.

Lana asking Hogan: "You brought me here?" about this nowhere bar on the lip of nowhere.

"You'll see. How's the leg? Let me meet you on the other side."

She is tired of the solicitude of others, a trait that seems to show up mostly when people need something because, from what she can tell, this is the quid-pro-quo fine print unfurled at the bottom of the social contract.

Right now what is needed is that she meet with some wizard but on the way to the meeting, Hogan has brought her to a bar, or maybe this pit stop is the destination, all recalling that unfortunate rape moment in Greece when two men had saturated her and Rose with ouzo at a pilgrim's progress of bars until the men turned rageful at the girls' refusal.

That said, in this moment it is not uncomfortable to ride in a truck with Hogan: the rebellion feels necessary, a flip of the finger at Rose and her idea about how Lana should behave, as an old friend or daughter, even as a mother, Rose with that particular non-mother vantage, one among the long parade of women who have acted as if Lana's mothering is supposed to be a constant game of structured bedtimes interrupted only by balloons, ginger snaps and intermittent zenlike perceptions by fascinating, well-coiffed, unsalivating children.

After eight on a Sunday night, her boys are installed in the Hope cinema with Dirk's suplicants and the judgments of Rose, destroying their minds by watching a movie starring sword-wielding wizards, good for at least three hours of mind occupation until the last phase of the anniversary celebrations starts at the hour determined by the exact second of the moon's ascension, an auspicious augury that will bless all participants for at least the next thirty-three years.

Who cares about any of that, I really am a bad mother, she tells herself inside Hogan's truck as he comes around to help her out.

"Sorry, didn't hear what you said?" he says.

"Nothing really," annoyed to sound so peevish, childlike. Where's the wisdom? as Rose had asked her that morning, what do you think you've learned since our Lola days?

"Okay." Hogan's grin again. "Why so worried?"

"I am?" smiling, as ever, under a fib.

Inside the bar, its sole customer is a man who in profile could have been anyone but who, when facing her, emits either unknowability or fame, somewhat like Vic who had taught her that fame makes someone easiest to enter only through a sideways glance, though Vic himself had stayed best known in a frontal shot, somewhere in his late thirties, taken in a second when he had looked roguelike up from the Spruce Street desk. Perhaps it had been Mary who caught him for posterity, his smile devious, this forelocked image of him staying the favorite likeness of the Mahler mystique, airbrushed like Che, Fidel, Mandela or Marley onto shaggies' T-shirts and even, she had seen, tattooed onto chests, arms, legs.

Famous or unfamous, in the bar, this bronzed fellow looks straight through her, impenetrable himself. He raises his drink as if for a toast. "Now, Hogan," he says, mock annoyed. "You never told me your friend's cute."

"Jim. This is Mahler's daughter."

She watches Hogan, a chameleon, assume a new aspect. People do this, shed skins so rapidly it becomes beautiful, a magic trick you could see as a child and call neat. Hogan's skin glows under the light, his eye sockets deep bulletholes.

"Office might have been better for us meeting," says Jim.

"Thought you'd want something less formal. Lana here's not your everyday gal."

EDIE MEIDAV

"I see. Sit by me." When she complies, Jim's grin twists. "So. Who's your favorite team?"

At first she thinks he must be speaking code so tries acing it. "I'm for whatever's better around the next bend."

"Then you're a Cubs girl? Must be a Cubs fan! Those guys haven't won a World Series in a hundred years!"

"You mean the Cardinals?" says Hogan but the man ignores him.

"So," smiling, as if going in for a broad Sinatra seduction, the smile one with his cologne, saying: "Think your dad's crazy?"

"I wouldn't call him that. Not all the way."

"But the governor should pull the plug?"

"That's my decision?"

"This one's a tough nut." The man looks over at Hogan, coughs. "You're really his daughter? Why'd you come anyway?" he asks, not waiting. "You know, I'd like to—"

"Hogan said I should." She tries to find a more important answer and locks weirdly into her asylum self, a sincere young girl. "He said you're important. That you could help."

This man stares before pushing her to have a Sunset, the drink so sweet it makes her gag but in her new mood she is dutiful in sucking it down. When the man gets up to use the men's room, Hogan nudges her. "Why hold back so much?"

"You want me to tell this guy the truth?"

Hogan rolls water around in his mouth, appreciative as if it were fine wine. "What would you say anyway? What would your friend Rose advise you to do?"

"She'd say whatever she keeps saying. I mean I can barely keep her from making it on some prison cot with my dad."

"Ouch. Drink makes you mean?"

"No," lying again, numbness filtering in over remorseful meanness, branches of seaweed atop her skin, rubbing her bones, "it's not drink, just I lost my old optimism, you know?"

When the man gets back to their table she aims for politeness again. "Must be great to have the state, I mean all the laws, behind you."

"It has its days." The man's smile boyish, almost a smirk.

"You feel you know the lives of the people? The ones you govern, I mean you feel you're looking down at a big anthill?" She wants to understand something about this smooth cowboy and smoother man-lizard, make at least some meaning from this night, because maybe something here could move and someone's pain could be eased, though probably too late for much easing of anything, not when she had already made too many mistakes, coming tonight one of them, wishing instead she could exit like the bad witch through a hole in the floor.

"Lady, who do I know? Not even this thug over here," waving at Hogan. "He's okay. But who ever knows anyone?" When the idea lands with a thud, he seeks some rectification. "Glad to meet you though. The Mahler case is closing. In a matter of minutes. Days."

"But why does everyone care how little time Vic Mahler has left?" Her palm sweeps Hogan's glass off the table, making him duck down to mop up the spill. "Just does anyone even care how long, for example, my mom has been gone?" It is as if Lana is talking about herself as a lifelong orphan: tears come forth at the idea of a girl entering the world motherless. She wishes, right then, that someone would still call her Jinga.

"So what you want," and the bronze wizard too caroms one hand off the other, a vertical slippage, "is for everything to go?" The slide of his hands echoes in her head, an eidetic blur: *go go go.*

"Not like I believe in taking anyone's life."

The man looks back, face so smooth all contact slides off, his eyes unblinking. "You and I should have met in some other zone. We could have said lots to each other."

"You think?" bobbing her head into the second drink he has ordered.

"Plus you blush and raise your eyebrows like a French girl does."

Now she knows things will work out whichever way she chooses, just as she is capable of seeing energy moving in a basketball game and predicting its end, just as her boys play with trains and with exquisite knowledge can switch tracks right as the other's engine tumbles down the ramp.

The sword hangs over her and she could choose for or against Vic. Tonight Mary feels so present that her very hands seem to belong to her mother. She waves them before her, long brown hands, trying to keep from total dissociation, some coquettish laugh not her own slipping out.

By evening's end she manages to avoid speaking one way or another about Vic. Even when Hogan presses, glaring, she says nothing decisive about Vic's insanity or her willingness to come forward or anything that would lube whatever Hogan wants her to lube. All of them seem lined up before her, the governor, the wizard, the pope, all the lackeys of the world awaiting the nod that will let them go with easy conscience into Vic's camp.

As they back out, Hogan takes one minute exactly to explain how thoroughly Lana has failed before he tries making a deeper point before sinking into a silence of pure frustration. Though he can't hold back. Once on the highway, he talks about the new legislation coming up, the referendum and how much she could have done. "I don't get you. It's like you beg to be housebroken or god knows."

"What do you mean?" Despite herself she is interested in some new form of torture opening up.

"You act as if you're hiding something."

"Did you ever really stop to ask whether I wanted this thing?" she says. And when the after-ripple makes no sense she adds: "I just can't take it."

Twenty miles later she tells him he's the one who needs to be housebroken, what, how could he expect her to be happy about all this?

"Well," he grumbles. "You'll get to go to that anniversary celebration at Hope anyway."

"I don't know."

"Your guy's leading it. Dirk. His trance bit."

"You're going?"

"You'd never catch me there. But it could be just the thing. Help ease your conscience. Sorry. But I think I should check out of you Mahlers now. For the most part I mean." He smiles in the half-dark. "I mean you're cool, I can tell you are, all that, but for now maybe I'll just leave everything to your friend Rosie. Now that lady, she is dynamite. Unstoppable."

An eye: it is a giant glowing human eye. Except that when it blinks, up pop new naked bodies, bathed in a light that turns skin every monochromatic hue from alabaster to dark purple, naked shoulders among shoulders. The eye as organism, made up of bodies of light, some bodies sitting and disappearing in unison, others popping. One group of people patiently, nakedly holding hands around the mass of the pupil, the ringbearers, guardians of the eye and its core, while inside the circle, more bodies continue to pop up only to disappear down, never still, all part of one organism scratching and stretching, the human race in its glory, microbes of light leaping from one out-stretched hand to another's shoulder, all sharing in phosphorescence. At the center stands Dirk, one more naked body directing traffic with his arms, the holy sitters and poppers.

Or this is the vision the girls share, knees hugged close far above the core, two girls seated on a ridge above the cherry-tree platform where the old tree tonight plays witness to the mass of light-covered bodies in the dark.

Someone had given the girls a drink of estorahuasca, *the shamanic drink lyric poets must drink from a wooden bowl* as the man—the computer millionaire—had intoned with a fake British accent as they looked at each other, giggling with the most delicious sincerity before sipping from the communal bowl. Together they took a plunge, together for the first time since they refound each other, here at midlife going for a leap.

I know this sounds crazy but I know what all those minds are thinking—

—and our awareness is higher than all theirs, Lana finishes her sentence.

Though it doesn't matter whether they spoke or whether they just share the thought while continuing to gaze at the spectacular vision of some two hundred bodies groping, moving, rising attuned to a drumbeat or whether the girls happen to gaze into one eye or the other in the desert night, since the great eye holds them, unblinking, always moving but also the same shape so who cares if they are special since they are also part of humanity, interdependent, connected with the eye and its bodies, the eye excluding nothing, no bad or good, no special past or future.

Could it be more perfect? Rose doesn't have to say a thing because between Lana and her lives an understanding sheer and electric.

Next morning, blood thumping, Lana does not remember the exact steps they took that led them to leave watching the great eye-dance though she does remember hitch-poking with Rose up to the dark of Rose's room. Sometimes they had been holding hands at point B but then had been still walking back at point A until they got shutter-framed into C, time a full illusion, and then Lana had actually tucked Rose into bed, Rose grateful like a girl-kitten gazing with sleepy love up at her one true mother. In Rose's room Lana had sat for a long time, rocking while the estorahuasca started to wear off. She rocked in a rustic wooden granny chair so she could watch Rose sleep truly as a mother would, loving the way her friend's lips parted and her cheeks were so soft, peaceful, Rose's ease of conscience palpable.

As the drug started to evaporate like tiny particles popping off in morning light, Lana's shin began to throb and there was only a grease-smeared empty pill bottle to be found in the bottom of her purse. The slackness of Rose's face became grating enough that Lana wanted to shake her friend, to wake her and talk off every single injustice. Lana could have had more of a right to a normal life and this is partly what she wants to tell Rose though how to start?

2001–2006

In many ways Lana was more imperfect than most.

For one thing, when she came back to her fiancé after nine months away—I went traveling, she said, I worked up north at the organic farm with my friend—when she came back toting twins with her, skin darker than his, she didn't tell him certain facts.

While she knew Kip was hardly averse to life's criminal stain, a man with his own attraction to crime, she preferred to bear the secret within. As if it were a substitute for pregnancy, her secret could almost equal an implantation and gestation.

You never told me you were pregnant when you left, said Kip.

And never had she ever told him how much she wanted a baby. Something of her own, sweet and tender with doe eyes. This had started to become a priority. Months prior to her departure she had seduced him. Later as a test of her own fertility, she'd even seduced one of his surfer friends, followed by a treesitter no local knew. To everyone she lied, saying she took the pill, but privately she'd come to the conclusion that all those abortions had rendered her infertile or worse, that during her hospital time, while she'd been under sedation, they had stolen her womb, prime evidence being that it had never again produced any blood and she now had some kind of alien womb, her punishment by an unfair justice, the non-irony being that she noted this bloodlessness just as she turned ready for a life swelling inside, wanting to play mother to some kid.

And of course she could have adopted but she knew from their single conversation on it that Kip was against that idea.

Not adopting a kid, he had said, end of discussion, let's have our own kids, c'mon, they'd be super cute.

So back from Oregon she came, months after she had left, returning to wake up the poor guy, tired at dawn, first birds of morning fish-like in streams above. To see the streaked sky she had roused him and brought him outside. He took all this, as she'd known he would, as a gesture toward reparations, a greeting-card return to courtship, an epiphany.

He had reached for her in blind instinct but she had put a finger on his lips and then pointed to the two boys asleep in the car.

Sedge and Tee, mouths lolled open, hands holding each other's tight enough to destroy someone else's tomorrow. Kip would later retell the moment: love for his sons fizzed his pores, a love he had never before known, as well as pride in the mother who had come back to him.

"You can't take the two apart," she would later overhear him telling a buddy, "you got to love the mother as much as the kids that come from her body. It's not like you quarantine love."

When he first saw the boys, she knew enough to stay silent, letting him put one and one together to get the idea of their four, of two boys now his. It took a second but to Kip's credit or detriment not long. He got it, hugging her skinny ribs tight and asking: "You stopped taking your pills?"

To which she'd smiled. She'd guessed the boys were a month old, had gone so far as to invent a birthday in her head but who knew?

All too easily Kip accepted this idea of her having worked and lived on an organic blueberry farm up north—that part was true—and that she'd needed to be internal, out of touch with him after the bad trash fire that had burned down the best part of their garden. Some mysterious inner call, he figured. Some female workings had made her want to keep the pregnancy under wraps while staying faithful to him: most of this was true.

Before she'd begun the long drive back to Yalina, she had needed to remind herself of Kip's abiding loyalty and couldn't that be enough to make their life together appear in someone's dictionary of the normal? Never in life had she been a full-on liar, not really, but her milky-compliance time in the sanitarium had taught her how to hold someone's gaze and deliver the thing without too many extraneous details.

She had been planning a return anyway. Southward just past the Oregon border, down the circuitous coastal highway from the tiny island where she'd stayed with an old college boyfriend now living on an organic farm and trying to get an acupuncture degree, she'd found herself in low spirits, questioning her purpose. Every song on the radio mocked her: *the way you sing off-key, no, they can't take that away from me.* Had she ever had anything solid enough that it could be taken from her? Had anyone ever really loved her? Even Rose had stopped. Lana wasn't getting any more of those beautiful, stirring letters that used to be forwarded from one of her Los Angeles addresses.

On a cloudy afternoon, having driven her determined chugger of an ex-pimpmobile for more than twenty-four hours straight, she'd pulled into a market's parking lot to get a bottle of water, a camel coming to an oasis of love.

This not being really any old market, rather more what people call a farm store, a place suggesting the purchase of family, the prediction of nostalgia and the racking up of summer fun. Provocative hay bales, half pints of raspberries, quart buckets of blueberries, cleavage-bursting bags of charcoal next to unstained wooden bird-houses stacked in front. Lots of families and kids entering and exiting, pushing mini-carts, happy to be connected, their purpose clear. Berry-gathering for the cave, her father would have derided the entire scene, stupid consumers of American bliss.

She sat in similar stupor gazing at the berry-gatherers, surprised to see a hazy nimbus around every figure, her eyes that tired from the drive. Angels, she thought. Not consumers: angels. No one sees it but these family people are made saints by the perfection of this moment, the artistry of their devotion to one another.

When she heard something cry out.

Later she would tell herself that no spirit had possessed her. Not five little ghosts, not the time in the asylum, no fear, no craziness, not the belief that the doctors, those aliens, had ripped out her womb. Instead—a pure cry.

In the next car, windows half rolled down, sweet cheeks full, tongues fluttering on a dream nipple, twin boys slept, blue-clad infants outside a supermarket on a main highway. Something unthinking must have given birth to them because how obvious that these children were unloved: you only had to stare down the facts. Two infants, heads sadly crumpled over the infant car restraint, abandoned in a car that defined disorder. Long wood antler slats roped to its roof and scrappy wind-battered yellow rope frayed from its end. She peeked her head inside and had to plug her nose at the garbage-truck scent, even with windows open, the interior with its hoary seats dirt-veined and on the floor a carpet of half-empty baby bottles flung over old mildewed newspapers with no blanket or toy to be seen.

Someone had left two babies: a surge of proprietary interest flooded Lana.

Who leaves kids in a car with the windows half-lowered so anyone could take them? Lana almost sputtered but would not give in to rage, and as she choked, a light flared around the car, the same energy capable of pushing a steam engine's worth of goodwill into her hands.

The surge in her said take and you will be given, paradise lost will be someone else's gain, metamorphosis always proves beautiful. Not that she would call anyone hers. Only that her care could create an umbilicus, a pump of vitality into two angels, motherly interest.

In the back of her car, her own stab toward order, she had a laundry basket filled with folded clean clothes. Already a method suggested itself, screwing her tight, so that if someone had interrupted her, her alibi stood ready—I wanted to protect them, they were crying—while a mechanical knowledge entered her fingers, her quickness in unleashing both from the carseats a way of helping someone avoid bad parents. Because before she lifted each up and smelled the scent, the wet-grass, dried-milk baby scent, she still had the thought that she might just take them to some local sheriff's office. But once that scent flared her nostrils, some milky vertigo opened a hole in time, enough to swallow all sense. She had never known the sugar of this moment, these two babies in her arms: a guard went and unlocked the mother waiting in her fingers, fingers that had spent so much time stroking the hair of grown men in consolation for the loss of their own mothers.

Twins fraternal, not identical, she saw, babies in such deep sleep they barely stirred. One held his hands as if still tickling the inside of the womb's walls, a bent bird-wing, while the other's neck strained against an invisible collar. For this long moment she held each before placing them down, patting them in, covering them with her fleece, hand steady on their bellies in a rush of pure atavism. Never had she been around anyone so young, anyone whose promise was still so much a question: you had to wonder how responsible the world would be toward such perfect creatures.

With folded shirts she braced their weak necks, not knowing this act of buffering against physical slights would turn out to be the easiest part of mothering.

And once they were secured, she continued south on Highway Five, driving with hands gentle on the steering wheel, deciding to forget about any sheriff and each marker saluting her. *I'm not crazy,* she thought, *I am helping* and it was beautiful how no other thought interfered, making for almost the best high she would ever know, everything confirming her, etched in bright knowing complicity, so that if she had sailed off a cliff right then, she would have flown.

Only briefly did she consider hiding. Hiding would be unclean, making her face the idea of unworthiness while having nothing to hide would be the brazen, right thing to do here when providence was finally trying to download into all her messed-up psyche without encountering any bottleneck. Could it be right to argue with such a force?

And how lucky that the boys stayed asleep until halfway toward Yalina when the coos of one woke the other. Not sure how to handle them, she pulled over at a convenience store, raising each onto her hip, carrying them into the lit space, their eyes scrunched, arms flailing. She read the instructions on a can of formula and with her smile apologetic, various bystanders, including an off-duty cop, helped mix the warm water in a cup, also unwittingly helping to birth Lana as a mother.

We're moving to formula, she said, loving this newly multiplied self, the first time in her life since Rose she had ever consciously said the word. *We.* The employees smiled lovingly as she mixed the formula, everyone suddenly so kind in helping her pour a simulacrum of milk into two doll-size bottles.

And if it was a simulacrum of milk, so what, so what if the boys would not get that immune boost: the stationwagon drivers hadn't promised more, she told herself, nor had her own mother ever nursed her, right? She brought the babies into the car, laying both across her lap. Already they were cued, one sucking in his breath, the other with lips smacking, knock-kneed, eyes crossed and then unfocusing in dream-love so as to slurp from the nipples.

Don't worry, she told these perfect amnesiacs. They needed the command more than herself. She would bring them to a paradise of clean air where all would be provided for.

It was as they nursed that their names came, providence again shining one of its faces upon Lana Mahler. Tee for the caramel-skinned boy who strained against the collar, Sedge for the au lait baby with hands folded into bent wings. She could have eaten them, little bonbons she placed back into their backseat laundry cradle but for now she would not stop to savor. Stopping would stem this amazing all-flowing power.

Already the dance of mother with children had begun. When she stopped, even at a traffic light, the boys cried because no way did they want to let trivia stop their journey of endless rocking. If their crying scraped every nerve, and why shouldn't it, still the hum of rightness filled her. Diapers, she thought, I need to find some diapers.

Somewhere around Eureka, right when her thumbs were losing most of their grasping power and her knees became rubber, almost unable to brake, the phrase she had never thought took over. *Thank you Lord*, she thought. A sustained ecstasy all the rest of the way down, along with another uninvited guest: *I am in thy holy hands.*

One of the things she'd loved about Kip was the way he took on challenges.

In this manner he had entered fathering. With a slow sizing-up of the reality of twin boys, and then, once he'd committed himself, with gusto. No one in Yalina, a town capable of hiding so many shotgun industries, ever needed so much as a birth certificate or social security record for her to begin giving the boys their tests and shots. At the underused, overfunded clinic, she'd say sorry, she'd lost the hospital records, and the pockmarked nurses, glad that at least one local bushmama chose not to depend on herd immunity, would fire away, as her own mother had not, with protections against diphtheria, hep B, measles, mumps, polio, rubella, tetanus, whooping cough, the alphabet of entry into civilization's ideas of how to organize a body as liege and protectorate. Lana loved this motherly risk assessment: you had to figure out which dragon sting would fend off greater dragons.

It's good for you, she whispered, a loving sadist, her boys' arms riddled with shots. Lana had never felt more serious or adult than when handing over the boys' crisp yellow immunization cards.

Did Kip ever suspect the boys were not his? She was almost sure he didn't.

Early on the passions in the two boys became clear: Tee avid, Sedge's enthusiasms more subtle, smacking his lips with less force as the bottle arrived to tickle above the upper lip. Which one takes after you? Kip asked her. Let's not use labels, she would say, the books say not to compare, and she would smile up at him, a pious mom following all feeding and nap-training protocols dictated by the priests of attachment.

Perhaps what had drawn her to the boys was that they did resemble Kip, didn't they? But she could not have guessed, not fully, how the kids were exactly what Kip and Lana had needed for resuturing or how they would help Kip bond to his own parents.

For parents who had been waiting year upon hope-defying year for their Californian son to grow up and give them grandkids, the twins ended up being the one right thing Kip had done, Lana temporarily relegated to cheering committee, starting with the way his parents loved quarreling over how best to furnish the nursery.

And because of the tidal force of the grandparents' love, Lana had to suffer the jokes: Big Jim liked to bring up the suppressed side of Jennie's Springfield ancestry, her mother's lineage of freed slaves, his smile crooking at what Jennie always mentioned just after, some story of the middle class Jennie had been forced to leave behind when she'd come with Jim to redneck hippieland in Yalina.

Lana did not dispute what they said, basking in the respect her in-laws shone her way. She was the mother of their treasures, and okay, she had left their son for a few months, she still had come back with the treasures. And none of the bushmamas of Yalina ever asked why Lana chose not to nurse though she could tell that in silence and horror they pitied a woman's sapped-out breasts or poor understanding of bonding.

And because she lived in the lie that she'd given birth to the twins, Lana began to remember labor. The pangs and how giving birth had sent her into a dark cavewoman part of her psyche: she could recall it in mirror shards, the moment so intense one immediately forgets the worst. This part she did let herself talk over with other mothers. And it was also true that she did occasionally finger the boys' navels, wondering over the stationwagon drivers whose kids had been spirited away and also why she never saw reports of their loss on the news, not on mailers or milk cartons, not on gumball dispensers. It was not that Lana failed to keep an eye out. It was that she did not wish to keep up with the news all that much anyway, given the unfortunate truth that occasionally some newscaster would also mention *Mahler v. State of California* and she'd have to overhear some bit about her father, his new appeal or the governor's stay, an exemption or barring, some evidence of professional misconduct or revision of legislative process, all that could smooth or stall the case of Vic.

His cause had been taken up by the one liberal radio station that got piped up the coast to Yalina:

You got this guy who may have been demonstrating the ultimate in personal choice, I mean that's how I see it and here at Men's Liberation Hour we all know a crime out of impulse is bad, nothing to replicate in civil society but then you got to consider if you have a tree and its roots are rotten and then you got this guy standing at the tree trunk trying to prune the whole thing but who's just like everyone getting fed by the sap in the poisonous fruit and the sap acts like poison in the system, doesn't give anyone real recourse to understand what it means to be a man in our time, I mean where does it all cohere, and you're stuck in this convention of matrimony and you come from a whole different era, I mean we're talking a guy scarred by an entire European world war so where you going to point your finger first? The origin of war? The first cavemen? What men are taught to become? No one has any real modes of communication in the ongoing gender war, am I wrong? And so all we ask today here at Men's Lib is whether it's society to blame or Vic Mahler? I mean this is a guy actively trying to change the system, guy a Trojan horse in the academy trying to explode it, did so much for swarms of people, men and women, guy who became way more than a philosopher, a bona fide cultural hero, and in this way helped women too by trying to blow people's assumptions apart, the whole thing. We're asking our listeners this—if we had Mary Mahler as some kind of desperado, Mary and not Vic Mahler, wouldn't she have ended up a feminist hero like Angela What's-her-face rather than on death row?

And so Lana did her best to avoid 94.1 on her radio dial, instead choosing to listen to bad honky-tonk filled with girlish yelps and cries.

Perhaps the stationwagon drivers—that was how she thought of them, not as parents—had been relieved. Perhaps she had been a delivering angel and they could now return to their stacking-up of mildewed newspapers, finding better jobs or who knows what. Perhaps she had been a necessary instrument in a desired change. She didn't want to linger too long on the idea of what she called not crime but *passage*. She had helped Sedge and Tee entertain passage into a more orderly life. She would pay attention! She would be a good mother! Those two sweet-faced boys passed into the glistening hall of what she had never gotten and what the drivers probably could never have given. She would become their nun of devotion, making these twins' lives really matter and in the process become, for the first time, someone.

Long ago she had noted a mathematics to the way people had children. Some seemed to do it out of unthinking societal algorithm or a desire to multiply themselves narcissistically out of a fear of solitude or death and this could have been the case with the drivers—were they kid-collectors or former druggies? Did they pop out babies just to feed them sugar water? These were the kind of people who might have anyway been seeking a good foster family so they could, as shaggies liked to say, sort out their own heads.

Growing up in Berkeley, Lana had known lots of kids with parents like that, uncertain parents giving birth to quick-witted and likable kids, to foster kids like Rose. Just think what would have happened to Rose if she hadn't been adopted.

Plus, when you actually have to *take* something, Lana kept telling herself, doesn't it become more real than if your body just hands it to you? And hadn't she anyway known the march of conception, *five times*, when none of those moments had been right? The ripe full crankiness of early pregnancy had always made her stride toward the nearest clinic. Hadn't she been in school, too young to be a good mother?

And what anyway were all the celebrity moms doing, going to Russia, China, Malawi, Vietnam to adopt babies? Airlifting children into lives they considered better. How was having the law mediate this sort of transaction any different?

Plus she had not asked for her insane asylum to administer an abortion or worse a hysterectomy as she suspected had happened. Didn't the universe owe her a small bonus?

Lana among the mamas never lingered long on the pains of labor. She just nodded sympathetically when they spoke of it. She mentioned her ghostly own and then moved on into discussing child-rearing techniques. Ultimately didn't it all come down to nurture, not nature? Look at her own family: did Lana resemble her mom and dad one bit? And consider the genetic hex: if she had gone ahead and birthed her own child, would the child have turned out as twisted as Vic Mahler? Didn't that Nazi guy Goering's daughter sterilize herself?

So much better to bypass nature then, to impress upon herself the importance of *nurture*. You could bear down on aspects of child rearing as much as you bore down to give birth.

Earnestly Lana read everything, letting it inform life, grinding up organic baby food with the zeal of the baker of communion wafers. She helped foster independence, letting the babies hold spoons, mush dribbling down their chins, always trying to give her best and then some, at the end of the day more satisfied than a prelate after the rigors of ritual.

Sometimes in the tired-soldier look she and Kip shot each other, at night after they'd stoked the woodstove for lighting the next morning, the twins in bed, she knew a peace she hadn't felt since she'd been a girl back in her Lola days, that giddy froth. Did Kip ever shoot back a flare of suspicion? If he did she didn't notice—these were his kids and to them he was a good father: a morning's rough warmth, a nighttime patience.

And once they started living in the guesthouse on his parents' land, she had to work fewer hours at the market. In that guesthouse, with Kip still around, she couldn't have asked for a better time, the boys toddling, falling, laughing, making little burps, holding items up for inspection, causing chaos. Sedge always turned to her to see whether she noticed while Tee drove straight ahead into any new commotion.

Did she deserve to be this happy?

One of the things she'd liked least in the asylum—or whatever people called the hellhole in which she had weathered nine months, enough to birth a baby, she'd marveled—was watching her fellow inmates' behavior at the salad bar. It reminded her uncomfortably of her lost college years. By the gravity of the patients' sashays near the salad bar, you could tell which girl had a strong father making her a puppet. Each girl's choice came weighted with severe predictions regarding success or fall-on-your-face failure. Choose the wrong legume and you faced a dearth of love, existential abyss, death by fat. While Lana hadn't been given the choice of an abortion, her fellow inmates had been choosing vinaigrette.

In this way Kip could be patient. Whenever Lana would get into her salad bar/hysterectomy riff, most often in her tiredness after a stint at the supermarket, he tried soothing her ideas but never once ridiculed her. And she learned why: in an especially tender moment, long before she brought the twins, he did admit that he wondered if he might not have been subjected to something equivalent. One bad night after a 'shroom trip, Kip had been taken up into a spaceship, losing his dignity to aliens and returned to earth with the sense that nothing would ever again be the same. At first she'd found the comparison a condescending insult. Then she took it at face value: he believed in his alien probe while she knew she'd received an unwilling abortion or worse. What mattered most was sympathy, his hands fond over her hip, not just locating her but fixing her in space, better than any global positioning system used by his harvesters.

Before she had left him to go up north, Lana had to keep some part of herself safe, having to protect herself from Kip and his parents, from his father's tales of wholesome prairie life, from his mother eyeing how Lana handled the heirloom blue-laurel china. If Lana ever made the mistake of speaking ill of his parents, Kip exploded. Then she withdrew even deeper, becoming an automaton avoiding his gaze as she passed him in the corridor, feeling as if with a magic wand he had managed to turn her into Mary at her most cold and abstracted. Kip would protest, voice loud late into the night. *You didn't tell me I was getting involved with an ice queen, did you?*

Later she told him that the worst of their arguments had led to the angry sex he couldn't quite remember. And all had led to the conception of the twins the night before she cut out. It's like the twins came out of whatever hope we used to have, she said. And the reason she'd left in the middle of the night? To make sure she could cool out her head. This last part was true. And he liked the idea of her picking berries not far from the Salmon River while her belly grew fat with his spawn.

At least you still have a womb, he'd say, patting her belly while she winced, your doctors never took your female parts out.

Okay, so she had disappeared on Kip but her reconciliation package included that after those eight-odd months she had returned not empty-handed but with twins springy-haired and big-eyed, an echo of Kip's legacy.

Which is all a long way of saying she had not hedged. She had done the most she could to fetch those boys far from the rim of doom.

Rose has her hands on her head, eyes bleary, ears agnostic. "Please. You don't think you told me enough?" Peel away the layers and be worshipped, this is what Lana seems to want. A curbless street toward forgiveness. An incomprehensible incident forgiven.

"Well, it will all be in tomorrow's papers anyway, Rose."

"Really?"

"No." Lana not combative but reeling her in. "You don't get you're the only one I could tell?"

"No." The ordeal now stretches before Rose: there will be no time for interrogation or unscrambling. This confession has left her unravished, obtuse, at a loss.

"So was I wrong?" Lana only now starts to exhibit nervousness, rocking back and forth in her chair, sensing her audience might not wish to grasp the credo just set forth, her Rose not rising to the fly.

"I must be unlucky. What, you want me to tell you everything's okay? You might as well have just gagged me or dropped me in a ditch." The secret horrible confession already bursts Rose's head, making her move inside all spoken words with the speed of love, hearing a black ringing with no idea how to proceed, just banking on a certain willingness in herself toward conversation with this woman sitting up in bed, her pupils huge.

"Well, maybe I just told you that stuff as kind of an adjustment

thing? Maybe I didn't read the cues right. Our situation here's temporary. You know how a person gets tired of being the weakest link?"

Something makes Rose dead from the neck up. "Lana. You don't
get it? You just made me your witness. Practically an accomplice.
Almost as guilty as you are." She rises abruptly to go sit on a chair.
The stillness lucid between them, the only moving thing in the room
is Rose's hand, her fingers attacking the chair's wicker arm, piece by
piece, shredding it into the carpet, the pieces falling on the carpet in
some illegible writ about her clod's fate.

And yet there is a great astringent charisma to Lana right now, a
mystery of her violating self, her lips red as a doll's now breaking the
lull. "But Rose, who needs to know?" A smile unfit for human consumption, arousing. "Just say I didn't talk to you, right?"

At least one of them in the room is slowly being driven insane.
"You aren't that scary a person."

"What are you saying?"

"You have no idea how this works." Rose looks around the room,
feeling as if it has shrunk into a cannibal's lair, greased and ready.

"Wait. My eyes hurt. Like someone put acid in them." Lana rubs
furiously for a second but when she gets no response, she leans forward. "I'm saying you always asked me to open up more to you?"

"Well," Rose must prowl some limit inside, not sure where the
terrain drops off until she comes to a rough edge, "that was a long
time ago." Years later when she remembers this moment she won't
recall how the anger started. But for so long she had kept Lana as her
rich flowerbank, Rose the bee always there for the Mahlers, as if in
their silence the family had kept her feasting on their bright golden-
ness so she stayed buzzing but barren, filled so many years as part of
their importance, self-sealing, airless, her fate never to be satisfied by
the nurses and soldiers of the world but rather only by the Mahlers.
Something in this drone's anger gives her strength to dare imagine
the thin gray shadow of the mother of the twins, the cardriver ostensibly giving birth to sons, bearing them between her legs and trans-
porting them somewhere only to return to her barren car and even
emptier home. When the cardriver had seen her babies stolen, had
she panicked? Had she immediately resigned herself to having the life
she meant to have siphoned off by an unknown Lana?

All these years Rose had held aloft her unquestioning admiration for Lana and the Mahlers and had therefore buzzed toward and away from so much. How admirable her friend had seemed in her heedless female criminal joy—but here Rose had come somewhere she could not follow, to someone who took her lack of caring to the nth degree. Fulfill yourself, yes, that was what Vic had preached, but what happens if your fulfillment makes you stumble over other souls in your way?

Most other people would have given up on the family long ago. Lana must know, doesn't she, how Rose has kept her central, as if no other hue could rival the carnival colors of Lana and the Mahlers, these past saviors of Rose robbing all present savor from life, giving her now a deathbed weariness.

Hadn't Rose asked for something else? Not for this Hogan, this Lana, these boys. This whole time at Hope had wrought exactly the opposite of her wishes. The cocksure possibility of Lola seems to have distracted Rose and spun her away from actually helping Vic. When who had helped create Lola? Who had been the first to breathe the prospect of a love golem into Rose's life? *Vic.* Again she could have been more helpful to Vic and once again she had failed. She would blame Lana but can't, her shock at the real badness too great.

"Hey Rose. Come on." In the way a deer could just sidle up to another, Lana could make one right move but it is already too late. Rose is heading toward the door, opening it for herself. "Come on Rosie. Don't let this be the thing." Lana stops, a victor who understands timing, one with a final baffler. "I mean—your whole thing about my family. Aren't you the one who loved," waving, "all that Mahler stuff?"

"Jesus." The look that Rose turns on her old friend could freeze ichor. "Stealing? It's so permanent."

Lana wants to blot out this last part, jumping as quickly as she can to hop over and lean into this particular Rose, a woman looking through her with a face fascinated but unsolvable, a million miles away. Lana does what she can to pump life back into her, giving her the same massive hug Vic had once given Mary, years ago at Hope, the kind that breathes into another's qualms while gushing at warpspeed into Rose's shoulder. "I mean that drug we drank? Seriously. Maybe this was all just to get some kind of rise out of you?"

All could be relinquished: what great freedom could be found in letting go. Rose has no practice in it, the room falling outward but the place too small for whatever lets her shiver out of the embrace. "God, I am sorry." And she is, even with her hand on the knob tugging the door open against a desert gust.

"Don't get unreal on me. Come on. Hey now." From the way her lips and eyes move independent of each other, Lana could be starting her first conversation with her friend, trying all over to lure her back in.

In the dark chill of Lana's room, Rose cannot help but consider her reflection. Odd that instinct had made her sprint up here rather than just out and away into that better-adjusted realm in which she had never tracked Lana Mahler to Hope and all her memories of being Lola at least would not have gotten shot through with fissures. Vic had once told Rose that a friend who betrays you makes your epistemology shake your ontology or was it the other way around? While what Rose feels is as if this recent period marks having fallen through some previously unknown looking-glass back into the lair of the Mahlers, their ontology screwing with her epistemology, finding it hard to trust anything, least of all the report of her senses, and perhaps it is this that had made her run straight back into the lair of Lana, having left her friend bewildered in Rose's room, likely to hitch-poke up here any moment. In the room, the fig perfume steals Rose's breath. All Rose needs is one bit of independent confirmation, some proof one way or another.

Because clearly Lana's confession was not just some drug-tale: its moments had been recalled and told a little too clearly. Lana had un-bosomed herself, thrown it all out, clearly wanting to be seen in true colors. But how could she have had such little conscience? Never mind the dark hints she had offered of an asylum stay: could an adult woman have stolen two boys?

Flagrant with guilt, Rose concedes everything. She had tried weaving a rope with sand and where was she supposed to go now? Join far-off protestors on the distant hills? Or march, solo and failed, to the prison and just beg for entry as if at the face of heaven? *Dear Vic, I seem to be made of clay and wish to make myself all over again.*

And how much easier to just melt away and go home. To pretend she had never heard of the Mahlers. Surrender them in all their basic unprocurability. Let her instead be true to the lesser planet of stasis, sleep with a silk pillow over her head to muffle the faraway hint of a man in a bloodbath. Having lifted only a half finger in his direction, she could just drive away, five days before slaughter. The giddy unwisdom of this all offered a beautiful requiem.

Of course she would like to blame Lana for her distraction, though the evidence grabs her around the throat: Rose in the labyrinth of Lola had become an impostor of Rose, playing perjurer to any altruistic urges, following up poorly on Vic. And if she were really honest, slakeless thirst rather than self-sacrifice had led her to Hope. Adulthood had coveted the lightness she once knew with her friend and this hope too now seemed impossibly juvenile, the pall of time thrown over it.

In only one sense she recalls herself as Rose. She is struck by the urge to find a computer, to get on the web, to madly contact every single lover she had ever known. This whole trip now seems a fatal mistake as if she thought she could tour some country's canals and leisure zones only to find herself awaking in a gulag, the frame larger than its original conception. You love playing with fire, she tells herself, wanting to hold on to the giddy power she had felt for just a second in her room, the freedom of relinquishing Lana. And what should she do now, go ask Hogan for help, answer questions, be forced to say a formal goodbye?

How come Lana always gets to flee, leaving no trace?

Rose's finger runs with no incarnational logic over the dresser's maroon textured scarf while her pulse blasts. There must be a pattern here but she cannot hold the scarf in the same sphere as the story. What had Lana meant with such a blatant project of exposure? She had meant it as an unfolding. Could the Lana who had chosen this scarf also have done what she claimed? Rose stands, one minute of life putrefied, putrefying, staring at the totem of herself in the mirror. Dare double dare. Lana had been so free-speaking, offering revelation up as a contagion. It was ostentatious how little she cared about Rose, offering no token, dropping Rose in the middle of the Mahler enigma. *Their loss doesn't have to be mine.* A great relief starts to creep in at the edges, a breathing space inside Rose, one she has never known.

It is not hard for Rose to open the dresser drawer, the top, eyes turned upward like a midwife or a coroner dislodging the guts of a terminal patient until her fingers close on that empty, ratted bead purse, both keepsake and jackpot enough that her grip fastens.

You lost me, she tells Lana, hanging the purse around her neck and inside her blouse so it brushes her breasts softly before she goes out the door and shuts it with no bashful joy, these last honors both cussed and freeing.

Rose in a skirt, heaving her duffel bag into the backseat of an over-heated car. For this second, however, Rose is grateful: she seems to have lost her need to read signs everywhere. Nothing right now speaks to her in code or command. Everything is just what it is, varnish stripped. Only to jump at the figure coming in her sideview: Lana stumbling.

"You need your crutches!" says Rose, pity rushing her. Without meaning to she startles out of the car, the ratty purse still inside her shirt.

"That's your car, Rosie?"

"Well. Thought I would go—"

"Somewhere for the day?" Lana forces a smile. "Not to tattle though, right? Not like you're heading straight to your lady lawyer or someone."

"No." Rose vast and beyond could still be startled that this mirage might not think beyond herself. "God."

"What."

"Just how you still want a partner in—" and Rose waits, with ungrudging respect for their past. "Your partner in crime."

"Thanks. I knew I could tell you. Hey you forgot this?" Lana presents her with something in brown paper. "Found it under a heap of towels in your room." Brown-wrapped, marked LOLA, the scrapbook from the long-ago time when they'd come to Hope. "You take this wherever you go?"

Rose can't speak; her throat scalded, no new words forming.

Lana looks toward the burnt hills across the highway. "You know what? This will make you happy. I am going to try to meet with my dad after all."

"Great." Rose still on automatic. "He'll love that. But you know it doesn't matter now."

Her friend stares back.

"What you did. You can't exactly testify." With no more to say, having used up all their possibilities. "Actually Lana, keep the book. It should be yours."

Lana looks at it, beaming for a second, seemingly glad to feel generous in thrusting it back. "No Rosie, you made it. Come on, take it with you."

As Lana watches her friend pull out the driveway, car weighted down, headed toward the southern on-ramp of Highway Five, she hums her own half-fairytale: she'll be back, she'll be back.

Sedge is trying to convince Tee of the reality of the need.

"BON-kers, man," says Tee, a direct quotation of some adult somebody from TV or not. "That's straight out wack."

Sedge doesn't point out how direct the mission could be given that it is too important to convince Tee of the main point. His space robot Lestrion has come to Sedge and told him the need. Should the twins falter, they are done for.

The task is this: aliens have elected them to tie up Dirk. This is the essential part. Tie Dirk up with a length of frayed orange cord marked 200 amp, the one they found yesterday on the refuse pile out behind the reptile cemetery.

And though Sedge doesn't really want to let on to Tee the origin of the information he has received, he knows one part of convincing Tee lies in divulging sources. His vision had come just the way that he'd heard adults in hot tubs up north say they get visions on seven-day desert quests when all they get to eat in their tents is a single fig a day. Sedge's vision, asleep the night of the trance dance, had seen Dirk gagged and bound and their mother liberated of her hobble, rushing with them in a car toward where? A water playland amid this hot desert with slides and pools. After which they'd return to a normal house on a block with fences, lawns, helmets and bikes, convenient playgrounds, monthly menus of the kind of food too long suppressed in their childhoods, both in Yalina and here at Hope, cheeseburgers and popcorn chicken and tacos at a school cafeteria, a paradise of normal.

On this normalcy question Sedge feels himself one hundred percent aligned with their mother. They'd go somewhere he'd guessed about, have fireman friends, someplace he has glimpsed on verboten television where franks and marshmallows get toasted over perfect campfires. In this place you kick Halloween leaves in thick clusters and a kid gets to be mediocre and play paintball and though he can't quite say it, he knows his mother has been on the wrong track with the wrong people, especially men. Only he and Lestrion know how to liberate her.

"If we don't do this some other guy could capture her," is what Sedge squeaks now to Tee in his special-agent urgent voice, knowing the force of illogic can trump all.

Probably it has distressed Sedge more than Tee to see their mother so fallen, taken with someone they know could never be any kind of father, this Dirkster guy, and probably it has distressed his space robot Lestrion even more than Sedge, though Sedge was disturbed for sure. Seeing her fall for huckster Dirk had made him feel as if someone was slowly amputating parts of his body—his neck, his shins—with a cleaver determined to hack apart any real future for their family. This is why binding seems just retribution, better than the other ideas Sedge and Lestrion had entertained. As he had heard the Dirkster tell their mother only two nights ago, bind what you don't like, release what you do.

In the never-dark of the prison's incandescence, Vic considers confines
and stumbles. The cell's walls echo the birth into selfhood. There
you go, he thought. Leave the dark of the womb and you enter blaring
existence, locked into the self's skin. How much freer to be stripped
of skin and cell, to exorcise envy of air, to embrace the protoplasmic,
evaporate into ether and enter the easeful embrace.

He cannot decide whether it is real or not that all night they have
been pouring cement into the boundary wall between his otherwise
empty cell block and the rest of the world, trying to get him into a
crypt and slowly block off his air, the cement made of pulverized dust
from native skeletons unearthed by archaeological digs. On the other
side of the wall, Javier is having sex with multiple partners and ignoring the simple buzzer request Vic keeps making.

Someone inside his chest is talking about choice. Saying that
choosing to die would outwit everyone else's game and would be
understood in the right way, not as an adolescent rebellion against a
system that had swindled him, not as a case study of a psyche gone
wrong but as a true declaration of independence.

And yet could there be a devil working the world, someone who
would insert such a charter in his head, who with private lapses had
dreamed up the Christmas cookies offered in the max-security prison,
leaving for other devils tricks of refinement: the panopticon and
chicken-wire, the bullhorn and shower, solitary confinement relieved

only by an hour a day in the dog-pen, the insidious libertine luxury of prisoner Web sites, the alarms during which he must drop to one knee.

Has Vic not relied on at least one constant? His self or that habitual selfish way of seeing the world, the constancy a granter of the mortal, satisfying illusion of permanence, letting a person vault over any irregularities whether they be orphanhood or emigrancy, success or imprisonment.

A flash of his daughter and her friend: once on horseback for Lana's birthday on the beach they had answered, after he riddled them about whether they showed the customary female streak of competition that they lacked selfishness in their friendship because they were in it together and for the long haul, linked in endless generosity of the spirit.

It doesn't matter where she ends and I begin, his daughter had said, *this is one thing I know for sure, we're together forever.*

And he might have wished he could have known at least once in life something like this friendship but also thinks such an ideal might have been born of the Romantics if not the Sufis before them, all of it dying in a blaze near the middle of the twentieth century, somewhere within the troika sustained by the war, Stalin, McCarthy, that precious foolish period when cars became smooth as women and he had come to America hoping foolishly for perfect union, the possibility of his self transcending all its prior cages, a Lebensraum for his one self, giving him rope enough to hang himself.

The twenty-first century, lost in it, that's what keeps him pressing the buzzer, it would be wonderful to talk any of this over with Javier if only the guard could be pried loose from the clawlike, sore-ridden legs of multiple sex partners, Vic's guard and ally engaging in twenty-first-century coitus in a nation thinking itself a copulative empire in a state the coital apotheosis of the American dream in the coital zone of the state that is itself the coital zenith of coitus trying to annex everything while Vic must lie stationed in a solitary anticoital cell which stands for all the ways prisoner #4267 or whatever his number is, he can't recall, has been tricked by everyone else's peaks. Too dark. At the peak you topple. This may be Vic's first truly clear thought in at least half an hour or maybe a day and night.

As a surfer, he used to wait for the ocean's strength to return.

You wait and it comes back so that next morning his strength comes back tidal, leaving him a clear-thinking man again. Javier has been able to undo the cement wall and has showered all the love juice off.

"Sure you want to do this?" Javier asks, hair oiled slick.

"I'm not the one making the choice." Vic's pen over the form, signing for NO APPEAL, NO STAY.

"Your lawyer will want to talk to you about this."

"Please. That joke. Don't I have only a couple of days left anyway? Whatever the appeal is, it's out of my control. If it's going to fail, which may be the case, I'd rather spend my last days not being uncertain. Three more days on my own say-so with carte blanche to think whatever I want."

"Five."

"Fine. Please allow me to go lawyerless into the masses. I need wider berth."

When Javier presses him on this, Vic wants to explain but again his tongue falls dead, a slug. It is that he wants the saltwater wash that will induce ultimate conductivity, the electric calipers a surrender of the charades everyone likes to play. No more letters sent to various helpers and lawyers. No more attempts to get a college degree by studying old pre-college exambooks:

blood is to life as

a) rules
b) edicts
c) legacy

is to institution

And might there not be an ecstasy at the exact border between life and non-life when the self gets to release into the great vacuity, or *the great buckwheaty* as Vic's Bolivian mentor from old surfing days used to call it?

The mind as it had been constituted encounters the mind that cannot be and finally gets the ultimate chance at freedom.

And yet as Javier helps him this morning to the shower block, the light slants with such gorgeous specificity into Cell Block A it almost makes a person want to keep living.

"Hallelujah," whispers Vic.

"Pardon?" asks Javier. "Today you want liquid soap or a bar?"

Vic will not give them what they need.

For one, this being one of many topics for which he lacks time enough with Javier to discuss: no one will get the succor of thinking they serve a perfect last meal.

The hypocrisy galls.

These are my last hours, he tells the rain of water in autocratic tones, imperial in knowing Javier won't hear, manning the controls and politely averting his gaze, allowing another male his skinny dignity, interrupting only to ask: what, hotter? You'd like it hotter?

Somewhere in these few days his peace with a good decision will be marred only by an unsettling video apparition, though he cannot tell whether he has hallucinated Rose Lemm, his daughter's old friend: he remembered her as having an appealing bruisability and this specter would have softness only between her legs. If this was a waking dream, then so be it, he must be certifiably crazy. If it is real, in the parlance of the few prisoners he has come to know, this is a true mindfuck.

An odd fellow had come with Rose, a fellow who seems to at least know Javier, producing for him not his daughter but this Rose, a girl who says she has been writing letters and sending science magazines for years. She talks from a remote screen, engineered by Javier, so conceivably could this not all be a cruel hoax? Even Javier might be out to get Vic. Like their inmates, wouldn't guards be prone to lapses, drawn to the same vaporous line between good and evil?

Or has Vic forgotten so much? If only he could define the contours of his amnesia, he'd be in the clear.

To the video apparatus, deciding he has little embarrassment to lose, right before the video shimmers shut, he croaks: "Get me to see my daughter."

The jolliest of guards could have the greatest number of secret deals going on. This must be only forty percent Vic's paranoia, however unverifiable by outside source. Now he debates whether this had in fact been a dream. I just want to see my daughter, he tells his solitary cell walls, lying down between the rough sheets, showered and clean as a lamb.

A mindfuck indeed. At first he'd taken this twitching apparition named Rose to be his own daughter, his Mopsy.

Among the vital leftovers colonizing at least a few synapses is his little girl—he cannot remember if his daughter had ever visited him here in this place but what he does remember is Mopsy swinging on a hammock saying something about pineapple. What he wouldn't give to smell such a fruit.

Maybe only this last year he'd begun to forget even what ammonia meant when he was first brought here, the scent that used to raise all scents, better and more appealing, even sweat on a guard's uniform or on a fellow inmate's body after a basketball game. To combat ammonia Vic used to train his nose to understand degrees of mildew, a spectrum running from the warmth of old underwear all the way toward rained-on cat. And now even ammonia smells friendlier than the acids excreted by his own pill-gagged body, and while his nose deceives him, still his fingers carry the memory of stroking his girl's little dry elbow, her banana scent, head leaned against his shoulder, her length apparent even back then in her stretched-out bones. He can feel the elbow as if he'd touched it only two hours ago.

In a parallel universe lives a room of last touches in which he still strokes his daughter's arm before a father had to start pushing a daughter away.

In a crypt as in the crib, what you have left is this: embracing nothingness, embracing whatever nothing led to whatever act had led to yet another greater nothing. NO APPEAL, NO STAY fits him better than anyone else's sentence, the syllables themselves tallying nicely into a Yankee Doodle Dandy he sings, one more attempt at an endlessly self-propulsive lullaby. When has anyone before him ever found the grandeur to proclaim to a lover no appeal?

If he could just will spontaneous combustion, he would have found an ultimate trick, able to make his life take on perfect annularity, the shape of a marriage ring.

"C'mon, this is our moment," Sedge tells Tee, earnest, trudging ahead of him on the path, checking the plastic watch shaped like a duckling, one of a pair his mother had once won from a shoot-em-up carnival that had come to town. Tee had long ago lost his duck watch.

"Our moment? What the hell?"

"I mean carpet dee 'em," says Sedge.

"You ripped that off from Hogan."

"Carpet!"

"What's gotten into you?" asks Tee, following his twin wonderingly, knowing Lestrion could have taken over his twin's body. At moments Tee can believe in the powers of Lestrion though in grumpier seconds he derides his twin for having invented a babylike imaginary friend.

"You know it's cool how mama never made us dress in the same twin clothes," says Sedge.

"Why's that?"

"Because I would've thought I was you. Too scary."

"Okay, give me a chance."

They've gotten to the top but true dusk holds off, each hilltop bruised by shadows, crowned with a last bright crescent.

"You're not scared of lions?" asks Tee.

"Not anymore," says Sedge. Until now he has been good at suppressing that memory of this place but at the reminder, Lestrion has to take over and speak for him: "I'm giving you aerial overview for our recon. Look down."

Down where the thirty-third anniversary of this place continues: little twinkling Christmas lights, a tribal cry rising over drumbeats.

"Our target is there—" Sedge has started to talk in what Tee thinks of as robotspeak, his lips stretched in a wide smile, teeth tight as if mission control allows Sedge only the most covert consumption of oxygen. Sedge points to the round yurt, its windows lit red, a glow-bomb. DorAlba, the owners here, have returned but Dirk is using that space. At least this is what Sedge has understood.

"We'll make the mission simple. We're storming."

"Tell me again, man?" Tee actually loves his twin's whole other crazy made-up life though it doesn't mean he's above teasing him in a good way.

"You agree mom's been hanging out too much with everyone else?" Sedge waits but his brother only shrugs. "With her old friend."

"She left this morning."

"Rose? You sure?"

"I saw Rose carrying some bags."

"But anyway mom's been hanging out too much with other people." Sedge pats Lestrion in his pocket. "This way we get her back."

"How?"

"We get the cord. Hanging outside the red housing. We're going in. Plan is seize the subject, tie him up—" Sedge must sense Tee's disbelief is too big a wall. "Tell me we don't have our reasons?"

"Whatever." This is the thing about twinhood according to Tee. You go along for the ride when it suits you and it doesn't exactly un-suit Tee to tie up the man who has been sticking parts of himself into their mother, far as he understands that enterprise ·from the penis page in the dictionary and older boys' gossip. "I get your mission."

"Our mission."

"Okay, but I think we should trick him into it."

"How?"

"Let's call it a meditation." In full fiendish rapture, both realizing the gift Tee had just summoned, the boys freeze. "A meditation." Tee cannot help but giggle, relishing his genius. "That part let me talk."

"So what are we waiting for?" says Sedge, beckoning, almost slipping backward down the trail. When they get closer, they hear the made-up words of music pounding out the amps:

Gitchi gitchi gaga yaya!

It is not hard for Sedge to position his twin right outside the red yurt and go peek around the rear door, half ajar. Past a scarlet curtain the intruder Dirk sits on a round moondisk pillow facing a triangular mandala, sandalwood incense wafting out, their quarry sending smoke signals as he awaits supplicants. "Okay, so is this not a sign?" whispers Sedge to himself, a direct quotation of their mother, cord heating up in his hand.

A bit into the act, Sedge thinks this guy could not be weirder: their mother's suitor is so easily bound.

"We heard about this new meditation," Sedge had begun, pre-empting Tee.

"Yes?" Dirk had asked, humoring them, well-regulated. "You know I love new meditations." His impatience visible only around the edges. "It's nice you boys are interested."

"You want us to teach you?" Sedge had gone on. "The meditation?"

"It has to do with freedom," Tee had said, inspiration kicking in. "First we have to bind your hands though. The most important thing is keep your eyes closed. And you breathe the whole time. Deeply into the belly."

After he did this, their big lion breathing, they tied the kerchief around the eyes and roped his hands and legs, Sedge mumbling to himself to recall his best knots: over and under for the clove hitch and cuckold's neck, loop through for the manrope, tight for the clinch.

"How long you want me to do this for?" Dirk asked, keeping his part of the bargain, eyes closed.

Then they stuffed the silk from one of his mandalas into his mouth, Tee swift in tying it at the back of his neck. "It's important not to talk," Sedge had intoned, echoing Dirk's timbre of voice from one of his workshops.

"Ooo. Look, gross, his wiener just went up," Tee whispered into Sedge's ear. It was true but Sedge did not let the sight sway him from the mission.

"Now do what you can to breathe in freedom," Sedge had said, unperturbed.

"Yeah. Through the nose. Just like Houdini."

Something about the mention of Houdini was the first misbegotten word from Tee in the whole enterprise. Hearing it made Dirk start to strain, first with a few subtle caterpillar movements to make sure he could get free of two nine-year-old boys' hijinks. Then Dirk had gotten mad, crimson flush under his brown skin, neck veins bulging, still doing his best to keep some kind of meditative cadence to his burbling.

Being cautious, the boys tiptoed around their would-be stepfather, taking especial care to blow out all the candles in the red yurt, whispering quick commands to each other in the dark.

Lucky that no early supplicant roamed outside or at least none knocked at the locked door. With Dirk secured, Sedge leaned over and whispered something about Lestrion into the captive's ear but Tee couldn't hear that part, already thinking of the next step. He brought Sedge out to the small stairs where they barred the yurt from the outside, placing in front of it a sign that Sedge with superior word powers had made saying: NO DARSHAN WITH DIRK UNTIL NEXT WEEK.

Happy boys, sweaty in jubilation, having tied up an adult man, they shine what Hogan calls their most shit-eating smile toward a supplicant they pass coming up the path, ready for Dirk's blessing before the big evening. The boys can tell who the lady supplicants are because they wear long white dresses as if trying out for the part of Halloween ghosts, wearing garlands of lavender or big rocks around their neck, scented with some hippie version of old-lady perfume, not like their mom who always smells delicious.

As they pass the first clump of supplicants, Tee asks, "Now what?"

"Lestrion was strict, said not to say."

"Aw come on. Be serious."

"He says wait. The first part of our mission is accomplished."

Tee grabs his twin's fist in his and gives it a happy pump. "You're crazy."

Sedge shoots back a secret smile. "Tell me you're not."

Hogan is getting up before the crowd, which he hates to do, saying: "Look, folks, thanks for coming. Dirk should be here soon."

Restless, the crowd stirs, hungering to be released of all hungers.

TWENTY-FIRST OF DECEMBER, 2008   5:46 P.M.

Vic in a head that sees everything with a bit too much pain since at least lunch is listening intently to Javier talk about his day to another guard down the hall. There is some kind of stoppage along Highway Five, which everyone calls the interstate. "Excuse me," shouts Vic. The color of the sky through the slit at the top of his cell is like tapioca, bland, everywhere and unreachable. "Jesus, Joseph and Mary!"

When that doesn't work, he hits the call button.

Javier had confided in him that he had to be put on suicide watch—or is this another mind twister? Whatever the case, Vic has been granted this special, direct-hit call button: does it beep only at Javier or does the signal sing forth on magical invisible electrical waves to the Commissioner of Prisons, buzzing the governor and then finally his daughter?

When the corrections officers—not Javier—installed it, they said they trusted he wouldn't abuse it.

"You left me here," says Vic to his guard's face once it appears, slotted vertically so it looks like something a person could buy, an intriguingly wrapped plastic parcel of humanity. "I was calling your name. There was this commotion and no one heard. Why do they all want me to lie here and die in my own waste?" He is crying now. "I have some things." He is struggling to even form the words. "Some things I need to tell you."

"You want to change that paper you signed?"

"No." Vic waves this away, impatient. "It's about the flagellation of Jesus and how it links with the question of longing for the father. I have some interesting theories."

"Tell me."

"First tell me something."

"Anything, boss."

"Why do they all want to murder me? There is that man, the owner of an important duck farm right behind this wall. He's in control and wants to buy this place. Could you talk to him about why they want to leave me here to die in my excrement?"

"You're right here, in your own cell."

"That part I know. There is a good water system here. When I go, please tell my daughter she won't suffer for lack of water. You and she both just have to be careful if you go on any trip because this place is surrounded by people who can't hear."

"Whenever you need me, Vic, please, use the button. Like you just did."

"Why did you leave me?"

"I'm sorry." The guard's hands flutter open, letting free a dove Vic can't see. "Do you need a wash?"

"No, what I really need is coffee. Can you ask someone for some coffee?"

"I will."

"Not the motor oil they use to inflame my bowels." He is trying to ask the guard for a different promise but can't quite locate it. "Don't go please. You're a father." Now finally it comes to him, how to keep his guard there. He is not sure the words will come though the simultaneity of the picture appears to him in full rainbow, the story he has never before told anyone. Yet—as he always thinks— like their inmates, wouldn't guards be prone to lapses, drawn to the same mist between good and evil?

Vic will not start by blaming it on Berkeley. He could but won't.

He knows it sounds strange, crypto-religious, but he'd wanted to have a last dinner with his wife. The idea of lastness. To appreciate her, knowing it would be their last before some grand departure. But how many ways can you spell lastness? He was going to tell Mary he would move out of the house.

But the banality! After years spent putting up with her failings, charred dinners, sacrificial offerings, slights at dinner parties held in his honor. He could list them so easily: her absentminded, poor folding of laundry, the slimy handles on cabinets. A real hypochondriac and germ-phobe, she never replaced a toilet paper roll and had known far too many madcap falls from ladders while changing lightbulbs. She'd painted his office an intolerable eggplant hue and was always getting blocked by someone's car in driveways, requiring rescue. Many times she couldn't pull a key from the ignition or had to change everyone's plans just so she could save some cat, a raccoon, a bird's nest. A person couldn't believe what he'd put up with. While what she tolerated seemed minor by comparison: his nail-clippings like shed moons scattered over the bed or his own perpetual tardiness, a proclamation few seemed to hear, as if life had slighted him by deigning to start in his absence.

Put in a shaker and everything had come to this? Yet the idea of leaving—to leave, to leave behind—had its own life and tentacles, offering specific outcomes related to lastness, an enshrinement. He wanted to take her to dinner, announce the woeful truth of his leaving and in this way enshrine his martyrdom. He wanted to see her prepare for dinner, casting a look of wistful anger toward the hall mirror while he knew it was the last time, *il n'y a pas de plus*. He wanted all stations of lastness: to watch her chew dinner without tasting it, to see eyebrows grown a bit too close, gray and tufted, cherishing all elements because they were final and she'd be wearing that flower-pompom cap that still reminded him of that very first moment he'd spotted her at the university pool, limbs shooting out of a bathing suit from those delicate thin canals at the delta of her thighs, and how she had crowned the outfit with a ridiculous bathing cap sprouting pink floral excrescences, perhaps one of her Japanese customs, to not throw open the wind-gates by removing a cap too often. But the hat habit didn't seem to keep with her Yokut half which would have had her—do what?

He had to admit how little he knew about her origins which didn't mean that, in their worst moments, he hadn't yelled at her *not just mixed but mixed-up!* while secretly thinking her hybridity gave her a leg up, so to speak, alluring and untraceable, a trickster-coyote length and strength, the doubled roots denied him by orphanhood. Yet whenever he chose to name it, he could also see her pompom hat as an emblem of the greater problem. She kept her heat too close, not sharing well enough with others (but for the one horrible, notable *sharing* with which she had scorched his ears).

Not once in their thirty-four years had he inquired about the hats.

He could have. A cuckold could do lots of things. A cuckold could also ignore any hunger for the finality of a last meal. A cuckold could suggest the pair go, borrowing the lexicon of self-help books, *rediscover* each other. But such rediscovery was insuperably foreign to Vic. What he wanted was a graceful last dinner, a parachute out, all termini announced by him.

First they would sit. In a perfunctory manner she would ask about work, this courtesy her vestige of courtship. He would sink back into his usual silence. Then he would say *I'm leaving*, just like that, so he could watch her face fall, knowing he'd never see her and her silent recriminations again.

Leave, he would just leave—because what held him to Berkeley? Not her, not their almost-grown daughter with her talent for still prickling his heart, not the vestiges of his students. Students! What had he ever taught them? He'd rather live in a damp thatched hut on a lonely Irish moor or speak philosophy over sangria with lined ancients after midnight in the white-plastered caves of Granada. If he returned to being not a teacher but a learner, no one would trace him. Of its own his reputation could revive and he could thrive or moulder in the reds and greens of a life he alone had chosen.

This craving for lastness struck after a bad day in his decades-old office, filled with the sediment of papers, dust suturing pages together, grayed rubber-bands gone brittle, stripped of tensility. Where was his new thought? What did he have to say given that the neural network theory had been toppled?

> This soul is a penis. The hero of the dream is a phallic double, or phallic personification of the whole body. Having a soul, the hero with a thousand faces, is the same as having genital organization—to take the penis as the "narcissistic representative of the whole personality."

He used to be in favor of the exponents of the brain-as-spark model, the experimenters who liked ripping out sensory-input portions to steal input from the cortical map. Later he had been a proponent of the brain-as-soup theory and even later the parallel-processor theory but what did it matter when all his most favored thinkers were now considered outmoded, ancien régime, only antique William James bandied about these days as the pioneer in conceptualizations of the brain, a predecessor leaving Vic feeling superannuated.

Better to be an astronaut who sends commode contents off onto a garbage satellite circling the earth in an ignored but dangerous vessel or better to stay landbound and contribute paperwork directly to the recycling heap. That must be the ticket! Go directly to recycling without stopping at any ink-on-page intervention. At least one could later say one was cited in the logbooks of some eco-virtue station. How easy to be rendered irrelevant, how simple to see the slow decline in the life of emeritus. Does it get any lonelier? Could you make an anagram of *erstwhile* out of *emeritus*? And how weak was his mind to wonder that?

Vic still had the occasional homeless man who sought him out, especially a strange last shaggy with his arcane sign HOW MANY BA- BIES ARE YOU GOING TO STUFF INTO YOUR SOUP CAN AND SELL TO TEXAS? And still occasionally encountered the odd student on a special project of exhumation. Each year when Vic taught his one lecture course, on the first day he still packed the halls, the students coming not, to use their lexicon, for *content provision* but out of reverence for his reputation, youth using his twilight as high romantic backdrop, a creep and droop to gloss their own vitality as if he were the backdrop in a Caspar David Friedrich painting and they could turn their backs on him since what they came for was fame no matter how erstwhile, for the shamanic aura of fame this old man could bestow upon the lucky. Fame to them seemed to mean the love of the many, a delicious concept, a multiheaded idol of celebrity with which they could copulate rather than with the staidness of any single idea.

So much so that students now had the rude habit of sidling out mid-lecture, mid-sentence, going to great lengths to climb over the pylons of stuffed backpacks and letting the door slam behind to echo in the hall like a verdict. For this generation with its flea-circus attention span, Vic Mahler turned out to be but a glyph on their screen. Once he spoke a single sentence, they already sighted his fame down to its micromeme, absorbing its absolute value, needing then to scurry out to obey the pressing needs of their id while leaving Vic suspended. *The Age of Rude Entitlement* indeed (cf. Mahler, 1987, a prescient work). How could he blame them given that youth of all eras made haste to find a better mirror for longings primarily hormonal in origin (cf. Mahler, "Perennials of Socialization," 1963).

Sure, he too had taken on habits he would have mocked had he been young. For one, whenever he saw protocol was not being followed, he could not keep from swearing. And yet he had a right to be angry, didn't he? In the shadow-realm of his reign, his contributions— not to mention all those committee meetings, my god!—were not adequately recognized. He had cleaved to the centerline of virtue, had not been an alcoholic and in the main had not seduced female youth, having tried to the best of his ability to ignore concupiscence, all the soft cups offered up.

Though he remained cognizant of the inverse proportionality between youth's esteem for him and his actual chronological age and though he'd been somewhat capable of reinventing himself for each succeeding generation of students, on this particular day, Valentine's 1989, he'd known the exact longitude and latitude of his irrelevance.

Irrelevant to students with mainly mating on the mind. It was a wonder any adolescent read any book at all, given how haywire the hormones went at this age, granting all the youth around him the appearance of Blakean fire for a brief moment before the professionalization of habit and streamlining set harder tracks into the five percent of their brains' total utilized capacity.

On the fourteenth of February, 1989, Vic had gone to refill his water decanter down the hall and had spotted that curvy redhead succubus in the green sweater and cowgirl boots who sprang up everywhere on campus. Now she thrust forward those shapely arms, the better to dance with a long-haired boy in a pink shirt, the shirt being a frontal attack, meaning something utterly different than it had back in Vic's time.

Your categories are not mine, the shirt screamed at Vic, this boy consenting to tango down the institutional halls with a supple coed, a boy with a shapeless body whose main attributes were his youth and puppydog loyal eyes ready to play, his barrette and clear willingness to forsake traditional gender roles. Why else would a pink puppydog get to tango with a girl you could tell would be a tigress, a girl who would enjoy one's eyes upon her, a girl who would quickly lose interest, seeking the next conquest to add to her low beltloop under her creamy belly, so that even restlessness formed part of her nympho charm.

While it was also true that, mostly faithful to Mary, those few times he had strayed, it had been with girls not unlike the redhead cowgirl. Of course, these digressions had occurred back in the days when he'd had more hair on his head, his eyebrows less ostentatious in telegraphing decrepitude, all the girls an evolutionary obstacle placed in his moral path, some sort of stepping-stone necessary for the teleology of the other side.

Why did the professor sleep with his student? To get to the other side.

Valentine's was clearly a bad day because the students were in their element, on their side of Hades, busy having some school-sponsored sex-positive party down the hall. A party replete with enough childhood elements that everyone could pretend sex was an innocent pleasure. So did they think they had invented the garden of Eden? Did variety of sexual experience matter so much? Did they think they were alone in choosing a few select able-bodied types to participate? *O Knowledge!* he felt like shouting, a cranky old lion in winter. *Go fuck yourselves!* occurred to him as well, a phrase all too apt. Because all they wanted was to be released by the laws of their elders to go fuck themselves. Or rather they were energized like reverse magnets away from the law of the elders toward fucking.

He pondered this: hadn't society taken a downward turn when *fuck* turned into an unfortunate transitive, possessing a wholly negative valence? *Go fuck yourself*: an unfortunate phrase, like Bay of Pigs. What had early colonists said? Go imbibe hemlock? Go fig yourself? Now pink streamers and balloons flanked the hallway leading to the big conference room where the kids joined up—what was the term, *hooked?*—in a buzz of fig-happy frivolity. Might as well be pigs in pink-streaked mud, hooking. Pairs of international students entered this pleasure-dome with some sheepishness, the open sexuality of the American students making this question live in their gaze: was *this* the way to go or would it be better to obey the old-world law of one's elders imploring them to shun Babylon?

False idols, friends! was what Vic could have shouted at all the tables bearing pagan-pink glitter glue and card-decorating, an exhibition of hot pink sex toys, someone demonstrating massages on a pink table, everything pink pink pink, smoke wafting over the whole scene, sage sticks burning from a tribe with an identity long buried by the sands of fuck-happy New Age kids. In her genteel way his Mary would have been distressed, so easily horrified by an ad showing a tearful Indian watching trash come ashore, by the reiterated booms in turquoise jewelry, the rise in sweat lodges, the cheap polymorphous love shown the idea of the Indian, licked white like a candy cane by heedless pink kids. They want to consume the idea of us, Mary had said. Just past the toddling age, her daughter had listened carefully.

I come from a candy cane? Am I striped?

No, but no—Vic had laughed, Mary laughing even harder, slapping his hand to try to stop her own laugh, the moment so rich. That had been back when their Lana had been a more tractable quantity, some sixteen, seventeen years earlier. Since that time, since Lana had been about four, what had not slipped away? Some witch had come at night to steal their daughter. A rude theft, he muttered to himself, stealing someone he and Mary had brought into the world, the world exacting its penny for the miracle bounty of a child. How quickly a daughter's essence could disappear, how subtly, and so easy not to have noticed when she'd first coughed, looking away, asking the dinnertime *may I be excused?* that now lasted an eternity.

Mahler filled his decanter and peeked in again on the students. The music of his daughter's generation: loud, sardonic quotations of his era. Who could work to that parody?

I could tell you about real sex, he might have roared at them. Direct, no-holds-barred sex, the kind where you slam your partner down, thighs grasping, everyone entering primal abdication, moving through the senses to lose them. And afterward the tender muted apology a gentleman uses to stitch himself back to his lady. The polite thing to do after is swallow the urge to run since later you get the reward of a hilltop postcoital moment of solo reflection, calm sight: where you have been, where you are going, the lady and your romancing her a ladder up that hill and back to yourself.

Even old tenderfoot Sinatra knew more than any aggregate of these students, too busy with ornate forms of procreative dance to listen to old Vic Mahler, too busy with importantly self-appointed tasks, the pink decoration of cookies shaped like vulvas and penises, a boy stretching rosy plastic over a friend's face. Mahler returned to the threshold of his door to shake his head and of course no one noticed the vestigial professor.

Why were their tasks any more important than his? Who among them wasn't acting out the great march of neural determinism?

And yes, he had argued, the brain had its plasticity, up to a point, but there were also biologically determined coordinates that functioned like bitumen if one were to consider the ideas of his colleague Gallagher, whose ability to create elegant, modular theories Mahler had once admired. Perhaps, had his theories been more like Gallagher's, Mahler might be more relevant to these kids today.

Was that plastic a new form of a condom? Flat plastic? Could that be a woman's condom? When did these kids become so sophisticated?

Back to the office, back to its sediment he went, slamming the door on the beat, as loudly as any first-day kid leaving his lecture. Clearly to them Victor Mahler lived mainly as a quotation, while everything he once considered the forefront of human connection— *reverence, civility and gratitude*, he'd told Mary at the start of their courtship some half-century ago—was up for question. No center held and how revolutionary were these kids anyway?

How different were they from any previous generation, the ones who just wanted to knock up a girl, knock the sexual power out of her, get her caveward, barefoot and pregnant as the cliché would have it, so that she would knead bread dough and tend babies, an endless life of *Kinder, Kirche, Küche*?

Was this the harbor his own daughter headed toward? A girl lost in the universe of that first year after college, barefoot and swishing through rooms, padding about, most definitely a padder and swisher. And if he couldn't quite see the outcome of whatever she was doing, you had to have faith that a kid could work it out, steered by whatever muddled hope this generation offers as a ticket out.

At his desk at school, this new breed of sex-positive Valentine's loud and intruding on his consciousness, Vic had tried returning to the task at hand. What had he been working on? His daughter. Clearly, Lana, as she'd asked them to call her somewhere at the start of her high-school career, *Lana* had a pressing need to defer the real world. One way of putting it: she wished to delay the world of linear task-reward systems in the vocational sphere (cf. Mahler, "Work Force and Neural Imprinting," 1969) in order to create an illusion of her own world (cf. Mahler, "Delayed Adolescence Among American Youth," 1982).

Spontaneous, loopy, improvisational, that was what his offspring needed to be, or rather, Lana's neopallium demanded of the inferior archipallium the illusion that it could make territorial claims upon the future.

He settled himself. Even thinking about the neopallium had rendered his own calmer, allowing him to read a book on intelligence by one of these new computer guys, Hank A. Fearnley. He tried but the words swam: too many footnotes! Instead he thought he should close up and nap on the chaise longue—once carmine, now browned—that had been his wife's gift to him so many moons ago, on his fortieth birthday, the age he sometimes thought was still his before the usual self-inventory intruded: a man of sixty-two, arteries only semiblocked, circulation reaching his toes, a bit of plaque on the brain but appetites still occasionally feral. At forty he'd started thinking of himself as an old man given the mystery of his own birth-father's age at death—the closed archives of Liechtenstein obscuring his own genetic sentence—offering Vic the gift or theft of a faceless clock. How long did his genes predispose him to live?

He could be a healthy sort (the thought usually easing him toward sleep) and yet, because students insisted on celebrating sex so loudly, no nap for Vic! He would have to go home, his mood not leaving him the whole drive back, still cranky as, once inside his front door, he cuckooed his usual *Mary?* No one greeted him and for this small respite he was glad, upstairs finding himself almost content to lie down on his study's tattered green couch so that when he awoke, rested as the legendary giant, a teakettle whistling downstairs, his mood found a decent hum, perhaps because he'd had a dream that set things aright, part of the brain's brilliance in its electrical spark or soup. Half asleep, he had the impulse, if not to make amends for whatever slight he had inflicted—was he not usually in the wrong with Mary?—at least to make an appeal. He had some tricks, some roundabout methods for achieving bonhomie, a moment of better repute in her eyes.

And he was pleased that well-being warmed his limbs, a boon often denied him. Get closer to death and you no longer enjoy the slumber of youth; the best you get is to linger in somnolent halfness. Halfness because some dim reminder buzzes in the corner of the psyche, the deferral of some pressing appointment with mortality as bad as the awful scent of wet tweed suffusing the room, some new unclassifiable form of mold, something he'd have to talk to Mary about—but then he heard her downstairs, Mary talking with her hard-chinned assistant Sherry, continuing the mystery: what did women always have to say to each other?

Sherry to Mary, Mary to Sherry, Sherry who had stayed around the longest of the long retinue of assistants, who'd gone through grad school and yet despite the rigors of classes, orals, defense committees had helped Mary with her research, interviews, the typing up of field notes, charts and statistics. Sherry who, like Vic and Mary, had understood the unpatented holiness of work.

To Sherry, Mary felt she owed her success. More than once he'd heard Mary's whispered refrain *what would I do without her*. From upstairs he heard some similar whisper run through the women's speech, a clandestine train punctuated by sharp outbursts of laughter before an arrival at concord. *What compels women to talk on and on*, he thought again, mood slipping notches toward grumpy. Had Mary ever confided in him with such tones? In the hall downstairs Mary said goodbye to assistant Sherry, and, after one more embrace, closed the door. *Sherry, ma cherie*, he mouthed upstairs, capable of farce even half-asleep.

The only other person his wife would hug with similar susurration—sincere, slow, a small purr escaping—was their friend Mosh, the one friend they'd ever truly shared, a ruddy man full of tales of mushroom-hunting, duck-trapping, cheerful moose escapades. Years ago Mosh had given the Mahlers a silver-plated gun at which they had laughed, thinking it a quaint relic of some night of syrah, vermouth, palaver. For years they had kept Mosh's gun, dusty, locked but loaded against intruders, heavy and unused in the upper shelf of the china hutch in the hallway, behind the teapot, away from the prying dustrags of cleaning ladies who under California law were as illegal as black-market firearms. They had kept the gun even after Sherry had told Mary that she thought the Mahlers should get rid of it—*the leading cause of gun fatalities among white males is suicide*. Which Vic thought a convoluted way of saying the obvious: keep a gun and naturally one day a person considers its applications.

He was fully exiting the dream-zone. Listening to Sherry's car start up outside, Vic thought he might wait an interval before he came downstairs, wishing for casualness, his limbs loose, a harmless spider hovering, caught in its own breath.

The nagging thought returned: hadn't things been pretty much all right? Hadn't Mary and he evolved a pattern of being cordial when others were around? Across a room at a party he could sight Mary laughing, ducking her head, the flash of her well-preserved poitrine, a lighthouse of a woman, and fondness would return, his pride a heartburn inseparable from their histories of dispute, however rare it was that during the day around the house they engaged much because there was always work, the never-failing excuse and binding ethos simultaneously an invocation and shared god.

Finally awake, he thought: no casualness, just go down and surprise her.

Surprise how? Perhaps he could offer Mary something; some prick of delight might penetrate. But she'd already eaten all the birthday chocolates mailed them by their Belgian friend. What then? Like a spill seeped onto a beachhead, the fullness of the memory slammed on him: her news. What she had told him three nights ago, what he had been good at suppressing, her news which these past numb days had waited like a half-remembered appointment now rose, a phantom spiraled into rage.

Cuckold, lost to the cockfight, he was a cuckold.

His plan will have him make the announcement gently: *Mary, I've decided to leave.* Or just *I'm leaving.* He will be nothing but dignity: *but I'll leave you the house.* His nobility will be the perfect punishment, given that, three nights ago, ten o'clock at night, wearing her sleeveless nightdress with the eyelets that made her look like an Indochine lady for hire, she had told him about her years-long affair with Gallagher. *Maybe I always loved him?*

He would have preferred Sherry as the object of lust. Anything but Gallagher. One can't help the ignition of rage: it is hard-wired. Unable to linger in his nap, he bolted up in bed, tramped down the worn stairs to find Mary wearing reading glasses, poring over a journal, wearing a man's denim shirt and seated in the living room's blue glider.

"Sorry," she said, a paltry attempt at reparations, "didn't get dinner started yet."

"No problem," he replied, disarmed and uncertain: he found himself holding the globe that had been left, mistakenly, on the stairs. The globe—he looked at it quizzically before assuming the cheery face of a postcard husband.

"How about Ozzie's?" he suggested, placing the globe down carefully. Ozzie's was a reference to a dining moment they'd enjoyed one day after having seen a brutal matinee together, the kind of shared trauma that brings some couples closer, a movie about a Dutch woman buried and her frantic husband seeking her.

Her eyes lifted for a second: she understood the attempt. Over her face passed the shadow of washed-away hope, a crest after a small death, the shadow of a decision she must have come to years ago when she must have started believing Vic could only spell a galaxy of disappointment.

Nonetheless they dined, a pair of tongues and stomachs in aging bodies with greening livers, the couple led by courtesy and convention. Late afternoon at the old pharmacy at Russell and College, the one that had restored its soda fountain, senior hour at Ozzie's. The shaggy who still stalked Vic with the greatest passion dismounted from his motorcycle outside the window and waved, smiling and holding his usual ramshackle cardboard sign on which today he had painted HOW MANY BABIES ARE YOU GOING TO PUT INTO YOUR SOUP CAN AND SELL TO TEXAS? Vic waved back as if he too could be jolly, enough to satisfy this harmless shaggy and help him move on to other important stations. The married pair without comment turned back to their meal, good American food hearkening back to imported tradition while Vic tried to locate what he wished to tell her. The diner seemed helpful, friendly, a testament to civilization with its chrome-plated stools, a malted for him, a club sandwich for her, the dainty cellophaned toothpicks festooning her plate, petite flags of surrender.

"It's great they've fixed the place up," she said after she had finished. "The new owner's from New York."

"It is great." He stared into the bill, gloom enveloping him. Now would be the time to pounce, to tell her if he could, but his plan had turned sour in his mouth, here in a place made up of prefab nostalgia. Did he think he could fool anyone? As the prospect of leaving her neared, it seemed impossible that Vic could separate from a lady with whom he had shared so much. He would not be able to leave either of them happy; the revenge would not be sweet. It was all as impossible as if someone had said all of individualistic, rebellious, quarrelsome Berkeley could be sold into the hands of a single greedstruck developer who could glass-plate everyone's mind. Impossible.

"What are you thinking about, Vic?" she'd said, this woman who'd been the receptacle for all of it since almost the beginning.

"How—beautiful you are," he lied.

She looked through him unconvinced, pulling off her knit cap only to put it on again, all rather uncharacteristic, he noted, dully. When he hadn't been looking, she'd been busy accruing new habits. What was that reddish mark on her neck?

Then it was that she struck her blow.

He was just about to say something magnanimous—he was working up to it—when she chose to issue her own pronouncement. "You know, I've been thinking, it would be best if you left."

"Left here?"

And then—his fate!—he understood how readily the wronging party meant to unauthor his idea, undo him. *She* would be the ejecting agent. She had cuckolded him and now she would doubly cuckold him, telling him to leave her and their Spruce Street abode, a home that had seen the beginning and middle of their marriage, a house that had contained them, the silent inviolable witness to the birth and death of Vic and Mary. Unthinkable. They'd been there so long; they'd moved there when Berkeley had first offered him a job as a lecturer. They'd raised a daughter in the house. His house. His money. His hard work.

In the beginning of their courtship he used to want to devour her limbs, push his head inside her long confusing hybrid body, but now the rage that filled was its pure twinned absolute, an ice poison.

As they'd driven home in the most brittle silence of their lives together, in the vintage leather-seated Porsche, south to north in their idyllic college town, he'd almost had an accident. Not hard to do, given all the narrow one-way roads and shortcuts winding between overgrown rosebushes and oaks, the hairpin turns that meant one car suddenly faced down another: so many decisions a person had to make to avoid mutual destruction.

In retrospect, he might have bypassed the act. *The least original thought will often be exactly the one that seems to you inevitable and necessary!* he used to tell his student researchers. *Never believe you've arrived at confirmation before you're willing to utterly abandon the hypothesis!*

But what originality could have refuted the imperfection of her choice in ejecting him? When does one mark the onset of brutality? And who put the music on the stereo? As if to make one more sally in a decades-long argument they had continued, over the worth of music over pure quiet, Mahler's Eighth had entered the room.

The act happened on stairs where their Lana had first learned to walk as a toddler but their hug might have erased it all, a pleat of desperation, a death-grasp as in coupling's early days.

The unwelcome scene tended to visit him whenever he most needed sleep. In the language of the courts, he must have *premeditated*, the spontaneous act foretold by the tranquility of choice. For had he not used both globe and gun, items not exactly borrowed from anyone else's universe? Random chance, of course chance had played a part: chance had swayed his hand, chance whose doctrine he used to preach to adherents, chance as well as a few improvised elements, most of them products of the hindbrain with its knack for hellbent inspiration.

At a crucial moment, when things could have stalled, if not gone backward, she'd asked what he thought of as the haunter, the question almost enough to have spun him out of forward momentum (and what awaited, the future of regret stored in the forebrain, the future when he would try to put Mary's face into a sealed-off carton).

Have you taken leave of your senses?

Later her last question would seem most apt. He had taken leave. His volitional mechanism had exited the sensory apparatus, which really could be another way to define marriage, right? Not union but rather exit. Your will exits your senses or maybe the opposite: your senses exit your will. If he could just stick with the facts, she had denied him the leavetaking he'd wished for, which made him in turn leave the contours of his usual self. That day, he found himself murdering more than one thing, piercing that flimsy bubble of Vic Mahler who would choose to be a rational being and it was unfortunate that his second and third shots then proved brutal premeditation.

in one of the moment's variations is when he parks outside their house and doesn't know what to do. Their cat Medusa sits outside on the lawn, hunting new spoils, tail unfurling, her gaze admitting no need to her human couple. The two do what they usually do which is to enter through the front door.

Vic rushes Mary in or does he push? He locks the door behind them. Without considering, he hurries to the stereo to press, somewhat arbitrarily, the triangle of PLAY.

"Stay there," he says.

Play! No choice really. Play! The violins speed on. Mary looks at him, confused.

"Just wait," he says.

"What?" she asks. The blaring music makes her churlish. Disgust crosses her face as if the whole setup might signal some new tediously kinky turn. The dusty gun in his hand before he realizes it, Mosh's silver gun. Violins thundering, rage in his loins. Whatever she says is not wholly addressed to him but to the invisible spectators who now people their marriage. She shouts *turn it off* and also *what do you think you are doing?*

But she is not the only one who knows how to shout.

With any other pretext, they might have dropped the act altogether, might have grappled only to fall over the two stumble-stairs separating entrance from living room. Yet this was no ordinary fight. The thrall of cellos, his marrow gurgling, an itch. Something else pilots him.

Long light stretching through the plated glass by the entrance hall puts him out of time.

Have you taken leave of your senses? asks Mary and then repeats herself, neck strained against the scarf from her sister, some scent of milkshake emanating. Seconds earlier the scarf had hung on the doorhandle, an afterthought now tight around her throat.

In her eyes the same terror and hope he'd seen on their wedding day at city hall: *will you won't you be my savior or destroyer?* The Mahler in the background, riled up, the Eighth always speaking to him, one thousand instruments required for full orchestration. First his hand is grabbing the globe and using it in a manner never intended by cartography. Next his hand fires, old duck-hunting knowledge entering, shaken into two more rounds. And then the act finds an end that will become no end after all but rather endless intermission.

He walks. Leaves the scene, absents himself. Leaves her there. Locks the house, rushes by the intrigued cat, keeps walking. Uphill past the cypresses to their trusted neighbor Carol's house where he lets himself in the back. On Carol's granite counter lies a circus-themed ad for a corner pizza store. Without thinking he picks up the phone, dials the number, waits through circus music, peeks outside to see the number of Carol's house, talks to a foreign-accented woman to request delivery of a small cheese to the house, using his neighbor's name, asking for no trimmings. Hungry because he hadn't touched his malted and because a hole bores through his gut. There at someone's kitchen island he watches the clock, drumming fingers on Carrara stone while having the nonsensical thought that now he might never get to see Carrara. The pizza delivery takes exactly nineteen minutes.

As he used to tell his daughter whenever she herself was obscenely tardy, nineteen minutes slanted toward death.

Vic takes money from his neighbor's ceramic kitty, tips the buck-toothed delivery boy too generously. Not wishing to be recognized, he closes the door in the boy's face. Poor devil. He writes an IOU to Carol but forgets how to sign his own name. Sits back at the table, chews a hot slim triangle in half, disgusted by the island shape of sauce on his shirt. Closes the box. And then makes the first conscious choice: he doesn't wash his hands before picking up the phone, dialing 911, this time no music to wait through, this time calling the police on himself.

In court he blames that earlier morning's reading. He hadn't been footnoted in a recent article in *Science*. Who in court could understand what plagiarism means to an end-of-career academic? No one. How to shore up your future? He floats the idea over their lowbrow heads, knowing they cannot understand how a footnote might become almost a life-or-death matter.

Nor does he mention the students' sex freedom, their celebration of Saint Valentine. He does make himself mention the affair that Mary had described with such viscosity, telling the blank faces on the jury that his wife had been seventeen years in love with another man, someone he had known. Worse, a colleague. Worst, someone he'd thought a shared friend. And not just an affair. His wife had known an all-consuming love, perhaps the closest to pleasure she'd ever had. When naming the culprit, she had given off a little love-tremble, as he had noted, one that plunged Vic down into all their unhappy recent years. Of course it made sense only if you believe that sense is sadistic.

After her confession, the sole satisfaction left Vic was the apocalyptic grimness of a scientist who, the last living human, proves his sad hypothesis that an evil world-eating bacterium he had predicted had triumphed: the scientist gets the lonely conquest of *aha!*

Because he had been cuckolded by someone with a sniveling laugh from a neighboring department: Gallagher!

Gallagher who had elegant theories but who had vetoed Vic's requests. Who had been notorious for being the administration's darling, an officious prig in a suit with a baby's face, beard and mustache, his blue eyes notorious for unctuous flattery of power-mad superiors, Gallagher who even after tenure actually kneeled by chairs in the faculty dining room so as to exchange civilities eye to eye, lick to lick, Gallagher which could almost rhyme with cuntlicker, who wished to be seen as important and busy, who apparently had lusted after others' wives despite the amazing civility of his own tolerant Dutch wife, mother to two compulsively excelling children, a woman who made homemade jam at the slightest excuse. Gallagher who didn't deserve any woman, his name rather more like sputum: Ga-lla-gher! More than an affair: it was as if Mary had guerrilla-conscripted Vic to a life of polyamory.

In court, finishing up, Vic sees that what he has just said might work against him so he finally offers them what they expect: *it was self-defense. Look, we had an argument, the heat of the moment, the usual man-woman thing, you know?* all this his attempt to try to speak contemporese when their faces have already snapped shut and they will let him undo no early bravado, refusing to understand Vic and his European flair.

Already his fame, as the judge has hinted, works against him: Vic can feel fame smothering him. And of course no notoriety ever could compensate for the cuckold's gutburning shame, fame's eviscerated cousin in which your skin peels and your innards spill out. Could he now write a whole new corpus on shame?

Be indifferent to your enemies.

On the one hand, sure, he had probed Mary for all the grimy details. Had Gallagher held her by the back of her neck, her hair spilling over? Had he loved the obtrusion of her hipbone, her long flanks? Had he called Mary at work, murmuring? Had they eased into familiarity like a married couple? Or had it always stayed new between them, seventeen years fueled by the dynamo of taboo?

Over my dead body. Vic could understand that idea from every direction, Mary and Gallagher frolicking over his body, Vic's entrails powering their dance, making him need to end the unwilling troika. Would Gallagher one day contact him? Unlikely when the man was a flame-haired narcissist. Had the man shed tears over the Mary now denied him? Or could he have understood any part of Vic's act? The guy probably at that exact moment was still kneeling somewhere, licking up to someone in the faculty dining room, just like Vic on his one knee during yet another all-prison alarm.

If Mary had been just a bit forthcoming—but Vic couldn't blame her. Still, if Vic had known just a few more details, she would not have unmastered him: rather, Vic would have mastered this new idea of Mary as a cheater, Vic her cuckold, and his motor neurons might not have excited him in such untoward fashion. But right after the most vicious part of her confession she had chosen to stay mum, saying little. Just as if, a young immigrant in his early twenties, a new parishioner of America, someone had prevented Vic from studying in the low-cost college in Los Angeles or as if every book he'd tried prying open had remained glued shut. Mary and her Gallagher were keeping him from knowledge when knowledge is experience and experience is ultimately innocence, as he used to tell his own daughter and her friend, encouraging them to steal out for one of their nighttime walks.

During Vic's turn in court, he tried explaining how little he had chosen his horrible act.

"I loved her," he said. "My instinct to save her was strong. Say a car had threatened to run over Mary, even after her truth-telling, I still would have jumped before the car, I still would have sacrificed my life to spare hers. Without hesitation. In this case, however, her idea of reality could coexist neither with my own nor with the past of our reality.

"And given what I used to believe about what happened after death—namely, nothing—would I have chosen nullity for either of us? No.

"And though I'm not proud of sadism, I still would have preferred her to live through the torturous screw of realization so she would at least feel what I did. So that at the depth of her womb she would know the nastiness of her deceit, the grim fact of all she undid by cuckolding me.

"Especially when one of the best parts of being a father was the romance of laying a seed in my own velvet, the womb like a marriage ring, despite creation always being vaster than its players. You could say we found a higher redemption in my daughter.

"And my daughter, past the baby stage but before self-consciousness came at night to murder the child I used to hold dear—somewhere around age eight, I think—my child showed me that thing we could call the sparkle of creation, the way she held duty and independence, whimsy and intelligence at a perfect fulcrum. Some of you must be parents. Tell me there's anything better than that?"

After he spoke, the jury looked hung in space, even more unconvinced.

"Mister Mahler, do you feel regret?" the assistant prosecutor had asked.

"Well, regret kills," he had answered, honestly.

The lead prosecutor had then tried to make it seem as if, in right mind, Vic had chosen to murder Mary.

What did they want from him? For him to say outright that he was a bad person? Would it put their own demons to rest? He actually asked them this: *what do you want?* Knowing they would turn a deaf ear. Of course Vic, whose shaggies had shown him how much people needed to believe in chimeras, understood why they needed to call him evil.

"I tried," he said, before his last-ditch attempt when he chose to single out his daughter's friend Rose, asking her to stand and speak for him. He could have been gobbling and hooting since whatever he said mattered little to any of them. "Just like all of you. I did the best I could."

Lana stands in the corridor plugging her ears against the fire alarm, watching the guard named Javier speak energetically with the prisoner said to be her father though she cannot recognize Vic in this bag of flesh-encased bones. This bag cannot rise by himself from his bed: his shins are blue-mottled sticks, his hips a child's, his torso bends forward.

"Try again?" says the guard.

A moving, dancing, gesticulating skeleton. She sees Vic's back; he doesn't see her.

The guard lays a hand on the skeleton's shoulder and then bursts from the cell, locking it behind and pulling the door shut. The fire alarm has stopped, at least for now.

Lana asks: "Is this a fire drill or some real threat?"

"Look, if this were just a drill, you couldn't be standing in here." When he sees Lana's confusion, he explains. "They were about to turn you away. We had an emergency? Basically I abandoned protocol to let you in. He scratched you off the list. Now we got to get you out. They'll call it a security threat. Or I'm not sure what, but no one's answering the radio and Mahler wasn't on Cell Block A's count."

"Okay," she says, unconvinced.

"It means officers will come looking. I let you in not knowing the full scope. I thought I'd get you in and out. Not exactly the best time for a family meeting. He has to get to the courtyard."

"Okay."

"Because say it's a real threat and the wind picks up—I'll need to call for a gurney. One of his legs doesn't work well. Anyway he's not in his best mind right now."

"I can help."

"I'm sorry, too much to explain. Please come with me now."

"You can't break protocol? Just once?" she asks, looking into this guard's pretty face and understanding his gentleness has been a boon to her father. The sirens have been replaced by a series of low warning beeps. "You've been working with my father how long?"

"Six months? Four?" The guard cracks a smile for the first time. He is too pretty for her taste, inspiring admiration more than seduction. "We know each other some." He waits. "Guy's been living to see you. Why I let you in. But my mistake. They'll write me up. You should probably exit now."

She wants to cry at this man's gentleness. "Just for a second?"

He signals with his shoulder the camera behind them in the corridor.

"No, I see." She tries for patience as bulwark against the beeps. "But if there's a fire, who's looking? Unusual circumstances, right?"

"He's been refusing his meds," he tells her. "He doesn't want to eat. Yesterday he got an infection from his catheter but won't take his antibiotics. The infection puts him in another world. I think he's saying his goodbyes."

"You've been good to him," says Lana, surprised to find some tears coming out of her eyes. For years she hasn't cried. Now she loses some control and can't help it: she shifts, awkward on the saucer device in her boot. It upsets her that Vic, with whom she hasn't talked for years, refuses medicine. Finally she manages: "Sorry. He was lucky. I mean to get you."

The guard considers. "Okay," he says. "We'll call it emergency procedures. Don't know what the hell's going on."

She taps the gate closed behind her, hearing the click of the lock. The face Vic turns on her is deep-set and scary, purple bruises around eye sockets. His fingers fly to his cheek in salute, bloated violet stubs with yellowed rot ripping away from the tips. She tries to smile. He looks into her and then says: "Nice to see you."

"You too."

"Here in this library our parents gave us."

"Oh." She had not counted on the possibility of his mind being so hazy. Or is he tricking her? Does he really think she is some long-lost sister?

But he looks sincere. "That nice fellow outside helps service the library. Come, sit near me. Soon I have to get dressed for the wedding."

"Whose is that?"

"They didn't tell you I'm marrying the daughter of the priest? I thought you came to help. Or who'd you come to see?"

"We don't have a lot of time. I basically came for—" For what? For pardon as much as for anything. She sits in the chair by his bed, deep in the oyster waft of old male urine, there with her tentmate, jailmate, cradlemate. As if scratching herself, she reaches down inside her boot, under her heel. Together they are building a stone idol out of this moment, one that cannot be taken down, though she is not yet sure the proportions of the idol's face. "How could I help?"

"Don't lift a finger in my direction." He surveys this effect. "Or tell me what kind of grandparent I have been to you."

His optic—or trick—has shifted, though the gaze stays aquarelle, too watery for guile.

"You know, I wasn't sure you would recognize me," she says, unready to take up any gambit while still sorting her own. "Right away, I mean."

"Of course I do. Come closer." He squints as if to better render the portrait. "You're the good nurse. You haven't done anything bad. Today's the day of the ceremony, isn't it?"

She pushes the chair just a few inches closer, obedient. He could not be joking, not now. Or could this be some last frictionless duplicity? You mock life enough, you gain eternal life, he said once, back when he had been a wholly other person, living a wholly different truth. He used to shift quickly and was known for being a trickster but never like this: old Vic never went so abruptly from being present to being so crazily specific. She cannot help but cough from the smoke now threading near the hall ceiling, a grisaille in which float calipers and a league of tiny heads, the guard outside urgent in his beckoning, waving at her with one of her crutches.

"What ceremony?" asks Lana.

"The one in the great temple. Kick against the pricks, as the good book says. Today's not the day? Help me. You look intelligent. We can figure this out. You know, this is the day when they convert goats to cows. Something about the mother cow."

"Vic. Papa. Are you confused?"

"No," he says, patient. The old scientist comes to the fore, under a skin rubbery and stretched, through eyes watery caverns. "You really don't know about the ceremony?"

They are in tune, just this second. "I came to talk to you about your daughter," she says.

"I do have one. Is she coming?" He waits. A light in his eye, confessing. "You know sometimes I escape from here?"

Lana's head shakes, a congenial tremor with no real mandate.

"I go with colleagues. Quite friendly. We go to a hospital to talk among ourselves as if we're back in the medieval era." His chest puffs. "My colleagues and I are working out the names of god."

She tries smiling.

"The work's going well. Terrific. Quite pleasant."

"That's great."

"You know my daughter's not a bad person. She's an angel. But she never visited."

"Never?"

"Maybe. Were you there?" He peers up from that deep-set brow with suspicion.

"No," she lies.

"She's a good girl," he says. "Like her mother."

"How?" Choking more on his words than the smoke.

"Burdened by good looks and good manners."

"Your daughter?" Incredible. What memory can he hold? One of the things he had always stormed about was Lana's lack of manners, all her uncouth American ways. She becomes sure that whatever happens, he won't remember this meeting.

"When does the ceremony start?" He waits. "I am ready to get out of this place already."

"I think in about an hour. What were you saying about your daughter?"

"She could play the violin. Beautifully." A smile runs across his face. "You have no idea how celestial her playing was. She had a real gift. Straight to the heart. The tongue of angels. But she made a mistake. Should have kept up with it." He becomes an old man again, eyes confused. "What's happening now? What's that racket?"

"A siren."

"Oh. I thought it was something like thunder. Dry and sterile with no rain."

"There's a fire but it's contained. Or maybe," she dares, "some protestors are coming to free Vic Mahler?"

"Why would anyone want to free Vic Mahler? I told them Vic was ready. They are the ones forcing me to wait now." Something like a sob escaping. "So." A different smile returns as if they are strangers standing in line. "What sort of thing do you do to keep body and soul together? What's your calling?"

"I have two children but I don't really have a calling."

"Do you drive a big car?"

"No, an old undercover cop car. Not a minivan."

He thinks about this. A minivan. "Then you should populate your minivan more."

"People still care about Vic Mahler," she says, her own squeak escaping.

"Vic Mahler means the same to them as a minivan or police car does to me. An idea. Don't get upset." He is tender, his hand upon hers. Someone keeps making her cry, letting her head fall onto that bony chest, her hand on his rickety shoulder, his voice reverberant. "You are a sensitive, emotional person. I can tell you are a person of great worth and capable besides. Do you have a husband?"

She tries but cannot stop. Her hand wet on the device, the innocuous cup, the miniaturized plastic egg-poacher Hogan had pressed on her last night. "I can help you get out of here," she tries, lifting up.

Now he beams. "You could?"

"You really want out?"

"I'm sorry," he says. "This is probably not the right time. You should go now. I need to take a nap but let's set up something soon. Next week maybe? You know there are some French bandits waiting to tie me up. You see them right there in the corner of the room?"

"There are no bandits," she says. "You're having a hallucination."

"But I see them and can hear their whispers. They're crouched right there."

"Like you always said. The mind is powerful. It's playing a trick on you."

He studies her dimly for a second, appraising her understanding of reality, before nodding. "Well, I find it hard to believe you. But I do accept the possibility of your proposition." He has stayed so open, almost a child in his ability to take on another's way of seeing: he accepts what she says despite the report of his senses. And yet their moment seems to be passing since he focuses now less on her than on his fingers, performing some slow ghost dance that entertains him, entwining, unbinding, waving.

As if she were Mary utterly alone with this man. As if Mary lived in her for the first time. How lonely to have been her mother, married to this man with this particular daughter. To be Mary and have kept him ticking along in civil urbanities while denying her other wishes: to tear him apart and find his root, rip off the mask of coffee parties and clubs, to find in herself the lost scapegrace, bearer of an original sin she had so successfully tried forgetting.

Lana sees the bulge on the chest, as promised no bigger than a trinket pushing forward through the shirt. You won't even have to touch skin to skin, the man had said, sniffing her response, eyes a ferret's.

Only if she could get Vic out of his cave would she do it. "You know I've never been very good at speeches. I'm not a flowery kind of person. It's hard for me to tell you how important you've been to me."

And he looks up from his fretwork with his fingers, his tiny ghost dancers, seeing her as if for the first time, an openness in his eyes she can't remember having ever seen. "Don't worry. You are my first-born." He listens to the weight of the words. "You are my only child. A melody can play all the time and it never needs a single word." Inside her is a wall with tears going down; she could move just one bit toward that fountain and drown. "You know, sometimes I cannot help but really miss your mom."

"Papa."

"I can't help it. It's a little thing. Scarcely of consequence to anyone else. But I loved the way that when we made love she—"

"Vic."

"She liked giving this little hoot. I can't imitate it. I'm not talking about something volitional. More a sneeze, I can't explain, I'm just sharing this with you. Really that hoot was a pinprick, a nothing, a drop in the ocean of everything else. But that little cry. In many ways that cry was what cursed me. Or all of us. Because inside all her self-improvement and tightness, did you know your mother still showed some abandon—"

She takes his hands. Not to shush him, not fully: she is right now of the same matter as he is, missing the one she could have had, the mother she almost had, every word he utters carrying her forth on the same wave so they swim together.

And yet he is wrong; she must correct him, she craves a chaste truth down to the marrow. "I don't think it was the cry that cursed you guys."

He is wrongly pleased. "You don't?"

"Maybe it was," and she chokes, "having me? Your daughter? You know," and she has never said this to herself or another, "you really have no idea," and for one moment seeing she has buffeted others and carried them along in herself, "how bad I am," collapsing, not meaning to have said this but unburdened, for this second simple as a child with this boy king in prison. How bad and how good to not be defended against her badness, to not have to justify to anyone.

"Mopsy," he says, knowing her as he used to, his fingers bloated but intentional, knives stroking her hair, her head fallen. And his stroke lets her own hand find its purpose, no more tinkering, letting the saucer cup climb, the egg-poacher reaching unpoaching, all of it letting her find the mercy in herself to place the ungiving thing firmly on his chest, to hold it three seconds over the left ventricle just as the man had said, the miniaturized plastic will be undetectable in your boot, no one will think it anything but heart failure. This is your gift to a person, given his recent wishes spun by the new factors complicating his case, not just a statute but the history of prosecutorial misconduct, Vic's whole case about to become a mess, caught in the courts for years. So she has only three seconds to give someone fully what he needs and what only she can give.

This will be done. Vic letting out a surprised little *oh!* before falling over on her as if to rest in a deep sleep while mortar continues to fly around, a man finally safe and free.

She doesn't realize if time has passed, one second or ten minutes. The guard has come, name forgotten, giving back some crutches, telling her not to worry but she must exit down the left corridor now, no time to lose as he will stand by, a weak smile already on him as if he halfway understands how responsible she just made him for Vic.

Far off beyond the sirens she hears hooves. She could use a friend, at least an ally right now, but anyone she would call a friend has been thwacked away. "What's happening?" she manages.

"We'll know." The guard almost smiles. "Don't worry. Please, now you must head out that corridor. Follow the exit signs. Don't stay, get yourself out. Anyone sees you, say you got lost."

"You're so calm," she marvels.

"I'll stay. Dispatch will get my call and send someone down with a gurney. For now I am standing by in case he needs exit."

Exit. He had asked for it and that was a needful act. Later, on the road, she will believe her whole life had brought her to that second and that maybe if she had not been such a bad person, she could not have fulfilled her father's will. At the critical moment she would have lacked stamina no matter how many times, back at their apex, he had made her promise to keep his dignity intact. The salmon, having spawned, fulfilled its biological function. Was that not the self she should respect most? Honor your parent by honoring the clear-thinking one and not the other selves. And I came not for revenge, she will remind herself, I came to help and when I was with him, did he not give some confirmation?

She will begin to tell herself that she could know what he wanted better than he might have ever known himself. A good death. As she knows from her own kids, only children know best who a parent is. Only children can give the punishing gift of themselves.

She had her knowledge of him to deliver and it belonged to nobody else living. Even if the state of California had gotten a thousand depositions from a thousand tributaries, what would it have ever known about her family? And if the sin lived in her having taken another's life rather than granting it, shouldn't she have been the one to accept the sin rather than some random jailer?

In the blue safety light of the communal kitchen, the boys find their mother fixing tea, padding about in bare feet and wide slacks. This is the mother they know. As if she has managed to escape a spell that had forced her in this last period to use crutches and be touchy, to not pad about much. Now their real mother swishes by under artificial moonlight, a recognizable mother, the yummy one who used to sing random folk songs and take them to the ocean with their dog Cad running near where rocks pushed up from the foam like a bunch of stranded bowling balls. This same mother always carried them slung on her front and back and now long-spined in the kitchen, their mother like an angular barn mostly withstanding time, her neck straighter than anyone's, this mother theirs in her silver hoop earrings and hair full over that long neck.

For a second Sedge gets adult vision, able to see their mother as she exists apart from them.

Dirk had been calling their mother an Amazon but Sedge thinks that means Asian because once she'd mentioned her mother had been part-Japanese. Anyway Sedge finds the idea of Amazon upsetting: he knows Amazons slice off half their chest and that man–eating monkeys come from the Amazon while pasta comes from Asia and pasta he can handle but not the other chest stuff.

So struck by the sight of her, at first Sedge, thinking Amazons and Asians, says nothing. She looks up from her tea and smiles, the most exuberant, beautiful sight in the world. Sedge's tongue lies heavy, which is something of a relief; paralysis means Lestrion has not forsaken him. Sometimes Lestrion can forsake him for weeks and these times are bad—Sedge ends up gravityfree, spun out into a galaxy, lacking a compass. Other times he knows Lestrion is manning the controls even if the space robot has his mischievous side. If Sedge doesn't cup his hands and whisper to him every once in a while, Lestrion can grow unruly, his behavior embarrassing.

So now Sedge stands, hands hanging, staring at his mother, tongue stuck.

Tee stops too, struck not by Lestrion but by his twin's paralysis. Much as he would never admit it, Tee uses Sedge as his own compass.

What Sedge's tongue can't bridge, what he can't translate, is the awesome good luck of finding their mother making tea, their mother with her access mostly oblique now seeming available and ready for customers. Once, trying to take her in, when she'd been working her market job late hours, Sedge had inhaled an onyx from her dresser and had to be taken to the emergency room and then his mother had come so soothingly too, belonging to him with her quick laugh and sharp wrists, her banana scent: how quickly she could understand before you ever opened your mouth.

We all need to leave he wants to tell her now.

He imagines them pulling off the road to a rest stop. He would casually say to his mother *you know, we never really liked Dirk.*

She would smile the way she was smiling now only to admit *you know, me neither* and she would belong to her boys but especially to Sedge, creamy and compliant. She would heed their requests, taking them to a water playland where they'd never leave or at least never have to return to the zone of Yalina, their old home against which they'd already been brainwashed.

On the ride down to Hope, hadn't their mother muttered *been there, done that?* One day they would live in a big house where their grandparents would come visit. They'd have a sprinkler on the front lawn, tons of extra fancy rooms and many new and interestingly submissive friends. Sedge stands there in the kitchen's blue light wondering how to transmit the vision and get his mother to understand that now is the time to leave.

Instead what he says is: "Ma, we did something bad."

She kisses the top of Sedge's head then Tee's, truly in a good mood.

"Would you like some of this delicious tea someone made?"

"Chamomile?" asks Sedge, diverted, screwing up his face.

"No, something else. You'll like it, I think. Cinnamon," she says, "cayenne," licking her finger, "honey?" Not finding mugs, she gives them each a big bowl. "It's how the French drink," she tells them for the millionth time. On high stools at a butcher-block island in the half-dark kitchen, they sit a threesome again.

To hide his pleasure, Sedge lifts the giant drink to his face, hearing their mother tell them how her father used to love drinking from big bowls: this is the first time she mentions her own father without any pressure from their questions about cereal boxes and other facts. Of course Sedge had been curious, had wanted to know who their other grandpa was, but she had never surrendered much of a satisfying answer. *A parent can put a spell on you*, she says.

Which all matters less than that, in the bowl's reflection, wrinkles form around Sedge's eyes and mouth and ears, magnified by a trick of light. He is a monster and cannot retreat from this central fact. The intruder Dirk sits gagged and bound with an orange cord and Sedge is the most evil person ever invented this century or ever.

"I'm sorry, mommy," he blubbers. Tee looks over at his twin, disgusted.

Lana's eyes upon the two don't waver. "Sorry for what?" Her voice warm and tender, unjudging, her good mood floating above everything. "I just had the best exorcism of my life." Exercise, schism, they don't really understand what she just said, so Sedge tries to bring some clarity into the picture, mumbling toward the middle of the room. "Mama, maybe someone messed things up."

"Try more of this yummy drink?" Their mother has a serious dream in her voice. And here is where Lestrion must have understood Sedge's wishes enough to finally help his mother make a good choice. "Maybe we should just pack our bags and go."

"Go?" squeaks Tee. "What about goodbyes? Zabelle? Hogan?"

"How about we'll write them cards." She tousles his head; Sedge must work to keep himself from spluttering; she barely notices. "Let's go make our own fun. Seriously. Let's drive—" She founders, seeming not to have thought beyond the idea's brink, just as they'd had no real plan for what would happen to their gagged Dirk.

"To Mexico?" says Sedge.

"That's a great idea. How about Isla Mujeres? Or La Paz? We could get a house by the beach. You guys could learn Spanish. We'd play on the beach. I'd homeschool you. You'd get good at listening. We'd catch our own salmon for dinner. Sardines."

"I don't like sardines. What about Colorado?"

"Maybe let's just drive for a bit and figure out where we're going?"

"Road trip!" Tee's fist punches the air.

"But keep it our secret, right?" and in the way she raises a finger to her lips, in her wide-open eyes, in how she says "just the three of us?" they love their mother all over.

SOON

they place him in a departure lounge where he is pleased to be neither in the past nor the future. They call out numbers of departing
flights but his will not be called for a while. A sense of well-being
floods his toes. When Mary had first suspected she might have Lana
inside her, she had been lying on her back and had girlishly awakened
him to say a warmth had entered her from the toes and traveled up to
her belly. A spirit just entered me, she said, to which he had said back:
that's your Catholic schoolgirl voodoo speaking!

Having spent much of his life pooh-poohing others, now he gets
this last joke: he is experiencing a reverse pregnancy, an undoubling,
a womb turned inside out. His spirit is slowly traveling up from his
belly so as to lodge, temporarily, in his head. Troubling that he still
has some theories about Jesus to share with whomever will listen,
though only a chair mars this departure lounge.

The way of silence is not only death but incest. Paracelsus says, "He
who enters the kingdom of God must first enter his mother and
die." The silence which is death is also our mother. The matrix in
which the word is sown is silence. Silence is the mother tongue.

What will be left will be this giant head, its bones and sockets
hearing but not seeing, thoughts coming, going, shrinking him into
a mere homunculus. Then the involuntary act of breath will cease

along with the thoughts and the thinker will leave, going where? The girls walk toward him in identical yellow tank tops, happy he has not boarded his flight yet. You like the shirts? No one's lips move. How many more moments of pleasure do they want him to string together? Does it matter if they want him to have five more moments or ten? Why are they all so voracious?

The woman in charge of Decedent Affairs winks like a mother. "Right this way," she says. "You must have been close. You came despite Christmas."

"I am," admits the visitor. "Or I was."

"He's going to have a good time with you, I can tell."

"Sorry?"

"You'll see," says the woman. Gold script on her chest spells out her name. Eileen Lynch. "You were his only child?"

"Yes." The visitor's hand waves the idea of filial kinship away like a phantom.

This Eileen Lynch seems to be someone who flanks descendents of the dead and probably doesn't know Vic's background. Eileen, a person of official warmth, clicks down the long gray hallway with its lighting flat, its doors closed, and tries changing the subject.

"Anyway, ever seen a dead person before?"

"I guess not."

"Prepare yourself. I always tell people hold on to something when we open the door. Take a breath. You got to will yourself to breathe. Otherwise we find ourselves trying to join our friends on the other side."

"Pardon?"

"You faint. It has to do with your will for life. What helps is if beforehand you create your intention. First, want to be alone with him?"

"Probably. What did you mean when you said that about him having a good time with me?"

Eileen is out of breath, these corridors making her mount private hills. "You don't want to hear my personal history."

"I do," says the visitor.

"Okay. You asked. I was seventeen, I died and then came back."

"No way," says the visitor, not knowing how else to respond.

"Fell out of an apple tree. A doctor pronounced me dead and I saw my body from above. My grandma crouched over it. That whole bit. The tunnel, vague figures from the past. My third-grade teacher, the beckoning figure of light. They said I was dead for an hour and covered me with a sheet. Then I decided to come back. Because I had a purpose."

"What—you mean—you connect people to the dead?"

Eileen gleams, tugging at her collar. "Well, I didn't know it then but now I see spirits hovering around people. The dead connect me to people like you."

"Like—now?"

"Your man is hovering right near you. I knew all about you before you came in."

"Then what's the point of going to see the body?" she asks.

"It's for you, not them. You go, say your goodbyes. Because we hold on to sight but the dead hold on to hearing. Even after their vision goes they can hear everything. We stand on the shore and sing our goodbyes. You're not an opera singer are you?"

"Why?"

"I once had someone go and launch into an aria. But never mind."

"No," says the visitor. "I'm a terrible singer but I'm okay at following other people's tunes."

She is at the door. She has not been in the same room with the dead man free for years. Maybe never.

"Well, anyway, the other important thing is don't go in and lose yourself," says the woman. "The undertow can suck you in. Some of them love to give life but some love to steal it. There's no real constancy."

"Should I wait?"

"Well, I tell people it's like memory or breath. Goes in and out and there's never a perfect time. It's like they go in to join a tribe of dead people. You need to sit a second?"

"I'm sorry."

"Just take a moment. That's what this bench is for. It helps. But whatever you're scared of brings the greatest gifts, right? Because would you want to live life without jumping in? Sometimes your moment comes and you got to know when to seize it."

"I'm sorry, what?"

"We're in bigger currents we can't name. It's like fish."

"I do want to get what you're saying."

"A fish doesn't say okay, give me a second, I'm choosing not to go into the mouth of that whale."

"You're saying the dead are the whale?"

"Just that no matter what happens in life you find very few absolutely wrong moments."

"I should go in. I'm almost ready."

"Because you're getting a gift. The chance to say goodbye. It's like hello. Not everyone gets that chance. If we're all members of one family, one body, let's say, you back off, it means you're backing away from life itself. Like you grab a golden ring but fall off the horse."

"I'm falling off?"

"A long time ago I found life's short. No guilt or regret. You get the chance, call it luck, you leap. Want me to help you up? Someone in there has been waiting a long time. That person wants you and no one else. Can't you see now is your time?"

Hogan's hand on Rose's belly: "That's kicking all right. She's strong."

"She?"

"You don't think we're having a girl?"

"I do," and her smile up at him swallows the sky and dusty mountains, the prospect of calm.

LATER

they rinse the back of his eyeballs in hot light so he may finally stand before them in a beautiful suit, ready to lecture, irradiated and weary. He waits until the right moment to ask the question they never forget, the one forever drumming their core. For the first time he does want their answer. Are you happy now?

ACKNOWLEDGMENTS

Thank you to the editors of both *Conjunctions* and *Guernica* for publishing early excerpts.

The great generosity of the Lannan Foundation, the Bard Fiction Prize and the Howard Foundation all helped create favorable conditions. As did liberatory paragons Mary Caponegro, Robert Kelly, Brad Morrow.

A–Z plus a legion of students.

Thanks for the gift of place: Liv and Dan Leader and Leigh Stevens, offering orange-walled welcome; Marla Walker for proposing Joseph Cornell–like charm; and Lois Guarino, Livi and Stan Lichens for providing the miracle of a medieval nunnery in which to work.

For humanity toward this particular book: Rebekah Aronson, Sue Austin, Dianne Belfrey, Liza Birnbaum, Leon Botstein, Norman O. Brown, Sylvia Brownrigg, Jim Brudvig, Eugenie Cha, Carolyn Cooke, Mariah DeLeon, Shaun Dolan, Michèle Dominy, Gabriella Doob, Daisy Doro, Deb Durant, Cindy Herchenroder, Michael Ives, Dana Kinstler, Jane Korn, Evelyn Krueger, Marcus Leaver, Amii and Linda Legendre, Yasmine Lucas, Paul Marienthal, Joe Mathers, Vern Miller, Donna and Tony Monaco, Eric Myers, Mischa Nachtigal, Carol O'Day, Lisa Pearlman, Marcey Pollitt, Ira Sachs, Julia Sforza, Mercedes Sidor, Noel Tepper, Adrienne Weiss, Gena Wilson, Lisa Wolfe, Liza, Hedy, Katya. For dazzling endgame succor: Snapdragon Films, Kevin Salem, Tara Shafer, Larry Bensky, Sharon Guskin and

Michael Ravitch as well as FSG's production crew and jacket designer Jennifer Carrow. The late Ellen Margron and Carla Zilbersmith.

For immeasurable enthusiasm and unflagging support: Mae Ziglin Meidav.

For brilliance and inspiration: my editor, Eric Chinski, and my agent, Bill Clegg, showing their usual kindness in helping drive the cattle back to the meadow at the foot of the mountain while enlivening the journey with music on the lyre.

In memory of the benevolent lost grace of Tsvi.

The seed family: Stan, Eliana Esther Zoe, Dalia Elodie Rafaela.

EDIE MEIDAV

LOLA, CALIFORNIA

Edie Meidav is the author of *The Far Field: A Novel of Ceylon* and *Crawl Space* (FSG, 2005). Winner of a Lannan Literary Fellowship, a Howard Fellowship, the Janet Heidinger Kafka Prize for fiction by an American woman and the Bard Fiction Prize, she teaches at Bard College.

Visit www.ediemeidav.com for links to a film and score composed for this book.